Diamond Bonds

The Runics Series

JEFF KISH

Diamond Bonds by Jeff Kish

www.runicsbook.com

Edited by Tim Kish

Book Cover Design by ebooklaunch.com

ISBN: 978-0-9976784-1-3

10   9   8   7   6   5   4   3   2

Dedicated to my fun and lovely wife

Who surely never expected to have a fantasy book
dedicated to her!

NOTE TO THE READER:

Maps and a diagram have been provided starting on page 314. These can be referenced at any time without spoiling the story.

They are also available at www.runicsbook.com.

CHAPTER 1

It strikes Era mid-jump that perhaps a train raid isn't as easy as he had been led to believe. Rope in hand, the teenaged thief smashes into the side of the train car, clinging desperately to his lifeline as his horse veers away. The stinging wind forces his eyes shut as terror seizes him, but a hand grasps his wrist and gives him the assistance needed to climb to the roof.

Era collapses to his knees, his heart pounding in his ears. "That could have gone better, huh?" he calls out over the deafening roar.

Without responding, his masked companion places her open palm on the surface of the wooden roof, and a coating of frost creeps from her hand. Once the area is sufficiently frozen, she shatters the surface with a sharp kick and jumps inside without hesitation.

Era scrambles to peer into the dark car, only to find his partner safely alone and impatiently motioning for him to join her. Obediently, he slides through the opening, but his backpack snags the jagged edge of the shattered roof before coming loose and dropping him to the floor below.

"Hey, watch it," his partner cries in a hushed voice while examining the pack, aided by the moonlight. "You have to be careful with this! You don't want it tearing."

"I know that. Next time make the hole bigger," he whispers in defense while rubbing his backside.

"Next time make your own ice," she mutters, satisfied the pack is intact. "I got through without any issues."

He opts not to push the issue. "Regardless, it looks like you were right about the layout, Jem."

The girl's brown eyes sparkle. "Of course, I was right! These types always load their valuables in one place, which means the prize is in the next cargo car."

"You say that like it's not our first train raid," he says in amusement. The treacherous boarding may be over, but he has no idea what to expect as they plunge forward. "Biggest haul ever, huh?" he mumbles, recalling his partner's comment the previous day.

"Darn right it will be," she says as she unsheathes her dagger and moves to the door. "You thought that haul three months ago was good? Just wait till you see this. You ready?"

Era nervously nods, and she swings the door open, flooding the car with cutting wind and the earsplitting thunder of the train on the tracks. Jem boldly steps along the coupler to the next car, slams the door open, and charges recklessly into the unknown, leaving her partner scurrying to catch up.

By the time Era is inside, Jem is already clashing with a bewildered guard. The thief dumps his backpack and kicks Jem's opponent from behind, allowing her to land an elbow to the side of his head. Their victim collapses, unconscious, and the teammates bump fists before realizing two more guards are charging them with swords drawn.

Jem deflects the leading guard's swing as Era hurriedly draws his dagger and intercepts the second guard. Sparks fly as the foe slams his sword into the thief's smaller blade, and the bruising impact makes Era think his hand may well fall off if struck again. He seizes the chance to grapple the guard, only to be forced backward into a row of crates. Though wincing, he manages to deflect a fatal thrust, forcing his adversary's sword into one of the boxes. Era mercilessly bashes his handle over the vulnerable guard's head to finish the fight, and he breathes a grateful sigh of relief.

A girl's shriek pierces the air, and Era rushes to Jem, only to find her standing over her unconscious opponent.

"Geez, there were more guards than I was expecting," Jem complains. "And what's with you pulling your dagger after the fight began? Haven't you learned anything about-"

"Never mind that," Era interrupts, sheathing his blade. "What's wrong? Are you hurt?"

"No, they barely touched me," she replies in confusion. "Why?"

"Well, you screamed, so I was worried."

"Oh, that wasn't me. That was her," she says while pointing a thumb back over her shoulder. On the ground is a young teenager, her wrists tied to a chair flung to its side in the chaos. Overwhelmed and sobbing, she yanks at her bindings in a vain effort to escape.

"What the-?" Era exclaims as he shoves his way past Jem and kneels next to the girl, who shrieks in fear of the masked intruder. He shoots an angry look at his partner. "Jem, why didn't you help her up?"

"You have a long way to go if you want to be a master thief." She strides to the wall of crates, bouncing with excitement. "This is why we're here!" she says as she begins digging through the first box.

Era ignores Jem and studies the captive. Her button-down blouse and knee-length skirt remind him of a school outfit, and her long, blond hair is the purest color he has ever seen. She squeezes her teary eyes shut while trembling from the turmoil. Her wrists are tied to the chair arms, but she appears uninjured. Era unties her ropes and carefully sets her against the wall. He rests his hand on her head and says, "I'm sorry my mean partner knocked you down with all that fighting."

The youth opens her eyelids to reveal brilliantly golden eyes. Even in the dim light of the lanterns, the unusual color catches him by surprise. "Wow, how beautiful! I've never seen eyes like those." He removes his handkerchief mask and offers a goofy smile to cheer her up. "Who are you? Why were you tied up?" he asks, but she just stares at him fearfully.

Puzzled, Era stands and turns to his partner. "Hey Jem, I-waaahh!" he screams as he suddenly trips and lands on his face with a thud. He looks back to find his new acquaintance clinging tightly to his legs. "Hey, what are you doing?"

"They took me... They took me from school!" she cries as she chokes back tears.

Startled, Era sits and places his hands on the girl's shoulders. "You were taken? Kidnapped!?" She nods with a whimper and starts crying.

Jem snaps at her partner. "Hey, calm her down before she draws attention! There could be more guards in the next car over." Motioning to the empty boxes around her, she adds, "I'm getting frustrated over here! Come help me."

"She needs help, Jem. She was kidnapped!"

"Would you stop using my name? Rule number one is to never use names on a job." She returns to her rummaging and says, "Put your mask back on and leave her be! It's not like we can do anything about it."

"That's cold of you," he huffs.

"How do you expect to get her off the train? We'll barely manage on our own! So leave her be and come help me."

Era ignores her and looks back at the schoolgirl. "We'll take you with us, I promise." The teen glances at Jem, then back to Era and manages a weak smile.

"Agh!" Jem shouts as she throws her hands in the air. "This is useless! It's all low-grade weapons in bulk."

Era grimaces at another job turned sour by poor information. "I told you it was just a shipment to the military. No wonder it was headed to Satari."

Jem argues, "Hey, Satari is home to more than the military. Collectors, dealers, the wealthy…" Slumping to the floor, she leans back on her hands and groans. "This was supposed to be a great load. Why is there nothing here?"

"How did you even find out about this?" Era asks.

"I heard it from a train scheduler at the Yugar junction," she recalls. "He said the Smith's Hammer scheduled transport on short notice. They sent it up to Hensi, which is a known guild repository. Things coming from there are usually the good stuff: jewel-encrusted swords, engraved hilts and blades, even diamond-tipped edges!"

Era glances at the empty boxes in disappointment. "If not the shipment, maybe it's the girl?"

Jem swings her head around, taking interest in her for the first time. "The girl?" Excitedly, she jumps to her feet and runs over. "Of course, the girl! The girl must be worth money, right?" She squats and gets in the captive's face. "Hey, are you valuable? Did they kidnap you for money?"

"I don't know," she replies in bewilderment. "They just took me from school, and-"

"Yes, yes, they took you from school, we heard that earlier," Jem impatiently interrupts. "Who are your parents? Do you have a last name?"

The girl sits silently, unsure what she should say. She looks at Era, who gives her an affirming nod. Staring at the ground, she mumbles, "My last name is Venelli. My father is is… He's the mayor of Canterin."

Jem's eyes widen, and she cracks a wide grin. "She's the daughter of the mayor of Canterin!" she whispers in Era's ear, not making much effort to keep her voice down. "That city is huge! No wonder they kidnapped her. Think of the ransom!"

She again squats in front of the girl and places a hand on her shoulder. Her demeanor completely changed, Jem says, "Don't worry, little one. These men have done a terrible thing to you. We'll get you back home. I promise."

Though the girl is taken aback by Jem's sudden empathy, she releases Era's leg and excitedly hugs her new friend.

Era can tell Jem is already dreaming of a hefty reward, but at least now she's more accommodating toward bringing the kid along. He feels like it would be wrong to leave her behind.

"Well, it's not quite what I expected," Jem says to Era, "but I'm glad we're getting something for our trouble."

He nods as he looks to the unconscious guards, and he squints in the faint light of the lanterns. "Jem! These guards... Are they wearing military uniforms?"

She smirks confidently. "Why would the crown be ransoming one of its own cities? This is a standard customs trick. Even the guild has to pay railroad taxes, so this is just an attempt to pass it off as a military shipment."

Her words fail to ease his concern. "To the capital? Jem, what if-"

"Stop worrying," she insists. "It's a Smith's Hammer train, I'm sure of it. Military trains look different."

"I suppose you're right about that," he says, trying to shake off his concerns. "It's just, you know, getting on the military's bad side would make life difficult."

"To say the least," Jem agrees. "Either way, no turning back now! Let's get this princess back to her castle."

He looks to their new friend. "What's your name, little one?"

For the first time, she acts irritated with Era. "I'm not little. I'm almost fourteen! And my name is Di."

"D?" Era repeats, confused. "Like the letter?"

"No, like D-I."

"Oh. Is that short for something?"

She shakes her head in frustration. "My name is Di!"

Era happily ruffles her hair, much to her dismay. "Well, nice to meet you, Di! I'd tell you my name, but my boss here won't let us use our names while on a mission."

"And how many times have you used my name?" Jem grumbles as she retrieves her bag.

Beckoning Era to lean close, Di loudly whispers, "The lighting makes it hard to tell, but isn't your partner a... She's an..."

"Yes, I'm an Allerian. Got a problem with that?" Jem abruptly calls out.

Di jumps in alarm, but Era says, "Easy, Jem. I think she just now noticed is all."

Jem holds her hand out, comparing her skin's darker tone to Era's. "I guess it's hard to tell in this light." Shrugging it off, she looks at her pocket watch, surprised by the time. "Era, your watch is official. I show about ten minutes."

Era checks his watch, quietly amused by the use of his name. "Ten twenty-four, to be exact."

"Okay, let's get ready for the drop off." She heads to the door with an obvious spring in her step.

Di studies Era, squinting in the light. With a warm smile, he says, "Don't worry, I'm Valvoran, and Jem is a good friend. You can trust her."

She nods. "That's fine, it's just that I've never been so close to one before."

Era decides to change the subject while strapping his backpack tightly around his shoulders. "Anyway, this part might be scary. We have to get off the train, and we don't exactly want to wait for it to stop." The teen swallows hard at the thought, but her eyes reflect a determination to go along with her saviors. She grabs Era's hand and follows him to the back of the train car.

*   *   *

Commander Galen finds himself enjoying the small taste of extravagance by reclining in such a luxurious dining car, the likes of which would never be found on a military train.

The young soldier sports a high rank despite his age. As with all officers, his dark blue coat is buttoned tightly over a leather tunic, and his slacks match the color of his outer jacket. Always one to take in every detail of a mission, he flips through his orders yet again, his keen eyes carefully pruning every line for a hint as to the nature of the task. His directive is to deliver the schoolgirl directly to General Graff at the nation's capital. Further adding to the mystery, the order called for her to be bound. To his frustration, no other details were provided.

The seasoned train conductor enters from the front of the car. Revealing his discomfort around uniformed officers, he stops a good distance from the commander and stutters out, "M-Mister Commander, you requested regular updates about the arrival time. We're currently four hours from Nadar."

"Very well," he says firmly, glad to watch the civilian hurriedly retreat. In addition to the lack of details, the order came down with such immediacy that it required chartering a train from the Smith's Hammer guild. The lack of discipline and protocol from the train staff has been painful to endure. "Private, inform the others of our arrival time," Galen orders to a nearby soldier.

"Yes, sir," the subordinate says. He exits the rear entrance of the train car, only to hurriedly stumble back in. "Someone took the girl!"

The commander leaps to his feet and shoves his way past the private, stepping across the gap between cars and into the room where his men are unconscious. His eyes fall to the opened crates before he charges toward the back. "They didn't come through us, so they must have left this way. Come!" The private scurries to follow after his superior.

The commander leaps through to the other car. Finding it empty, he notices a ladder leading to the roof, and he hoists himself up without hesitation.

*   *   *

Era looks at his watch. "Three and a half minutes!" He rubs his hands together in a futile effort to warm himself amidst the rushing winds. "It's cold out here!"

"Be quiet!" Jem screams. "The guards may be waking up, so let's not give away our position."

"Shouldn't you follow your own advice?" Era shouts back, annoyed by his partner's constant criticism.

"Shut up! I have half a mind to shove you off right now!"

Though they don't see it, Di cracks a smile at their bickering, and she wonders if this is their usual team dynamic. Suddenly, she sees a menacing figure climbing the ladder behind Jem and Era. "Look out!"

Jem grabs the dagger from her waist and spins to find the officer charging with sword drawn. She manages to deflect his blow, but the force of the attack sends her stumbling backward.

Era draws his own blade, but the experienced combatant kicks it away before he can fully grip it. The dagger slides off the rooftop and plummets to the rushing ground below. Era backs up, and they find themselves rapidly running out of room as their aggressor exerts his pressure.

"Give me the girl!" he bellows.

Desperately, the thief stuffs his left hand inside a sack of dirt at his side, digging his fingers into the elements within. He concentrates on the form of the sandy mass and wills its shape to twist and mold into a narrow blade, constructed from the dirt that once filled his pouch.

Galen furrows his brow. "An earth sword?"

"Don't get cocky because of your little trick!" Jem warns, but Era sticks his hand out, holding up a finger at a specific angle. She knows the signal, and she gives a subtle glance to her timepiece.

Undaunted by the feat, the commander lunges forward and swings down over his opponent's head, but Era parries the attack with his thin weapon. Convinced the elemental sword will crumble with enough force, Galen presses down with all his might, hoping to slice through both weapon and wielder.

With a smirk, Era leans away and boldly releases his grip on the dirt sword. It instantly disperses into a cloud of sand, and the commander falls forward from the abrupt lack of countering force, his blade barely missing its target. The tricky thief kicks his vulnerable opponent's weapon away and pushes him backward.

As Galen regains his footing, he breaks Era's hold and creates space. He pulls his sleeve to his elbow and withdraws a black stone from his pocket.

"A rune?" Era immediately recognizes the object, but there's no telling what type it is. He backs away, counting down the seconds.

The commander taps the stone, and it erupts into flames. The fire dances furiously with the wind, but it refuses to be extinguished as it engulfs Galen's forearm. Though his sleeve singes at the edge, the fire shaper himself remains unharmed.

Galen presses forward with his arm extended. Era is forced to cover his face from the searing heat, leaving him defenseless against Galen's sweeping kick, which takes him to the train's roof. The commander stomps on Era's gut and holds his burning arm near his reeling victim.

"Stop!" Jem yells as she prods Di to the edge of the train. "Or I'll shove her off!"

"What!?" Di screams.

Galen glances back to the private who followed him to the roof, but his trembling subordinate is too petrified to be of any use. Growling, he turns to the masked thief and calls out, "Let's make a trade, then."

"Fine, you can have her! She's not worth it!"

He beckons while easing his torch away from Era. "Bring her here."

Suddenly betrayed by her would-be rescuer, Di struggles to escape Jem's grasp, but the Allerian leans close and whispers, "Don't worry, I've got you." Jem checks her watch one more time and glances ahead on the tracks. She grips Di tightly and, holding her breath, throws herself off the train roof. Di shrieks as she's taken over the edge.

Galen instinctively rushes to the edge of the train in horror. However, his shock turns to rage when he finds that the swindler timed her jump perfectly, making her leap when the train was crossing the bridge extending over Haloran Gorge. She's using the compressed air of a pressure pack to carry her gently to the treetops below.

The commander spins to face Era, who is scrambling to his feet. Realizing for the first time that this one is also wearing a pressure pack, Galen charges after him, but the thief hurriedly leaps off the other side of the train.

Galen can do nothing but watch helplessly as the engine crosses the gorge and carries him away from his asset. Once the thieves are out of sight, the commander releases his control of the flame, allowing it to dissipate into the wind as he yanks his sleeve down and storms past his useless subordinate. "Stay up here. Indefinitely," he grunts before returning to his cabin.

CHAPTER 2

Safely supported by a strong jet of air, Era watches the train whisk his powerful opponent away. It was the first time Era had fought with a fire shaper, and he shudders at how helpless he was against the searing flames. He's relieved the gorge came when it did.

The pack's forceful, downward gale offers a gentle descent into the darkness, and Era uses the handheld jets to aim for a clearing below. However, a strong wind blows him off-course, and he gets dragged through a cluster of branches before he manages to cling to one. When the winds attempt to yank him off his perch, Era desperately rips open the pack, releasing a small black rock that whizzes past his ear. It rips through the area, ricocheting off tree trunks before disappearing into the darkness of the night. Relieved, he climbs down and releases his grip, and his feet hit solid ground.

With that, the adventure is over. Era finds himself laughing aloud. He can hardly believe the escape went as planned, not to mention the boarding. Jem and Di soon emerge from the darkness of the woods, and he pumps a fist in the air. "We did it!"

"Wasn't that a rush?" Jem exclaims as the two energetically bump fists. "I told you those pressure packs would work, but you were convinced they'd get us killed! I guess I was right once again, huh?"

"That thing did almost kill me," Era tells her. "I had to release the rune before it flung me back into the air."

Jem's mood dramatically shifts as she rips off her mask. "Do you have any idea how much that thing cost? First you lose the dagger, and now the pressure pack! I'm taking all that from your share."

"Share?" he asks. "Share of what? We didn't get anything."

His partner nods her head at Di, then mutters through clenched teeth, "The reward money," as if to somehow prevent the teen from understanding.

14

Era laughs. "Come on, Jem, she lied about that." Jem grimaces as he looks at the schoolgirl expectantly. "Right, Di? You aren't the daughter of some ritzy mayor. You just wanted us to save you."

Jem glares at her. "Is that true?"

Di looks back and forth between Era and Jem in confusion. "No, my father really is the mayor of Canterin. That's my hometown."

"Listen, Di," Era says calmly, "I promise we'll take you home, so just tell us the truth."

"But I *am* from Canterin," she insists. Era's jaw drops, and Jem's goofy grin returns. Di adds, "I know you're expecting Daddy-erm, Father to pay you a reward for taking me back, and that's okay. You two did rescue me from those villains, after all."

Era manages a weak smile. "Well, okay then. I was sure you were making all that stuff up."

"Wait, you thought she was making it up but still took her along?" Jem gasps. "I swear, Era! You're far too soft for this lifestyle."

"Saving a little girl makes me soft?"

"Hey, I'm almost fourteen," Di interjects.

"Yeah, Era, get it right," Jem snidely remarks. "So then, are you too kindhearted to accept reward money?"

Era shrugs. "I mean, if her old man wants to pay us for taking her home, I certainly wouldn't turn it down."

Jem begins pondering their options. "We'll need to approach Canterin cautiously. The guild will definitely lay a trap for us there, assuming they know she's Canterin's princess."

"I'm not a princess," Di corrects.

"You have a last name," Jem retorts. "That makes you nobility, so close enough."

Era scratches his head. "Actually, Jem, something's bugging me about that fire shaper. You're certain that was a guild train?"

She crosses her arms in contempt. "Didn't I already say this? Valvoren wouldn't be blackmailing one of its own towns, unless Di's father is planning a rebellion."

"Daddy would never do that!" Di exclaims.

Jem shrugs. "Then his uniform was a ruse for tricking inspections."

"He sure seemed like the real deal to me," Era mumbles while rubbing his skin where the burning sensation lingers.

"Sure, he was talented," Jem agrees, "but he bore the insignia of a commander. Someone his age could never be so highly ranked."

Still not convinced, he turns to Di and asks, "Any idea who those guys were? Or where they were taking you?"

"They said they were with the military and they were taking me to their barracks in Satari, but that's all I know."

"Obviously a ruse," Jem insists, "but that guy was a tough fighter. He was probably in the military at some point, so the uniform might not have been just a prop." She rests her hand on Di's head with confidence. "Either way, we'll get this one home, collect our reward, and be on our way." Turning to Era, she adds, "And we'll buy a new dagger from your share before we leave town. Plus another pressure pack."

"What?" he balks. "We don't need another one. How does that make any sense?"

Ignoring him, Jem points to the bridge high above the gorge. "Did you notice, Era? The train never came to a stop. We'd be able to hear the brakes screeching for miles."

He pauses at the realization. "Why wouldn't they stop?"

"Maybe they think they'll have an easier time finding us if they report us?" she guesses. "We incapacitated their forces on the train, after all. Either way, we should get moving."

Era glances around in the darkness. "Where did we leave our bags? It all looks the same at night."

"Pretty sure it was over here somewhere," Jem states as she follows her compass deeper into the woods. After a brief search, they find their hefty backpacks stashed inside a fallen log.

"I just can't believe this worked according to plan," Era says, still giddy as he brushes his bag off.

Jem pulls out a compact lantern and brings it to a soft glow. She next withdraws a map from her bag and spreads it out on the ground. Studying it, she traces out various paths before settling on an attractive route. "Okay, Canterin is on the northern coast. They'll probably expect us to take her home, so we'll take an indirect path, avoid trains, cross the hills south of Ugorzi and…" She stops when her finger hits a mountainous region near the sea. "I don't want to hike those mountains near Maya, so we'll stay along the coastline, avoiding the guild with our expert maneuvering. It should take fifteen days altogether."

Di gulps. "Fifteen days? Why not take the trains?"

"Because it's the most obvious way to get you home," Jem answers, annoyed by the challenge. "Any other objections?"

Era shrugs. "Sounds like you've got it figured out, so let's do it." As Jem packs her map, he turns to their new friend. "I didn't introduce myself earlier, though you've probably caught my name by now." He extends a hand and says, "My name is Era. This is my partner, Jem."

Di shakes his hand. "Pleased to meet you, Era. Thanks for saving me."

"I'm glad we found you. Kidnapping like that... Some people have no shame," he says in disgust.

"Come on, let's go," Jem calls out, compass and lantern in hand as she starts her march.

Era and Di follow their energetic and confident leader as she charges through the brush. The gorge is filled with thick foliage that takes considerable effort to traverse, especially in the darkness.

"So what's an Allerian doing in Valvoren?" Di asks, breaking the silence.

"You're sure concerned about that, aren't you?" Jem asks, getting testy. "I'm a wanderer. Have been most my life. Valvoren, Alleria... They don't matter to me."

"But how did you even get across the border? I've heard it's well-guarded on both sides of the river."

"What is this, an interrogation?" Jem snaps. "I came over during the war, when there was plenty of chaos."

"Oh," Di says. "So, you've been here a while then? I guess that explains your lack of accent."

Jem walks in silence, not interested in continuing the conversation. Era picks up on her demeanor and decides to change the subject. "So, you were kidnapped from school?" The youth nods in affirmation. "What school did you attend?"

"The Arcane Three Pillars Academy."

They halt in their tracks, and Jem swirls around with wide eyes. "You? Are you even old enough to go near the place?"

"I'm almost fourteen," Di says with a huff. "I'm older than I look."

Era scratches his head. "Sure, but the Arcane Academy is elite. I was assuming they took you from Canterin."

Di puffs her cheeks. "Daddy sent me there to study. I've been there almost two years now, and I haven't even been home once since first arriving."

"You haven't been home once?" Era asks in disbelief. "I mean, that's impressive devotion, but isn't that a bit much?"

The schoolgirl frowns. "That's actually quite normal for Academy students."

"Even so, that's too extreme," he argues. "Couldn't you have taken a short break to go home?"

Di grows quiet, apparently embarrassed by the answer. "Well, my father never sent for me, but I was busy with my studies, so it's not like I could have gone home if he did."

Jem crosses her arms in doubt. "Okay, little Miss Arcane, let's see what you can do."

Di is indignant but obeys. She holds her arms out with open palms and focuses. Jem's shoulder-length hair starts to blow as a small gust of wind extends outward from Di's hands. She works up a nice breeze before dispersing it. "Is that enough for you?" Di asks as she wipes the sweat from her brow.

Jem fakes a yawn. "You're an air maker, and that's all you can do?"

"I'm an air *shaper*, not a maker," she corrects. "I can just push air around. Make it bend, twist, and... Well, that's about it."

The Allerian looks back at Era. "Okay, that's actually impressive. Most air shapers are worthless when it comes to making even a simple breeze."

"Air is the most difficult element to shape, after all," Di smugly brags.

"Still, you could make a better breeze if you were a maker," Jem says. "Makers are superior to shapers, after all."

The comment irks the girl. "Hey, I-!"

"Shapers can't do a thing if they don't have the elements available. Makers can use their abilities anytime, anywhere!"

Before Di can object again, Era places his hand on her shoulder. "Relax, Di. Jem is an ice maker, so she's biased."

"Ice maker? Elementalists aren't instantiators," Di says with a pout.

Era looks at her blankly. "Come again?"

"People who control ice and other derivatives are called elementalists," Di explains. "Elementalists aren't makers or shapers."

"Yeah, yeah, enough with your academic jargon," Jem interjects. "I make ice, so I consider myself an ice maker."

"You're not a maker!" Di insists. "Elementalists are special. They're not common elemental manipulators like Era and me."

Jem beams at her partner. "Did you hear that, Era? Elementalists are special!"

Era grimaces at Di. "Hey now, don't be giving Jem a big head. No need to feed that ego."

"But an ice elementalist is rare, Era!" Di exclaims. "There were only a few ice elementalists in the entire Academy."

"Ugh… I won't hear the end of that anytime soon," he mutters, noticing a proud grin on Jem's face. He turns to Di with a gleam in his eye. "So, you noticed I'm an earth shaper?"

"Yes! You seem talented for someone without proper training."

Era fails to hide his delight. "I'm happy with what I can do, but Jem says it's not beneficial."

"What's the point of carrying around a sack of dirt that takes ten seconds to open and shape?" she asks.

"It doesn't take ten seconds."

"Plus, it's fragile."

"It held up against the fire guy."

"Just use a normal blade! And next time don't lose it."

Era laughs and turns back to Di. "See what I mean?"

"Actually, elemental blades aren't a bad idea," Di says. "The masters can shape their elements sharper than a metal sword. That takes decades of practice, though."

The thought is a tantalizing one for the young thief, but Jem reiterates, "Decades, Era. Decades."

"Hey, she said I'm talented. Maybe I could do it in a year or two."

"The masters *are* talented," Di clarifies. "It would take a century otherwise."

Jem continues her original march. "Come on, let's keep moving," she says over her shoulder. "We should probably cut the chatter, just in case."

Di obediently follows along in silence, doing her best to keep up with Jem and Era, who demonstrate a knack for traveling through the wild. The night air is cool and crisp. Despite the lantern and moonlight, the ground is difficult to see, and trampling through the foliage makes it difficult to move too quickly. Not accustomed to traveling in the wild, Di jumps several times at the sounds from various forms of wildlife. She grabs Era's arm and holds it tightly.

After a lengthy period of travel, Jem comes to a stop and looks around. "This should do nicely," she says to herself as she drops her backpack, and Era does the same.

Di watches in confusion as they rummage through their bags. "Wait, what's going on?"

"We're spending the night," Jem explains. "This is a good location. There's direct moonlight, and we can start a fire over here."

"Shouldn't we travel to the next town?" Di asks in a panic. "I don't want to sleep in the woods. We'll get eaten by an earth bear!"

"There's no town for at least another day's travel," Jem responds casually. "And really, Di? Earth bears? Those things only live south of Maaman."

She glances around in the darkness. "Is that true?"

"That's the truth," Era chimes in with a mischievous grin, "but wild shock boars, on the other hand…"

Jem smacks him in the back of the head. "Stop giving the princess nightmares. Go find us some firewood."

"Okay, sorry," Era says as he rolls out his mat and heads into the darkness. Jem pulls out a canteen, enjoys a long drink, and offers it to Di. The weary hiker gratefully takes a sip, her eyes still darting anxiously around the clearing.

Era returns and prepares the firewood. He pulls a black stone from his bag and holds it down in the kindling. He presses on it, prompting a flame to appear, and the fire quickly takes form. "Thank goodness for fire runes, eh?" he asks Di in an effort to make her more comfortable. She politely smiles and sits next to the fire, but Era puts his hand on her shoulder. "Don't worry, I'll sleep on the ground. You can grab my mat. Sorry if it smells."

Di nods in thanks and slides to his mat. As her guardians fall asleep, the youth places her arms behind her head and stares into the starry sky above. Her breath trembles as she fights back tears from the day's events. Somehow, she feels safe with Era and blushes at the sight of him lying nearby. *'Even if his mat does smell,'* she thinks with amusement as her eyelids grow heavy.

*   *   *

"It was a bold but effective escape," Galen disdainfully explains to his subordinate. "Haloran Gorge is vast. It wasn't an option to stop and search."

The young Lieutenant Commander Bowen places his hand to his brow. "I just can't believe they jumped from the bridge like that. And you say the Allerians are involved?"

Galen throws a hand up to clarify. "She had a mask on and it was dark, so I couldn't confirm. Regardless, I personally believe they were simply riff-raff thieves who stumbled onto the girl."

"What makes you think that?"

"The other thief was Valvoran, and the small stock of weapons the train contained had all been rummaged through, as if they were looking for anything valuable. They were not there solely for her, if they were there for her at all."

"Even then, raiding a military train is a blatant offense," Bowen points out. "Thieves tend to leave our trains alone."

"The mission came on such short notice that we had to charter transport from the Smith's Hammer," Galen says. "It's not unheard of for a guild train to be raided."

Bowen rubs his temple. "So, what now?"

"I'm going to contact Commander Talkem," Galen says. "He'll arrange several platoons to station themselves at Canterin. I'm also going to ask him to assist in engaging local Merc Market resources."

"Wait, *you* want to engage mercenaries?"

"Do you think I'm happy about it?" he barks. "We don't have enough troops in the region, and this mission was classified as life-or-death. That girl must be found."

"We've been engaging the market more and more lately," Bowen points out. "Using them requires us to turn a blind eye to their infractions. Many of the hunters are wanted for a multitude of crimes. Some are even assassins!"

"The market isn't entirely illegal, plus they have an information network the military simply doesn't have," he grunts. "We're going to use every resource we have." Reluctantly, he adds, "I'm also canceling the western train network until she's found."

Bowen cringes. "That's really not going to go over well."

"And do you want to be the one to explain why we didn't do everything possible to find her?" Galen asks. "I've not failed an S-ranked mission, even dating back to the war, and I don't intend to start now." He storms into the outer hallway and calls out, "We'll arrange the meeting for tonight at the western tower. I want you there as well."

He bursts into the streets, his frustrations mounting as he marches to the nearby beacon tower in the light of the sunrise as it peaks over the mountains. The bustling trade city of Nadar lies in the lowest part of the Impal mountain range, determined to be the path of least resistance for building the tracks that would connect the western train hub to Valvoren's capital, Satari. As the gateway between the two halves of the country, its growth has rivaled even that of the capital, and the market resources available in such a city may prove to be good fortune for the desperate officer.

*   *   *

Era awakes to someone vigorously shaking his arm. He shoots up in alarm, bashing Di in the forehead.

"Gah!" he yelps as he falls back against the hard ground, rubbing his head as Di does the same with a whimper. His early-to-rise partner is still sound asleep, and he groans as he realizes the sun has barely risen.

Teary-eyed from the impact, Di leans back over Era and whispers, "Era, I need to… I mean, I have to…"

Era offers a sleepy gaze. "You have to what?"

Di blushes and lowers her head. "I have to pee."

"And?"

"And I don't know how! In the woods…" Di softly mumbles, upset with Era for making her explain.

Not showing much sympathy, Era points around and says, "Go find a tree. There are plenty around." Seeing his suggestion isn't well-received, he offers, "But hey, you can wake Jem and ask her for help if you want."

Unsettled by the thought, Di heads into the woods on her own. Era rolls over and squeezes his eyes shut, hoping to return to his slumber before Jem awakes, but he cringes as he hears her sit and stretch.

"That was heartless of you," she chides, sounding plenty awake. "Don't you know how to be delicate about sensitive things? She's not a boy." Giggling, she adds, "Find a tree…"

Era lies still, hoping she'll let him go back to sleep, but Jem walks over to him and leans close. "Nice try," she whispers. She stomps on his foot, and he yelps in pain. "Come on!" Jem says with a chipper tone in her voice. "The further we make it today, the sooner we get paid! I put a lot of thought into it last night, and I'm already thinking this could be a six-figure sum. Can you even begin to imagine?"

Reluctantly, Era sits and groans at starting so early. He pulls his canteen from his bag while mentally preparing himself for a full day of hiking.

*   *   *

The noon sun shines down on the intrepid adventurers as they hike up the tree-covered hillside, finally taking their exit from Haloran Gorge. Each one drenched with sweat, they stop to take a break in the shade of a large tree. Jem takes a swig from her canteen and sits with a huff. "Why is it so hot?"

Exhausted from hiking, Di collapses next to Jem. Era grabs a drink from his own canteen, then hands it to his inexperienced companion and replies, "Because the sun is out? There are no clouds?"

Jem isn't amused. "Shut up," she moans as she flops backward, lying on her back and staring at the blue sky.

Di finishes and hands the canteen back to Era, who takes one last swig and stuffs it back in his sack. "Are we taking a rest, then?"

Jem plants an arm over her eyes as a cool breeze sweeps in. "Sure, let's take a short break," she concedes.

For a few minutes, they silently take in the breeze. Era looks back down the hill they just climbed and counts the days it will take to arrive at Di's home.

"So why are you two thieves?" Di abruptly asks, a serious expression planted on her face.

Jem waves a hand in the air, annoyed by the question. "Hey, we just make use of the resources we come across, that's all."

"Uh huh," Di says with skepticism. "Sounds like thievery to me."

"I survive off the land, Di. I don't consider myself a thief," Jem explains. "Thrill-seeker, adventurer, explorer... Any of those works for me. Now that guy over there is a different story, but he's an anomaly in many ways."

Era gets excited. "I'm a thief alright, and I'm going to be the world's greatest some day!"

"Ugh..." Jem groans as she rolls over, covering her ears. "See what I mean? Now you're going to get him talking, which kills any chance I had for a quiet rest."

Era waves her off. "Jem's jealous of my heritage. I come from a long line of master thieves, and I'm training to become even better than my ancestors."

"A long line of thieves, he says!" Jem shouts. "Come on, Era, you claim your dad is a hot-shot, but I've never heard of him."

Di's curiosity is piqued. "What's your father famous for doing?"

Era raises his head as he brags, "My dad is none other than the Dark Cloak!" Di doesn't offer a response, and Era frowns. "Don't tell me you haven't heard of him, either?"

"I've never heard of any thieves, other than you two," Di admits. "But he sounds cool! What's he stolen? Anything big?"

Era excitedly exclaims, "He stole the Jewel of Nerwal! And some other major artifacts, but I shouldn't brag about those. Pride comes before the fall, after all."

Di eagerly leans forward. "What about you, then? You're following in his footsteps?"

"I am," he answers. "My dad once told me, 'Son, a weak man strives to achieve his dreams, but the strong achieve their dreams through the efforts of others!'"

Di's excitement disappears, realizing Era isn't joking. "Your dad... He sounds like quite a man."

Era blushes at the forced compliment. "I'm going to be exactly like him, but I've only just started. He's off doing great things, so I'm training under Jem here, who's going to teach me everything she knows. That should only take another couple months, then I'll move on to-"

"Hey!" Jem snaps. "Show some gratitude, would you?"

He laughs and waves his hand. "Kidding, kidding." She turns back with a huff, and Era says, "Jem's actually a genius when it comes to living off the land. She's been training me for quite some time, now."

"Hmph," she grunts, "I'm just waiting for you to make up for all the jobs you've botched."

Di looks back and forth, unsure of what to make of their relationship. "So, are you two lovers?"

Era is speechless as he turns beet red, and Jem's face matches his as she stammers, "W-We aren't like that at all! The moron wants my tutelage, so I've graciously given it to him." Era nods fervently.

Di raises a suspicious eyebrow, but she grabs Era's arm and says, "Good, because he's just my type." Looking up at him, she scolds, "Well, except for the thief part, but we'll get that worked out of your system."

Era awkwardly smiles, but Jem isn't amused. "You're thirteen years old, and Era's seventeen. What exactly are you thinking could happen?"

"I'm almost fourteen! Daddy says that's old enough to go on a date." Slyly, she asks, "Or is it possible you're worried about the competition?"

"Competition? You can have him! He's good for nothing whatsoever."

Era laughs aloud, breaking up the spat. "I am pretty useless. That's why it's good I have an amazing teacher!"

Jem is taken aback by the compliment. "Yeah! Your good-for-nothing father set you on this path and abandoned you. You're lucky I came along."

Era looks at Di and says, "Lucky for you, too. It was Jem's idea to raid that train, though we thought we were getting some shiny new swords or something." He laughs and adds, "We got more than we bargained for!"

Jem stands and stretches. "Okay, let's keep moving. We have an outside chance of making it to the next town by dark. I'd think the princess would appreciate an inn over sleeping in the woods again."

Though exhausted from all the hiking, the thought of sleeping in a bed gives Di a burst of energy. She jumps to her feet and drags Era off the ground. They gather their things and stroll after Jem, with Di still clinging tightly to Era's arm.

* * *

A lone figure approaches the designated tower with caution in the light of the setting sun, and she instinctively checks her back several times while approaching. The door swings open, and she's hurried inside by the guard. "Name?"

"Fire," she grunts as she removes the deep red bandanna covering her head, revealing dark hair that shimmers a hint of blue. The soldier observes the short market operative disdainfully; her hard leather vest sits over a dark under tunic, and he wonders what weapons she's hiding under the wrappings at her waist.

She's led into an inner room of the stone tower, furnished with small chairs facing the front. Several others are already present, and not one is seated. Her sights lock onto one hunter in particular, a stocky fellow with a dark leather jerkin. She offers him a coy smile while tying the bandanna back over her hair. "Hello, Jaras."

Slamming his clenched fist against the wall, he dramatically points at her and yells, "You have a lot of guts to show your face here, Fire!" Despite the stares from the others, he bellows, "I told you what I'd do to you if you showed up in Nadar again. Now I'll have to make good on my promise."

"Typical Jaras," one of the other hunters mocks, prompting chuckles from around the room.

"Oh, we're already at this again?" another chides as she enters.

His anger fueled, he replies, "You can all mark my words. You wrong me, you pay the price. And this monster," he stresses, jabbing his finger at Fire, "will be my example."

"We don't need you to tell us," a portly hunter offers. "Her reputation speaks for itself."

26

Fire eyes the mercenary with a smirk. "You mean like yours does, Shem?"

"And what's that supposed to mean?"

"It means that not all of us need fancy toys to get the job done," another hunter chimes in.

"And most of us can get a job done alone," one adds, looking specifically at Jaras.

"You're all just jealous of success," Jaras sneers. "I'll grab this bounty however I want. Just you watch."

Fire stifles a yawn, whether real or fake is hard to tell. Jaras clenches his fist in raw hatred of his adversary while trying to ignore the amused snickers of his peers.

Commander Galen abruptly charges into the room and heads straight to the front, where he faces them with his arms behind his back. "We have three fugitives we want brought in. They're useless to us dead, so they are wanted *alive*," he says, stressing the point. "Two females and a male. Male and Female #1 are in their late teens. Male is just over six feet tall with loose brown hair, and he is an earth shaper. Female #1 is average height and has shoulder-length brown hair. She may be Allerian, and she's likely an ice elementalist. Female #2 is in her early teens, has long blond hair, and responds to the name 'Di'."

He briefly pauses, annoyed no one bats an eye at the prospect of hunting someone so young. He continues, "The trio was last seen nineteen hours ago in Haloran Gorge, and, though their intentions aren't known, they are potentially headed northwest with a destination of Canterin. As for the bounty," he pauses for effect, "twenty thousand venni. Each." Seeing every eye widen in surprise, he adds, "One contingency: no rewards will be distributed until all three are in custody." The caveat fails to stir a reaction. No one was planning to collect less than sixty thousand venni.

"That is all the information I have," he concludes. "I will again stress they are to be taken alive. If anyone has anything to do with their demise, the twenty thousand bounty will be transferred to you, and there will be no quick death for you once arrested. You're dismissed."

As the room clears, Bowen approaches Galen in shock. "Twenty thousand? Per person? That's unreal!"

"It's the highest bounty we allow," he agrees. "Where is the roster?"

Bowen hands it to him and recounts, "Twelve altogether. At least a couple are wanted for assassinations."

Galen reads, "Blane, Wolfgar, Fire, and Shem? We attracted some ruffians." He crumples the paper and says, "We should have arrested half of them. I swear, Bowen, if a mercenary finds my asset, I'm not sure I'll be able to bring myself to pay."

"But shouldn't you have offered more for the girl? She's the one we care about."

"That would be tipping our hand," he explains. "If the Allerians are involved, there might be information out there about her. Directing their attention to the girl would give them reason to consider shopping around."

Bowen crosses his arms in frustration. "Did you send a message to the general about all this? We need to know why she's a VIP, just in case there's information that will help us track her."

"I sent a courier to report to the general directly," Galen answers. "I have not yet received a response."

"Not even by beacon tower? That's a mild reaction considering the mission rank."

"Yes, it is," Galen says. "Until we receive new directives, I want you to organize the propagation of information to the major towns between here and the Lidoran Sea. I'll check in with Commander Talkem by beacon to see how his efforts at Canterin are coming." Confidently, he adds, "We will find her, Bowen. It's just a matter of time."

CHAPTER 3

The early morning light breaks through the treetops, stirring Era from his deep slumber. Groaning as he sits, he wonders how much sleep he had after Jem pushed them so far into the night in an attempt to make it to Hougur. He glances over to the small girl curled up nearby, still fast asleep. She had been as adamant as Jem in making it to an inn, but exhaustion eventually overcame them all and forced them to retire in the wild once again. He's impressed with the endurance Di has thus far displayed, but he knows the worst of the hill country lies before them.

With a shiver, he grabs the last of the firewood and places it on the smoldering embers from last night. Igniting it is a simple task with the help of the fire rune, and the flame soon comes to a roar. He stretches and yawns, breathing in the crisp morning air.

Humming a tune to herself, Jem emerges from the woods, her hand gripping a line full of fish slung over her shoulder. "Whoa, you're up on your own?" she teases as she trots over to the camp. "Good timing with the fire. I brought breakfast!" She holds the fish out for her partner to see, waiting for his admiration.

Era enthusiastically approves. "You found a stream? How'd you catch so much?"

Jem frowns and sits on the log next to him. "Honestly, Era, you need to learn how to live off the land if your goal is to be a so-called master thief." She uses her dagger to start scraping scales and says, "It's important to disappear after a high-profile job, so being able to procure food in the wild is a must."

Scooping some dirt from the ground, Era forms a small earth blade and starts cutting up the scaled fish. "Sorry, master, I guess I'm still learning."

Jem shoves chunks of fish meat on a stick and extends it over the fire, yawning as she watches over it. "I was actually excited by the prospect of sleeping in a bed last night. Sometimes this life isn't so glamorous, huh?"

"No, but it has its perks, right? I mean, moving about as you please, and a gourmet breakfast every morning," he adds as he shoves a pair of skewers into the flames.

She laughs. "I'm surprised you haven't gotten scared off by this way of living. How long has it been now, anyway?"

"Almost a year and a half, if I remember right," Era recalls.

"You two have been together that long, and you haven't fallen in love or anything?" Di calls out. Startled, Era and Jem spin around to find the groggy teen up on her elbows.

The partners sit in awkward silence, and Di stands and brushes off before joining them on the log. She slides herself between the two, forcing Jem to scoot to the side. Di's long hair is disheveled, and her golden eyes are dazed as she gazes into the fire.

Era hands her one of the skewers he's been cooking. "Careful now. It's done, but it might be hot. And mind the bones."

Di is unsettled by the offer. "Ummm… I'm not supposed to eat this, am I?"

Jem smacks her lips loudly. "What, the Canterin princess doesn't eat meat?" she chides with a full mouth.

"Stop calling me a princess, already," Di says while wrinkling her nose and staring at her breakfast.

"And to think that all you did yesterday was complain about stale bread," Jem continues. "I'll have you know I got up over an hour ago to catch those, so you'd better not be a snob."

"I eat fish, just not half-cooked fish-on-a-stick, thanks," she says with disdain.

Era bites into his food, amused by the conversation. "Well, better get used to it. Canterin's, what, two weeks away? You should learn to enjoy a bit of variety."

Di looks suspiciously at Era and Jem, who seem to have already forgotten about her as they tear into their meals. Sighing, she plugs her nose and takes a bite out of one of the chunks of meat. She chews it for a second before spitting it out in disgust.

"I guess she really is a princess," Jem says as she reaches for seconds.

Not giving up, Di takes another bite, but she doesn't last any longer before spitting it back out. With a determined look in her eye, she takes a third bite and immediately swallows it.

"Whoa!" Era says with no small surprise. "That's some willpower, there."

Di stares at her meal for a few moments in silence, and her face starts to lose its color. She gets up and, with as brave a look as she can muster, walks quickly back into the woods. Jem and Era do their best to stifle their laughing at the sound of her heaving.

"This is going to be the worst two weeks of her life," Jem says gleefully.

"I guess she should stick with bread," Era says as he snatches another fish. "Oh well. More for us!"

*　　　*　　　*

With their belongings packed, the travelers resume their hike, and they soon find themselves traveling a thickly wooded trail. Di's queasy stomach growls, and her legs ache even as she begins the day. She's envious of her guardians' energy despite a solid day of hiking yesterday, with no end to it in sight.

Era eventually drops back to check on their lagging companion. "Sorry we haven't taken many breaks, but now Jem wants to make it past Brentan and out to Werran if we can. We need to move without unnecessary stops." Di's heart races in Era's presence, and she marches briskly to keep up with him.

Jem abruptly stops and throws a curled fist into the air. Era plants his hand on Di's shoulder, who waits in confusion as Jem and Era focus their senses. Finally, Jem signals to her right, and she leaps into the designated bush. Era grabs the oblivious Di and dashes into the foliage to join Jem. He dumps her to the ground and starts whispering with his partner.

Di is about to raise an objection, but Era meets her eyes with a stern gaze, his finger planted firmly against his lips. She eventually hears the trotting of a distant horse, and she's amazed Jem had picked up on such a faint sound.

While they're well-hidden, the brush is too thick to see the road. Dissatisfied with her viewpoint, Jem breaks the silence by pushing into the bush as far as she can. It feels like an eternity to the inexperienced Di as they wait for the carriage to pass. When Jem sticks her hand out of the bush to give the all-clear, Di gasps for air.

Era looks at her in confusion. "Were you holding your breath? You didn't need to do that."

"Not on purpose," she retorts. "How do you two do that? I felt like I was going to die trying to be still and quiet for so long."

Jem emerges fully from the brush, plucking twigs and leaves from her hair and clothes. "Hey, keep it down. No reason to risk anything." She gives Era an eager thumbs-up. "It looks good! Packing some luggage, too."

Di is once again left on her own to figure out what they're discussing as Era's excitement builds. "It's been a while since we've taken a carriage. How many?"

Jem holds up three fingers. "Driver's an old man armed with a sword, but he didn't look fit for a fight. At least two are inside."

"Whoa, whoa!" Di cries with her hands outward. "You want to raid them? I thought you were thieves, not bandits!"

Jem shoots her a dirty look. "I told you I'm not a thief, Di!"

"And besides, the difference between thieves and bandits isn't exactly clear-cut," Era adds.

"Either way, they likely have food and water, which could save us from entering a town during the day," Jem explains. "We need to remain inconspicuous while we travel."

"All the more reason not to raid a carriage!" Di objects.

Era plants his hand on her head. "Sorry, but this is what we do! We'll just take what we need. It's not like we're going to hurt them." When she continues to pout, he suggests to Jem, "Maybe Di should stay here. We'll come back for her once we've made our raid."

"No, I'm coming too," she insists.

Jem grimaces in annoyance. "Look, do whatever you want, but stay back so you don't get involved." Di takes a deep breath and nods, nervous about the undertaking despite her insistence to be included.

The two thieves hurry to catch up to the carriage, and Di trails, doing her best to keep up. As they approach their target, Jem puts a hand out to signal Era to stop, and they communicate back and forth with hand signals while Di catches up, out of breath. However, before they can leap onto the path for a rear flank, shouts break out from up ahead. A strong gust of wind blows through the area, and the horse lets loose a whinny as the carriage tips over, crashing to its side.

The thieves stick their heads into the path, and Jem smacks her forehead in disbelief. Three bandits are swarming the tipped carriage, and, as predicted, the driver is doing a poor job fending them off. A lady from inside the tipped carriage shrieks when one of the bandits squeezes inside. They overwhelm the driver and start celebrating their victory with cheers.

"Unbelievable," Jem mutters, relying on the ruckus to hide her voice. "What are the odds?"

Era shrugs and turns away. "Well, that's that I guess. We were too late." Jem nods in disappointment, and they step away from the road, intending to go around the commotion.

Di peeks at the scene before turning back to the others. "Hey," she half-whispers, "we have to help them!"

Jem and Era look at each other and do their best not to laugh. "We were going to raid them! And now you want us to help them?" Jem whispers back. "Let them have their prize, they've earned it."

"Earned it!?" Di yells, far louder than intended.

"Who's there?"

Di nearly jumps out of her skin as one of the bandits approaches. "Hey, it's a girl!" he yells to his companions, having spotted her blond hair easily through the foliage. Visibly shaking, Di freezes in place as she watches him come at her. "You alone, girly?"

Jem and Era spring into action, charging the bandit at full speed in order to frighten him off. As desired, the brigand dashes back to the carriage, yelling for his allies. Era cuts over to Di and hoists her over his shoulder in an effort to make an escape. Jem follows, but a forceful breeze blasts her from behind. She loses her balance and falls as the bandits close in on her.

"Jem!" Era yells, and he dumps Di in order to race back to his partner. The girl lets out a yelp as she hits the hard dirt.

"This is just great," Jem mutters as their three aggressors converge on her with swords drawn. Undeterred, she unsheathes her dagger as Era joins her side.

A gruff and weathered bandit extends a palm outward. A blast of wind escapes from his hand, taking Era's legs right out from under him.

The air maker's allies charge in. Jem leaps at one with her dagger, clashing blades and pushing to stay on the offensive. The other bandit ignores his partner's situation and raises his sword above Era's head, trying to finish him while he's down. However, the earth shaper digs his fingers into the dirt below and pulls out a long blade. He slashes upward in time to intercept the strike, stunning the bandit who thought his victim was unarmed.

Taking advantage, Era sweeps his opponent's legs out from under him and leaps onto him. He punches the bandit in the face, but the air maker blasts him away with another strong gust. Era rolls behind a tree to take cover, and the leader unleashes a strong gale on Era's hiding place, intending to keep him pinned while his dazed ally fumbles for his sword.

Meanwhile, Jem's opponent grabs her arm and tries to shake her dagger loose, but the ice elementalist grabs his wrist with her other hand and begins to freeze it. The sting of frostbite startles the bandit, and he releases her with a yelp. Taking advantage, she kicks him into a tree and smashes his forehead with the handle of her blade, knocking him out.

"Oh for the love of-" the older bandit cries out in exasperation, still focusing his wind on keeping Era pinned behind the tree. "Forget him! Go get the gir-RRRUUAAAHHH!" he screams as the earth beneath him abruptly gives way, and he tumbles into a pitfall.

The thieves don't waste any time. Jem grapples the remaining bandit, and Era helps her shove him into the hole. Their captives yell and squirm in the compact space.

The partners bump fists as Di runs up and hugs Era tightly. "I'm sorry! I'm so, so sorry!"

"Hey, now, it's okay," Era says reassuringly as he pats her head. "See, we don't lose easily." Di holds him tightly with tears in her eyes, and she smiles in relief.

Jem sheathes her dagger, her attitude far less forgiving. "You'd better not do anything like that again! How stupid do you have to be to-"

"Give her a break, Jem," Era calmly says. "It was a mistake. She won't make it again. Right, Di?"

Relieved at Era's graciousness, Di nods enthusiastically. She releases him and looks back at the pit, where the bandits are scrambling around each other below. "We sure were lucky the ground gave out beneath him. What are the odds of that happening?"

Era and Jem crack up laughing. Di just watches them in confusion until Era holds out his open palm. "Earth shaper, remember?" He beats his chest and gloats, "I can do more than make dirt swords!"

Di's jaw drops. "Then, when you were behind that tree, you were shaping the ground?"

"Yup!" Era points along the ground between the tree and the pit. "Don't step anywhere along there, or you'll fall in too."

Jem hops over the invisible line, making her way back toward the path. "That's not the first time he's pulled that off in a fight. Don't feel too bad, Di. I thought it was sheer coincidence the first time, too."

Di trots after them and exclaims, "No Era, that's… That's too strong! You can't do that without years of practice!"

"Well, it did take me years of practice."

"No, I mean years and years!"

"More like it took him years and years to bother doing it," Jem remarks. "Why didn't you do it at the beginning?"

"Hey, I needed over a minute to do that."

"So start sooner!"

Era knows there's little point in arguing further with his partner. He turns to Di and says, "The technique is mostly useless. Minutes don't just happen in the middle of a fight. I was lucky he opted to pin me instead of push the advantage."

Di cautiously asks, "So, you don't… You don't kill people, right?"

Jem shakes her head. "Stealing doesn't seem so bad in comparison, right?"

Di laughs and looks up, realizing they've come back to the path with the ransacked carriage. Era and Jem pause, and they signal for Di to stay behind them. Creeping up to the carriage door, Era peeks in to find a young woman, the driver, and a guard all tied up.

"Whew!" Era exclaims, wiping his forehead. "I thought they might've killed you all. Want some help getting out of there?" he asks as he leans in and starts working at the ropes binding the woman.

"Who are you?" the guard demands. "Are you really here to help us?"

"Seems that way," Era answers. "We were passing by, saw the bandits, and took them out for you." He gets frustrated with the ropes and scoops up some dirt to form a small blade, then makes quick work of the bindings.

Once freed, the woman stands and hugs Era before he can help the others. "Oh, thank you so much! I can't believe how lucky we are you all came along!"

Era blushes as she continues to hold him. "Sure! You're welcome, Miss...?"

"Andrea!" she exclaims, releasing Era from her hug. "What are your names?"

"I'm Era. That's Jem and Di."

She offers the girls long hugs while Era unties the others. He can't help but notice the guard eyeing Jem with suspicion, but it's not uncommon for the foreigner to draw attention to herself. Allerians are a rare sight this far into Valvoren.

Andrea, on the other hand, doesn't seem to balk. After releasing Di, she says, "My, you're a small one. How old are you?"

Di proudly stands as tall as she can. "Almost fourteen!"

"Fourteen! Ah, to be young again. Fourteen is dating age, you know?" She offers Di a wink, and the schoolgirl gives Era an awkward glance. "So what are you all doing in these parts? Isn't it dangerous to travel alone like this?"

Jem crosses her arms, humored. "That seems an odd thing to say, given what just happened to you."

The gruff officer points at Jem and barks, "Careful there, missy. I'd have liked to see you put up a fight being in that carriage when it got blown over." Looking around, he asks with a suspicious tone, "What'd you do with the awful lot, anyway? How'd you take them out?"

She shrugs. "Era here's a hired guard for me and Di, and he single-handedly scared them off. They're probably long gone by now."

Everyone turns and looks at Era, who seems as surprised as they are. He scratches his head and explains, "Uhh... yeah, I guess I know how to put up a fight."

The guard looks him over. "With just that tiny blade?"

Era tosses the small earth knife at the man, who cringes before he's showered with loose sand. "Earth shaper," Era explains smugly.

The guard growls in response, but Andrea claps her hands ecstatically. "Okay, okay, we have plenty of time to sort it all out. You must be my guests tonight! You won't get much past Brentan before dark anyway, especially on foot. I'll feed you and give you a change of clothes, and you can sleep in my guest suite."

Di gets an excited look on her face before Jem breaks in. "Sorry, we need to keep-" Her eyes light up as she processes Andrea's words. "Wait, a guest suite?"

"Yes! And I'll have my butler whip up a fine meal. Please stay!"

"A butler?" Jem repeats as she offers Era a goofy grin. "Sure, why not?"

Di claps in excitement, but Era knows full well what Jem has in mind. Rarely is a thief invited into a luxurious home.

*   *   *

"What an amazing fight!" Andrea exclaims after Jem finishes an embellished version of their conflict with the bandits. "I can't believe you'd risk your lives like that for strangers!"

Jem sits opposite Andrea in the carriage as the men out front continue to guide them on their way, gleefully telling her story. "Well, we did get lucky, but it all worked out in the end. Era's a good bodyguard. So strong and manly, after all," she says, not hiding the sarcasm.

Andrea excitedly gasps. "So, are you two-"

"No!" Era and Jem emphatically state in unison.

She frowns. "Oh, you two just seem so perfect for each other." Looking at the blushing Era, she asks in a disappointed voice, "So you really are just a hired guard?"

Era nods fervently and gives the answer he'd been scripting in his head. "Jem and Di are sisters who were visiting relatives in Yugar. I was hired to escort them back home to Hensi."

Di panics at Era's terrible lie, and the maiden glances back and forth between the Allerian and Valvoran in confusion.

Jem quickly adds, "We're adopted sisters, obviously."

Her curiosity piqued, Andrea says, "I'd love to hear about it over dinner. Still, that's quite a journey for sisters so young. Why not travel by train? If you have the money to hire a guard, you could surely afford a few tickets."

Jem shoots Era a nasty look for having to patch so many holes in his story. "My sister's stomach is weak and can't handle train rides," she explains. Di puffs her cheeks at being used for such an excuse.

"Oh my," Andrea says, taking everything they say at their word. "Well, you two have a good guard for the journey, at least. And an earth shaper? I don't think I've met one before today."

Era beats his chest and brags, "Yep! My father was an even better earth shaper, too. One day I hope to be as skilled as him. He's one of the greatest... ummm, bodyguards who ever lived!"

"Your father sounds wonderful," Andrea says.

He nods enthusiastically. "He told me once that the world is full of lovely women, and I should always stand up to protect them. But only the most beautiful ones!"

Andrea laughs, taking it as a joke, but Di decides he must be serious. *Just what kind of man is his father?'* she wonders.

"Oh no!" Andrea gasps, grasping at her neck and shoulders. "My necklace! I just noticed its absence, it must have come off in the commotion!"

"Oh, Andrea," Jem moans. "I'm so sorry, but I think I saw one of those nasty bandits making off with a necklace in his hand."

Andrea groans. "That's so sad. That necklace was made with imported emeralds!"

"Imported? From Alleria?" Era asks. "I've never heard of importing things like that."

"There's certainly a market for such things, and emeralds are only mined across the border." With a sigh, she says, "Well, I suppose it's not worth stressing. The important thing is that we're all safe."

That the wealthy woman could shrug off such a loss sickens Jem. The Allerian leans her head out the window to find the road winding through croplands. "Didn't realize the hill country was so rich with crops," she comments.

"Oh my, yes," Andrea replies. "This year is important, too. Next season is the year of the dark ravagers."

Di raises an eyebrow. "That sounds ominous."

"Naturally, you would be oblivious to the plight of the common folk," Jem snidely states. "Dark ravagers are little flying bugs with major appetites. They show up once every seven years, devour our crops, and lay eggs that will hatch in seven years."

"Ew!" Di exclaims, wrinkling her nose.

"That's why the sixth harvest is so important," Andrea adds. "Our storehouses must be packed or we will face starvation."

Jem shields her eyes from the setting sun and asks, "Is that Brentan up there? I didn't know you had such an impressive wall."

"We're proud of it, for sure. My father funded the project ten years ago. It keeps our village safe from brigands and the like."

"That's impressive," Jem says with interest. "Is your father the mayor or something?"

"No, no. Father is a businessman from Nadar," she says. "He made his money when they moved the capital and established the road through the Impals. Business flourished, and he benefited. He retired here right before the war started."

Era glances at Jem, whose eyes have already glazed over as she envisions a lifestyle entirely opposite her own. It's hard not to envy those who stumble into such luxury, and the thought makes him wonder about Di. The Academy student must have a noble heritage.

"It's a humble place to retire," Jem remarks as she watches the farmers packing their tools for the night. "Your money must have tripled the local economy."

"It's certainly been a boon," Andrea says proudly. "The wall's construction was started during the war, both to keep the economy going and to protect us in case the Allerians-" She cuts herself off and offers an apologetic glance to her guest.

Jem laughs aloud. "I'm no stranger to these conversations. Given how far the Allerians made it past the border, the wall was a good idea."

Andrea looks relieved. "Well, it wasn't used during the war. Its construction took longer than anticipated, plus the truce was drawn so abruptly."

Di looks confused. "Why was it abrupt?"

"The late king was killed in a battle across the border," Jem says flatly. "The Valvoran army was thrown into chaos, the Allerians pushed in... Don't you know your history?"

"I knew all that," Di insists.

"Really?" Jem smugly asks.

"Yes! The new king mustered his forces and defeated the Allerians west of Maaman," she says in response. "He offered a truce, supposedly in spite of a significant strategic advantage."

Andrea chimes in, "I was just a teenager at the time, but I can still remember the fear melting away from the hearts of the villagers. It was most fortunate timing."

Era glances to Jem, who has turned to watching the passing crops. She doesn't like talking about the war, and he has long wondered about the nature of her sensitivity.

The carriage slows to a stop at the town gate as a guard makes an inspection. He chats with the driver and proceeds to open the carriage door. "G'evening Miss Andrea-" He abruptly pauses when he sees Jem.

"Good evening," Andrea replies. "Please accept Jem here, as well as Era and Di as my guests for the evening. They saved my life in an act of true courage today."

Jem offers a self-satisfied wave, but the guard doesn't return the gesture. He reluctantly closes the door and waves them on. The carriage starts to move again, taking them into the town.

Andrea appears distraught over the encounter. "My, I didn't realize you would cause such a stir."

"I cause a stir wherever I go," she says proudly, placing her hands behind her head. "People love me."

Era grins. "You never fail to draw attention, that's for sure."

The road leads into a wooded lot, and the carriage pulls up to an impressive house built into the city wall itself. It stands two levels high, and its roof meets the top of the wall. The second story has a smaller footprint than the rest of the house, providing a walk-out deck that can be accessed from the top floor.

Jem lets loose a whistle. "Woods in a walled city?"

"I thought we were getting out of the forest," Di mutters.

"There are probably fewer trees inside the house," Era points out.

The driver and guard hitch the horse to a nearby fence post and head back toward the main city. As her guests stretch, Andrea approaches her front door, which is made from the same stone as the wall, and it swings open to reveal a lanky servant. "Miss Andrea, thank goodness," the butler exclaims as he embraces his mistress. "Aren't you quite late? You had me worried!"

40

"Oh, Connor, stop it," Andrea says while pushing him back. "We just had a late start this morning is all. How are you this evening?"

"Quite well, thanks," he replies as he gives a suspicious look to the three hungry strangers behind Andrea, eyeing Jem in particular. "And you are?"

Jem crosses her arms. "Hey, don't be so cold. We saved your lady's life today."

His eyes widen as he looks at Andrea. "Saved your life? What does she mean?"

Andrea waves it off. "It was a bandit attack, but Era here fought them off!" She grabs the supposed guardian and shoves him forward, prompting Jem to tap her toe in regret for making him the sole hero of the story.

Era awkwardly endures the butler's cold stare. Scratching the back of his head, he stammers, "I-It was... ummm... Well, it was all in a day's work! I'm a bodyguard, and we were passing by, you see..."

The butler loses interest and turns back to Andrea. "Madam, are these strangers to be our guests tonight? You know how your father feels about such *fellows*," he stresses, not hiding his disdain for Jem. "He's in the market presently but shall return home shortly, and he won't be pleased."

"I'm not a child, so I expect you not to speak to me as one," she responds. "I've already given my word, so we have no choice." She turns the butler around and pushes him inside. "I'll handle Father, so you go work on dinner," she commands, leaving the three to wander into the luxurious manor on their own.

The foyer's walls are adorned with glamorous canvases, and two towering sculptures loom overhead, as if standing guard. An intricately woven rug extends down the main hallway, and an impressive staircase leads to the upper floor. Jem gawks at the remarkable sight, and she shares an eager glance with her partner in crime.

Their host reappears and claps her hands. "Jem and Di, come with me!" She grabs their wrists and pulls them up the stairs. "Era, you can just wander around or something. Girls only!" she shouts as they disappear.

Era feels a shiver of excitement at being alone in such an extravagant home. The corner of his eye catches Jem sneaking back to the top of the stairs. She throws him a signal before excitedly disappearing again. Era smiles to himself, glad his partner is as impatient as he is to get started.

CHAPTER 4

"Di, your outfit is in tatters," Andrea observes in horror.

The schoolgirl looks herself over in dismay. The white blouse is dirty and stained, and her skirt is ripped to shreds. "It's not the right kind of outfit for traveling," she laments.

"Didn't your relatives give you better clothes?" she asks as she runs her fingers along the tattered skirt.

Di swallows hard as her innocent brain works to perpetuate the lie. "Well, actually no, they said I should buy some along the... I-I mean- Of course they did! But I lost them in a... in a river?" Jem cringes at the horrible attempt.

"I'll remedy that," Andrea declares, too excited to notice Di's fabrication. After searching her wardrobe, she withdraws an outfit and says, "I know I have more old clothes in my second wardrobe downstairs. Try that on, I'll return shortly!" she calls out as she hurries from the room.

Di anxiously reaches to unbutton her blouse, but Jem stops her. Di's brow furrows. "Hey, why are you-"

"We're leaving, naturally." Jem starts touring the extravagant room, finding all kinds of knick-knacks to stuff in her bag.

Di watches in dismay as the crook makes her selections. "Jem? You can't possibly be comfortable stealing from Andrea!"

"Shush! Do you want to get caught? That would make leaving even more awkward."

"But-"

"Do you honestly think our gracious host will even notice these trinkets are missing? She's checking her second wardrobe for you!" She snags the outfit Di was about to try and says, "Here, I'll take something for you, too. You're welcome."

Di wants to argue, but she finds herself speechless as Jem crams a few last items into her bag.

"This is going to be too easy," Jem mumbles as she walks out onto the balcony. Like the house itself, the balcony connects to the town wall, with the top of the wall resting just above her head. She hops up and finds that she can reach the ledge.

Di's heart races as she glances around Andrea's room, trying to somehow note what all was taken. It's as if she realizes for the first time she's been traveling in the company of a thief.

"Uh oh, looks like Daddy's home," Jem says as she glances to the yard below. "Get out here!" she calls to her lingering companion.

Di hesitates, torn about whether to go with her guardian. It's the first time she's had a choice, and the option of staying with Andrea isn't entirely unwelcome.

"Hurry up!" Jem barks in annoyance.

Di hears shouting break out from downstairs, meaning that Andrea's idea of hosting an Allerian is probably not going over well. Suddenly worried she'll be blamed for her alleged sister's thievery, she darts out to the balcony where Jem is crouching with a cupped hand. She takes the boost to the top of the wall, and Di looks over the edge to find a steep drop awaiting her. She lets out a shriek and grips the wall tightly.

"Ugh... Di," Jem quietly growls as she heaves her bag up and over the ledge. She jumps and pulls herself up, however, upon seeing the distance of the drop, she also finds herself grabbing tightly to the stone. "Okay, that's higher than I thought."

Di nods furiously. "Let's find another-" To her horror, Jem throws herself off the ledge, and she lands hard on the ground below. The Allerian hops up and down, dancing off the pain.

Another thud sounds out as Era's bag lands a short distance away. The thief himself is the next one to land, having found his own means of escape.

Jem shouts, "Come on, Di! You're running out of time!"

Di starts to swing her legs over the ledge, but her face turns a bright shade of crimson as she presses her skirt against her legs. "Era, turn around!"

"Turn around?" he asks in confusion. "But why-"

Jem physically spins Era to look the opposite direction. "Okay, he's not looking. Now come on!"

The terrified accomplice squeezes her eyes shut and drops her legs down while still clinging to the ledge.

"Di!" Jem snaps.

Startled, she falls with a shriek, but Jem catches her as she lands. She looks to her Allerian guardian with gratitude.

Jem immediately releases her, and she falls with a yelp. "I swear, Di! You're making this trip impossible."

"Can I look now?" Era asks.

Jem slings her bag onto her back. "Yes, you can look. Now let's move."

They make their escape into the darkness of the surrounding woods, rushing away from their crime scene with expediency. The forest isn't as thick in these parts, and they can spot the town's surrounding farmlands through the trees. They avoid any possibility of human interaction by staying off the main paths, opting to travel across the natural terrain as the sun makes its way below the hilltops.

After what feels like an eternity, Di slows while panting heavily. Straining her eyes in the soft light of the moon, she struggles to keep up with Jem and Era, who seem to have no intention of stopping. "Era, wait!"

The two shadowy figures ahead slow down and start bickering with each other. Jem sits with a huff, and Era returns and rests his hand on Di's shoulder. "Too tired to continue?"

She nods. "When are we going to set up camp?"

"I was planning on another two hours," Jem calls out. "We rode in a carriage half the day!"

Di collapses to her knees at the notion, and Era looks back to his partner. "Easy now, Jem. That carriage ride helped us make good time today. We'll get to Canterin soon enough."

"That ride was our chance to make up for lost time," Jem insists. "Di's so out of shape that we can't even hike a full day. I want to get paid!"

"All you care about is money!" Di cries. "I can't believe you stole from our friend like that."

"Our friend?" Jem scoffs. "We saved her life! She owes us a far bigger debt than what I collected."

"She was going to repay us with dinner and lodging!"

44

"That helps me for one night. These trinkets will keep me going for a month. It's no comparison."

Di tugs at Era's shirt with pain in her eyes. "She's a horrible, horrible person, Era. Why do you travel with her?"

Era avoids eye contact and sort of shrugs, but Jem starts laughing. "Oh, I'm so horrible, am I? Era's such a nice guy, right?" Turning to her partner, she says, "I figure I landed around three thousand's worth, not counting the emerald necklace. How much did you get?"

"Wait, you took her necklace, too!?"

Jem maintains eye contact with Era. "Well?"

Era glances nervously between Jem and Di before admitting, "Probably between two and three."

Jem smugly raises her head, having made her point, and Di turns away from him in anger. Annoyed, he asks, "What do you want? I already told you I'm following in my father's footsteps. I couldn't just stay in a place like that without making off with something."

"But Era," Di argues, "how can you save her life and then steal from her?"

Era smiles softly. "It was nothing personal. Jem and I... We can't pass up an opportunity like that. To someone like Andrea, she'll barely notice those things are missing. But that's food and clothing for us! It's not petty thievery."

Di puffs her cheeks and averts her eyes. "That doesn't make it right."

"You live in a fantasy land," Jem says. "This is the real world out here, rich girl. We don't have last names. We don't know where we're getting our next meal, and we don't know whether we'll survive the night. But don't worry, we'll have you back to your castle soon enough, and then you can go back to your dream world."

She resumes her hike and says, "We'll slow our pace, but we can't stop. The town's police may be in pursuit, and a campfire would draw them straight to us." Era glances to Di, but he opts to follow after Jem without another word.

The emotional schoolgirl walks in silence, regretting the type of people who rescued her. Her heart aches as she mulls over it all, wondering if she should have taken the opportunity to stay with Andrea.

*   *   *

The walled town of Brentan is known for closing itself off to strangers and travelers. The gate is always shut promptly at sundown, locking locals in for the night, and forcing any weary travelers to find somewhere else to lay their head. This landed a certain weary bandit in the town of Hougur, a few hours' walk to the east.

The husky brigand enters his quaint room at the inn having just returned from the bathhouse. A towel wrapped around his waist, he sits on his bed and rubs his shoulder, silently cursing his poor fortune.

"Well, well, I didn't expect it to be you, Orlan." The towel-clad air-maker extends his open palm to the window, where he finds a short mercenary smugly leaning on the sill from the outside.

Orlan lowers his arm. "So it's you, Fire. Finally decided to come after me, did you?" He walks to the rack in the corner where his clothes are hanging. "At least let me dress before you kill me."

"Kill you?"

"I've been hearing of your accomplishments," he says. "Figured it was just a matter of time before I saw your face in my window."

"Tch, same old Orlan, it's all about you," she says as she slides in. She pulls her sweat-drenched handkerchief off her head to reveal short, dark hair extending to her chin. Hidden weapons clink around at her waist, covered by a sash that enwraps her torso.

"I assume you're here for the money," he says, "but I sure don't have that anymore."

Fire shrugs. "Forgot about that long ago."

He watches her quizzically. "Really? That was a lot of money I swindled."

"I just pulled the same scam on a rookie hunter, so consider your debt indirectly paid." She crosses her arms and adds, "Still, doesn't change the fact that you're a dirty hustler."

Orlan slides his shirt over his hairy chest. "Leave me alone, I've had a rough day."

"So I've heard. Sounds like you were in a scuffle with an earth shaper. Maybe a couple others, according to the drunks you chatted up at the bar earlier tonight."

"You're as resourceful as ever," he grunts. "What about them?"

"Tell me where you saw them and where they were going."

46

"Those kids? You're joking, right?" Fire continues to wait expectantly, and Orlan's interest escalates. "What are they worth?"

"Three hundred."

The experienced bandit rolls his eyes. "Who do you think you're fooling, Fire?" Before she can respond, he adds, "Tell you what, you let me get dressed in privacy and I'll take you to where we fought. Least I can do after what I did to you and your teammate. What was her name… Hallie? How's she been?"

Fire clenches her fist. "We split ways," she mutters. "Haven't seen her in a while."

"That's a shame," Orlan says sincerely. "You two made good partners. You should find her and make amends."

"Little late for that," Fire says as she ducks out the window. "Don't keep me waiting, old man," she warns before disappearing into the dark evening.

He yanks the curtain shut. "Old man? Ugh… Maybe I *am* getting too old for this."

*   *   *

Orlan swings his lantern back and forth as he strolls along the open path. "It's got to be around here somewhere. Where'd you go, Fire?"

At first there's no answer, but Fire's voice eventually whispers from the dark forest behind him, "Shut up, Orlan! And put out that lantern. You want to draw attention?"

Orlan chuckles. "Little lady, you're far too paranoid."

"I'm good at what I do, and screaming 'here I am!' to a five-mile radius isn't a good strategy. Now put that thing out!"

Sighing, he continues forward. "Well, like it or not, we'll never find it without the lantern." Arriving where the carriage tipped, he hikes back into the woods. Sure enough, a giant hole stands off the path, its gaping mouth waiting for some unfortunate forest creature to fall into it.

"Found it," he calls out. Fire emerges from the woods and stoops to study the hole. Orlan grumbles, "He got me good. I sure didn't expect something like that."

"You said a teenaged kid did this?" Fire asks in disbelief. "It takes decades to learn this kind of control, doesn't it?"

"Well, it sure took *me* decades to learn that kind of control," Orlan huffs. "I had him pinned behind that tree over there," he points out. "It took him a while to pull it off, but I was keeping him trapped while my boys tried to knock out his Allerian girl partner. Never saw it coming."

Fire finds a stick and pokes at the ground between the hole and the tree until she jabs the right spot, and a crevice opens. As she continues to drag the stick, she opens a long path carved into the earth that makes a direct connection back to the tree. "Well, it was definitely him who did it. That's some powerful shaping."

"Is that why you're after him?"

"You know how it goes. You never know why you're after someone. All I know is what he's worth."

"And what is he worth?" Orlan asks. "If the price is right, I'll offer my services to you."

"Sure, come along," she coldly replies. "I promise I won't feed you false information about how to get paid."

"I can take a hint," he grunts as he picks his lantern off the ground. "Well, that's all I have to show you. Embarrassing as it is to admit, it took me the better part of an hour to get out of that hole, so they were obviously gone by the time I got out. As best I could hear, they made nice with the people in the carriage and took off with them. It was late in the day, so they were probably headed to Brentan."

As he leaves, Fire calls out, "Thanks, old man! You're pretty useful when you're not swindling me."

Orlan shakes his head and turns back toward Hougur. "And to think I showed you this for free." Waving a hand in the air, he calls back, "We're even now, Fire! Don't come asking for any more favors."

"Like this makes up for ten thousand venni!" she calls out, knowing full well it might. She tromps back into the woods, following the path from a distance as she traverses the dark terrain. There will be no sleep for her tonight.

*   *   *

The travelers hike conspicuously along the open path, enjoying the midday road all to themselves. The morning was a quiet one for the group, as a sullen Di has continued to wrestle with her conscience. The relatively flat journey starts to become more difficult as they enter the hill country, and she moans as her legs complain about the inclines. "Can we take a break? Going uphill is hard."

Jem doesn't turn around as she continues her march. "Hills cover half the way to Canterin. It's not going to get easier anytime soon, so get used to it."

Era nods in agreement, providing no relief to Di. The cusp of the hill is in sight, but seeing the distance only makes it harder to hike the path. She trudges onward, slowly, until she collapses with a huff, her face and hair a mess of perspiration.

"Hey Jem, better hold up," Era calls out.

She forces an aggravated sigh. "Seriously, Di, do you even want to go home?" Jem yells as she storms back. "Look, you're not even carrying anything. Era and I have to hike with these ridiculously large bags," she notes as she loudly smacks the side of her backpack.

Di rolls her eyes. "Of course I want to go home! You want me to go faster? Fine!" She jumps to her feet and hikes at an accelerated pace, overtaking her two traveling companions. Though she attempts to maintain her lead, Era and Jem easily pass her at their normal walking pace. Not having any experience living in the wild, Di just can't make her legs move like she wants.

Jem stops as the sluggish traveler makes an honest but pathetic attempt to scale the incline. "Alright, Era, what are we going to do about that? We'll never make it to Canterin at this rate."

Era walks back to his lagging companion and, without asking permission, scoops her up in his arms. Di lets out a small "eep!" and smacks him in the chest. "What are you doing?"

"I'm carrying the princess back to her castle," Era informs her.

Blushing, Di crosses her arms in contempt, but she doesn't object. Despite looking weak, Era's strength and endurance continue to impress her. He catches up to Jem, and they continue to hike the trail.

"S-So," Di stammers, trying to become more comfortable with the situation. "I've decided you two shouldn't steal anything else while you're escorting me back."

"And if we do?" Jem asks, hardly interested in the conversation.

Di takes a deep breath and says, "If you do, then I'll tell my father not to give you a reward."

Jem glances at Era, but she can't keep a straight face. "So wait, you're saying you'll be worth nothing to us? Doesn't seem you've thought this through. Aren't you supposed to be smart?"

Di glares at Jem, but Era says, "Look, Di, we'll do our best not to make you uncomfortable. But if it means getting you back home, doesn't that make it alright? I mean, if it's for the greater good and all that."

"I just…" she starts, unsure how to defend her values in such a scenario.

"Besides," Era says, "I need the practice. Jem keeps nagging me about that! Practice is a must, so of course I can't pass up an opportunity that comes along." Di punches Era in the chest, doing her best to pout while enjoying his embrace.

Upon coming to the crest of the hill, Di leaps from her guardian's arms and hurries down the incline on her own. As the others follow, Jem leans close to Era and whispers, "She's trying so hard to crush on you, but you're making it difficult."

Era shrugs. "Maybe it's for the best. I think she's a little young for me."

*　　*　　*

"Okay Era," Jem concedes in annoyance. "Time to go get her again."

Era looks back at their struggling companion. "We're almost to the top. You don't think she'll make it?"

Jem crosses her arms. "Listen, I'm all for making her carry her own weight, but I also don't want to age ten years before we get her home." Impatiently uncorking her canteen, she takes a chug of water and immediately spits it out. "Blech! When did this get so warm?" She tips the canteen and sticks her finger in to frost it. Taking another swig, she wipes her mouth with a satisfied smack of her lips. "Ah, much better! You need more ice?"

Era takes a drink of his and says, "Nah, mine's good. I had you load it up last time." He looks back and calls out, "Di, you want a drink?"

Di catches up to her guardians, out of breath and drenched with sweat. "I could… use some." She takes the canteen and collapses at his feet.

"Geez Di, you're a wreck," Jem says as she adds more ice to her canteen. "Isn't exercise a requirement at the Academy?"

Di finishes chugging and wipes her mouth. "Quite the opposite. Everyone sits inside all day studying and practicing elemental arts. No one's in good physical shape there."

"At least you're young," Era offers. "You still have hope of not growing up to be fat and lazy."

"The elemental masters aren't lazy," Di insists, staring at the sky. "It was an amazing place to study. No one in the world is as skilled as they are."

"Isn't there an Academy in Alleria?" Jem asks. "They're probably just as skilled there."

"Not that there's any way to know," Era comments, "seeing as the border is locked down."

Di furrows her brow. "Actually, the two Academies are able to send communications through the border, and in some cases, the professors even travel back and forth. Though, admittedly, the last time that happened was just before I came to the Academy."

"Whoa, really?" Jem asks. "So the Academy *is* that special."

Era takes another swig of his water. "What's so special about sitting around all day studying?" He squats and places his palm on the path, forming small pillars of dirt all around his hand. "You learn plenty just by using the elements."

Di smirks. "Think you can beat me in knowledge?"

"What's there to know?" Era chides. "Water, ice, earth, fire, lightning, air..." he trails off trying to remember the others.

Jem sighs. "Light and wood! Geez, Era, don't embarrass yourself in front of an Academy student. You make me look bad as your mentor."

"So which ones are core elements, and which are derivatives?" Di asks.

"Derivatives?" Jem repeats. "I'd guess... ummmm..." She pauses, hoping Di will interrupt, but the Academy student just watches in amusement. Sighing, she admits, "Okay, so I don't know the fancy terminology. What's a derivative, oh wise one?"

Beaming, Di starts drawing in the dirt with her finger. "The core elements are earth, fire, air, and water," she says as she draws twelve small circles, themselves arranged in a large circle. "This is called the Elemental

Dodecagram. The four core elements are each assigned a quadrant with three circles. Two of these are dedicated to the control of each core element, which is divided into 'instantiation' and 'contortion'. Or, for the uneducated, 'making' and 'shaping'."

Jem is annoyed by Di's subtle insult, but Era doesn't get the hint. "I've never heard those terms before," he says with interest.

Di practically glows, enjoying her spotlight as she etches two symbols into the sand next to her drawing. "This symbol represents instan- err... making, and this one's shaping," she says as she points to each one. She then fills two circles in each quadrant with the symbols. "Let's say this quadrant is earth," she explains as she points to a group of three circles, "then these next quadrants are fire, air, and water. Since you have both making and shaping for each of the four core elements, you have eight primary elemental manipulations."

Era looks the drawing over, having never seen anything like it. "So what are the four empty circles?" he asks, pointing to the remaining ones that haven't been designated by a symbol.

"Those are the derivatives!" She etches a third symbol into the sand under the previous two. "This symbol means 'derivative', and each element has one." She fills the last four circles with the third symbol, completing her drawing. "Water has ice, air has lightning. Fire has light. Earth has wood. That makes for twelve elemental instances: eight cores and four derivatives."

Era studies the drawing with fascination, and even Jem finds herself drawn in.

Di flops back against the ground. "Everyone is born in possession of a single instance, though most people never put in the effort to develop their talent. Those possessing core instances are called manipulators, while those with derivative instances are known as elementalists. Elementalists are much rarer than manipulators, plus they have the ability to both make and shape the derivative element. Core manipulators can only do one or the other, never both."

Jem nudges Era in the side. "See, I'm special! You should show more respect."

Era grimaces. "Sure, but she said you should be able to both make and shape ice. You can't shape ice, so maybe that means you're not talented."

"Sounds like you want to drink warm water the rest of the way to Canterin," she snaps.

Di adds, "Well, I should specify that some of that is theory. Based on our understanding of elemental structures, elementalists should be able to both instantiate and contort, but that's rarely been documented. As it stands, elementalists are generally split into makers and shapers, just as with core users."

"Next time tell me that sooner," Era complains, hoping Jem forgets her warm water threat. "So can Jem also control water? Being a water derivative and all that?"

Di shakes her head. "Only one instance per person. What nature gives you at birth is what you have all your life."

"So how does nature decide that?" Jem asks.

"There are many theories, but we still lack a firm understanding of that."

Era laughs. "All those smarties studying this for hundreds of years, and they don't even know how we get our abilities."

The schoolgirl wants to object, but Jem squats and brushes Di's diagram away with her hand. "Okay, break's over," she orders.

Di groans, but Era scoops her up. Before she can argue about being carried again, he eases her concerns. "Don't worry, it's just for a minute. The hilltop is right there, see?" Di relaxes and enjoys her water as Era carries her up the last leg of the hill, and he sets her down when they reach their destination.

Finishing off the rest of Era's drinking water, Di's eyes grow wide as she takes in the sight of a massive gorge right on the path. "My, how beautiful! It looks like the road carves a path right through that hill," she exclaims. The path runs alongside a river with cliff walls towering on either side, providing relief from the seemingly endless stretch of hills.

"Don't get too excited," Jem warns, "because we're not going down there."

Di frowns. "But, if not down there, then where?"

A sadistic grin spreads across Jem's face. "We're going up there!" She points to the west side of the hill, indicating the travelers will be hiking off the trail to go over the valley. "We'll need to wade through the river here as well, while it's still narrow."

Di's jaw drops at the thought of both wading through water and then climbing the highest hill yet today. "Why would we do that? Why wouldn't we take the easy path?"

"Bandits," Era answers. "They love that terrain. It might be unlikely, but it's not worth the risk of an ambush just for the sake of taking a nice stroll."

Di slaps her forehead and glares at Era. "You'd better be planning to carry me up that *mountain*." She stomps down the hill, enjoying gravity's help one last time.

Era laughs as he and Jem follow. "I was already planning on it, princess."

"And stop calling me princess!"

CHAPTER 5

Di can hardly believe her eyes as the trio emerges from the woods to find a ridge overlooking the gorge. "Truly amazing. It makes all that hiking worth it!"

Era hunches over, sapped of his strength. "How much hiking did you even do? I carried you most of that way, including across the river!"

"I've never seen anything like this in all my life," Di marvels, ignoring Era's remark. The gorge spans a wide distance, and the rumble of the river below echoes off the canyon walls. Di creeps to the edge and looks down, spotting the path that would have otherwise carried them through the area. The ridge slopes at a steep angle, all the way to where the path and river lie below. "I guess I'm happy we didn't stay way down there. I wouldn't have seen this view!"

"Well, hurry and take it all in, because the whole point in coming this way was to remain inconspicuous," Jem reminds her. "We need to stick to the other side of the tree line. Don't forget what we said about bandits loving this terrain."

Di looks back slyly. "The big bad bandit girl is afraid of bandits?"

"I'm not a bandit," Jem insists with a huff. "Or a thief, or anything, so stop trying to label me."

Di looks back down the slope. "But why do bandits love this terrain? There's no way they could ambush anyone on that path from way up here, is there?"

Era steps next to Di and looks down. "It is steep, but I'll bet I could skid down it if I wanted to jump a caravan or something. There's a gentle grade at the end." Di grimaces at the thought of intentionally jumping off the ledge.

"If there are bandits around, we're not doing ourselves any favors by sitting out in the open like this," Jem warns, motioning for them to come. "Let's move."

Di sneaks one last peek at the view before ducking back into the underbrush. They hike in silence as she silently tallies how much further to her home.

"Yeow! Stupid bugs," Era yelps as he smacks the back of his neck. "Something just bit me!"

"More like stupid *woods*," Di gripes. "I'm sick of trees and branches and leaves and bugs."

Era pulls a small object around to see. "Uh... Jem?" Instead of a bug, he holds a feathered dart. "I dunnn thinnnk..." With that, he stumbles and collapses to the ground.

"Era!" Di shrieks.

The experienced Jem grabs Di and spins them behind a tree.

"Jem! Era's-"

"Shush!" Jem covers Di's mouth and stays quiet, ignoring Era's plight for the moment. A hush falls over the wooded area, and Jem listens intently.

Di obediently remains silent, though she doesn't have much choice since Jem's hand is still clamped down on her mouth.

Jem takes a cautious peek around the trunk and notes Era's condition. *'A poison?'* she wonders, but all she can do right now is hope it isn't a lethal dose.

Two projectiles plunge into the trunk next to Jem's head, forcing her to whip back behind her refuge. "We're pinned down," she whispers to Di. "Come on!"

Jem dashes from the tree, running away from Era and their hidden aggressor. Pulling Di by the hand, she races through the woods, dodging trees and leaping over fallen logs. She cuts and runs back toward the clearing next to the ridge, intending to force their pursuer into the open.

As the trees thin, her plan works, and a petite figure with a bandana emerges from the brush. Jem whips Di around and gives her a hard shove. "Get back!" she orders as she withdraws her dagger and turns to fight.

Fire smirks at the inexperienced target challenging her to a knife fight. She engages head-on, skillfully dodging a swing and kicking the dagger from Jem's hand. She swiftly swings around and punches Jem square in the jaw. The Allerian stumbles back, and the assailant lands a solid kick to Jem's gut, knocking the wind out of her.

Fire stands over her opponent as she collapses and gasps for air. "What makes these targets so valuable?" she mutters to herself as she begins unraveling wire.

"Jem!" Di cries out as she recklessly tries to tackle their aggressor, who snags her wrist, punches her mercilessly in the stomach, and tosses her onto Jem.

"Seriously, what's up with you three? Are you really the right ones?" Fire asks in disgust as her two victims writhe. Powering through the pain, Jem makes a weak attempt to sweep kick Fire's feet, but the mercenary easily steps over the attack and brings her own leg down hard at Jem's head. However, instead of making impact, there's simply a loud thud.

Jem finds Fire's foot suspended in midair mere inches from her head, pressing against a solid but invisible surface. It's as if a sheet of sturdy glass suddenly appeared, protecting Jem from Fire's attack, and it's clear Fire is just as confused. The two look at Di, who has her palms outstretched and pressed against the clear shield, the air at her fingertips shimmering.

"What is this?" Fire shouts as she continues to stomp, but the shield holds sturdy. Di grunts with every hit, struggling to maintain the wall. She squeezes her eyes shut in an effort to focus, but it's clear she won't be able to hold it much longer.

Shaking off her confusion, Jem springs into action. Without giving Di any warning, she grabs her waist and hoists both shaper and shield into the air with enough force to knock Fire backward.

Not done, Jem swings Di's torso and holds her like a battering ram. "Hold that wall!" she cries out as she pushes forward like a plow, shoving Fire toward the ridge. Di squeezes her eyes shut as she concentrates on maintaining the wall of air.

Fire panics when she realizes the error of her positioning. Jem continues to barge forward with Di's shield outstretched, pushing their assailant closer and closer to the edge. The bounty hunter frantically tries in vain to catch her footing and reverse momentum.

"Hyah!" Jem grunts as she makes one final shove, forcing Fire over the ledge. In desperation, she grasps up and manages to snag the top edge of the solidified air. Her weight topples Jem, who's already off-balance from thrusting Di forward, until Fire's feet press against the nearly vertical cliff wall. Though their precarious position prevents a fall, it's clear they're slowly moving the wrong way.

"Di, let it go!" Jem grunts, straining to keep her hold on the air maker. Yet despite their impending fall, Di continues to maintain her barrier. Just before reaching the tipping point, she hits her limit and releases the shield with a gasp.

The compressed air disperses into the environment, and the two opposing forces are torn apart from each other. Jem and Di stumble backward to the ground, safely atop the ridge, while Fire hits the steep hillside, shrieking as she tumbles helplessly.

Not giving any consideration to their aggressor, Jem retrieves her dagger and yanks Di to her feet. She races back into the woods, dragging the air shaper behind her. "Di, what in the world was that? Were you trying to take us over the edge? Do you have a death wish!?"

Exhausted, Di gasps for air as she stumbles along to keep up with Jem. "I... I'm sorry, I just didn't want to..."

Jem stops and faces Di. "Didn't want to what?"

Tears in her eyes, she blurts out, "Jem, you shoved her off that cliff! You said you're not a killer, but you... you...!"

Frustrated, Jem resumes her dash. "Sometimes you do what you have to do to save your friends, Di! Did you forget about Era?"

The girl's heart sinks as she remembers Era's plight, and she runs harder so as not to slow Jem down. The two soon arrive at their fallen friend, and Jem dives next to him to check for breathing. Di bends over and gasps for air while watching Jem closely.

After a few excruciating moments, Jem says, "He's feverish, but I think he's okay. At least for now."

Di collapses in relief and tries to catch her breath. "Do you think that girl was alone?"

"Seems like we'd have seen any friends by now," Jem replies as she snags one of the mercenary's robust needles embedded in the tree. "A spike?" She then searches through the dead leaves until she finds the barb Era had pulled from his neck, and she slips the projectiles into a side pouch on his backpack before tossing it toward Di. After grabbing her pressure pack, she also dumps her own bag next to Di, who realizes what's going on.

"Wait a minute, Jem! I can't carry these!"

"You want to be the one to carry this instead?" she retorts as she straps the pressure pack to Era's back and activates it. The gush of air lifts his torso off the ground, and she starts dragging her partner by his legs with considerable strain. "This is what pressure packs were actually made to do, but he's still heavy."

"Jem, are you sure you can-"

"We have to make it to the next town as soon as possible," she grunts. "I don't know what poison she used, but he's alive. I want him to stay that way."

Di feels each bag, surprised to find Jem's bag is heavier than Era's. *This girl is a beast,'* she realizes as she slings the bag onto her back, watching as Jem stomps across the uneven terrain with her partner. She heaves Era's bag over her shoulder and hurries to catch up.

*   *   *

"That's it?" Galen screams in reaction to Bowen's report. "Twelve villages? It's been nearly forty-eight hours since we sent word out by beacon tower, and only twelve villages have sent back a report?"

Bowen takes a deep breath, having expected the reaction from his superior. "Only twelve villages have reported back, but that doesn't mean word hasn't spread. Our forces are actively looking for them."

"There are dozens of villages across the hill country," he states. "Twelve is unacceptable. We need to find her immediately!"

"Yes, you do," a voice booms from behind Bowen.

The commander's eyes bulge at the sound of that voice. Bowen jumps aside, making way for the new arrival to enter the quaint office. "General!" Bowen hurriedly salutes.

Galen also salutes. "General Graff, sir! We weren't expecting you to personally-"

"I'm here to see for myself what your efforts are producing," the general interrupts. His short, graying hair reflects his veteran experience, as does the blue coat decorated with enough ribbons for an entire platoon of soldiers. "You're dismissed, Lieutenant Commander," he says, his eyes still fixed on Galen. Bowen hurries to retreat.

The general glares at his commander in silence. His powerful presence alone is enough to assert his authority, and even Galen has a hard time meeting his gaze. Eventually, Graff leans against the door and rubs the bridge of his nose. "Commander, your operation was a simple one. Retrieve a schoolgirl and return her to the capital."

Galen swallows hard. "Sir, I-"

"You do not fail an S-class operation," he barks. His deep voice shakes the walls, and Galen wonders how many people outside can hear the conversation with clarity.

The general folds his arms and informs him, "My official report stated that the girl wasn't at the Academy, that she had left for Canterin shortly before you arrived."

Galen's eyebrows furrow. "But sir, why would you-"

"Nayl," he says, using Galen's first name, "the king has expressed great personal interest in the recovery of this asset. This embarrassment will not reach His Majesty's ears. Do I make myself clear?"

"Yes, sir," Galen affirms. "I'm doing everything in my power to retrieve her, but I need more information. Why does the king want her?"

"The king was presented with quite a claim," he replies. "Supposedly, the girl knows how to access ancient Third Kingdom technology."

"Third Kingdom?" Galen repeats in surprise. "Do you think that's true?"

"I'm obviously hesitant to accept such an assertion, but we have a certain form of evidence," he says. "We've found a cavern entrance, sealed by a wall we cannot scratch with even the sharpest blade. Supposedly the girl knows how to open it."

"I've never heard of such a thing," Galen says. "Do we know for certain she's from Canterin?"

Graff sighs. "We should assume nothing about her, which means it's possible she isn't headed to Canterin. Unfortunately, if she's not headed there, she could be going anywhere."

The commander grimaces. "Even to Alleria?"

"That's a possibility," he admits. "I read your report about the thieves. While I doubt the Allerians are involved, we must allow for that possibility."

Though discouraged, he salutes and says, "Yes, sir."

"Galen, you may be the youngest of the commanders, but there's a reason I chose you for this," says the general. "I expect you to complete this operation with dignity and success." Without awaiting a response, he retreats from the office with footsteps resounding down the hall.

Galen sinks into himself, his breath trembling with frustration. The asset's importance is nothing like he suspected, and the general's information only serves to confuse his search parameters. He walks to the map and moves certain pins, realizing he needs to place greater emphasis on the route to the border. Vowing to find the perpetrators and make them adequately atone is the only thought that brings him solace.

*   *   *

Fading in and out of a lucid state, Era finally opens his eyes with enough awareness to make out Di's tear-stained face.

"Era? Era, you're awake!" His companion jumps onto his bed, hugging him and burying her face into his shoulder.

Jem comes running into the cozy room. Relief washes over her upon seeing her partner conscious once again, though she contains herself and turns away to wipe her face.

Era looks around in confusion. A window on the adjacent wall tells him the sun has long set, and his personal effects are stacked on a table in the corner. He glances down and realizes he's not wearing a shirt. He silently hopes he's wearing something under his covers.

Leaning against the wall, Jem folds her arms and says, "Hey, next time wake up sooner. Sleeping all day is unacceptable! I mean, I knew you were lazy, but this is-"

"Give it a rest, Jem," Di blurts out. "You were just as worried, so quit trying to hide it."

Jem scratches her cheek. "Okay, fine, so the bum got me a little worked up."

Summoning his strength, Era asks, "What happened to me?" Noticing his partner's swollen cheek, he adds, "And what happened to you?"

Jem cocks her head and smirks. "Yeah, I took a good punch," she says, rubbing her wound. She pulls the barb from her pocket and says, "We were ambushed by a professional mercenary. You took this straight in the neck. It was laced with one heck of a poison."

"Indeed, it was," an elderly fellow interjects as he enters the room behind Jem. "I am Doctor Lansen. Pleased to meet you, young man."

"Doctor?" Era sits up, easing Di off as she continues to cling to him. "But wait, how did I get here? You two took out the- Did you say mercenary?"

"No, I said *bandit*," she says, eyeing the doctor, "and I used the compression pack to lug your sorry hide to the nearest town. You cost us a lot of money, I'll have you know. Pretty much everything we took from Andr- our savings! This doctor is expensive."

The physician eyes her, and Era notices a disdain in his expression he's become all too familiar with in his travels with Jem. "Young man, Era was it? You were hit with a specialized and dangerous toxin, one which can easily end your life," he explains. "It's a particularly effective poison made of pollen from the iterial flower, but the user needs to utilize perfectly-dosed injections, otherwise the stick could be fatal. I've seen enough travelers who get ambushed by bandits and receive too strong a dose, and they end up dying."

His patient swallows hard. "Sounds like I'm lucky," he says, wondering what must have transpired over the last several hours. Though it sounds like he almost died, he'd never guess it based on how he feels. He stretches his arm and says, "Well, I feel fine now."

"Despite the danger, the symptoms tend to end quickly," the doctor says. "Men are more likely to survive; the few women I've seen affected were not so fortunate. Overall, should you survive, the lingering effects are light." Turning to leave, he adds, "I charged for the night, so you might as well sleep here. You're cleared to leave in the morning. Just be warned: a second dose so close to the first will be fatal, even if small. So steer clear of any more bandits." He glances again at Jem before closing the door behind him.

"Steer clear of bandits?" Jem mocks, throwing her hands in the air. "What a useless doctor! He looks you over, tell us he knows the poison, then charges us an arm and a leg to set you in a makeshift bed and check on you every hour. He did nothing! Plus he clearly has a thing against Allerians. I should demand-"

"Thanks Jem," Era interrupts with sincere appreciation. "You saved my life."

His frankness takes her aback. "What are you talking about? You're my apprentice, so it would look bad if you died on me." Sternly, she adds, "Though you owe me yet another pressure pack. Mine ran out of air just outside town. And I thought you were heavy beforehand... yeesh."

He chuckles. "You were strong enough to stand against a market mercenary. Carrying me couldn't have been a challenge."

"Well, joking aside, we wouldn't be standing here if not for Di," she says. "Kid saved the day."

Di's face turns crimson. "It was nothing."

Era is about to laugh it off when he realizes Jem is serious. "Really Di? I didn't know you could hold your own in a fight. How'd you do it?"

"Yes, Di, let's talk about your little talent," Jem says. "You owe us a serious explanation."

"I-It's nothing!" Di stammers. "I already told you I'm an air shaper, so it's natural that I can mold air to-"

"Di, everyone knows air shaping is the most useless elemental ability," Jem says. "And the reason it's so useless is because you can't do anything substantial with it."

"I'm confused. What are we talking about?" Era asks.

"Show him," Jem orders.

Di reluctantly stretches her arms over Era, her palms pointing toward the ceiling, and the air at her fingertips shimmers. "There," she grunts in exertion.

"There... what? I don't see anything."

Jem slaps her forehead. "It's air! What do you expect to see?" She grabs his bag and tosses it over his face. Era flinches, but the bag lands with a loud thump. The air maker grunts from the strain on the glass-like shield, trying not to topple from the load.

"See what I'm talking about?" Jem asks Era, slapping the solid platform. "Rock solid!"

Era runs his hand along the solid air. "I've never seen anything like this."

Proud of her demonstration, Jem drags the bag to the floor. Di releases the shield and stoops to catch her breath.

"Takes a lot out of you, huh?" Era asks. She nods, wiping the sweat from her brow. "That's quite talent, for sure!"

Jem puts her hands to her hips. "Era, you're completely missing the point. This girl is an air shaping genius! No, not just a genius... This is unheard of! And she's been hiding it from us."

Era shrugs. "We knew she was from the Three Pillars Academy, so she had to be talented. I mean, I'm not an expert on air shapers. I don't know what's typical and what's not."

"She's special, Era," Jem insists. "I guarantee it, and I also guarantee it's why she was kidnapped from the Academy." She turns to Di and asks, "Or do you deny it, Little Miss Arcane? You know the typical limits of an air shaper."

Di reluctantly admits, "Yes, I have more control than most air shapers."

"And why did you hide it from us?" Jem barks. "We're risking our lives for you here. We need the whole story!"

"I told you what I knew about the kidnappers! I just... I didn't know whether I could trust you at first. I don't want to be sold to a circus for being a freak. I just want to go home."

Era is quick to chime in. "Well, can you trust us now?" Di nods fervently. "And do you have anything else to tell us?"

"There's nothing else," she answers without hesitation. "I don't know why I have this level of control. No one at the Academy had any clue, but they worked with me to develop my talent. The faculty pulled all kinds of air shaping experts to come in and spend time with me."

"Okay, okay, that's a nifty skill," Era interjects, "but how did that help you take out a mercenary?"

Jem throws her arms in the air and starts motioning. "That hunter girl had us beaten down at the gorge's ridge when-"

"Wait, the merc was a girl?"

"Stay focused, Era!" Jem gripes. "Di threw her wall up as a shield between us, and I... well..."

Di points at Jem. "She used me as a plow! She grabbed me and... and..."

Era smiles. "What'd you do, push her off the ledge?" To his surprise, Di nods emphatically, unable to find the words to express her disapproval. Jem beams with pride at her heroic exploits, but Era frowns. "Did she survive?"

"Don't you dare get on your high horse," Jem warns. "You weren't there, Era. I had no choice. It was kill or be killed." He averts his eyes, and she hurriedly adds, "What's with you two? Geez, if it helps then maybe she survived. The slope wasn't a straight drop, and I didn't stick around to check."

Era slowly shifts his attitude. "If you say it couldn't be avoided, then it couldn't be avoided," he reluctantly says.

"It couldn't," she insists. "Regardless, the Smith's Hammer guild apparently took our little raid seriously enough to send a hunter after us. And where there's one…"

Era sighs. "We'll need to lay low from here on out, huh?"

"To think we'll be dealing with this level of talent," Jem groans. She tosses Era the needle she retrieved. "She used these against Di and me, it's called a spike. Fortunately she missed, but that would have hurt. It sunk into a tree."

He observes the projectile, about twice the length of a finger and thick enough to offer good weight. "So let me get this straight," Era wonders aloud as he crosses his arms. "The merc wanted us alive, right? Poisoning me, not poisoning you two since girls die to this stuff…"

"She was unraveling wire at one point, too," Jem recalls. "She was ready to tie us up and herd us along somewhere."

"But why alive?" he asks. "Why not kill us and take Di back if she's so important?"

Jem shrugs. "Who cares? It could just be some kind of vendetta thing. You know the routine: capture us alive, make us wish we were dead, and so on."

Di shudders at the thought. "How can you be so nonchalant about this? Someone just attacked us! With poison!"

Jem pats her head. "Silly Di, you have no idea what this means to us, do you?"

"It means you're worth a lot of money, Di!" Era explains with enthusiasm. "We found a good haul after all." Though he expects a smile, she storms from the room and slams the door behind her.

"Was that too much?" Jem asks.

"Maybe," he admits. "She'll get over it."

Jem sits on the edge of Era's bed. With Di gone, the air in the room takes a dark turn as the two thieves ponder their predicament.

"Jem, do you think we're in over our heads?" Era asks. "We can put on a show for Di, but we've never had to deal with Merc Market professionals. We came out alright this time, but it sounds like it was entirely thanks to Di."

"Neither of us have had actual bounties on our heads," Jem agrees. "I mean, other than a few small towns offering twenty venni for us, or whatever."

Era nods. Their map has black X's over certain towns, marking off where they had best not return, but nothing has ever followed them. Sighing, he admits, "I guess if we want to play with the big dogs, we need to be willing to dance, or something like that?" Getting only confusion from Jem, he says, "My point is that we can't stay unknowns forever. If we continue this lifestyle, we'll end up aggravating the wrong person eventually, or we'll end up marking every town in Valvoren with an X, right?"

When Jem seems uncharacteristically deep in thought, he asks, "You know my famous father? Have I ever mentioned him? He gave me a lot of good advice in life, but maybe none as important as this little gem: 'When life gets rough, just go into hiding. Eventually even debt-collectors give up and stop looking for you!'"

Contrary to usual, the advice seems to strike a chord with her. "This time, when the job is done, let's really lay low for a while," she says. "You know, like we were supposed to do after the last job."

Era nods in agreement. "Sounds like a good plan."

Jem stretches and yawns. "Well, good night. For all the money we just donated to this farce of a clinic, you're the only one who gets a bed. You'd better enjoy it." She leaves and closes the door.

The patient stretches and swings his legs off the bed, happy to find he was wearing his undergarments. He bounces a bit, finding he really does feel back to full strength. He finds his sack of sand and forms a dense sword from the soft earth, wishing he could have been there to help fight the skilled opponent.

He looks out the window, wondering if Jem killed the bounty hunter. If she survived the fall, and she knows he was poisoned enough to warrant medical care, it seems to him she'd know where to find them. Absent-mindedly shifting his sword, he ponders whether he and Jem should leave Di behind to scout the surrounding woods. However, the moment he considers calling for Jem, he remembers her demeanor during their conversation. The encounter shook her more than she'd care to admit.

Era instinctively rubs the back of his head, remembering where Jem hit him the last time he went solo without permission. "I'll just make one round," he whispers to himself as he throws on his cotton under tunic.

*　　*　　*

Jem wanders the hallway in a vain attempt to clear her head. Era has a way of cheering her up, but doubt continues to plague her. He almost died in front of her, and she was powerless to do anything about it. Lost in her thoughts, she eventually finds herself on the front porch of the humble clinic.

"I'm still not talking to you," Di calls out, catching Jem by surprise. She hadn't even noticed the schoolgirl sitting against the outer wall, her arms wrapped around her knees in front of her.

"Well, if it isn't my little money bag," Jem boasts. "How are you feeling? Valuable, I hope."

"You put up such a front, Jem, but I know the truth about you."

"The truth, huh? And what's that?"

Di looks to the starry sky. "Back on the cliff, when I refused to let that ruffian fall? You held onto me, telling me to release my shield-"

"You really want to bring that up again?" Jem interrupts. "Trying to take us all over the cliff like that... You'd better not pull something so stupid again."

Affectionately, Di says, "That's just it. 'Taking us all over the edge'... Jem, she wasn't holding on to you. She was only clinging to me. You could have let me go and saved yourself, but you didn't." Jem looks at Di blankly as she continues, "No one cares about money that much. Not enough to let it pull them over the edge of a cliff. So... thanks. You and Era, you're a great team. I feel safe with the two of you."

Dejected, Jem leans against the wall. "Di, I'm not sure... I mean, I can't guarantee we're going to get to Canterin safely. Not if they're sending professionals like that after us. Era and I may make a great team, but we're just not at that level."

Somberly, Di realizes, "Climbing steep hills in peace suddenly sounds like a dream."

Jem turns to head inside. "Well, hanging out here isn't a good idea. Let's turn in for the night. I think the doctor has a soft spot for us! He even gave us a pillow to share."

She contentedly waves her hand. "Sure, be right in." Jem reenters the clinic, leaving Di to wrap up her thoughts. The emotions from the day finally catch up with the young traveler, and her eyes well up with tears as she longs for her father's embrace.

CHAPTER 6

Perched atop a sturdy tree branch, Fire resists a shiver and rubs her hands together, keeping a close eye on the village entrance as the town lights are put out one-by-one. If not for the moon approaching its full phase, she likely wouldn't have a chance of tracking anyone leaving the city. She massages her tender leg, which seems to have absorbed the brunt of her fall. By all rights, tumbling down the bluff should have caused significantly more damage.

She stifles a yawn, fighting against her exhaustion. Not surprisingly, the exorbitant bounty has a way of keeping her going, especially now that she has confirmed her targets are authentic. Thinking back to all her experiences with air shapers, she has never seen anyone with near the ability to create an unbreakable wall of air. Despite her small frame, Fire is more than confident in her ability to deliver a sharp kick, so that wall should have easily shattered. To her, the girl's abilities are confirmation she has the right trio.

Still, they act as though they aren't aware they're being pursued. They travel in the open. They interact with others. They even make fires at night. Given the male's condition and their poor decision-making, it's almost certain they found the nearest village for treatment. Once Werran is asleep, she'll visit the town doctor and, with any luck, finish the job.

A distant branch snaps. Fire's heart skips a beat. She listens intently until, to her amazement, her poison victim enters her field of view. *'How is he moving already?'* She grips her throwing spikes, but he moves behind a tree as he poorly sneaks through the area.

As he moves away from Fire, she decides he must be baiting her toward his friends, and her lips curl in amusement. It will be easy to drop him and deal with the others afterward, just like last time, though she reminds herself she can't risk using a second dose of poison.

She drops from her perch, but her injured leg gives out on impact. Biting her tongue, she snags a thin branch to catch herself, but it snaps and sends her loudly to the ground. She hurries to her feet, forcing back the pain while cursing her failure to keep her stealth. Hugging a tree, she grips her spikes and waits, confident she can yet get the drop on him.

"It's you, isn't it?"

The voice startles her into staggering backward. She clumsily flings her needles at the source, but the figure ducks behind a log. Again cursing her mistakes, she spins around the tree to take cover. To her delight, her opponent recklessly charges her, and she reaches for more spikes. However, she finds only one remaining, a reminder that she lost most of her supply in the tumble down the cliff side.

Drawing her dagger at the last moment, she intercepts an earth club aimed at her head, and her leg barely keeps her upright as she deflects Era's clumsy strikes. Despite her tactical disadvantage, her heart races with excitement at the sight of her target.

To her fortune, Era disengages and backs off. "Listen, I don't want to hurt you. Just tell me what-"

Fire interrupts the speech by lunging at him with blade extended. Whether by skill or luck, Era manages to intercept it and continue deflecting her follow-up strikes. "Wait!" he calls out, huffing and puffing. "Hey, I was trying to-"

The skilled hunter's blade shatters Era's earth sword, and she swiftly kicks him in the gut. Era hits the ground and rolls to his back in pain.

Not letting up, Fire leaps onto his chest, but Era slams her in the chin and rolls them over to position himself on top. He firmly clamps her two wrists above her head and shakes her dagger loose. Cringing from his injury, he barks, "Now, listen! I want to know who you-"

Fire headbutts Era in the forehead. He reels back, and she uses her legs to flip him over her head. However, the move does more harm than good as Fire grabs her injured leg in agony.

Wiping the sweat from his brow, Era snags his downed opponent's dagger, shocked she was able to shatter his earth blade with it. Even his opponent on the train, with full force behind a sword, was unable to pierce it. As Fire scrambles to her knee, Era clears his throat and says, "I need you to answer my questions."

"What is it you want to know?" Fire asks while subtly reaching for her side pouch.

"Deep voice for such a small girl," he muses, pleased to finally elicit a response. "I want to know why you're after us. Tell me who put the bounty on our heads! Oh, and also what the bounty is." Uncertain, he mumbles, "What else should I ask?"

Fire glances around, wondering where the other targets could be. They should have engaged by now if they're nearby. "So, who's the girl?"

"She's just someone we- wait, no, I'm not answering your questions, either!" he exclaims. "Now start talking or-"

She flings her needle at him, which plunges into his right arm. As he yanks it out, she staggers toward him and punches him in the gut, then swings him to the ground. As she brings her good leg up to kick him in the head, the dirt below her shifts and forces her to stumble. The earth shaper pulls a blunt club from the soft ground as he stands, snaps it into two pieces, and flings one half at her.

Off-balance, Fire instinctively brings her arms up to defend, but loose sand is all that hits her. She furiously rubs the dirt from her eyes as Era lunges forward and jams his club into her stomach. With Fire gasping for air, he grabs her arm, swings her around in a circle, and sends her careening toward a tree. She glances off the trunk and spins to the ground.

"That's what you get for that sneak attack!" Era yells, rubbing his bleeding arm. "Fight fair!"

Fire trembles with disdain for her amateur opponent. However, before she can get fully recover, the tree branches above swoop down and wrap themselves around her. With a yelp, she swats the limbs aside, but one snatches her ankle and hoists her into the air upside-down. More wrap themselves around her wrists, completely restricting her movement.

Era watches the whole event in awe. He steps away from the tree that sprang to life and looks around frantically for whoever just interrupted their fight.

He doesn't need to wait long, as a bellowing laugh emanates from behind the tree. Walking around the trunk, the newcomer beams at his prey and crows, "Long time no see, Fire!"

"Jaras?" she gasps. Struggling to escape, she barks, "Let me down, you incompetent sleazebag! How are you-" She notices his palm planted firmly on the tree trunk. "You're a wood elementalist? How is that even...?"

"What, did you expect something else? Oh, that's right, I had you convinced I was a terrible water shaper. How you were dumb enough to fall for that trick, I'll never know."

Fire grunts as she tugs at the branches. "Jaras, you scum, if you steal my bounty from me, I'll tear you to pieces!"

"Ah, yes, the bounty," Jaras whispers as he turns his attention to his valuable target.

Era has backed off, watching for an opportune moment to slip into the shadows. With the hunter's eyes now on him, he awkwardly scratches his head. "Who, me?"

Jaras sees thousands of venni flash before his eyes. "I'd expect nothing less of Fire than to track down such a high-priced target in two short days."

Realizing he's in over his head, Era keeps an eye on the new arrival as he prepares to run. Jaras stares him down but doesn't move a muscle, maintaining his hold on the tree and, by extension, Fire. She grunts and struggles with all her might to escape the branches. "Jaras!"

Jaras gives an annoyed glance to his captive. "Shut up, Fire! He's not yours anymore, so butt out."

Era seizes the opportunity to dash into the dark forest, and Fire lets loose a rageful howl. "Do you have any idea what I had to do to track these guys down? I'm going to gut you for this!"

Without so much as a twitch, Jaras makes the tree lower his dangling victim to eye-level. "Want to hear something funny, Fire?" he asks. "There's a twenty thousand venni bounty in front of me, and yet I'm more interested in you. I really didn't expect that." A tree branch whips Fire across the face, spinning her around. "I'll catch up with the kid. For now, let's have some fun. Just the two of us."

Fire twists and spits in his face. "You don't have the guts to kill me."

Jaras calmly wipes the saliva off his cheek and strikes Fire in the stomach. "Who said anything about killing you?"

*　　　*　　　*

The leaves crunch loudly under his feet as Era races back toward town, anxious to fill Jem in on all this and escape town while the hunters are fighting with each other. However, as he rubs his needle wound, he finds himself concerned for the mercenary who was captured. Though he tries to shrug it off, her plight continues to nag at him. If she dies, will her blood be on his hands?

Frustrated, he slows to a stop and smacks the back of his own head. "Idiot!" he cries in his best Jem impression. "Now's your chance to escape!"

"I know," he moans. "It's just that-"

"No! You'll never be a Master Thief like this! What would your father say?"

It doesn't take long for his idol's voice to echo in his mind. *'Use others' misfortune to your benefit.'* Everything from his training and experience screams that he should run, yet he finds himself unable to shake his concern. With a sigh, he turns around and whispers, "Sorry Dad, I'm still not very good at this." He runs back toward the hunters, taking care to move silently.

As he approaches, he hears a loud whip snap followed by distant voices. He moves with greater urgency, and he can soon hear their conversation.

"Come on, Fire, just one scream. You owe me that much!" Jaras yells as he again whips Fire across her back with a limp tree branch.

Era takes position behind a bush. Forming a club, he wonders about the best strategy for battling a wood elementalist. So far, all he knows is that he can bend trees to his will. There's no telling what other tricks he has at the ready.

"I'll have you know, Fire, that I pride myself in my ability to hunt without killing," Jaras brags. "I'm not a filthy assassin like you are."

Era's jaw drops. *'An assassin?'*

"I do what I have to do," Fire utters. "You're too weak to understand."

Jaras unsheathes a dagger and presses it to his prisoner's neck. "I hadn't planned on killing you, Fire. I intended to make you repay what you owe me, but when I think about it… I'll only regret letting you live. So tonight, it looks like I play the role of assassin."

"That's not assassination. That's murder," she responds. "Your incompetence is breathtaking."

"Let's find out if the market agrees with you. I remember seeing a few digits on your head, and I don't recall any mandate to bring you back alive." Fire doesn't blink, daring him on with her icy glare.

"Stop!" Era yells, dashing from the darkness of the woods.

Jaras spins to find the newcomer panting a short distance away, out of breath from running. "Wait a second, aren't you the target?" Jaras exclaims before looking back at his captive. "What are you trying to pull, Fire? He's an ally of yours?"

Fire finds herself at a loss. She watches the scene in silence, hoping it creates an opportunity to escape.

"I'm your target, but I couldn't just stand by and let you get away with killing her," Era declares. "Let her go."

Jaras scoffs in disbelief. "Don't give me that! There's not a chance in the world a twenty thousand venni criminal would do something so idiotic."

Era's heart sinks into his stomach. "T-Twenty thousand?" he weakly stutters.

Maintaining his hold on the tree, Jaras sheathes the blade in his hand and reaches to his ankle, pulling a different, smaller dagger out. "If you're a friend of Fire's, I'm going to give you the same treatment. I'm not as good a marksman as her, but I still know what I'm doing," he boasts while flinging it at Era.

The darkness hides the incoming projectile, so Era spins aside in hopes of evading. The sound of a thunk behind him allows Era to breathe a quick sigh of relief.

"You idiot! That's-" Fire tries to yell as Jaras makes a tree branch smack her across the face to silence her.

Era looks to her in confusion just as a branch slams into his side. He hits the ground and glances up just in time to see another branch incoming, and he frantically uses his earth club to intercept the limb as it pushes down on him. Stuck on his back, the earth shaper can do nothing but hold the branch at bay. "What the-?" he grunts. "How are you controlling a tree you aren't touching?"

"Your friend isn't so smart, Fire," Jaras gloats in triumph. "I'd have guessed you would have better trained your pupil."

Fire stares at Jaras, dumbfounded as to how he's now managed to convince himself that Era is her student. Still, she notices his brow heavy with perspiration, no doubt from the exertion of holding two captives with his elemental control. She pulls hard at the branches, finding their hold on her to be weakened.

"Oh, no you don't, Fire," Jaras growls, and he refocuses on keeping her held.

From his position, Era notices a rope extending from the aggressive tree back to the elementalist's hand. *He's controlling this tree with a rope? How is that possible?* Squeezing his eyes shut, he presses a hand on the ground and focuses on the earth below.

Sweat dripping from his chin, Jaras pushes his limits by moving a branch to Fire's neck. She chokes for air while tugging on her wooden shackles, but she can do nothing to escape.

"Farewell, Fire," he sneers as he watches her consciousness slip. However, the ground at his feet abruptly shifts. With a yelp, he stumbles backward and drops his rope. Both trees spring back to their original shapes, which drops Fire to the ground with a thud.

Jaras scrambles to stand just in time to find Era rushing in on him. The mercenary digs his fingers into the dirt, and the earth below Era tears open, releasing a network of roots that enwrap his legs and trip him. The elementalist watches with delight as his trap works its magic. Era fruitlessly hacks at the brush and roots as they overwhelm him, eventually locking down his arms and forcing him to drop his weapon, which crumbles upon loss of contact.

Without moving from his crouched position, Jaras wills the mass of plants to stand Era upright. The roots work their way up to his victim's shoulders, and they begin wrapping themselves around his neck.

Jaras glances over at Fire's motionless body. "Seeing as your boss may already be dead, you're going to tell me everything you know about the actual targets. If you do, I promise I'll let you live."

"Heartless monster," Era grunts.

"You have five seconds," he warns.

"She thought I was one of the targets and engaged me yesterday," he answers, quickly fabricating a story. "We agreed to track the actual targets together and followed a lead to this town. That's all I know!"

Jaras scowls. "That demon will betray you in a heartbeat when it comes to money. Though you probably already knew that." With a pause, he asks, "She did tell you about me, right?"

"Can't say she mentioned anything about you," he answers honestly.

The bounty hunter clenches his teeth in anger. "That makes me hate her even more!" he cries while wrapping the roots tighter around Era's neck. "Don't worry, I'm not a killer. But I don't need you following me, so it's time for you to sleep."

Era gasps for air as the roots tighten. He concentrates on the small amount of dirt around his hands, racing against time to free himself. Just before losing consciousness, the roots around his shoulders break with a loud snap. Before Jaras can realize what's going on, his captive grabs the roots around his neck and snaps them off with nothing more than a touch as well.

The hunter reacts as quickly as he can, pulling more roots from the ground to contain his victim. This time, instead of struggling, Era simply touches the plants, and they crumble to pieces. He finishes the job by freeing his legs, after which he scoops a fresh pile of earth and lunges at his adversary.

Jaras grabs his sword just in time to meet the dirt blade. Though Era makes a few quick strikes, he allows his opponent to go on the offensive, and Jaras takes advantage, pressing hard against the fragile-looking earth blade. His trap sprung, Era leans away and dispels his weapon, causing Jaras to lose his balance and stumble forward. The shaper then sweeps the vulnerable hunter's feet out from under him while simultaneously scooping up more earth, and he cracks Jaras over the head with a newly-formed club. The dazed bounty hunter tries to crawl away, but Era yanks him onto his back and shoves his club into his opponent's face, forming it into a sharp blade.

Jaras throws his hands up, his eyes wide. "How?"

Era cocks his head. "How what?"

"How did you escape my root trap!?"

"Oh, you couldn't tell? I mean, your roots were covered in dirt." When Jaras continues his blank stare, Era adds, "So I used the dirt to cut your roots to pieces."

Jaras is aghast at the realization of what Era had done. "You used the dirt around the roots?"

"Yeesh, and Jem thinks I'm slow," Era mumbles to himself. "Now, tell me what you know about us. Are we really worth twenty thousand venni?"

"Wait, you *are* the target?"

"Answer the question!" Era yells, aggressively poking the hunter's forehead with the point of his sword.

"Okay, okay!" he yelps. "Yeah, you got two others, right? You're each worth twenty."

"Each?" Era repeats in alarm. "Who put that kind of bounty on us?"

"Some commander guy who really wants you, okay? Commander Galen, I think that's his name. It was a military posting."

Era's legs grow weak as the suspicion he had on that first night is confirmed. Jem was wrong; the military really did kidnap Di.

Noticing his interrogator's distractedness, Jaras grabs his sword and makes a daring dash away. Era takes a lunging swipe at him, cutting the mercenary's shoulder as he makes a tactical escape into a thick brush. Unable to risk plunging into a web of branches, Era takes the long way around the foliage, only to catch a glimpse of his wounded opponent as he disappears into the darkness of the deep woods. Era kicks a rotting log in frustration at letting his captive go so easily.

Remembering the fallen mercenary, Era kneels beside her to check for a pulse, and he's relieved to find her alive. Up close, he's surprised how small and fragile her body feels given the force of her attacks, and he finds she must be about his age. He scoops her up over his shoulder, wondering what her story is.

He strains his ears one last time to ensure Jaras isn't returning. Satisfied the forest is quiet, he makes his way back toward Werran. The many weapons at Fire's waist clink against one another, alerting Era to their presence. "Mind if I do something about all those?" he asks his unconscious companion. As he starts working at that, his thoughts turn to crafting an excuse to give Jem for all this.

CHAPTER 7

General Graff marches briskly down the barracks hallway. Every soldier he passes stops and gives him a salute, and he returns a subtle nod to each. He prides himself on military protocol, remembering there was a time when he had superiors. Still, despite his rank, there remains one authority above him. Having been summoned by Valvoren's young king, the veteran leader doesn't dawdle in his response.

The barracks had once existed in the basement of the palace, but it was relocated during the war's intense period of mobilization. Now attached to the palace's west wall, the separate establishment provides more space for training exercises. Though convenient in its own way, it creates a labyrinth of hallways within which many a lost soul has wandered aimlessly.

Graff remembers his own training in the catacombs of the palace. There was a time he was forced to endure menial exercises, and now he is responsible for all operations. The military is, in his opinion, running as efficiently as it has ever been run. After nearly a decade of recovery since the last war, he has confidence in his ability to mobilize his forces.

He finally finds himself in the palace receiving hall. On the right side towers the pair of throne room doors, each stretching to the ceiling and inscribed in gold with five seals of the royal family, a reminder that the Haran family has been in power five generations. On the left is a much humbler wooden door, leading to the royal meeting room the king uses for conducting business.

"Well, if it isn't old man Graff," the captain of the royal guard says with a salute.

The general exaggerates a look of disgust. "The oldest active serviceman is calling me old? I should dig myself a grave."

"My apologies for making such a remark," he says. "I suppose I should be grateful that my guard isn't part of the military, or the 'old man Graff' comment would have been considered insolence."

Graff salutes and says, "Good to see you as always, Captain Larimar."

"And you, my lad." The experienced guard sports a deep green coat with the royal seal embroidered in a brilliant gold. What's left of his silver hair is cut short, and his left arm twitches from an old injury. "His Majesty is ready for you."

"Thank you, old friend." As Larimar opens the meeting room door, Graff observes those on duty and adds, "Your troop is vigilant as ever. My compliments." With that, he boldly enters, and Larimar closes the door behind him.

A mix of candle smoke and mildew permeates the windowless space, as the aura of departed monarchs and nobles of past generations effuses the stone-walled room. Timeworn tapestries line the walls, and an isolated oak table stands for each of the monarch's four advisors. Even now, the king is finishing a meeting with the foreign minister at his respective location, his table covered in documents carefully sorted. A pair of Larimar's royal guards stand at the ready, eyeing the general with less respect than his soldiers in the barracks.

Graff kneels and says, "Your Majesty, I have come per your request."

The young monarch raises an eyebrow in amusement. "Formal as always, General."

"It's the way of the old guard," the young foreign minister says with a hint of disdain as he collects his meeting notes.

"Minister Reece, if respect is old-fashioned, then consider me happily obsolete," Graff retorts as he stands.

"At ease, gentlemen," says King Haran, his hand raised. "I'd appreciate a meeting without thinly-veiled barbs, for once." He motions to Graff and says, "General, thank you for joining us. As you might suspect, Meskel and I would like an update regarding our special schoolgirl. You sent word she wasn't at the Academy, but what does that mean for her retrieval?"

Graff chooses his words carefully. "The child is from Canterin, and we have several platoons mobilizing there as we speak. We will retrieve her within the week."

"I suppose it will have to do," Haran replies as he anxiously adjusts his crown. Fashioned from gold and silver, the diadem is molded with one large peak in front and four smaller ones around the base, each representing one of his ancestors. "Unfortunately, our informant has yet to show himself again."

"Sire, we know nothing of that cretin or his motives," Graff says. "He is presenting us with a carrot, and I don't know where he intends to lead us with it. This has been a major distraction for my command staff."

"And what choice do we have?" Reece asks. "If such a weapon exists, we must claim it."

"I agree," the king says. "We need it to enforce the peace we worked so hard to attain."

Reece eyes the general. "Is that what you'd use it for, General? A weapon of the Third Kingdom, intended for peace?"

Graff cringes at the comment. "You know well my opinion, Meskel. Even now they muster their forces. It's just a matter of time before they get the itch for Valvoran blood."

Haran rubs his temple. "General, must we go through this again? Let a generation or two pass without another war."

"We won't have a choice when the mongrels attack us," he counters. "If there is substance to this informant's claim, we should preempt their strike. Slay the dogs before they can bite."

"If we hold the largest stick, the dogs won't try to bite us," Haran insists. "A military can be used for more than war, after all."

"Which brings me back to my concern," he says. "My officers are distracted at a critical juncture. If the Allerians attack-"

"Do you not trust His Majesty's treaty?" Reece asks. "Or do you also doubt my ability to maintain our relations?"

"It remains to be seen what will happen when King Trapak passes," Graff states. "The Allerian prince is not like his father. He will not respect your treaty, Sire."

"Which is why we haven't demobilized, General," Haran says. "We will continue to maintain our troops, and we will hunt this Third Kingdom relic. We are doing the right thing."

Graff bows his head. "As you say, Your Majesty. I will alert you as soon as we have the girl." Before he leaves, he inquires, "And how is Her Majesty, the queen?"

"I'm afraid she isn't feeling well, again," Haran answers with regret. "I'll tell her you asked about her."

"Please give her my warm regards," the general says before taking his exit. After offering a wave to Larimar, Graff marches back to the barracks, deep in thought. Despite his aversion to this exercise, his greater concern lies in Haran's attitude toward the Allerians. He's far too trusting in the treaty he forged.

After a lengthy march to get back to the barracks, Graff opens the door to his office, and he scowls at an unexpected visitor sitting at his desk. The young informant's dark eyes sparkle as he flashes a devilish grin. "So good to see you, General."

"Ares?" Graff barks. "Where have you been, and why are you presenting yourself before me, of all people?"

He adjusts his mantle, clipped across the front with a silver chain. "I've grown tired of the other advisors. Not one of them is the least bit interesting," Ares replies, apparently not at all concerned with Graff's hostile demeanor. "You, on the other hand, seem to grasp what my discovery means for our nation."

Folding his arms, he replies, "You're wrong. The only thing I grasp is how you've romanced His Majesty and the others into believing this Third Kingdom nonsense."

"You don't believe it? Despite the evidence I found?"

"I don't know what trickery is behind your discovery," he admits, "but I do know that this is all a distraction for my military. Therefore, I'd advise you to take your information to someone who isn't bothered by your mere presence."

"Then allow me to try again," Ares says. "I choose to present myself to you because you are the strength of this nation. You and your army brought the war to a conclusion that favored Valvoren in spite of a dead king, something no one would have guessed possible. So, if I've offended you, then I apologize, because you are worthy of my respect."

Graff fumes at the attempt to stroke his ego. "His Majesty ended the war, and it was he who forged the first treaty between our nations in recorded history."

"Ah, yes, despite Valvoren's military advantage," Ares remarks. "A shame the king opted to lay down arms. Don't you agree?"

Eyeing him carefully, Graff says, "For someone so critical of his king, you seem to have no qualms aiding him."

"To aid the king is to aid my country," Ares says while offering the same confident grin. "That is what I want, General, as a loyal Valvoran. But if I may ask, what is it you want?"

"What do I want?" he repeats. "I want to do what I've spent my life doing. I want to protect this great nation from its greatest threat. And I could accomplish that better without you sending my troops on wild chases."

"Then I would advise you to give this a chance, General," he says. "Either way, how went the hunt? Did you find her?"

"Of course," Graff says. "She's in custody now, and we're-"

"Lying doesn't suit you, General. I know you lost her," Ares interrupts as he stands.

A shiver runs down Graff's spine. Something has always seemed off about this enigmatic visitor. "How would you possibly know such a thing?"

"I'm an informant, am I not?" he asks with a bow. "That, by definition, makes me a master of information." As he heads toward the door, he adds, "You had better hurry and find her, General, before someone else does. I'd hate for the king to find out the military failed such a simple task."

Furious, the general grabs Ares by the collar. "Is that a threat?"

"It is simply an observation of what could happen if the weapon falls into the wrong hands." Calmly, he adds, "Worry not. We are on the same side."

Graff glares at him long and hard before releasing him.

Ares rubs his neck. "Quite a grasp you have there, General. Try not to let the girl slip through it again." With that, he throws a wave in the air and makes his exit.

Graff slams his palm against the table. Ares has all the appearance of a youngster in way over his head, yet he has the backbone of the most veteran of soldiers. He contemplates sending someone to trail him again, but even his best scouts had already failed to follow him beyond a few miles. The cur is as elusive as he is cryptic.

He starts jotting notes to add to his personal compilation of what he knows about Ares, frustrated he has to deal with such a character in the midst of a decisive moment for his nation. He hopes Galen can quickly find the girl so this matter can be resolved and his focus returned to those of military affairs.

*   *   *

Sunlight streams through the window, waking Jem from her deep slumber. She can't even remember the last time she'd slept later than sunrise; she usually leaves that routine to Era. Finding Di curled in the corner of the cramped exam room, she grumbles, "Useless doctor takes all our money for this."

She tries to rub out the wrinkles in her clothes. With the sun as bright as it is, she thinks it must be at least midmorning. Loud footsteps approach their room, prompting Jem to grab her dagger off the ground. The door slides open, revealing Era on the other side, holding papers in his hand. Jem breathes a sigh of relief. "Oh, it's just you."

Era practically gloats, "Wow Jem, sleep in much? Here I've been working and getting ready to go, and-"

"Yeah, yeah, shut up. What's with you barging in here? What if we'd been dressing?"

"Hadn't considered that," he admits, "but this is important. Look!" he exclaims as he hands Jem the three papers in his hand. "We're worth twenty thousand venni! Each!"

Jem's eyes nearly pop out of her skull as she grabs the papers from his hand, and Di stirs from the commotion. "What's going on?"

The Allerian's shock fades to annoyance as she mutters, "Let's see... Drawings that could have been made by a toddler, the word 'bounty' is misspelled on one of these..."

"R-Right! Just like real bounty papers!" Era insists. "Because they're real bounty papers, that is."

Jem glares at Era as she holds a paper up. "And scribbled on the back of that old doctor's notes?" She smacks Era in the chest and yells, "You nearly made me faint, you idiot! What's the big idea? Do you think this is funny?" She throws the papers aside, leaving a curious Di to collect them.

Era swallows hard. "I guess I thought it would cheer you up? I know you were feeling down last night, so I wanted to take the edge off. I guess."

"By pretending we're worth the world's weight in gold?" Jem shoves Era into the hallway and slams the door shut. "Wait outside!"

Di reveals the last of the pages with great amusement. "He drew you with a scowl on your face, Jem. That's kind of accurate!"

Jem snatches it and is ready to rip it to pieces, but looking it over one more time, she can't help but find some humor in it. "The idiot got one thing right, huh?" She grabs her bag and retrieves her emerald necklace. "At least I got to keep something of Andrea's," she says while slipping it on.

"Ugh, you're going to flaunt that?" Di groans.

"All day long," Jem says with delight as she admires it sparkling in the sunlight, until she takes notice of a growing crowd noise from outside. "Apparently not," she mutters as she removes the necklace and wraps it around her forearm, hiding it beneath her sleeve.

Di looks to her guardian in confusion. "What is-"

Jem cuts her off with a finger held up in silence. "Stay here," she whispers as she leaves the room and heads toward the front of the clinic.

As she turns the corner, she bumps into Era, who was hurrying back toward her. "Oh, sorry Jem," he apologizes as he grabs her arms and turns her around. "Maybe you should stay back in the exam room."

Jem glances at him suspiciously, but as the clamor grows she begins to figure it out. "Ah, so the welcome party's finally here, eh?"

Era grimaces as they hear the front door open. He turns and takes a defensive position in the narrow hallway, shoving his hand into the pouch at his waist. Soon enough, three husky individuals walk around the corner. Though unarmed, they do their best to act intimidating.

"So it's true," one mumbles as he turns to his cohort. "Mayor, sir, what should we do?"

The elder glares at Jem. He points past Era and shouts, "You're not welcome here, Allerian. Get out of our town!"

While Era plays the role of bodyguard to Jem, she crosses her arms in defiance. "Oops, I didn't realize I wasn't welcome. I wouldn't have stayed if I'd known," she says, her words dripping with sarcasm.

The mayor narrows his eyes at Jem and then Era, sizing them up. The exam room door behind them opens as Di peeks out. After looking all three of them over, he orders, "Just get out of here before you bring trouble on yourself."

"Seems it's too late for that," Jem banters. "Or is that crowd going to nicely create a path when I leave?"

"Let's just say you'd do well to exit the building before we allow the crowd to come in after you," the mayor growls as the three turn and leave.

When they open the door, the cries from the crowd outside stream in. It sounds like the entire town is outside waiting.

Era scratches the back of his head. "I don't think we should go out the front door."

Jem gives him a shove. "Thanks for your infinite wisdom. Go get your stuff, we might not have long."

Era scurries back to his room as the doctor comes around the corner. "I'm most sorry, but once the people heard there was an Allerian here, there was nothing I could do."

"And just how did they know an Allerian was here?" Jem slyly points out.

"I treated your friend and let you stay here well into the morning," he replies, his words laced with disdain. "You'd best not frown on my generosity."

"Yes, thank you for your excellent hospitality," Jem sneers. "Funny you have such problems with Allerians, and yet you took an Allerian's money without remorse."

"Just get out!" the doctor huffs before leaving to join the crowd.

Jem waves him off as Di approaches from behind. "Jem, why are they being so...?"

The Allerian places her hand on the innocent student's head. "The real world is tough sometimes. You probably don't see anything like this at school, huh?" Di shakes her head and hugs Jem as she explains, "Some of these towns were deeply affected by the war. Maybe there was a battle here, or it's possible that some beloved local was killed in action. Either way, it's just another town to add to my blacklist."

For a fraction of a second, Di sees sadness in Jem's eyes as she says all this, but it quickly disappears as the Allerian offers her classic, reassuring grin. "Come on! Let's ditch this dirty town."

Era comes out of his room, his bag slung over his shoulder. "We can get out through my window. No sign of the mob in that direction."

"Move out!" Jem shouts, shoving Di back towards Era's room.

As the trio hurries through the back alleys, the sound of the crowd at the clinic dies away. Di follows Jem as she skillfully ducks from wall to wall, choosing her path carefully so as to remain unseen, and she wonders how many times the Allerian has had to sneak out of a situation like that.

Jem's words linger in Di's mind. She's long known about the war that ended when she was only six years old, but there's always been a mystery to Allerians. Jem had skillfully avoided Di's interrogation when they first met, and Di burns with curiosity about the foreigner's past. She's so lost in thought that she barely even notices as the buildings clear out, leading way to a brightly-lit forest.

Jem breaks the silence by abruptly smacking Era in back of the head.

"Ow!" he cries out. "What's the big idea?"

She plants her finger on his nose. "You still haven't explained your little prank this morning. Don't think I buy for a second that you were trying to cheer us up! You were up to something."

Era averts his eyes while rubbing the back of his head. "You're right. I'm not sure how to say it, but…"

A rustle of leaves from a nearby bush reveals the gang isn't alone. Boldly emerging is none other than Fire, her arm bandaged and in a cloth sling.

"You!?" Jem shouts as she unsheathes her dagger and shoves Di back. "Era, this is her! The one who poisoned you!"

"Oh! This is her?" he responds uncomfortably.

His lackadaisical response doesn't go unnoticed, nor does Fire's relaxed stance. Glancing back and forth between the two, Jem barks at Era, "What's going on?"

"You haven't told her?" Fire asks, amused.

Keeping her dagger ready, Jem glares at her partner. "What haven't you told me?"

"And now I see why he didn't tell you," Fire says. "Good to know who's in charge of this little band."

"Shut up or I start slashing!"

"It's okay, Jem. We're on good terms," Era eases, bracing himself for physical punishment. "We met last night."

Jem looks at her partner in stunned disbelief. "You went out last night?"

"I just wanted to see if she was still out there," Era explains. "I'll admit that I didn't expect to find her, but then I did and it got complicated! This other guy jumped in the middle of our fight, and he was about to kill her. So then I saved her life, and I-"

"I had the situation under control," Fire interrupts. "The idiot here jumped in before I took my opportunity to strike, is all."

Era waves it off. "Sure, we can go with that. Either way, I ended up fighting off the other mercenary and helping her recover."

Disbelief washes over Jem's face as the two recount the previous evening's activities, bickering over the details as if friends.

Era turns his attention back to his two companions. "So anyway, after I beat back this crazy root-controlling guy- oh Di! I have to ask you about him later. But either way, Fire here… Her name is Fire, by the way. Cool name if you ask me!" Collecting his thoughts, he slows himself and continues, "Anyway, Fire was unconscious, so I started carrying her back to town. My plan was for her to recover in the medical clinic, but she woke up and tried to attack me, even though I was helping her."

"I woke up to you carrying me. What did you think I would do?"

Era laughs. "Guess it's a good thing I tossed all your weapons."

Fire grits her teeth. "Most of those were tools. And besides, was that really such a good idea if you want to hire me?"

"Hire her!?" Jem screams at Era. "Are you saying you befriended and then tried to hire the bounty hunter who's been hunting us?"

"Actually, it turns out she's an assassin," Era quietly corrects.

Di jumps back as Jem's eye twitches. Fire adds, "And, to be clear, there is no befriending happening here."

Jem smacks Era repeatedly in the shoulder. "Idiot! Moron! What are you thinking?"

"It makes sense," he argues, rubbing his arm. "She's injured, so she's out of the hunt. Di's worth money if we get her home, so now Fire will help us rather than telling all her friends where we are."

Fire places her good hand on her hip, already bored from the conversation. "Are we doing this or not? Because I'm not interested in dragging it out."

"We are not doing this," Jem insists as she jabs her dagger toward Fire. "We're tying you up and leaving you behind."

"Just try it," Fire dares.

"Wait, Jem," Era pleads. "Look, I don't think they were lying about the twenty thousand bounty. Twenty thousand! Do you think Fire's going to be the last assassin we see?"

"T-Twenty thousand?" Di stammers.

"Each," Fire corrects.

"Sixty thousand venni?" Jem mutters to herself as she lowers her dagger. "But Era, we can't let her come with us! If we're worth that much, she'll backstab us the first moment she gets."

"Ah, I see what's going on here," Fire interrupts. "You enjoy being the queen bee of your little hive, and you don't want another queen entering the picture. But as I see it, you don't have a say. The moron here is the one who's hiring me for his share of the reward money. I assume it's fifty percent?"

"Actually, it's thirty-five percent," Era sheepishly admits. "I give Jem some of my share for her tutelage."

Fire gawks. "For tutelage?" When Era offers a shrug, she grumbles, "Fine, I'll do it for thirty-five. Girl's worth sixty thousand to the military, so we should be able to hold out for thirty from a town like Canterin."

Di starts to object, but Jem jumps in. "Wait, the military placed the bounty on us?"

"Yep! Turns out I was right about that," Era beams.

"You knew!?"

"Oh yeah," he admits, "that other assassin guy mentioned it during our fight. I guess I should have mentioned that."

"He's just a bounty hunter," Fire needlessly corrects. "So, let me see if I fully grasp the situation. You two," she points at Jem and Era, "don't seem special, so my guess is that you're chump thieves who stumbled into this entire deal. You ended up with the girl, who's a VIP to the crown, and you kidnapped her-"

"Saved her," Era corrects.

"Well, you unwittingly 'saved' her from the Valvoran military," she reminds him. "You really poked the hornet's nest, you know? Commander Galen himself placed the bounty on your heads. Sounded like he personally saw you in action."

Jem rubs her temple as her head spins. "Ugh, this is bad."

"So now you're taking the brat back home, thinking all the while you're doing a good deed for a small reward," Fire continues. "In reality, you're in far, far deeper than you can possibly imagine." With a cocky smirk, she asks, "Still think you can go it alone?"

"Jem," Era interjects, "I know it's risky inviting her along with us, but isn't it just as risky to do it alone? There could be ten, twenty, a hundred professional hunters chasing us down right now. We need to do something."

"Well, what good is she in a fight?" Jem asks. "Her arm is broken, so there's no way she could-"

Fire steps forward, kicks the knife from Jem's hand, spins around her, and grapples her neck with her good arm. Jem starts to fight back, but Fire just shoves her into Era. "There's plenty I can do in a fight," she says.

Jem rubs her neck. "I hate this girl," she whispers to Era. "Fine, come along, take Era's money. You're going to scout for us too, I hope?"

"I'll be scouting, that's a given. But first, a few rules," she declares as she holds a hand up and starts counting fingers. "Number one, no more towns. Number two, no more roads. And number three, no more fires. You three are like a herd of horses romping along, leaving a trail a mile wide for someone to track."

Jem musters a smile. "Sure, anything you say. You're the expert."

Fire sizes Jem up and says, "Just head west. I'll keep an eye on the path ahead. Try to keep up."

Without waiting for a response, Fire dashes into the foliage. As she retreats, Di can barely hear her footsteps disappear into the distance. The way she moves is different from anything she has seen before. "Are we actually teaming up with her?" she squeaks.

To her dismay, she's ignored yet again. Jem turns to Era and gives him a look that sends chills down his spine. Without saying another word, she turns and stomps to the north.

"Uh, Jem?" Era shouts as he stumbles after his partner. "Fire went that way." However, Jem continues marching in silence. As her companions chase after her, Era realizes just how much trouble he's in from both sides. "Oh man, Fire isn't going to be happy about this."

CHAPTER 8

"Come on, say something already!" Era cries out, tired of Jem's silent treatment. "I'm ready. I can handle it."

Jem tucks her canteen back away and withdraws her compass. Despite already moving at an accelerated pace, she picks up her speed in an effort to keep her distance.

Era sighs in frustration, wondering whether Jem will forgive him for this anytime soon. Still, there's little else he could have done. Even if he hadn't tried to hire Fire's services, she would have reported them or otherwise started tracking them again. Bad arm or not, he has no desire to reengage her in combat.

They come to the clearing where the local train tracks make their run. Jem storms into the open, recklessly revealing herself to anyone who could have been traveling along it. Era creeps to the edge of the clearing and glances around before again darting after Jem. The tracks remind him of their epic raid, though that success is becoming a distant memory in light of their current woes.

Frustrated, he determines their safety is compromised by the lack of communication. Dashing to get in front, Era turns around and extends his arms out to block Jem's path. She stops and glares at Era, giving him a lump in his throat as he weakly utters, "Look, I know you're mad at me, but not talking is going to get us into trouble."

"On the contrary, your new best friend told us to be more inconspicuous," Jem counters. "Traveling in silence is a good idea, right?"

Era swallows hard but remains firm. "Jem, I'm sorry, okay?"

"For what, exactly?" she demands, her gaze fixed on him.

Her partner stares at her blankly. "Well, you know... For hiring Fire."

Jem rolls her eyes and walks around the roadblock.

"What is it?" Era yells as he chases after her. "What do you want from me? I'm sorry for trying to hire her help, but I had good reason! She was-"

"You think that's what I'm upset about?" Jem barks. "I'm used to that kind of thing from you by now. Try again."

Era wasn't expecting that response. "Then what are you... Wait, are you upset I left you behind last night?" Jem continues to stomp away, but Era grabs her hand. "Jem, is that what you're-"

"We're partners, Era," she interrupts. "We're a team, and teammates don't go solo like that." She yanks her hand from Era and jabs him in the shoulder. "What made you think to leave me behind?"

He struggles to come up with a reply. "Well, you were pretty shaken up after the-"

"I was *what?*"

Era doesn't back down. "I know you pretty well by now, Jem. You weren't yourself last night. You were upset, and I could tell."

"Okay, so you decided to go solo because I was shaken up due to you being nearly killed? Use your brain, for once! What if she'd poisoned you again? You'd have been killed!"

"I'm wanted alive, right? I figured she wouldn't risk poisoning me again."

"Wow, you figured she wouldn't poison you again. Great plan."

Hoping to turn the conversation around, he says, "But we learned so much information! The military, the bounty size..."

Jem's eyes narrow as she mutters, "Don't even get me started about your bounty papers stunt this morning. Were you even going to tell me you went out, or were you going to hide it from me via some other screwball plan?" She holds a hand up and says, "You acted on your own, went behind my back, and then lied to me about all of it. I just... I don't want to talk to you right now."

With Era finally at a loss for words, they stand in awkward silence until the sound of huffing and puffing approaches from behind, and they find Di, drenched with sweat, trudging through the underbrush. She pants and wheezes her way up to Era, then collapses at his feet, her hair a mess of leaves and twigs. She glares at her guardian indignantly, but she doesn't waste any breath to berate him for leaving her behind.

"We'll take a break here," Jem grumbles before heading further into the woods.

Era flops down next to their tagalong, staring after his partner until she disappears into the brush. Apologetically, he tells Di, "Sorry for leaving you behind there. Jem and I were hashing things out."

Di pants, "I know. I could... hear you hashing..."

He grimaces. "Maybe Fire is right about the 'herd of horses' thing. We don't put much effort into stealth."

The exhausted hiker sits back against a tree. "Is Jem alright?"

"Not sure," he admits. "Jem hates it when I go solo for some reason. I guess I should start considering her feelings more, even if they don't make sense to me. She also hates the military, so I'm sure that's not helping."

"But you did fine on your own," she says. "You deserve credit for that."

"It was more luck than anything. That other hunter's involvement might have saved me. I was hanging in there, but she's a better fighter for sure." Pausing, he adds, "So, you're worth a lot of money, it seems."

Di squeezes her eyes shut. "I just... I don't understand." Earnestly, she meets her guardian's eyes and says, "Era, that makes no sense! I don't have any idea why they would be willing to pay so much for me."

Era doesn't seem troubled by the notion. "Hey, this could be a good thing for us. If you're worth that much to the military, maybe you're worth that much to your rich dad."

The girl's eyes widen. "Era, that's a lifetime of wages!"

"But they wouldn't be asking for that much if you weren't worth it, right?" He stares into the sky as he searches for answers.

"Wasn't there something you wanted to ask me?" Di asks, desiring to change the subject. "Something that happened during the fight?"

"Oh yeah, well, I should start from the beginning for that. Once what's-his-name showed up... Jaras, I think? He trapped Fire by using a tree. I got away, but then I went back to fight him."

"Why did you do that?"

He wonders about this. "I decided I didn't want Fire to die, even if she attacked us."

Warmly, she says, "That's because you're a good person, Era. Try as you might, you'll never be a big bad thief."

Era smiles. "Sorry, but that's my destiny! I will surpass my father."

"Who no one has ever heard of," Jem remarks, reemerging from her short walk through the woods. Era prepares for more verbal abuse, but she twirls her finger and says, "Go ahead, finish your story."

Reluctantly, he continues, "Well, I went back and Jaras had done a real number on Fire. He was a wood shaper, and-"

"Elementalist," Di corrects. "Wood is earth's derivative, remember? That makes wood users elementalists."

Era hesitates before nodding. "Oh, I remember for sure! So, he was a wood elementalist who used all the roots and shrubs and stuff to attack me. He wrapped me up tight, but I escaped."

"How?" Di asks anxiously.

Era beams. "I had a handle on the roots, which were all covered in dirt. I shaped the dirt and cut the roots to shreds."

"You cut the roots with the dirt?" Di exclaims in disbelief. "Era, that's unbelievable! Can you show me?"

Proudly, he yanks a young sapling from the ground, revealing the earth-covered roots. He places a finger at the trunk of the root, and it slices in two.

A smile curls at the scholar's lips. "Era, between that and your hole-digging, you're pretty impressive! Only the oldest earth shapers at the Academy are that good."

Era rubs the back of his head, blushing. "Really?"

Jem groans. "Don't give him a big head! It's bad enough he thinks he's strong, but now he'll want to start earning a bigger share of our hauls."

Di frowns at Jem. "So, it's true he only gets thirty-five percent? That doesn't seem fair."

Jem laughs aloud. "How much do you get, Era?"

Era averts his eyes. "Forty-five."

"You lied to Fire about that?" Di gasps.

Era cringes. "I mean, I still wanted part of the reward. I didn't want to give it all away."

"But you said... you said you just wanted to protect me," Di squeaks, her voice trailing off.

Era hurriedly explains, "That's still very true, but remember that Jem and I have to survive on what we can get. Taking two weeks to return you home and not getting a venni for it would be kind of stupid." His words seem to have opposite the desired effect, and she starts tearing up. "But Di," he interjects, "your safety is important to me! Please don't think otherwise."

Di wipes her eyes and nods, but she fails to cheer up. Era looks to Jem for sympathy, but she just mouths the words, 'That's what you get.'

Getting an idea, he leans forward and taps the schoolgirl's knee. "But Di, that brings me to my question." She looks up with interest, and he explains, "You see, when I first approached the wood guy, he had Fire trapped in a tree. Makes sense, right? Wood user, his hand was on the trunk, so of course he can move it around, right?" Di nods, and he continues, "But then he threw a knife into the tree behind me, and it started to move! It didn't seem to be as nimble as the first tree, but it was enough to attack me. Turns out the knife had a rope attached that he was holding, and when he dropped it, he lost control of the tree."

"What a great trick!" Di exclaims, her mood eased by the academic exercise. "The rope was probably woven with wooden fibers. And the knife must have been wooden as well! My, what a great trick," she repeats. Era continues to wait expectantly, but she just asks, "So what did you want explained?"

"What did I...?" Era asks, not sure where the disconnect occurred. "Explain that. Explain the whole thing."

"The whole...? Oh!" she realizes. "Well, you can always control any extension of an element. If your earth sword touches the ground, you can pull more dirt into it. You already know that, right?"

"Sure, but that's dirt. It's all the same stuff."

"It is, but it isn't," Di corrects. "You're only touching a few grains of dirt and sand. You control the rest by extension, because earth touches earth. That's how you keep the shape of your sword even though you aren't touching the whole thing all at once."

Era nods. "I think I get it."

"Other elements are the same way. If he was holding a wooden rope, which was attached to a wooden knife, which was in a tree trunk..."

The sudden student slams his fist into his palm and exclaims, "...he could control the tree! Though not as well as the first."

"Elements are harder to manipulate the further away they are," Di points out. "I'm sure you've noticed that with your sword."

"Yeah, it all makes sense now. Thanks Di!"

She grins, once again happy to play the role of teacher, while Era looks back at Jem. "So, are we good now? You came back pretty fast."

"No, we are not good," she grunts as she grabs Di's wrist and pulls leads her into the woods. "I found a stream, and I came back for Di. We're taking a bath, so stay away!" Di glances back at Era with excitement, unsure why Jem thinks she needs to be dragged to enjoy a bath.

Era watches them disappear into the woods and mutters, "Man, I'll bet she isn't going to let me take a bath." He wonders how much longer Jem will torment him, hoping she'll miraculously forget her anger by the time she gets back.

He sits against a tree, holding a sword formed from the ground so Jem will be impressed by his readiness. Waiting patiently as the minutes tick by, Era becomes lost in his thoughts, and his eyes eventually droop. His arm slides to his side, and, as he slips into his slumber, the sword in his hand loses its form, turning back to sand grains that form a pile on the ground. A cool wind blows through the trees as the area rests in a quiet peace.

The moment doesn't last long. Era stirs and opens his eyes, and he yelps as he's met with Fire's annoyed gaze mere inches away. He scrambles to stand, but she shoves him back into the tree with her good arm and leans in.

"You're pathetic," she growls with a cold glare. "Do you have any idea how long I've been crouching here?" Era just stares in a wide-eyed stupor, unable to offer a response. "Stand up."

He complies while watching Fire closely, but she isn't acting like she's here for a fight. Finding his voice, he offers, "I'm sorry about ditching you like that. We... I think we took a wrong turn and-"

"Which was it? Did you ditch me or take a wrong turn?" Fire sneers. "Did you think I wasn't expecting that maneuver? It was obvious what your boss was going to do."

"Wait, you've been following us this whole time?"

"Like I told you earlier, you're painfully easy to track. I followed the girls to their bath to confirm they'd be out of the way while we talked."

Era finds himself at a loss for words. The mercenary had not only tailed them with perfect stealth, she planted herself in front of him without waking him. He absent-mindedly rubs at the tender puncture wound on his arm. *This one is scary.'

94

Sensing his discomfort, Fire wryly asks, "Realizing just how out of your league you are? Look, I'm here to find out if the deal is still good. I'm not interested in playing games." When Era averts his eyes, she barks, "You need to grow a backbone, you know? Make up your own mind, already."

Meeting her gaze, he insists, "Jem and I are a team. She doesn't trust you, so there's no deal."

"You realize I just ambushed you, right? That I could have tied you up with one hand if I'd wanted?" Fire asks, annoyed. "You'll never make it on your own. You're oblivious to your surroundings and naïve to your threats."

"Even so, traveling with you carries its risks," Era says. "What guarantee can you offer us that you won't betray us?"

Fire notably ignores Era's question. "Should've figured you'd back out. What a spineless wimp." Turning her back to him, she barks, "Fine, I'm done with you. Best of luck." With that, she disappears into the thick of the trees.

Era breathes a sigh of relief, deciding maybe this is for the best. However, as a thought strikes him, he yells out, "Hey, wait! Does that mean you're hunting us again?" The woods fail to answer him, and his head spins at the possibility that he just made the situation worse. Hoping he doesn't see anything he shouldn't, he runs to warn his companions.

*   *   *

Jem wrings her hair out one last time and sits to put her boots on. Di, sitting at the water's edge, is furiously scrubbing her feet. "Hurry and finish up, already," Jem urges.

"Can't," Di grunts as she continues to scrub. "My feet are disgusting! I had no idea hiking would make them so gross."

"Might as well get used to it. We're still far from Canterin."

Di wrinkles her nose in disgust. "No way, you told me this might be the last bath I take, so I'm cleaning my feet."

"You already spent an eternity on your hair," she grumbles. "You should let me cut it. Long hair isn't fit for traveling the woods."

"No!" Di nearly shrieks, startling Jem. "Daddy loves my hair. You're not touching it!"

Jem holds her hands up, surrendering to the display of determination. "Yeesh, you're as obnoxious as Era."

Di stops her scrubbing. "Why are you so mad at him? He did all that last night because he cares about you."

"No, he did it because he's full of himself and thinks he can do anything," she scoffs as she sits on a large rock. "He can't be a one-man army all the time! He needs to learn that."

"Has he done this before?" she asks, returning to her work.

"Oh, he used to do it all the time. We'd enter a new town and the first thing he'd do is try to steal something from the market. He'd fail, and we'd be run out of town."

Di enjoys the thought. "That does sound like him. He wants to prove himself to his unique father," she says. "Doesn't seem like he'll be working with you forever."

Jem leans on her elbows. "I know that. Era's strong. He won't always need me." Slamming her hand against the rock, she exclaims, "But he needs me now! Thinking he can take on a professional assassin, and then doing it! He's going to have such a big head after this. I need to make sure he regrets it."

As she finishes saying this, she sits up in alarm, startling Di. The schoolgirl waits anxiously, knowing better than to say anything. Jem grabs her dagger and jumps to her feet as Di hears the rustling of leaves. Her heart pounds while she watches the tree line.

Era stumbles out of the woods with a hand over his eyes, prompting Di to shriek and dive into the water.

Jem sheaths her blade with an exaggerated sigh. "Really, Di?" Though sheepish, Di keeps herself below the water.

"And you," Jem barks as she storms up to Era. "This is the second time you've barged in on us today. We could have still been bathing!"

"Fire's here," Era blurts out, peeking through his hands.

Jem watches the woods in concern. "Where? Did you see her?"

"She got the jump on me," he admits. "Said she's been tailing us this whole time. She followed you two here and then came back to me."

Jem raises an eyebrow and looks Era over. "Doesn't look like you had a fight."

"No, no fight," he says. "She wanted to know if the deal was still on, and I said no. So now I think she's back to tailing us."

"Great, Era! I swear this whole thing is your fault," she growls as she pokes him in the chest. "Now get out of here so the princess can get dressed again."

Era hurries back into the woods, and Jem beckons to the soaked Di. "Come on, bath time's over. Guess it's a good thing I snagged some clothes from Andrea after all, eh?"

Di cautiously emerges from the water, her school clothes drenched. She looks up into the trees and whispers, "But what if Fire is watching?"

"You can walk in those wet clothes for all I care. You'll already be carrying them so they can dry off, thanks to your spectacular maneuver."

The weary traveler looks one more time into the trees, then surrenders and retrieves Andrea's clothes as Jem packs her own things.

*   *   *

"Okay, so here's the plan," Jem says quietly to Era as they hike. "There's a town up ahead we can use for cover. We'll find an inn and act like we're spending the night. Then we sneak out after midnight, taking a path out of town that will give us good cover."

Era bites his lip. "Once she sees us enter the inn, she'll be watching it closely. And besides, she'll know what we're planning. I can't imagine she'll expect us to actually spend the night."

Jem grimaces. "It's not the best plan, but this is it unless you've got a better idea."

Di does her best to keep up, hauling her drenched clothes over her shoulder. She now wears an orange summer dress that Jem cut off at the bottom to make for easier hiking. "But she's injured, right? Won't you beat her easily?"

"You saw what she did to me," Jem recalls. "There's plenty she can do with a single arm."

"Okay, then why not go on the offensive?" she persists. "Era did a good job last night by himself. She won't be able to take you both on."

"It's not a bad idea," Jem says, "but how do we catch her?"

"Besides," Era adds, "we can't be certain she's alone. She had all night to round up help, after all."

"That's not the case," Jem declares. "If she had help, she would have attacked us this morning, not to mention while we were bathing. The fact that she didn't seize the opportunity means she doubts her own ability to take us on."

"Then maybe your plan isn't so bad," he agrees. "A main road will make her hesitant to attack, and the town is our best chance to lose her."

With glee, Jem says, "My favorite part of this plan is that it goes completely contrary to her orders."

"Ha, now we just need a fire," Era observes. "Erm, well, not the assassin kind, just the regular kind. You know what I mean." He scratches his head and admits, "That name is not convenient."

"Nothing about her is convenient," Jem states.

"Well, she has a small stature."

She raises an eyebrow. "Oh? You like your girls short?"

"I meant that it should help us in a fight," he clarifies. "Plus it made her easy to carry."

"Already enjoying some physical intimacy, I see. Anything else you like about her?"

"Besides her cold blue eyes of death?" He shrugs. "I guess I like her narrow face. It accentuates the piercing gaze."

"Ugh. You would."

Di pouts. "I'm plenty short," she mutters, though no one pays her any mind.

The three find the main road leading to Ugorzi, and they follow the path as it bends and winds through the hills. Era and Jem keep their eyes peeled, watching for their pursuer while staying on guard around the travelers they encounter.

Coming to the crest of a final hill, they find their destination. Nestled between two cliffs, Ugorzi is built alongside a river that carves its way through the hillside. The road goes straight through the town and continues out the other side.

Jem snaps as an idea strikes her. "Era, this is perfect! She would never enter such a populous town that only has two ways in or out."

Era frowns as he surveys the landscape. "But does she need to follow us inside? The cliffs offer a great view of the entire town, and those two entrances means she doesn't have much to watch."

"Sure, but what if we wait her out?" she asks. "We stay in an inn for a couple days, never leaving the building. She'll eventually have to sleep, and, when she wakes up, she'll have no idea whether she missed us or not. If we're lucky, she'll be chasing us west while we're still here!"

Era questions if such a plan could work. "In the same way, we wouldn't know for sure if she's gone or not, but I guess that might be our best chance."

The familiar sound of gasping and panting approaches them from behind. "Is that… Is that it?" Now using the damp clothes to cool her head, Di collapses to her knees as she looks down the hillside.

"That's it," Era proclaims. "Do you need a rest?"

Di shakes her head, tired of being out in the sun. She stands and runs down the hill, grateful to have gravity on her side and laughing with delight as she races toward the new town.

Era is amused by the sight, but Jem isn't happy as they start walking down the hill. "She doesn't know the meaning of the word inconspicuous, does she?"

"Do any of us?" Era quips. Getting serious, he quietly mutters, "Jem, remember what Fire said about the military?"

"Yeah, what of it?"

"Well, does that change anything? This isn't the Smith's Hammer anymore. We might be up against the entire army for all we know! We fought a commander on the train roof, and we-"

Jem waves her hand in the air, cutting him off. "First of all, unlike you, I don't trust everything that monster says. And second, even if it is the military, there's no indication they've sent a lot of troops after us. If anything, it seems like it's the opposite."

"Let's not make assumptions," Era cautions. "It might have taken a while to spread the word. We should be on guard."

Jem is impressed. "Look at you, being all thoughtful. You're right, though. If it is the military, we'll need to be wary of the town guards."

The two watch as Di reaches the bottom of the hill before collapsing to her knees again. Era finds himself both impressed and amused by the unfit schoolgirl's clash between willpower and endurance.

"Listen," Jem says in a hushed voice, "it's a pretty big deal if the military is after her. We can probably negotiate a higher price if we find out what makes her so special."

"Wait a second, I thought we were in this for the reward money. You're making this sound a lot like ransom money," Era laughs.

"Reward, ransom… they're the same thing when it comes down to it," Jem claims. "In the end, we bring Di home, we get paid, and everyone is happy. I just want to get as much as I can for all the trouble this has been."

"I won't disagree with that."

The two meet up with Di as she gets to her feet. With the sun at late afternoon, a small crowd is leaving the city. It doesn't take much for the three to mix into the masses, happy to have cover from Fire's watching eyes.

CHAPTER 9

The land surrounding Ugorzi's entrance has been heavily farmed and irrigated to take advantage of the river cutting through the cliffs. Even as the three enter the edge of town, local farmers are planted alongside the the road, their carts filled with fruits and vegetables. Each one loudly offers his or her delicious produce to the newcomers at discounted day-end rates.

They head into the market district, where the crowds are the thickest. Even more vendors line the street here, each offering something for purchase. Di can hardly contain her excitement when someone offers her two apples for a half-venni. She turns to Jem, who shakes her head and walks past. However, Era slips the girl a fel coin, and she happily trades it for the fruit.

The buildings are constructed from rock and mortar, an impressive feat for such a remote town. Furthermore, Era hasn't seen such a wide variety of produce in all his travels. That might explain the thick crowd, which is a diverse group consisting of shoppers from many different regions.

Following his companions, Era glances upward to the impressive cliffs that tower over the narrow city center. If Fire could find a decent perch, there's no doubt she'd be able to spy on the entire village. He catches up to Jem and says, "If we're going to stay a couple days, we need to stock up on food. It'll do us no good if Fire spots us trekking to the market each day."

"But we can't risk her seeing us buy two days' worth of food," Jem contends. "So go light. We have rations that can keep us going if we run out of the fresh stuff. You grab some veggies, and we'll grab some bread." Sternly, she insists in a hushed voice, "And no stealing. We don't need attention being drawn when you get caught."

He breaks off and dives into the thick crowd, muttering a subtle, "I wouldn't have gotten caught," for his own sake. Finding a stand with fresh vegetables, he makes a selection and exchanges his coins for the food.

As he turns, his eyes land on a soldier across the plaza, and he suddenly becomes aware of several such guards patrolling the crowds. They don't look like local police, but he knows some towns hire the military for such services.

Counting three in total, Era finds his friends and hurries to them. Jem catches his eye and nods her head toward one of the soldiers, indicating she's seen them. Era holds up a hand with three fingers extended. His partner affirms she gets the message, and she signals for him to keep his distance for now.

Jem finishes her transaction with the baker and politely asks him for directions to the inns. He points down the street, and Jem thanks him as she leaves. Di eyes the freshly-baked bread in Jem's bag with desire as she walks alongside, but Jem notices and switches hands, keeping the hungry traveler at bay. Era walks behind at a distance to avoid being seen as a group of three as they head across the river to another section of town. He watches the guards, but they don't seem to pay the group any particular mind.

Suddenly, Era realizes why Jem isn't drawing the usual attention. As he scans the crowd, he finds two other Allerians perusing the markets. To his recollection, this is the first time seeing an Allerian besides Jem outside a port town. Unfortunately, his hopes for remaining inconspicuous are dashed when Jem draws the attention of one of these Allerians. The middle-aged woman spots Jem and eagerly moves toward her. "Young lady," the Allerian woman calls out as she happily greets Jem.

Startled, Jem resists the reflex to draw her dagger. She subtly prods Di, indicating she should keep moving. "Hi?"

"It's so rare to see an Allerian that isn't a local!" she excitedly exclaims. The woman sports a long, plain dress, and she's holding a bag full of apples. Her darkened skin and facial features make it obvious she's not from Valvoren. "What is your hometown? Why are you here?"

Jem shoots a glance to Era to make sure he sees the situation, and he gives her a sign to keep moving. She rolls her eyes at the obvious signal and looks back at her new acquaintance. "I'm from Duroshe, and I'm here to pick up some fruit. For a festival."

"Oh, you simply must purchase apples from the vendor over here," she says, pointing behind herself. "And is your husband here with you as well?"

Jem's eyes bulge. "Husband?"

"Oh, well, I suppose I made the assumption based on your age. And besides that, every other Allerian woman I know in this region is at least betrothed."

"I'm not betrothed or married or anything," Jem insists.

"Are you free for dinner tonight?" the woman asks. "You can't make it back to Duroshe this late in the day, and I'd love to chat with you."

Tired of the conversation, Jem says, "Look, lady, I'm not sure why you think I'd be interested in having a meal with a stranger, but-"

"A stranger?" the woman gasps. "Absolutely not! We share a common blood, so we must offer support when we're fortunate enough to find one another."

"Why?" Jem challenges. "Why do you assume I want to associate myself with other Allerians?" Realizing she's drawing attention, she turns away and mumbles, "Sorry, but I'm not interested."

Aggravated, the Allerian woman turns away with a huff. Jem spots Era, happy to see he's keeping an eye on Di. Hoping she can avoid further conversations, Jem hurries along toward her original destination.

Several quaint inns line the street, each unlikely to have more than a couple rooms. Jem enters one to negotiate price while Era leans against the outer wall of the inn. Di paces, impatiently waiting for Jem to come back with the bread.

While they wait, a short, well-dressed man walks up to Era, apparently intending on making conversation. "Say, are you two looking to spend the night here in Ugorzi?"

Era ignores the solicitor, hoping that he'll take whatever wares he has with him when he leaves. However, Di obliviously answers the question in his stead. "Yes, we are. Why do you ask?"

"Well, I'm glad you asked, little one! I'm the owner of an inn of sorts. I was hoping to obtain your business."

"Which one is yours?" Di asks, glancing at the inns behind her.

"Actually, mine is on the west side, over there." He points toward the edge of town, but it's impossible to tell which building he means.

Era waves him off. "Get lost, we're already staying here," he says as he jabs his thumb toward the inn behind him. However, the angry shouts from within are a sign his statement is soon to be proven wrong.

"But you need to pay these innkeepers for their services. Whereas with me, I'll pay you."

"Come again?" Era asks in confusion as Jem stomps outside, annoyed to find her companions engaged in conversation.

"It's quite simple. I'll pay you two hundred venni if you accept," he boasts.

"Two hundred?" Era exclaims. "To stay in your inn?"

"An inn of sorts, I said." The businessman adjusts his suit coat and explains, "I happen to have a manor on the edge of town sitting vacant. I'll pay you the money if you stay all night."

"And the catch?" Jem asks.

"The catch is you'll die!" a nearby shopper calls out. The property owner scowls as the stranger warns, "Don't be fooled! This crook is trying to get you to stay in a haunted mansion. That house has claimed more lives than the war, it has!"

"It is not haunted," the broker insists. "I've personally examined it a dozen times."

"You go through there during the day, when it's safe. Nighttime is when it happens. That's when the last owners were killed. Even you won't inspect the house after dark."

Jem's patience is rapidly fading. "Let me get this straight. You want to unload this property, so you're willing to pay strangers to sleep there and prove it's not haunted?"

"The townsfolk all believe you'll die if you stay in there after dark," the dealer admits. "The last two owners of the manor were both killed, but they were probably murdered as part of a robbery. That could happen in any house!"

"Those weren't no robberies," the local insists. "The valuables were still in there after the killings. Not a thing was stolen!"

"Okay, I've heard enough," Jem interrupts, concerned about the attention they're drawing. "Sorry, but no deal. I don't want to stay in a scary haunted house, even if you pay me two hundred venni! Stay there yourself if you believe it's not haunted."

Dejected, he begs, "Please, won't you reconsider? I'll pay three hundred!"

"Get lost, little man," Jem growls.

The owner gives an angry glare to the local who ruined his plans before heading off in search of another set of visitors. The other man proudly waves as he departs, certain he just saved the three travelers' lives.

Di breathes a sigh of relief. "I thought for sure we'd be staying there when he said three hundred." Looking at Jem, she admits, "I don't believe in haunted houses, but this place sounds terrifying! I'm glad you think so, too."

"You're cute," Jem says as she pats Di's head. Turning to Era, she excitedly says, "Looks like we found our inn. Where did he say it was?"

"I thought you might say that," Era says as he points to the west. "Sorry, Di."

The turn in conversation shocks Di. "But you turned down all that money! Why are we staying there?" she yells.

"Keep it down, Di," Jem hushes as she prods her westward. "We're trying to remain inconspicuous, and what better way to do that than to spend the night in a place where no one would look? And for free, no less!"

"But you turned down the money," Di repeats, still bewildered by Jem's decision.

"If I had accepted it, that shady swindler would have bragged to the whole town we were out there."

"But I don't want to stay in a haunted house!"

"You just said you don't believe in haunted houses! Make up your mind."

Era places his hand on the frightened girl's shoulder. "Don't worry, Di. We've taken on bandits, assassins, and bounty hunters! I think we can handle a few ghosts."

Jem's brow furrows at Era's comment. "When did our lives get so exciting? You must be a curse to us, Di. You'd better be worth all this."

The manor on the west side of town is easy enough to find, standing taller than any other home in the district. The foliage around it is overgrown, and a few of the nearby houses have also been abandoned. The windows and front door are boarded up.

"No wonder that guy wants to sell this place," Jem comments as she sneaks among the abandoned houses. "Can you imagine the price for something like this? It's even bigger than Andrea's!"

Era holds Di's shoulder, guiding her along and trying to keep out of sight as he glances skyward. The cliffs offer visibility of this part of town as well, but with any luck they'll be able to avoid Fire's watch. They hurry to the manor's wall and slide along it, looking for an entrance.

Jem finds a boarded window and pulls at the planks until one snaps off. Pulling the other boards back, she beckons for Di to crawl in. Jem follows her inside, and, after making one last look at the cliffs above, Era ducks in as well.

The intruders find themselves in the living area of the house. A thick layer of dust lies undisturbed on the furniture and floor. It's obvious no one has been in the house for quite some time. Era dumps his travel and grocery bags and lets out a whoop as he jumps onto the sofa, creating a dusty cloud that erupts into the air. Jem coughs and waves her hand as she dumps her own bags and looks for a place to sit. She wipes a chair off as best she can and has a seat.

Di creeps forward, looking around in anxiety. "How long are we going to stay here?"

"Two, maybe three days tops," Jem replies.

"Three days?" Di exclaims with a gasp.

"We need to stay hidden," Era explains from his dusty couch. "Fire is likely watching the town from the cliffs above, so we'll wait her out. If we can outlast her, we'll ditch her."

"You didn't tell me that was the plan," Di complains. "This is not acceptable. I can't stay here for three days!"

"Spoken like a true princess," Jem contends. "Of course, we didn't tell you. You would have made a scene, and people would have overheard our plan."

"Don't worry, we brought lots of food," Era says in an effort to comfort her.

Di frowns at the bags tossed on the ground. "That's not enough food."

"Geez, Di, would you quit complaining?" Jem barks, growing ever more annoyed. "If we had bought three days' worth of food, and Fire had seen it, she would know our plan." Reaching into her travel bag at her feet, she procures a piece of dried bread and tosses it to Di, who manages to catch it. "Here you go, snack away. We have plenty."

"But I wanted to eat the food we bought."

"Okay, that does it!" Jem yells as she stands. "I'm going to explore. Era, you deal with the pampered princess." No one objects as she stomps off, leaving a cloud of dust in her wake.

Di looks to Era with disgust. "Why do you hang out with her? She's so mean."

"Complain if you want, but she's trying to keep us all alive," Era argues. "Not much to complain about when you consider that."

Di wants to object nonetheless. Disgusted, she drapes her damp clothes over a dusty wooden chair and sits in Jem's seat, noting the setting sun streaming through the boarded windows. "It happens at night, huh?" she says to herself, recalling the local's words.

"Don't worry about it, Di," Era says. "Nothing's going to happen. And if it does, I'll protect you."

Di smiles, instantly comforted by his words. As Era lies on the couch with his eyes closed, she realizes just how much she's come to rely on him. *'Almost fourteen,'* she tells herself as she leans back in the chair, her eyelids growing heavy.

*   *   *

Era stirs and awakens in the moonlit room, startled momentarily as he struggles to remember where he is. Looking over to the chair, Di also apparently gave in to her exhaustion, as she's curled in a ball and breathing deeply. Glancing around, he doesn't find Jem, so she's either still exploring or she found a place to sleep.

He swings his legs off the couch, again stirring up clouds of dust. Coughing and waving it away, he leans toward Di and whispers, "Wakey, wakey."

Di opens her eyes and smiles at her protector. "Hey there," she says as she sheepishly wipes away the drool. "I fell asleep? Where's Jem?"

"No clue," Era answers. "Looks like we both slept, so maybe Jem found a place to sleep as well." He stretches and stifles a yawn. "Let's go find her, or at least find some beds. That sure would beat sleeping on this furniture."

The two start exploring. It would be easy to call out for their friend, but the thick silence gives the house an eerie atmosphere, causing each to be hesitant about making any noise.

Di's heart races as they walk through the abandoned manor. Despite all the logic she repeats to herself about there being no such thing as a haunted house, she can't shake her anxiety. The local's warning continues to echo in her head.

Era steps on a board that lets out a long and loud creak. They freeze in place, but all they can hear is the sound of their own heartbeats pounding like drums in their ears. After a lengthy silence, they calm down enough to force a chuckle.

Suddenly, something jumps out and tackles Era. Di loudly shrieks and stumbles backward, tripping over a footrest to the dusty floor below. Era manages to grab the assailant and roll over, getting on top. When he does, he finds his partner under him, giggling uncontrollably. "Jem?"

Still laughing, she puts her hand on his shoulder and says, "Sorry Era. Couldn't resist."

Di peeks up from behind the piece of furniture she tripped over, relieved to see Jem in the moonlight. However, her reassurance quickly turns to anger. "Jem! That was so mean!"

"Come on Di, it was just a joke. Lighten up." She looks at Era, who's still on top of her. "Want to let me up, honey?" Era rolls his eyes and helps her up. She brushes herself off and offers a goofy grin. "I guess I let the kid in me take over. I was walking back when I heard the two of you heading this way. I just had to do it!"

Era knows there's little point in continuing to discuss it. "So, did you explore the whole house?"

"Yup!" Jem beams. "Aside from a very wet basement, there's nothing scary about this place. Found us some beds, too. Oh, and I also found this!" She withdraws a small cylinder from her pocket and fiddles with it until a beam of light breaks forth from one end. "It's a light rune!"

Era whistles at the find, and Di gasps and excitedly reaches for it. "Let me see it! Let me see!"

Jem hands it to her, and the student starts studying it. "I can't believe it! Light runes are rare." She shines it on the wall and ceiling and floor. "It works wonders compared to a lantern!"

"What's so rare about a light rune?" Era asks.

"Light is the derivative of fire, so that makes it less common than the core elements. Maybe one in a thousand people carries each derivative element, and even less work to hone it. That's all there is to it."

"One in a thousand?" Jem asks in surprise.

"Yeah, yeah, you're special," Era says, wishing Di would stop bringing up this particular topic.

"So then, can you teach me how to make a rune?" Jem asks with a gleam in her eye. "I'm a skilled elementalist, after all."

"Sure, you can make a rune," Di says. "You just need some obelite, then you program it and instill it with ice." Seeing only blank expressions, she realizes the need to explain in more detail. "Obelite is the dark rock-like material used to make runes. Once you have some, you have to program it by carving symbols into it. See?"

She hands Jem the light rune, who looks it over. "I know about the symbols on a rune. So by 'programming' you just mean drawing the symbols?"

"Right," she confirms. "Each symbol has relevance. There's a character on the side for activation, and one on the end for focus. There are a couple other standard ones on there, and all that together is called programming."

"And then you just need to fill it up, right?" Era asks.

"It's called instilling," Di corrects, "but yes, you can place about as much of an element into the obelite as you want using capacity symbols. The obelite holds the element and stores it for future use."

Era pats Jem's shoulder. "See, you could be making ice runes! You'd make some good money, too. I've seen freezers selling for thousands of venni each."

"Actually, it takes significant expertise to program something like that. You can't just release ice to keep a freezer cold," Di explains. "The elementalist is rare, but finding such a skilled programmer can be just as difficult."

Jem shrugs it off. "Can't say sitting around all day pushing ice into rocks sounds interesting, anyway." With a yawn, she says, "It's late and I'm tired. Want to see your rooms?"

"I know I do," Era replies. "It's been a long day." Di nods her agreement.

Leading the way through the decrepit house, Jem leads them upstairs and down a hallway, opens a door, and walks in with a "Ta-da!" The spacious room sports an unlit chandelier, and a spacious bed fills half the room.

"A guest room?" Era guesses as he walks in.

Jem grabs his shoulder. "Not so fast there. The princess gets the room with the chandelier. Yours is across the hall."

"Can I light it?" Di asks excitedly.

Jem grimaces. "Remember that whole thing about hiding? Lighting that thing will give away our location." Devilishly, she adds, "Though it'd be fun to see the townspeople freak out."

Di pats the bed and nods in satisfaction. Turning back to Jem, she asks, "Will you be staying in here too?"

"No way! I've got my own bed." Nudging Era, she adds, "Notice how nice I am, giving you two the rooms on this floor? Mine is all the way upstairs."

Era knows full well Jem does little in the name of self-sacrifice. "Yeah, I'm sure you're disappointed your room is so far away."

Di grabs her arm. "Please stay? I'll sleep on the floor!"

Sternly, Jem says, "Di, you'd better get used to this place. We're going to be here a while." She pushes her off her arm and leaves with the light rune, turning the room dark with her departure.

Era turns to leave as well, but Di grabs onto him. "Please stay with me?"

"Okay, okay, I get it," he says, and he pats Di's head reassuringly. "Don't worry, I'll stay with you."

Jem's voice echoes from the staircase. "Don't lead her on, Era!"

Era rolls his eyes in the darkness. "You notice she acts so tough and brave while taking the only source of light with her?" Di smiles as he leads her back into the room. "I know this old house is creepy, but it's going to help us get you home. Try and think of it in friendly terms."

Di nods as she squats down to lie on the floor, but Era scoops her up, making her heart skip a beat. "H-Hey?"

"The princess should sleep in her bed! Let her valiant guardian sleep on the floor." He carefully sets her down and goes to the door. "Let me grab the blankets from my room. I'll be right back." Di grins from ear-to-ear as she lies in the luxurious bed, not holding it back since Era can't see her. He sneaks back in and spreads out the blankets. "This dust might kill us before the monsters do," he jokes as he lies down.

Di turns to her side. "Thanks, Era. You take such good care of me."

"Naturally, I do! You're worth a lot of money."

Her heart sinks at his words, and she leans over the bed. "Am I... Am I just a reward to you?"

"I mean, it seems you're handy in combat, too," he jests.

"I'm serious, Era!" she yells, louder than intended. "Would you be helping me if I had nothing to offer?"

Era quietly ponders the question. "You're sweet, Di, but I'm not the kind of guy you think I am. I take from others. I value money over people. I don't risk my life for someone for free."

"You're not that kind of guy," Di contests. "I know you, Era. I can tell your heart isn't into being a thief. If not for Jem and your dad-"

"They don't control my life," Era argues. "I've made a decision to do what I do. I've done bad things to others, and I have no guilt about that. We all have our calling in life. You have your studies. My father is a master thief. I'm pretty sure Jem just wants to be left alone. And I... I choose to surpass my father. That's who I am."

An uncomfortable silence fills the room as Di rolls away from the bed's edge in anger. "So, you wouldn't have helped me get home," she mutters.

Era shrugs in the darkness. "I pulled you from the train without knowing I was getting anything for it. Maybe I'd have helped still."

"When you have your reward, I'll never see you again, right?"

"Oh, I don't know about that. Canterin is a big city, so I'm sure there are lots of high-profile things to steal. It could be the perfect place for me to make a name for myself," he chides. "I'll drop by from time to time, and maybe I'll even come to your house, seeing as you're the mayor's daughter and all. You must have a ritzy room or two in there for me to sleep in." Humorously, he adds, "Hey, maybe you can even unlock the windows for me? I wouldn't turn down the help."

Di laughs, much to her own surprise. "Yes, perhaps I could do that."

They lie in silence long enough that Era drifts off to sleep. Di places her hands behind her head and stares at the ceiling, her eyes adjusting enough to make it out. Her guardian's intentions confuse her, but she's grateful for his help. She chuckles to herself at the thought of helping Era break into her house. *I wonder what Daddy would think of that.*

*   *   *

A distant crash jerks the two sleeping travelers awake. Era starts for the door, but Di lunges across her bed and grabs his leg in terror.

Era places a hand on her shoulder to both reassure her and separate himself. He creates a blade from his pouch of sand and opens the door with a creak. As he steps out into the hallway, Di jumps out of bed and runs after him. He points back inside the room, but she silently pleads with frightened eyes. Relenting, he walks toward the stairs with Di clinging to him. Remembering how angry Jem was when he left her out last night, he opts to go find her. They head up a floor and start peeking into rooms.

Era finds his sleeping partner in the master bedroom, lying diagonally across the bed with blankets and pillows strewn around the room. He shakes his head when he sees the lavish bed, not to mention the size of the room. "No wonder she wouldn't stay with you," he says to Di. He stirs his partner awake and whispers, "Jem, get up."

She stares at him with heavy eyelids. "This had better be good."

"There was a loud crash somewhere in the house. Probably ground-level."

Jem listens in silence. "I don't hear anything."

"Might be an intruder. I'm going to go check it out. Stay here with Di and I'll-"

"Forget that," she says as she jumps out of bed. "I'm going with you. No way am I missing out on fighting with that... that..." Collecting herself, she says, "Come on, let's go have some fun." She energetically leads the way, her dagger in one hand and the light rune in the other as she trots down the stairs, boldly marching to the ground floor. Era remains on alert, keeping an eye out for a broken-in door or open window as Di clings tightly to him.

Jem makes little effort to move with stealth. She barges into each room, looks around with the light, and moves on to the next. After exhausting their search, they find themselves back at the stairs. "Nothing," she huffs in frustration.

"No sign of anything that crashed, either," Era adds. "I don't think anyone broke in down here. Should we check upstairs, or... Didn't you say there was a basement?"

"Sure, but there's no window down there."

"Worth a check," Era offers. Jem shrugs and heads toward the stairwell she had found in her earlier exploration. She opens the door, and the group is met with a dank odor emanating from within. Jem's light reveals hundreds of cobwebs littering the path downstairs. Waving a hand out front, she takes the lead and heads in.

112

Di crouches her head as she cowers behind Era, silently wondering how Jem had earlier mustered the courage to descend into these depths on her own. Finding the bottom of the stairs, Di's bare feet find a half-inch of standing water. The rock floor is covered with a slimy substance, and she almost slips the moment she steps on it. She snags Era's arm to hold herself up.

"Careful there," Era offers a bit too late. "Good thing I slept in my boots."

"Guess I could have warned you about the slime," Jem comments.

Holding tightly to Era, Di trudges through the water. Basements are rare, limited only to large manors such as this one, so she has no way of knowing if flooding is a common problem. She knows her father would never have stood for this if they'd had one.

The basement is a single room, built from brick and mortar on top of large slabs of rock. Wet furniture litters the place, an indication the flooding may be a recent development. Jem swings the rune around, finding nothing of interest until her light reveals a small opening in the corner, which seems to lead further. "Didn't notice that before," she mutters as she offers Era the rune. "Go be a man."

Trapped by her words, Era takes a deep breath and plunges into the tunnel, using his earth sword to brush the cobwebs aside until the makeshift hallway opens into a hidden room. He shines the light inside, finding wine racks toppled over and bottles strewn about. As he wonders if this was the source of the crash, he notices a slithering track straight through the center of the room, from one cracked corner to another.

Suddenly, he hears a loud rumble, followed by Di letting loose a shriek that echoes through the tunnel. He dashes back out to the main basement, his heart pounding. Di and Jem are both gone, and in their place is a large hole through which the water is draining.

Era shines the light down, and he's relieved to find his companions on a rock slab not far below the basement floor. "Are you alright? What happened?"

Jem brushes herself off. "The floor just collapsed on us! Give me the light." Era drops the rune. She catches it and uses it to reveal a cavern as the water rains down around her. "Too bad we just took a bath," Jem complains, her voice echoing. "We could have waited for the shower!"

Di gives her a terrified look, again in awe of Jem's ability to remain calm. "Where are we? How do we get back up?"

She looks up to Era. "Hey, can you stretch your sword down here? Maybe make us a little ladder or something?"

Era looks at the weapon in his hand. "Not enough dirt."

"Then go outside and get some more!"

"Can I have the light back?"

Jem stomps her foot and shouts, "You want to leave two defenseless girls in a cave by themselves without a light?"

Era sighs and stands, annoyed by the attitude. The basement is pitch black without the light rune, so locating the stairs is a guessing game. Hoping he doesn't find another sinkhole, he tiptoes around the void, carefully placing his weight down with each step.

Down below, Jem continues to explore. The cavern stretches up to the house's foundation, exposing the bedrock used for the basement floor. "Great, they just had to build this house on top of a big pit. How is it we're the first ones to fall in?"

Di steps out from under the dripping water and shivers as a cold breeze passes through. "This house really is haunted."

"No, Di, if this is what killed those people then the hole would've already been there. This is pure coincidence."

Di nods, her teeth chattering, and Jem starts to notice how cold she is herself. She tosses her soaked jacket aside and rubs her hands. "You couldn't have been a fire maker, huh?" she teases Di.

"Air is so much better," Di argues, taking the comment too seriously.

"Hey, chill out there," Jem puns as she turns the light and points it straight at Di. "I was just saying-" Jem cuts herself off with a gasp. "Di, watch out!"

Di spins to find a large blade about to descend on her. She screams in fright as she extends her palms upward, forming a barrier just in time to intercept the mysterious weapon before it slices her in two. The force sends her to the ground, but she maintains her hold on her air shield. The blade continues to press against the elemental wall as she struggles to maintain her protection.

Jem unsheathes her dagger and races to Di's rescue, but she freezes in terror when she realizes there isn't some*one* attacking Di, but some*thing*. A monstrous blob of water is looming over its victim, held aloft by a column of water extending from the floor. A tentacle is protruding from the main body, its tip formed into the blade trying to cut the air shaper in half. Even as Jem watches, a new limb forms from the mass and extends outward, another blade at its tip. This one strikes against Di's main shield repeatedly while the other one holds her down, leaving her with no options for escape.

Shaking off the fear, Jem dashes around Di and tries to intercept the blade. She holds her dagger out in an attempt to parry the strike, but the watery blade slices cleanly through the metal, as if it weren't even there. The strike narrowly misses her fingers, and Jem stares at her broken dagger in disbelief.

The blob forms a third tentacle and strikes at Jem, but she jumps backward to avoid the blow. Sheathing her broken dagger, she tugs on her companion, hoping to dislodge her from the pressure of the blade holding her down. "Di, angle it!" she yells in desperation.

Di tilts the shield, allowing the pressuring blade to slide along until it hits the ground. Jem yanks Di out of the way before the other blade can strike and drags her along in a mad dash to escape, clutching the small rune as she relies on it to light the way.

CHAPTER 10

Era stumbles along in the darkness, using his weapon as a cane to find his way around. As soon as he finds the stairs, he is met with a foot that connects with his chest, and his sword flies from his hand as he hits the floor. Disarmed, he scrambles away from his unknown assailant, slipping and sliding on the slimy stone. Di's shriek pierces the room, and he glances into the hole to see the light faltering, accompanied by bizarre noises.

He turns to his pursuer, intent on going on the offensive, and the flickering light is enough for Era to make out the face of his opponent. "Fire?"

She lunges and grapples him, but Era keeps his balance and shoves her aside. The mercenary swings around with a high kick, which Era barely manages to duck. As they fight, the light from Jem's rune abruptly fades, prompting the adversaries to step back as their eyes strain in the pitch-black chamber.

"What's the deal, Fire?" Era barks, noting he has been taking blows from two fists, and he deduces Fire's arm must not be as broken as he thought. "What did you do to Jem and Di?"

In response, she tackles him to the wet floor and attempts to slam his head against the ground. Instead, Era grabs her wrists and, gaining leverage, rolls over on top of her. "Fire! The hole!" he warns in vain as she uses her momentum to roll back around, and his body hits the edge. As he slides in, Era flails for the ledge, but he finds Fire's legs instead.

Fire desperately catches the floor and kicks to dislodge Era, but his grip holds tight. Eventually, her fingers slip from the slimy surface, and they plummet into the cavern below. Slow to move, Fire picks herself off the rocky ground, and Era shoves his arms through her armpits and pulls up on her shoulders from behind. She struggles against him, but her captor holds her tightly.

"Tell me what happened to Jem and Di," he demands.

"Don't know what you're talking about," Fire says as she kicks at him.

"Liar!" he shouts as he pulls on her bad arm. She winces in pain as he demands, "Tell me what you did."

Fire remains silent, and Era jostles her one more time for good measure. "Jem and Di fell down here just before I ran into you, and they disappeared right after we started fighting. You're telling me you aren't involved?" Facing more silence, Era forces her forward. "Fine, we're going for a walk until we find them."

*   *   *

Jem stops running and doubles over, gasping for air, and Di collapses at her feet. Jem coughs and pants, "I think… we lost it." Di rolls to her back, praying Jem is right.

"What was that thing?" Jem wonders aloud, her voice echoing off the cave walls. "Was it… Was it made of water?"

"I… have no idea… what that was," admits the elemental expert.

"Aren't you smart or something?" Jem snaps. "To think it sliced right through my dagger. My very expensive dagger!"

"It's an elemental blade," Di answers, catching her breath. "Remember what I said? Those things can be sharper than metal."

Jem draws her broken weapon. "Yeah, but Era's is like a noodle compared to what that monster was using."

"Era is good, but not *that* good," Di explains. "Only the best and most experienced contortionists can shape a blade sharp enough to slice through a metal sword, though I've never seen one slice through so cleanly." Dumbstruck, she realizes, "That thing is a better shaper than the experts at the Academy!"

Jem grits her teeth at the thought, wondering how to fight such a monster. They wait in silence, listening for any indication that the creature is still slithering its way after them. Content it's not immediately behind them, Jem swings around with the light to explore their new surroundings. "This is such a strange place," she mutters. "It doesn't look quite natural."

Di ponders this for a moment and exclaims, "It's not possible that… that thing made all this?"

"Not possible. It'd need to be slithering around for years."

"Try hundreds of years," Di argues.

"That just makes me more right," Jem mutters to herself as she finds a wall in their path. "Di, I think this might be the end of the road."

"What?" Di gasps.

"Come on," Jem beckons as she begins walking. "Let's make sure of it before we panic." They head over to the wall, the tension in the air building with each step.

Di starts to tear up. "This is it. This is it."

"You want to survive? Then shut up with the despair," Jem barks as she scans along the wall, finding a crack just big enough to fit a finger. She shines her light in, revealing empty space behind it. "See, there's a passage here! We just have to find a way to get to it." As she moves her light along the wall, she catches the reflection of moisture around the crack. "Just like the floors," she realizes. An idea strikes her, and she hands the light rune to Di. Placing both hands on the wet wall, she starts coating the area with an intense frost. The exterior of the wall crystallizes, and the crackling of freezing water echoes throughout the chamber.

"Your turn," she says to Di expectantly, wiping her brow.

Di frowns. "To do what?"

"To bust it open!" Jem answers as she snatches her light back. "You can make a wall of air, so surely you can make a giant hammer or something. Get to it."

Though doubtful, Di finds she lacks a better idea. Extending her arms out as if holding a large object, she concentrates on solidifying the air. Mustering all her strength, she winds back and hurls it forward, swinging the solid block of air into the iced-over crack. She hits the icy wall hard, making a loud bang that echoes all around. The ice shatters, taking a chunk of rock with it.

"Again!" Jem calls, excited by the success. Di repeats her motion, slamming the wall loudly once more. "Again!" She complies.

Panting, Di starts to wind up again, but Jem raises her hand to stop her. "Good work, Di. That should be enough." The air maker topples over, exhausted but pleased with the results. The crack is now a more manageable size, and Jem squeezes herself through the hole. After ensuring it's safe, she beckons for Di to follow.

Di emerges on the other side, and her face twists in confusion at the odd sight before her. Rusted, metal shelves are lined up throughout an enclosed room, and crumbled rocks litter the ground. The walls are flat and reflective, made of a different material than the rocky cavern. "Could this be metal?" Di wonders as she runs her hand along it.

"What is this place?" Jem mumbles to herself as she continues to explore with the light rune. A heavy door appears to lead out of the room from the opposite side, whereas their entrance point was a crack that had formed in the metallic wall. At their feet is a trail of water leading through a different, larger crack, indicative of a path the liquid creature had taken recently. "Is this where that thing came from?"

"Jem, give me the light!" Di exclaims. She hands it over, and the schoolgirl shines it at the rubble on the ground. "These rocks are... They're runes?"

"Not much left of them," Jem says. Looking closer, she notes, "Where are the symbols?"

"They're all gone," Di says in amazement. "Obelite softens over time, after all. But that would mean these runes are seriously old."

Jem looks around in awe. "So what is this? Someone's personal collection?" Leaving Di to salivate over the rune fragments, she walks to the door and pulls at its handle in vain. Pounding against it, she says, "Let's try our trick again, Di. This door may be our best chance of escaping that thing. Unfortunately, I don't think my ice is going to help us with this one."

Di resolutely forms the hammer again, hoping the creature doesn't show up before they can escape.

*　　　*　　　*

"Ow! Stop stepping on my feet!" Fire shouts in the darkness.

"Shut it," Era tells her, not interested in dealing with her sass. "Just be glad that's all the pain you're feeling."

"Oh, I'm so scared."

"Keep pushing it and you will be!"

"Try it!" Fire taunts. "You're a spineless wimp. If not for my arm, I'd-"

Era laughs, cutting her off. "I've beaten you twice now, so get over yourself."

"Twice!?" she exclaims, struggling against him until Era clamps down on her injury. Giving up, she grumbles, "You're not half the fighter I am."

"It must be miserable losing to someone like that, huh?"

"You have no idea," she says. "So how long is this going to take?"

"You tell me. If you fill me in, it might go faster."

"I didn't do anything to your comrades," Fire insists. "Next time keep a closer eye on them, yourself."

Era grows annoyed. "You showed up the moment they disappeared. It's not like they just wandered off on their own! I heard Di scream, I'm sure of it."

"Ow!" Fire yelps as Era steps on her feet yet again. "For crying out loud, your clumsiness is worse than your threats. Just take the flare rune out of my pouch and light it, already. Stop making me walk in the dark and stop stepping on my feet!"

"You've got a flare rune, and you're just now telling me?"

"Shut up and use it."

He releases his hold on the weak arm, hopeful she won't be able to try anything with it. He reaches to her side, looking for her pouch.

"You go any lower and you'll never see your hand again," Fire promises.

"Well, where is it?"

"Other side."

"That's a nice coincidence," Era snidely remarks. "So I'd need to free your good arm in order to access it."

"It's a coincidence that my pouch is where my good arm can reach it? Are you completely inept?"

Era takes a deep breath to remain calm as he reaches around Fire's torso. Locating the pouch, he pulls it closer and finds the flare rune.

"Why is this taking so long? Did you need a hug or something?"

"Would you shut up for just one minute?" Era growls as he fumbles around with the flare in his free hand.

"All you ever do is try to get me to talk," Fire retorts. "And now that I'm being conversational, you're mad at me?"

"Shut up, already!" Era barks as he trips the flare rune. It flies up and hits the ceiling, lodging itself in the rocks and illuminating their surroundings: the smooth rock wall, cavern floor, and, to their mutual awe, a bubbling pool of water swirling just a short distance away.

The two stare in stunned silence at the faceless mass, which somehow seems to stare back. Era slowly releases Fire as it extends a tentacle from its body and sharpens it into a blade. The two adversaries finally snap from their stupor and dash away at full speed.

"What was that?" Era yells as he runs alongside Fire. "Was it trying to sneak up on us?"

"How should I know?" she replies as she tries to outpace her rival. The flare rune's light fades, and the darkness swallows them up once more. The sloshing noise of the creature continues to echo behind them.

"Enough of this," Fire calls out as she pulls another flare rune from her pouch. "We have to fight that thing."

"You're crazy!" Era screams as she activates the flare. Fire turns to face the monster, and Era stops running as well. Hurrying back to her side, he prepares himself and says, "Okay, fine! Let's-" But the sly mercenary has already left him, racing back in the same direction they had been heading.

"You backstabbing sleaze!" Era cries as he races to catch up, kicking himself for falling for such a trick. "Come back here!"

*   *   *

Di collapses, exhausted from slamming her hardened air club against the door so many times, which hasn't budged in spite of the forceful collisions. Jem also leans against the wall, having aided Di as best she could by swinging with her.

"Can't... be done," Di pants.

"Not enough force, I guess," Jem reasons. "Whatever this is, it's a fortress. I'm surprised the back wall cracked."

Di looks back at the hole they used to enter. "That monster has been gone a long time. Do you think it's still looking for us?"

"Maybe it got lost?" Jem hopes as she peers through the gap with her light rune. She reluctantly slides back into the cavern, scanning the area as she does so. "I think it's safe. For now, at least."

Di follows Jem, but she slips on the ice and falls. "Ow," she mumbles as she rubs her side. "Your ice worked well on this crack. Too well."

"Yeah, that's because there was a lot of…" her voice trails off as she looks back at the ice-covered crack. "Di, I can only make ice, right? But the ice I made froze all the water around it?"

Di cringes as she stands, still massaging her side. "When you make ice, it's already at sub-freezing temperatures. It would naturally freeze all the water around it as well."

Jem snaps her fingers. "I think that's the answer! Come on, let's go find that thing."

"You want to find it?" Di asks incredulously. "What's your idea, to freeze it?"

"Exactly! It won't be able to shape the ice, right?"

"You're crazy!" she cries, but her arguing is interrupted by the sound of rushing water approaching. Jem steps behind Di as the short air maker prepares her shield, preparing for the inevitable. Shining the light ahead, Jem waits for the creature to round the corner and show itself.

Instead of the monster, however, Era and Fire race into the area, each blinded by the light rune as they shield their eyes. "Jem?" Era calls out.

"Era! And you?" Jem shouts at the sight of Fire.

Their reunion is cut short by the increasing sound of water rushing through the cavern. Having apparently done away with its previous form, a torrent of water rushes into the giant cavern like a river gone wild. Once in the middle of the room, it pulls together in the open space, stirring in a circle as it regains its form.

Jem slaps Era's shoulder and barks, "You went and got Fire? Are you insane?"

"She found me," Era corrects. "We were fighting and fell in the hole."

"Fine, let's feed her to this thing and hope it doesn't notice us slip by," Jem suggests.

"Want to try it?" she challenges.

"Guys, focus!" Di warns, her eyes locked on the monster before them.

Jem watches Fire disdainfully before turning to Era. "This is a dead end, so we either run till we collapse or we fight this thing."

"Fight it!?"

"Listen, this might be a long shot, but maybe I can freeze it to death," Jem says in a hushed voice. "I need to get close."

"Ah, so the queen bee is an ice queen?" Fire snickers. "Just give me your dagger and I'll carve this thing up in no time."

"You want to use this?" Jem asks as she flashes her broken blade. "I already tried."

Fire is uncharacteristically shaken. "That thing did that?"

"It uses an elemental blade, so it will cut right through a dagger," Di explains. "We have to use elements to battle it."

"What the- But my elemental blade doesn't do that!" Era argues.

"Not the time, Era," Jem retorts. "Just keep your blade sharp and you'll be fine, right? It won't be able to cut your sword."

Era's heart sinks as he's reminded he lost the dirt when Fire kicked him down. "I... uh... I don't have it..."

"Then just hold the light and be a distraction," she barks as she flips him the rune. "Here it comes!"

Having formed three bladed appendages, the creature advances toward the clustered group. Di's arms tremble as she raises them, palms extended, forcing the air in front of them into a shield. Era places his hand on her shoulder to help calm her nerves. Swallowing hard, she forces her legs to move as she trots forward to meet the threat head-on.

Fire watches the display of bravado in disgust. Her plan had been to sit back and wait for a chance to sneak by, but watching the three advance in front of her makes her burn with anger at the prospect of being protected.

The beast barrages Di's shield with its three arms. The defender winces as she focuses on the critical task of maintaining the barrier. Jem shouts, "Break!", and she and Era split off, running in opposite directions from Di's protection. The creature, choosing to split its arms, presses one down on Di while shifting the others to follow the two thieves.

Era works to keep the light centered on the beast while he dodges strikes from one of the arms, grateful its powerful attacks are slow. With it being made entirely of water, Era notices that the light refracts and illuminates the entire target regardless of the angle. He keeps moving in hopes of at least keeping one arm distracted, wishing he could contribute more directly.

Jem runs to the giant water blob, keeping an eye out for the inevitable attack from above. When it comes, she dodges and dives in, and she starts freezing the water the moment she touches the creature's body. As the ice creeps around the outside of the mass, a new fourth appendage takes a swing at the oblivious ice elementalist. Just before it hits, Fire sweep kicks Jem's legs out from under her, causing the blade to narrowly miss her head.

"Freeze it, already!" Fire yells as she dives backward, narrowly avoiding a strike from another appendage.

"I need Di!" Jem calls back as she stands.

Fire glances back across the cavern, barely finding the air shaper in the darkness, who is still holding back the single arm pressing against her. Dashing to the youngster, she slides underneath her barrier and barks, "The ice queen needs you."

Dripping with sweat, Di manages a grunt to acknowledge Fire's request, but it's evident she can do nothing about it. Reluctantly, Fire heaves herself atop the air wall and kicks at the giant appendage, but her foot just sinks into the water, its consistency like mud against her boot. She yanks it out and gives a glance to Jem, but she's not making any progress, instead spending most of her time dodging multiple attacking arms. Letting loose a battle cry, Fire jumps up and brings her good arm down hard on the watery tentacle. Her bare hand penetrates the arm, chopping it off at its tip and releasing Di from its hold.

Free from the pressure, Di releases the shield and collapses to her hands and knees. Fire, who had been standing on the shield, freefalls next to her with a yelp. Resisting the urge to smack her sudden ally, the mercenary wastes no time yanking her to her feet.

"How did you break it?" Di asks, but Fire gives her no answer as she drags the air maker to Jem.

When Era sees Fire leading Di toward the creature, he tries to run back to rendezvous with his allies, but the water creature slams one of its arms directly in his path, cutting him off. "Why aren't any of us water shapers?" he screams in frustration as he reverses course.

As he runs, he notices a substantial amount of dirt where the water arm last struck, and it occurs to him that it can only shape a single element. Any dirt that works its way into the water is quickly expelled due to the creature's inability to control it, which means it's actively depositing piles of earth as it moves. The water creature lifts an arm to ready an attack, leaving a fresh pile of mud behind. Era dodges the strike and scoops up enough dirt to form a knife. As he continues to move, he drags his small blade along the ground in an effort to draw more into it.

Meanwhile, Di raises a wide shield at the base of the creature to protect Jem as she works on freezing the main body. Several smaller protrusions form and attack the transparent wall.

Fire cringes as each strike against Di's barrier echoes loudly throughout the chamber. She watches Jem's slow progress and shouts, "No way will this work. At this rate you're just feeding it more water!"

"Got any better ideas?" Jem retorts.

Di looks past Jem, noting the hovering mass is only supported by a thin pillar of water from underneath. "The pillar? Breaking it should make the creature collapse!"

Jem and Fire glance at the pillar. "Consider it done," Fire calls out, and she steps into a wide chop of her hand, which plunges into the pillar. However, her hand gets stuck within as the creature swirl the water, and Fire finds herself getting sucked in. She pulls with all her might until she's suddenly released, but she staggers backward from the force and falls outside of Di's protection.

The blades seize the opportunity to assault the vulnerable target, but Di steps into their path and deflects the attacks with shields formed on each hand, demonstrating a ferocity as her adrenaline spikes.

Jem helps Fire up as Di restores their wider protection. "How did you think you were going to cut through that? With your bare hand?" Jem screams. Fire ignores her and hides a wince as she rubs at her hand.

A hard slam echoes out as the creature brings its three arms down as a combined club of water, flinging Di backward and leaving Jem and Fire unprotected. The club reforms into a blade and comes down on the dazed Di, but Era zips in and deflects the attack with a hefty dirt sword.

"Miss me?" he calls out.

"Era! About time!" Jem cries in relief.

The creature splits its arms once more and resumes its assault. Era intercepts one arm and then another as they continue to barrage him. Having his own elemental blade, he defends each strike without concern of the blades slicing through him, though the strain from such shaping takes its toll.

Fire joins him, running to his side and watching for an opportunity. As Era meets a blade, she slides past him, leaps into the air and comes down on the tentacle, chopping it clean through. Era is momentarily awestruck by the feat, but his attention soon returns to the other arms.

"Era, light!" Jem yells, and Era obediently flips the rune back to her. "Let's go," she orders as she grabs Di and drags her to the pillar. Di extends her palms upward, providing protection as Jem crouches at the central column and places her hands against it.

"You need to freeze it all the way through," Di instructs as she maintains the shield. "Any amount of water inside will keep it up!"

Jem is surprised by the amount of ice already swirling within the pillar. Deciding she must have made better progress than she thought, she pours her effort into finishing the job as her companions hold the creature's attention. She grunts and screams as she forces the ice further and further into the column. Just as she feels like she might black out from the effort, it freezes all the way through.

The suspended accumulation of water comes crashing down on Di and Jem, knocking them hard into the ground as the creature loses its form. Its appendages fall off as the entire mass rushes around Era and Fire's feet, but, just as it appears the waters are dispersing, a central glob of water pulls together in the middle. The creature, despite losing most of its mass, manages to display new life by pulling in much of the water from the ground, sucking Jem and Di into its mass in the process and trapping them within its watery confines.

Now half the size it was before, the creature no longer uses a column of water, but instead pulls its waters tightly together. Di and Jem struggle in vain within the waters, unable to gain any momentum against the torrent. Jem tries freezing it from the inside, creating chunks of ice that float to the top and fall out, but her efforts are insignificant.

Era tightly grips his weighty blade, knowing Jem and Di don't have long before they drown. Illuminated by the light rune swirling within, the creature again creates bladed protrusions and attacks its remaining opponents. Era and Fire split up, each trying to get in close, but the arms keep its targets from approaching.

Desperate for time, Era charges in recklessly, deflecting attacks and swinging hard at the base of an arm, chopping it off. As another of the blades meets his own, he looks at his trapped friends and sees a large, floating object near the top of the swirling mass of water. He strains his eyes, surprised to find it immune to the internal flows, maintaining its position relative to the monster's main body and separated from where it keeps its prisoners confined. "Fire, something is in there!"

"I know! Your friends!" she shouts as she nimbly dodges an attack.

126

"No, something else! Something floating in the middle," he grunts while deflecting a strike. "It looks important!"

"In the middle?" Fire repeats, spotting the dark object floating effortlessly amidst the currents. Locking onto the target, she zips toward the body, hoping to jam her fist in far enough to make contact. However, a tentacle of water lashes down and wraps itself tightly around her ankle. It yanks her into the air as every blade accelerates to impale her, but Era slices cleanly up through all the arms at once, turning the weapons into a harmless spray of water as Fire crashes to the floor.

Using his momentum, Era swings around and cuts down on the creature from above, pressing into the water with enough strength that he makes contact with the object. The moment he does, the mass of water again falls, washing out along the cavern floor.

Jem and Di hit the ground, gasping for air. Overcome by his exhaustion, Era's legs buckle as he releases his weapon, and Fire catches him as he swoons. He looks at her gratefully as she helps him to the wet floor. "You sure do get lucky," she says in bewilderment as she sits next to Era and massages her injuries, not sure whether she should be relieved or angry she was again saved by the amateur fighter.

Di rolls to her back, still coughing. "Please tell me it's over."

"I thought… I thought that was it for us," Jem pants. "How did you take it out?"

"I struck something floating in the middle," Era explains. "That was it. It just died when I made contact." He points and says, "That thing, there."

Jem snags her light rune from the floor to illuminate the object, and Di's eyes widen as she frantically crawls over to examine it. Shaped like a disc, the rock is about half the size of a carriage wheel. A deep gash stretches across the face of it, indicative of where Era's blade sliced it. "No way," she whispers in amazement.

"What is it?" Jem asks as she leans over Di.

Di can hardly speak as she squeaks out, "This thing… It was a rune."

Era's jaw drops. "A rune? I didn't know they could do that with runes."

"They can't," Di insists.

"Well, clearly they can," Era retorts.

"No, Era, they can't! This technology is way too advanced, even for Three Pillars researchers." Unable to take her eyes off it, Di says, "What I wouldn't give to take this back to them."

Jem snatches it and holds it close. "Well, they'll have to pay a pretty penny to see it."

"Jem!" Di shouts in offense.

"Hey, we almost died fighting that thing. There's no way I'm giving it up for free," she says as she studies it. "Say, Di, there are no symbols on this thing. Aren't symbols needed? You know, for programming and all that?"

"The symbols are there, all right." Di snags the light rune and points it at the disc, illuminating hundreds of thinly engraved rings concentrically marking the disc's front side.

"Nice try. You're saying a bunch of rings is all it takes to program something this big?"

"Look closer."

Jem peers close, shocked at what she finds. In actuality, each ring is a string of characters, so tiny and close together that, without close inspection, they blur together to form a solid ring. "That's... That's..."

"It's not possible, I know. That's what I'm saying," Di insists.

"No, Di! This thing will make me rich!" She puts it to her lips and kisses it with a loud smack, adding, "Sorry Di, you've been replaced as my new favorite thing."

"Jem, you can't sell it! You have to-"

"It's settled, Di. Might as well accept it."

As the two bicker, Era glances to Fire, who removes her bandanna to let her damp hair fall. She wrings out the cloth in a fruitless effort to start drying herself. Era blushes, now seeing a stark contrast to the cold-natured assassin he's been fighting. Water drips from the hair plastered to her cheeks, and her toned arms are defined through her soaked sleeves. "Hey, thanks for helping us," he squeaks. When she glances at him, he quickly avoids eye contact.

"Don't think too much of it. I was forced to do it," she responds frankly.

"Well, sure," he agrees, "but you could have run after the monster fell apart the first time. You stuck around and helped me save Jem and Di."

She slaps her wet handkerchief on her knee in surrender. "You saved my life. I owed you that much."

"Seems you have a sense of honor," Era chides. Glancing back toward his partner, he lowers his voice and says, "Look, I know Jem's not going to like it, but-"

"You want my help? Then tell the ice queen how it's going to be," she snaps. "For being so useful in a fight, I can't believe how spineless you are when it comes to that Allerian."

Era shrugs. "Hey, she's my boss, but I'll talk to her if you're still willing to work with us."

"Look, if not for my arm, I'd have no problem capturing you three. I'm just looking for a way to make a venni after all this." Glancing away, she mutters, "Thirty-five percent, right?"

"Sorry, offer's lowered to thirty." Fire looks back with a flash of anger, but Era says, "Should have taken the offer before you sucker kicked me down a flight of stairs, threw me in a hole, and had your life saved by me again."

"I did accept your stupid offer! You reneged on it!"

"Sheesh, do you want me to leave you in this cave?" Era flatly asks. "Because that's what it's sounding like to me."

Fire starts to protest, but she realizes Era likely is the only person who can get them all out. With frustration, she relents and says, "Fine, whatever. But if you don't pay up, I'm putting my own twenty thousand bounty on your head."

"Fair enough."

CHAPTER 11

Era holds a long plank of earth as his companions climb out of the cavern one at a time. Holding the form over such a long distance is exhausting, so he decides to sit down and take a break before climbing out, himself. He releases his hold, and the dirt rains down to the rock below.

Standing on the basement floor once again, Jem kneels and examines the disc with the light rune. "Pretty impressive," she says to herself.

"Is there any chance that thing can come back to life?" Fire asks. "That rune spawned a killing machine."

Di shakes her head. "I don't think so. Runes that have their programs erased or otherwise marred become expensive doorstops. I think we killed the... well, whatever that was."

'Yeah, thanks to Era,' Jem thinks as she shines her light down on her partner, wondering when it was he became so formidable. Were it not for him, she and Di would certainly have drowned.

As if reading her thoughts, Fire says in a hushed voice, "You undervalue him, you know that? If not for him-"

"I know that," Jem says in defense. "He's strong, I get that. But he's not smart, and until he is-"

"Uhh... Jem? I can hear you," Era reveals from the cavern below.

Sheepishly, Jem leans forward and says, "Era, you're alright. Thanks for saving us down there." Era blushes in the darkness and absent-mindedly scratches the back of his head.

"So, Di," Jem says, changing the subject, "did you grab enough rune shards? Just remember, I'm not carrying those for you in my bag. It'll be heavy enough with my big one, here."

Di looks at the crumbled rocks in her hands. "The symbols on these are almost entirely eroded. I'm not sure they'll have any value whatsoever to the Academy." Longing for the remarkable rune in Jem's possession, she says, "Come on, just let me have that! You're not going to do anything with it."

"Except make tons of money," Jem touts. "But hey, I'm impartial. If the Academy can offer up some venni, I'm all for giving it to them."

Ready to make his exit, Era again solidifies the dirt into a long beam and scales it. Hand over hand, he works to maintain the form of the earth with each grip. When he gets near the top, Jem reaches down and helps him the rest of the way. The moment he releases the plank, it loses its form and crumbles into the cavern below.

After brushing himself off, Era collects his courage and looks his partner in the eyes. "Jem, I know I'm not the smartest person in the world, but I have a good feeling about bringing Fire along. I've pledged part of my share to her, and I'd like it if... No, I mean to say that I'm hiring her services."

Jem is startled by the change in conversation. "Hey now, just because she helped us out down there-"

"No Jem, it's more than that," Era says. "I truly don't think we'll make it to Canterin without her help."

After a moment of inner-turmoil, she relinquishes and says, "Okay, it's about time I trusted you with a decision. I'm fine with her coming, as long as *you*," she emphasizes as she shines the light into Fire's face, "can swear, with absolute sincerity, that you will not backstab us."

Fire is surprised by the demand. "You do realize I could just lie about it?"

"I won't believe you either way. I just want to judge your reaction. Now look me in the eye and tell me."

Annoyed by the seemingly pointless exercise, she relents and says, "Fine, I promise not to backstab you or your little bees."

"And you're swearing off each of our bounties?"

Fire winces at the prospect. Her straight face gone, she visibly squirms as she forces out, "Sure."

Jem studies Fire for an uncomfortably long period. "Well, if you're earning most of Era's share, you'd best pull your weight."

Fire crosses her arms. "Of course, but now that I've played your little game, I'm setting ground rules. No more fires, no more towns, and no more roads. You will concede to my expertise or the deal's off."

Di watches the interaction nervously, wondering how smoothly this operation is going to go with these two egos vying for control.

"I'll go get my map," Jem grumbles, heading upstairs with her light.

As they follow Jem and her light, Fire turns to Era and says, "This thirty percent had better be worth dealing with her."

Era pats her shoulder, and she glares at him with a look that screams, *'Don't you dare do that again.'* Nervously pulling his hand back, he says, "Well, if you can get us to Canterin safely, I'm sure you'll never have to deal with either of us again. Think of it as a bonus."

Fire looks Era over with contempt, questioning her decision already.

*   *   *

Leaving the competing commanders alone to plan, Era and Di find furniture to use as beds. It feels to Era like a short nap, but when he's shaken awake, he's surprised to find sunlight streaming through the boarded windows.

"Get up already," Jem orders. "We need to be out of here before it gets too bright."

"Too late for that," Fire gripes. "We should have left an hour ago."

"Then next time don't spend so long trying to decide something so trivial."

"That was not trivial!"

Era sits in a daze, trying to remember the last time he was so sleep-deprived. After the skirmish with Fire and Jaras, not to mention the battle in the caverns last night, it's a wonder he's even able to keep his eyes open. Still, he shakes off the desire to lie back down, not daring to cross the dual leadership of Jem and Fire. He groggily stumbles over to the table where the map is sprawled out. Many penciled lines and scribbles litter the document, an indication of the intense debates he is grateful to have missed. The final path takes them far from any more main pathways or cities, and it leads to a harbor town called Kemplen.

"Kemplen?" Era asks. "I thought we were going to approach from the coast."

"And then what? Just strut into Canterin like you own the place?" Fire asks in disgust. "We need to get to Canterin by ship. Kemplen is the largest port town this side of the Lidoran Sea, which will keep our profile low. Naturally, they'll be searching the ships at Canterin, but smugglers have gotten good at their trade thanks to the tariff spikes."

Jem begrudgingly nods her approval. "She's right about all that. We should be able to smuggle ourselves in."

"Will Di even be safe once we get her inside?" he wonders aloud.

"Not our problem," Fire says coldly. "We get her in, get our reward, and leave. Her rich daddy can hire protection from there. This is the plan."

Era wants to object, but he acknowledges the first priority is to get Di home. "I guess I'm fine with that."

As Jem rolls up the map and collects her things, Fire glances at the sleeping Di and quietly asks, "Have you two considered the idea of just turning her in?" Jem stops her cleaning, and Era's brow furrows as she continues, "Look, I don't know what your relationship is to her, but with sixty thousand venni just sleeping over there, why not cash in?"

Era isn't swayed. "Sorry Fire, that's a negative. I've sworn to Di I would take her back, and I-"

"You value your honor over wealth?" Fire scoffs. "Aren't you a thief?"

"Thieves can have honor," Era insists. "Besides, Jem and I have bounties as well. It's unlikely we can turn her in and get the reward."

With contempt, Fire asks, "Do you think your bounties are just going to go away once this is over? You could negotiate with them, have them erase your bounties and give you the full sum. They'd do it in a heartbeat."

Era is caught off guard by the proposition, but Jem interjects, "For now we stick with the plan."

"Figured I'd at least convince you," Fire says, "but if you're out then the honorable thief over here is certainly uninterested as well." She shrugs and admits, "Too bad, I was hoping to make things easy."

Era's mind races while Jem silently packs. His dreams, his goals… everything he wants to be is contrary to this decision. Being a thief means becoming an emotional island, if his dad's words are to be believed. His life with Jem has, in some ways, helped him get closer to that state of mind, as she's always kept him at a distance. If he were to treat Di the same way, he could achieve the infamy he's always desired, plus cash in on a major bounty in the process.

"I'll head out first," Fire says, snapping Era's attention back to reality. "Follow the map exactly, and I'll scout out the path to ensure there's no one waiting to ambush you."

"Wait," Era says as he fumbles around in his bag. He withdraws a dagger and hands it to Fire. "You'll probably recognize that."

Despite her annoyance, Fire can't hide her delight at the sight of her old blade. "Thanks for keeping it. Ugorzi had a falling out with the Smith's Hammer a year ago, so there's no smith here." Looking back at Era's bag, she asks, "Got anything else of mine in there?"

"Sorry, that's all I kept," Era assures her.

"Sure would make this easier if I had my gear," she grumbles.

"Hey, at least you have a blade," Jem offers, drawing her own dagger. With the blade cut cleanly across the middle, she swings it around in dissatisfaction. "As if fighting against swords wasn't enough of a challenge."

Fire turns to Jem. "So, you're going to follow me this time?"

"We'll be right behind you," Jem promises as she sheaths her weapon. "Just do your part." With that, Fire heads to a window, pushes out the boards, and slips outside.

Jem plants her hands on her hips. "This had better work, Era. If not, I'm blaming you and-"

"Why, Jem?" Era interrupts with sincerity. "Why were you so fast to reject Fire's idea?"

Jem eyes him. "You're seriously asking me that? You?" Throwing two fingers in the air, she contends, "For one, there's no guarantee they'll give us the bounty since we caused this whole mess in the first place. For two, there's *this* whole issue," she adds, waving a hand over her face.

"So, if we could easily collect the bounty, you'd be up for it?"

She pauses before answering. "Money isn't everything to me, Era. The thought of helping the military makes me throw up a little in my mouth. I'm not sure I could bring myself to negotiate with them, even for twenty or sixty thousand venni." With a smirk, she asks, "So you have such a low opinion of me that you thought I'd sell out a lost child?"

"No, I... I guess I'm trying to decide for myself," he confesses. "I mean, if I'm in this for the money, doesn't it make sense to turn her in?"

"Since when are you in this for money?" Jem asks. "You're all about honor, honest thievery, etcetera etcetera, on and on... You never shut up about those kinds of ideals. Plus, you just gave most of your share to Fire for her help."

Era shrugs. "I don't think much about money, but Di asked me last night if we'd be helping her if not for the potential reward. I couldn't give her a straight answer, because I honestly don't know."

Jem scratches her nose. "Am I having a negative influence on you? There's no way you'd ever have debated something like this back when I first met you." Placing her hand on his shoulder, she meets Era's eyes with confidence. "I know you pretty well by now, and, in my opinion, you'll never have it in you to betray someone like Di. And that's a good thing."

Her words instantly lift his self-imposed burden. Di stirs, and Jem turns to her with relief. "Oh, thank goodness we don't need to wake the princess up. That's even more of chore than waking Era."

Di yawns. "Wha... What time is it?"

"It's time to get moving," Jem orders as she pulls her to her feet. "We're leaving in fifteen minutes."

*　　　*　　　*

Fire watches as the three ineptly sneak out of town, doing their best to blend in amongst the sparse early-morning crowds. Both Di and Era get distracted, hoping to buy some fruit from the traveling vendors while Jem yells at them to keep moving. Fire starts to give herself less credit for tracking them so well.

Perched high above the town once more, she laments her situation. The encounter in the caverns was a setback for her arm and leg, and Era has demonstrated himself as a formidable foe. Still, she can't help but be pleased with the way things turned out. By helping them fight that monster, she's managed to earn their trust. Now that their guard will be lowered, an opportunity shouldn't take long to present itself. Era may have saved her life twice now, but she insists to herself that it cannot cloud her judgment.

However, the situation is admittedly complicated by the fact that the girl could be worth serious coin to her hometown. Plus, though it is clear the bounty is directed at Di, turning in Era and Jem after returning Di home could add to her profit. She'll need to keep them all safe until she can capitalize, one way or the other.

A distant whinny prompts her to drop the thought altogether. She spots a pair of horses across the chasm, and one rider sports a familiar dark jerkin. "Jaras," Fire grunts, her anger already seething as she watches them steer their horses toward the trio. She darts back into the woods, racing to decide whether she'll use the opportunity to cash in on the bounty or simply to kill her rival hunter.

*   *   *

Di groans as she drags her legs, wondering what's become of her guardians. "They always leave me so far behind," she grunts to herself as she crawls to a stop, stooping to catch her breath. The uneven terrain is much harder to hike than the main pathways. She finds a fallen log and sits, sweat dripping off her face. Looking to the sky, she's crushed to find the sun has barely risen. The day is going to be a humid nightmare for her.

Hearing the familiar sound of leaves and twigs crunching and cracking, Di turns around, disappointed her guardians have already come back for her. She usually has more time to rest before being verbally whipped back into hiking. However, she realizes the emerging figure is a stranger, and she freezes in terror while the young man marches through the area.

The traveler spots her as he nears and offers a gentle grin. "You're a little young to be out this far on your own, aren't you?"

Annoyed, Di informs him, "I'm almost fourteen. I can take care of myself."

"Ah, older than you look," he says. His dark hair shimmers in the morning light, and his dark eyes are piercing. "I'm older than I look as well, so I know how that goes." Draping his mantle over his shoulder, he extends a hand and introduces himself. "My name is Ares."

Di finds herself captivated by the handsome visitor, and she blushes as she takes his hand. "Di."

"You go by Di? That's amusing." Di frowns at the strange comment as Ares' grin turns mischievous. "You know, there are some people who have been looking for you for quite some time, Di. Would you mind accompanying me back to Satari?"

Her eyes widen as she rips her hand away. Numbed by fear, Di tries to stand but only manages to fall backward over the log. In desperation, she does the only thing she knows to do. In the highest pitch she can muster, she shrieks and cries out for her guardian. "Errraaaaaa!!!"

The cry rips through the forest, and the sound of rushing footsteps prompts a sigh from Ares. "I had hoped to avoid a squabble," he says, placing a hand on a hidden weapon at his side as Di continues crawling backward. Era soon bursts onto the scene and positions himself between Di and the newcomer.

Ares fails to act threatened. Laughing aloud, he looks behind Era to Di. "This is your guardian?"

Era dips his hand into his pouch, trying to determine the stranger's intentions. He glances to where Jem is hiding nearby, ready to engage if needed, but he holds off from signaling her. "What is it you want?" he demands.

Ares merely shrugs in response. "This could be interesting. I think I'll let things play out as they are." He turns to leave, but he glances back and says with delight, "You're headed to Canterin, isn't that right? You're in for a real treat when you arrive." With that, he hikes back into the forest.

Perplexed by the encounter, Era lowers his guard as Jem reveals herself. Di pants to catch her breath, and Era looks her over. "You're okay?" She nods. "Who was that?"

"I have no idea. I was resting on this log when he just walked up and started talking. He was nice at first, but then he said there were people after me and he wanted me to come back to Satari with him. That's when I screamed."

"He didn't try to hurt you?"

"He didn't touch me. He never drew a weapon, though he was readying for a fight until you appeared."

Era flexes a muscle. "Guess I'm finally starting to look intimidating."

"Nah, must have been something else," Jem says as she stops watching after Ares. "We'll figure it out later. Let's go," she orders in a hushed voice. "No more falling behind, Di."

"Quit leaving me behind, then!"

Jem shushes the girl and leans close to her partner. "So much for Fire. What good is she if someone can just walk right up to Di like that?"

"To be fair, we weren't exactly watching her."

"So what? Fire's clearing the way, right? We shouldn't have to be as cautious."

"I don't think that's how it works," Era comments.

"But if that guy was after Di," Jem wonders, "why would he leave without-"

Her thought is cut off by a violent gust of wind that sweeps Era off his feet. He rolls uncontrollably until slamming into a tree trunk.

"Era!" Di shrieks as the wind dies. Silence again fills the area, and Jem seizes the opportunity to grab Di's wrist and make a dash. However, she's immediately yanked backward by Di, and the two flop to the ground.

"Di?" Jem scowls as she looks back, but she finds her companion's feet entangled by roots and undergrowth. Di panics as she realizes what's happening. The roots and plants are winding around her ankles, getting tighter as they move up her legs.

Jem backs away from Di, much to the captive's bewilderment. "Jem! Where are you going? Help me!"

"I am," Jem counters as she carefully scans the trees.

"Ew... ew... ew ew ew!" Di shrieks as the roots envelop her.

Jem continues to strain her eyes to find a culprit, and she sees motion as someone steps out from behind a distant tree. Before she knows it, an intense wind again fills the area, its source clearly the person who just revealed himself. Jem ducks low, but the focused wind is too intense, and she skids backward uncontrollably. Fortunately, Era reaches out and catches her.

"Thought you were down," Jem says with relief. "Roots have Di!"

"Roots?" Era exclaims. He jumps to his feet and starts to dash to his trapped friend, but the wind again knocks him backward.

Finally, the two assailants fully reveal themselves. Shem and Jaras walk to Di, who by now is entangled from head to toe. Both have swords drawn, and Shem's is a peculiar one: its handle and hilt are abnormally broad. "One down!" Jaras exclaims as he mercilessly delivers a sharp kick to Di's side, eliciting a painful scream. "See, Shem? Aren't you glad you ran into me? I told you I had a lead on them."

"That's him," Era affirms. "The one I fought in the woods. Not sure who the fat guy is."

Jem grits her teeth. "Come on, Di! He's not holding the roots anymore!" she half-whispers, hoping the air shaper will escape.

"Doesn't mean she isn't still tangled," Era points out, watching as Di fights in vain to break free. Clenching his fist in anger, he calls out, "She's just a kid! Fight me instead!"

"I'm not a kid," Di grunts.

"You!" Jaras declares in rage, gripping his bandaged shoulder. "You may have beaten me last time, but now I have help."

Jem leans close to Era. "So again, where is Fire?"

"Surely on her way," he hopes.

Turning her attention back to their opponents, Jem says, "One wood user, one air maker. Think we can handle that without her?"

Era grins. "You know, at first I was hoping for a day without a fight, but this is actually pretty exciting."

Jem rolls her eyes. "Just don't rush to free Di. That hunter knows your trick, so they'll be watching for it."

"You got it!" Era yells as he charges forward, screaming a battle cry as he clashes blades with Jaras just in front of Di. While they're exchanging blows, Shem turns and takes aim at Jem, who is circling around the group. He plants his sword's hilt into his palm and unleashes another torrent of strong winds at his target. She cuts behind a tree to evade the primary focus of the forceful gale and, when he shuts off the wind, Jem seizes the opportunity to dash around and lunge at Shem.

However, the hunter twirls his sword in his palm and unleashes a torrent of a different nature. A flood of water erupts into Jem as she approaches, and she slips to the ground as Shem continues to douse her with a merciless current. "Get her!" he calls to Jaras, and the two perfectly time a shift such that Shem slides in just after one of his partner's strikes. Suddenly finding himself in a spar with a different opponent, Era's confused hesitation allows Shem to go on the offensive. The stocky but skilled hunter continuously strikes at Era while stepping forward with each blow, forcing Era away from his friends.

Jaras rests his hands on the ground, digging his fingers into the soil before Jem can recover. As she tries to stand, she finds herself suffering the same fate as Di, struggling in vain as the roots and plant life enwrap her legs. She hacks at them with her broken dagger, but it doesn't take long before the plants overwhelm her. Jaras takes care to bind her arms to her side before placing additional layers of entanglement around her.

Era panics at the sight of Jem being overtaken. In desperation, he resorts to his trick to bring a quick end to his fight. As soon as their blades meet, Era leans back and releases his sword, allowing Shem's blade to pass by. As he stands and prepares to attack the off-balance warrior, he's met with an elbow to the gut, followed by a sweep kick that knocks his feet out from under him. Era barely manages to roll out of the way of a high kick to the head, and he scrambles to back away.

As Shem and Jaras approach Era, Fire emerges from the brush and charges Jaras with rage. She slices at the surprised hunter, cutting across his arm as he barely brings it up to defend himself. Before she can strike again, Shem knocks her away with a blast of wind, forcing the diminutive mercenary back toward Era.

Fire trembles with hatred at the sight of Jaras, but her thoughts are interrupted by Era joining her side. "Fire, you're-!" is all he's able to get out before Fire's clenched fist meets his face. The strength of her blow is enough to send him stumbling to the ground.

Era looks up at Fire in disbelief, but she points at him and yells, "Found you again, you filthy rat!"

Wincing from his wound, Jaras furiously scowls. "Trying to steal my reward again? I'm going to carve you up, Fire."

Fire's nostrils flare as she sets her sights on the hunter who nearly killed her. "You're not leaving here alive, Jaras. I promise you that."

Era stands, rubbing his sore jaw. *'Girl's got a nasty punch,'* he complains to himself while trying to piece together the current situation. Regardless of Fire, he laments that his dispelling maneuver didn't work on his opponent; Jaras must have given warning of his earth shaping tricks. Noting that he needs to learn some new tactics, he takes the opportunity to draw another earth sword from the ground, readying himself for more action.

"Stay where you are," Fire orders. "Once I take care of these two, you and the other targets are mine."

It dawns on him that she must be trying to trick her rivals. "Ha, like you can take me out so easily," he banters. "Your punches feel like getting slapped by wet noodles."

"Is that why you haven't stopped rubbing your cheek?" Fire asks, annoyed.

"Sucker punches don't count! I've beaten you in two fair fights, now, and I-"

140

"You have not beaten me in a fair fight!" Fire screams in anger, turning away from Jaras. "I'll be glad to show you if you keep insisting."

"Bring it on," Era counters, momentarily forgetting the real enemy.

Jaras curses Fire's untimely arrival. "Forget the target for now. Let's first double-team Fire and knock her out."

"No, the earth shaper will set his friends free. We have the advantage, so let's push it. How is your arm?"

"Fine," he grunts. "I'll take the backstabber, then. Let's move." As they approach, Fire and Era stop bickering and turn their focus toward their actual opponents.

Jaras charges Fire with his sword drawn, and she happily meets him directly with her dagger. "Unlike the targets, I can kill you," she taunts between blows. Jaras scowls in rage as he places more force behind his strikes.

Shem, meanwhile, stops well short of engaging Era's blade. He takes aim again, this time unleashing a wave of fire that his target dodges at the last second. Era retreats and looks back at the scorched earth, mystified by his use of a third element. He tries to work his way toward Di, knowing her shield would prove useful, but Shem is wise to his maneuvering and blocks his path with a wall of flames. Era pulls back in frustration, wondering how he'll manage such a combatant without a shield.

Wait... a shield! Can I do that?' Not wasting time, he scrapes his sword on the ground, pulling more dirt into it while he runs to avoid Shem's blazing inferno. Soon enough, his weapon is bulging to the point that he can barely run. Heaving it into the air, he shapes the mass to form a hefty shield. He rests it on the ground in front of himself, already fatigued from carrying so much weight.

The barrier meets its first test as Shem unleashes a powerful blast of fire into the wall of earth. Era holds onto the mass and concentrates on keeping its shape. Much to his relief, the shield withstands the attack without difficulty. Confident in his new protective wall, Era heaves it off the ground and charges at Shem, mostly off-balance as he tries to keep the heavy dirt aloft while moving. Shem shifts strategies and unleashes a concentrated water assault at Era's boots. His feet slipping, the earth shaper has no choice but to plant the shield once more and duck behind it.

Jaras slams his sword into Fire's dagger. "What's wrong with your arm there, Fire? Did you trip into a tree or something?"

The remark makes her blood boil. "Your arm doesn't look any better."

"And that's the last time you'll lay your blade on me!" he shouts as he swings all the harder, forcing her to use both hands. Fire does her best to hide her pain as she deflects each of the hunter's strikes.

Holding the barrage on Era, Shem starts to feel a rumble. He stops the water and leaps away from his location just in time to avoid a sink hole opening at his feet.

As Shem stumbles back, Era seizes the opportunity and dashes around his earth shield. Having no other choice, the hunter plants his hilt in his open palm and again unleashes a violent gust of wind that blasts his opponent away. Though at first relieved by his own reaction time, Shem soon realizes he blew his victim right next to the Allerian, and Era's skill allows him to snap the roots with just a touch.

Era helps his partner up. Jem brushes herself off and mutters a quick thanks as they turn to face Shem together.

The hunter is unable to believe he had accidentally blown Era in that direction. "Did he plan that?" he mumbles to himself. He dashes to Di and plants himself in front of his captive, intent on preventing Era from freeing her. He passes his hand over his hilt and flings a flaming fireball at Era and Jem, forcing them to split up. The blast hits the ground, once more scorching the earth as the grass kindles.

Era dashes to Shem's right side while Jem darts to the left, but the hunter simply blasts each in turn with a powerful gale to keep them at a distance. As they try to regroup, he sends a flamethrower to keep them separated.

"It's his sword!" Di shrieks as the winds die down. Shem kicks her hard in the back, knocking the wind out of her.

"His sword?" Jem mutters as she deciphers the secret behind his attacks. The only way he could command multiple elements is if his hilt is made from runes, and it would also explain why he's showing no signs of fatigue from abusing the powers so much. Looking at Era, it's clear he hasn't realized it yet, because he's still watching Di in hopes she can explain further.

"Era!" Jem screams as she holds up a closed fist. Catching his attention, she gives him three quick signs, and he nods in affirmation of the order. He positions himself opposite Jem as they run circles around their enemy, intent on creating a two-pronged assault.

Shem unleashes a wave of fire at Era, forcing him to abandon his trajectory and veer to the side. Knowing Jem is approaching from the opposite direction, he spins and takes aim, but he finds she's matched Era's trajectory as they continue to circle. Before long, the two coordinate another pincer attack, and Shem again takes aim at Era first, this time blasting him with wind. Era dives forward, clinging to small handles he shapes from the earth below. Despite the concentrated assault, Era maintains his hold.

Shem growls in frustration as he's forced to relent his attack to meet Jem, who's now closing quickly. She takes a swipe at him with her shortened blade, and he deflects it but trips backward over Di. Jem shows little regard for her ally as she leaps off Di's back and dives onto the downed hunter, her dagger aimed for his hilt. Upon contact, the rune unleashes a jet of water, the force of which sends the blade careening from Shem's grasp. He kicks Jem away and scrambles after his weapon.

Era wastes no time in moving over to Di and rescuing her from the roots. She brushes herself off and screams at Jem, "Thanks for using me as a stepstool!"

Jem shrugs. "You're free, aren't you? Good job, Era." The two bump fists.

Shem recovers his weapon as Jaras screams, "Shem, what are you doing over there?"

Shem shouts back, "Strong words from someone who didn't pick the earth shaper!"

"Back to my plan," Jaras calls out. "Forget the targets for now!"

Fire growls as she swings at Jaras. "I'll cut you both down."

Jaras deflects her overly-aggressive blow and plants his palms on the ground, hoping to snag her ankles. Aware of his tactics, Fire leaps forward and tackles the hunter, but she's instantly blown off him by an air blast from Shem. She scrambles to her feet, cursing herself for failing to finish Jaras off.

"Are you happy, Fire?" barks Jaras. "The targets are long gone now, so none of us will-"

"Jaras," Shem warns, motioning toward Jem, Era, and Di as they approach. Though Di stays behind her guardians, the three are moving toward them aggressively.

Jaras stares at them in bewilderment. "What are you three...? Wait, you're all working together?"

"Of course not," Fire insists before any of them can answer, giving Era a look that sends a chill down his spine.

Reminded of her ploy, Era points at Fire and exclaims, "No, we're going to kill all of you right here and now!"

The bluff falls flat, and Shem raises his voice in accusation. "His expression gives everything away! What are you doing, Fire? Why are you working with the targets?"

"I'm not working with them!" Fire continues to insist, but it's evident her ruse is no longer working. Shem and Jaras turn to each other and, mutually, turn tail and run away.

"Come back!" Fire screams as she gives chase. They dart into the woods, leaving the others behind.

The scene quiet once more, Di rubs her tender ribs and groans, "I don't know how much more of this I can take."

Era frowns as he watches after Fire. "Is she going to be okay on her own?"

Jem shrugs. "Far as I'm concerned, now's our chance to lose all of them. Let's go."

They turn and run in the direction they had been heading, leaving their hired mercenary to her personal chase.

CHAPTER 12

"Can't... go on..." Di huffs and puffs as she's pulled along by Era. Sweat drips from her brow as she does her best to make her legs move, but she ultimately collapses from exertion.

Era looks to his partner. "Do you think this is far enough?"

Jem slows down, out of breath herself. "It's hard to say for sure. The woods feel like they're crawling with bad guys."

It doesn't take long for a rustling of leaves to indicate they have company. Di instinctively creates an air shield while Era and Jem bring their weapons to the ready until Fire reveals herself to the team. The air shaper breathes a sigh of relief as she releases her shield.

"You morons!" Fire screams, prompting Di to momentarily reactivate her barrier. "Idiots! Nitwits!"

Era looks to Jem. "I'm confused. Didn't we win that fight?"

"We might as well have lost!" Fire yells, her face crimson. "Those two got away, and now they're going to report our alliance."

"They got away? From you?" Jem asks smugly.

"They had horses," she retorts.

"Why didn't you take them out with your poison darts?" Era argues.

"I don't have any darts, because some moron stripped me of all my gear."

"I returned your dagger. Why not chuck that?"

"Chuck a dagger? Do you know how weapons work?"

"Children!" Jem shouts. "We have bigger issues, so let's focus."

"Says you, Ice Queen," Fire growls, now turning to Jem. "I'll have a bounty on my head for helping you lot, and now... now I'll be..."

"…in the same situation as us?" Jem nonchalantly asks. "Why would we care? Especially after you let three people get through to us. So much for your worthless scouting."

"I let Jaras and Shem through because I knew we'd- Wait, *three* people?"

"Yeah," Era jumps in, "that guy who walked up to us before the hunters."

"His name was Ares," Di needlessly adds.

"Wait, when was this?" Fire asks in disbelief.

"Just before the other two attacked," Era answers.

Fire is aggravated by the suggestion. "No one could have snuck past me. Didn't happen."

"And yet it did," Era snidely insists. "He said some strange things to Di, but he left without a fight once Jem and I showed up."

"Hold on," Fire says, "you're mad at me for letting this guy through, and you two weren't even with the brat when it happened?"

"So?" Era argues. "Your scouting was supposed to prevent this sort of thing from happening."

"Isn't that what I said to you earlier?" Jem grumbles. "Look, a lot just happened. We have a plan, so let's just stick to it."

"No," Fire says, lowering her voice, "the plan just changed. If they report this to the military, a large force will descend on this area by the end of the day."

"Won't those two come after us again?" Era suggests. "That's what I'd do. Sixty thousand is too much of a temptation."

Fire places her hand to her chin. "I don't know. Jaras is a vengeful rat who would love to see me wanted by the military."

"But how does that change the plan?" Jem asks. "We're three days away from Kemplen. Changing course would add at least a day to the journey, and there's no guarantee we won't still encounter the military."

Pausing in thought, Fire reveals uncertainty for the first time since charting their course, and she kicks the ground in frustration. "You're right, we march for Kemplen, but we make good time," she says, looking directly at Di. "But in case I'm wrong about Shem and Jaras, I'll continue scouting. You three stay on course."

"Yes, and this time don't leave me behind!" Di cries.

"Then try keeping up for once," Jem counters.

"Just carry the brat," Fire huffs as she disappears into the brush.

Era laments the group's dysfunction. It might well take a miracle to make it to Canterin alive.

*   *   *

Jem leads the way as they continue to hike along their planned route. Di follows behind Jem a short distance, and Era follows the schoolgirl at the same length. The threat of being captured feels more real to Di, and that alone is enough motivation to keep her legs moving. For those times when she starts to lag, Era scoops her up and carries her briefly. Di no longer complains about the aid, and Era doesn't make fun. They move with a much more established sense of urgency.

Eventually, Fire appears from the brush. Wiping her brow, she meets the trio with a spring in her step.

"What'd you find?" Jem asks, noticing the enthusiasm.

"Something interesting," she teases. "I was scanning the horizon when I saw a sky boat descending just a few miles away. That could solve our dilemma."

She isn't impressed. "A sky boat? Those things are dangerous, aren't they?"

"What, are you afraid?" Fire asks with annoyance.

Di nods her head emphatically. "Yes! Those boats are just patched together with air pressure runes. They crash all the time!"

Jem speaks up in agreement. "It's true. I've even heard the military abandoned plans to use them."

Fire looks at Era. "Got anything to add, or are we done whining?"

Era shrugs. "I didn't know any of that. What's so dangerous about them?"

"They fall out of the sky without warning," Jem explains with arms crossed.

"Oh, so they crash all the time?"

"I literally just said that," Di mutters.

Fire rubs her temples. "So, to be clear, you each have twenty thousand venni bounties. You've been dealing with bounty hunters and water monsters, plus the military is likely descending on you as we speak. And you're afraid to go for a little ride?" All three nod an emphatic 'yes', and Fire slaps her forehead in disgust. "Look, a sky boat is exactly what we need. We're backed into a corner with no way out, and taking to the sky would not only get us out of a rough spot, but it could also get us to Canterin in a day. So, we're investigating this."

Jem and Di both start to object, but Era cuts them off with a wave of his hand. "Fire might be right about this. We should at least check it out."

Di isn't convinced. "Era, no offense, but you know nothing about those things! We studied sky boats in school as a case study for how *not* to use runes. A standard craft requires no less than twenty runes to keep afloat, and someone needs to manage all of them at once! If they were safe, there would be hundreds of them in the sky."

"But if they were completely unsafe, you'd never see any," Era counters.

"Sure, but-"

Jem places her hand on Di's shoulder. "I hate to admit it, but they're probably right. Even if the chances of surviving a sky boat trip are fifty percent, it might be better odds than making it to Kemplen alive by foot."

Era adds, "If Fire is right and those hunters are reporting our location, we don't have long until we have to start dodging troop deployments." Di puffs her cheeks but relents, accustomed to not getting her way with this group.

After an extended hike, Fire leaves the group to scout ahead. When she returns, she seems unusually excited as she points a thumb behind herself. "There's definitely a sky boat operation in the clearing over there. I'm not sure yet whether it's on the up and up, so we'll need to be cautious in our approach."

"I bed it's sketchy, considering it's buried in the woods," Era suggests.

"Not necessarily," Jem contends. "Sky boat operations are banned by most towns, aren't they? It wouldn't surprise me if they set up between villages like this."

"Either way, we approach cautiously," Fire again warns. "I'll stay back with the brat, and you two-"

"Whoa, whoa," Jem contests. "You are not staying alone with Di."

Fire smirks at the expected response. "Finally making a smart decision, Allerian? Fine, the idiot and I will go in and ask around. There are seven workers milling about, and four of them have weapons strapped to their sides. If there's a fight for any reason then we'll need both of you for backup. Understood?"

"Got it," Jem affirms.

"Okay, let's move," Era says, and Fire follows after him.

Di looks to her remaining guardian as the other two leave. "Jem, I really don't want to go in a sky boat." Her stomach growls, and she rubs it pitifully. "Also, I'm really hungry."

Annoyed, Jem pulls rations out for her whining companion. Di pouts at the paltry portion before reluctantly taking it, and Jem silently wonders if she'd rather hang out with the assassin.

After a quick peek through the trees, Era boldly steps out into the open, keeping his hands visible in an effort to remain innocuous. Fire follows, keeping an eye out for any signs of hostility from the workers.

A burly laborer drops a crate, spotting the two approaching strangers as he wipes his brow in the high heat of the sun. He calls out a warning to his associates as he meets Era. "What business have you here?"

"We're looking for transport," Era explains. "We saw your sky boat descend. Can we hire your services?"

The outspoken worker mutters, "You'll have to take that up with the manager. I'll send him out." With that, he retreats to one of the many tents scattered about, but the other workers keep their eyes locked on their visitors.

Era waits in uncomfortable silence, and his eyes fall on the sky boat at the center of the clearing. The main body of the craft resembles the carriage they'd ridden in with Andrea, though the wheels have been replaced with landing struts. The operator's seat is mounted up top in front of a command console, which houses dozens of runes of various shapes and sizes. A mess of tubes spills out from under the console and runs along the sides of the craft, providing the pilot different options for control.

Motion catches his eye, and he sees someone pop a head out from under the flap of one of the tents. Though young, her hair can only be described as silver, and she watches them with intense curiosity. Era doesn't have time to give her much thought as the manager arrives and makes his way over.

Short and dapper, the middle-aged controller walks with a cane and a limp. He sports a mustache and goatee, and a short top hat rest on his head. Contrary to the mood of the workers, he jovially steps up to Era and shakes his hand. "Welcome, welcome! What brings the two of you to my humble operation?"

"We want a ride," Fire explains as she steps in front of Era. "What would be the charge for a ride to Canterin?"

The manager smiles and shakes Fire's hand, much to her disgust. "Sorry there, young lady. I didn't realize you were the one in charge." Short enough to meet her at eye-level, he removes his hat and introduces himself. "The name is Poulton, and I manage this sky boat operation. We don't typically transport people, but we can certainly be flexible."

Fire crosses her arms, knowing exactly what he means. "How much?"

"One thousand per head."

"One thousand each!?"

"That's right. One thousand for each of you two, plus another thousand for the young lass behind you who keeps peeking her head out."

Annoyed, Fire offers, "We'll give you one thousand total for the transport."

"I won't go a venni lower than eight hundred a head," the manager insists. "I'll have you know my daughter is the sky boat operator. I need to make it worth my while to risk her safety."

Era glances over to the one staring at them from her tent. '*I guess that explains her.*'

"Sleazy old man, selling out his daughter like that," Fire mutters to Era as she beckons for the others to join them. Surprised by the request, Jem and Di make their way into the clearing.

The manager smirks at the new arrivals. "Ah, so this is why you wanted a flat rate. How many more Allerians are you hiding back there?"

Fire reaches a hand to Jem. "Give me that rune."

Though at first confused, she argues, "Hey, you're not planning to-"

"Do you want to walk to Canterin?"

"I didn't want to fly in the first place!"

"Jem, give it to her," Era pleads.

Annoyed, Jem swings her bag to the ground. She pulls out the rune she procured from the underground cavern, gives Fire a dirty look, and extends it close enough for the manager to study. "No touching."

Poulton raises an eyebrow. "And this is?"

"This rune was evaluated at eight thousand venni," Fire lies. "We'll exchange it for transporting the four of us to Canterin."

"This is a rune? It looks like a rock to me." He waves his hand to have Jem withdraw it. "Sorry, but I'm not a rune collector. Sell that to someone who cares." Jem smugly returns the rune to her bag as he adds, "If you don't have the money, then I'm afraid we can't do business today."

"Fine," Fire scowls as she turns to leave.

Era glances at the workers, who continue to watch the small group carefully. He wonders if this might be for the best.

The group walks back into the forest a short distance before Jem asks, "So what now?"

Fire's mood is soured as she recalculates the plan, giving one last glance toward the operation. "We head to Kemplen. The threat of the military swarming us is realistic, so we'll need to continue our fast pace." Di cringes at the suggestion, but she's silently grateful they're not flying.

"Fire, you seem particular disappointed," Era notices. "Could it be you were excited to take a ride?"

"No! Of course not," she sheepishly blurts. "I just-" She abruptly brings her finger to her mouth as someone loudly approaches from behind. Fire scales a tree while Jem unsheathes her broken dagger and steps next to her partner. Era forms a blade from the ground and steps in front of Di, and he's surprised to find the light-haired girl from earlier chasing after them.

She shrinks back for a moment when she first spots them bearing arms but, summoning her courage, continues her approach. Era has never seen a sky boat pilot, but her ratty, knee-length dress, leather leggings, and thick goggles resting atop her long hair certainly fit any mental picture he had of one. Her eyes are gray, their color matching her hair.

Holding a clenched fist close to her chest, she boldly says, "Excuse me, do you have a moment?"

Jem and Era glance at each other in confusion. Raising an eyebrow, Jem sheathes her dagger and asks, "Who are you? What do you want?"

151

"I'm the sky boat operator," she answers, relieved to see Jem put away her blade. "I can give you a ride if you'd like."

"Going around your dad's back, huh?" Jem asks with a certain respect. "Can't say I mind that. How much are you looking to make?"

The girl looks directly at Era, determination in her eyes. "I don't want money. I want a rendezvous."

Era and Jem's eyes widen in surprise at the request, and Di swings around from behind Era. "Wait, what?"

"I want a date. With him. Tonight."

Startled by the request, Era scratches his sandy brown hair. "A date? You'd take us to Canterin for that?"

"Canterin is too far," she quietly admits.

Fire abruptly drops from her perch, prompting a contained yelp from the pilot. She gets close and asks, "What about Kemplen? Would you take us that far?"

Though disturbed by Fire's appearance, she nods an affirmative. "Kemplen is fine." Returning her gaze to Era, she blushes and says, "I don't get to meet many boys my age. Take me to dinner and on a romantic walk. No rushing it, either! I want to have a nice time."

"Dinner?" he asks in confusion. "Where can we eat around here?"

"There's a small town called Lentien about an hour to the north," she explains. "We'll walk there and back, and I'll fly you at first light."

"First light is too late," Fire argues. "Fly us to Kemplen immediately after your little rendezvous."

The pilot shakes her head. "It's too dangerous to fly at night. We could hit a tree or land in a swamp. It has to be tomorrow morning."

Exasperated, Fire asks Jem, "How far are we from Kemplen?"

Jem already has her map out, wondering the same thing. "I just don't see us getting there faster than three days. And that assumes we move without much sleep."

"Wait, we're not actually doing this, are we?" Di interjects. "Jem, we don't even want to fly! There's no reason to force Era into something like this."

Jem reluctantly admits, "I think it's our only option, Di." As the crushing youth pouts, Jem leans close to Fire and whispers, "Can we sit idle that long?"

Fire shrugs. "It might actually throw them off our trail. There's no way they're expecting us to stop and rest for so long." She looks to their visitor and asks, "You sure you don't want the money? We can pay a thousand."

"I'm not interested in money."

Out of options, Jem extends her hand. "Guess you've got a deal."

The pilot ignores the gesture. "No, I want him to do it." Amused, Jem smacks Era's back and shoves him forward.

Era looks his sudden date over, recognizing she's about his own age, maybe a touch younger. Her silvery hair blowing in the breeze gives her an aura of sophistication, and he decides he might not mind this ordeal. Clearly blushing at this point, Era stammers, "W-Would um, would you...?" Pausing, he realizes he doesn't even know his date's name. Extending a hand, he says, "My name is Era. What's yours?"

The pilot happily clasps Era's hand between hers. "My name is Pearl. Pleased to meet you, Era."

More relaxed, he smiles and asks, "Could I treat you to dinner tonight, Pearl?"

Playing the part, Pearl exclaims, "I'd love to, Era!"

Di audibly huffs at her personal fantasy playing out before her eyes. Fire glances at Jem, curious to see if she shows any kind of jealousy, but the Allerian is sporting her usual confident grin, as if taking credit for the entire arrangement.

"So where should I pick you up, and at what time?" Era asks.

"You can meet me right here at six o'clock sharp," Pearl answers before turning back to Jem. "By the way, that thing you showed my father... Was that a rune?"

Jem raises an eyebrow. "Why?"

"There's an old rune expert just outside Lentien. He lives in a small ranch to the east. You should show it to him if you're trying to sell it."

Her interest piqued, Jem quips, "Sounds like a profitable way to spend the afternoon."

Her mission accomplished, Pearl calls, "See you tonight, Era," as she heads back to her camp.

Di plants her hands on her hips and sternly says, "This is a terrible idea! We're supposed to be going to Canterin, not going on dates."

Rolling her eyes, Jem grumbles, "Yeah, I'll bet you'd be this upset if Era were taking *you* on a date." Without waiting for a response, she asks Fire, "You good with checking out the town? We should probably scout ahead for tonight."

Fire nods in agreement. "I'll go ahead of you. Try to keep up."

"But it's an hour away!" Di gripes. "We're hiking there and back just to check it out?"

"What else are we going to do? The date isn't until six," Jem argues, annoyed by the constant complaining. "Besides, I want to see how much my rune is worth."

"Don't worry, Di," Era says in an effort to comfort her. "If this gets you home, I promise I'll take you on a date in Canterin sometime."

Blushing, she stammers, "H-Hey now, that's... I mean, that isn't necessary."

Era shrugs. "Well, we'll do it anyway. For now, let's keep moving. It'll be safer if we're not standing in one place, anyway."

Di nods, seemingly content. Fire dashes ahead, and the other three resume their previous formation as they turn north.

*   *   *

The remote town of Lentien consists of no more than a few dozen structures clustered together within the forest. A lightly-traveled road exits the east side of the town, probably connecting back to one of the main pathways between major villages. With only one path in or out, it's unlikely the town sees many passers-by.

In traditional form, Fire appears from the brush when they approach the outer border. "About time."

Jem ignores her and jabs her elbow into Era's side. "Getting excited for your big date?"

Era smiles awkwardly. "Yeah, I guess I'm actually a little excited. It'll be nice to forget this whole situation for a little while."

Fire frowns. "Getting a big head about it, I see. You do realize you were picked by default. I think you're the first clean-looking guy she's seen."

"And it's a good thing she didn't smell you before asking you out," Jem mutters, waving her hand back and forth while wrinkling her nose.

"You need to take a bath or she might call the whole thing off from the start."

"He smells better than someone else present," Di mutters, glancing at Fire. She replies with a snarl.

Era sighs. "This wasn't my idea, you know."

"But you just said you're excited," Di reminds him.

"You did," Jem adds.

Era is bewildered. "Why am I being ganged up on, here?"

"Because you're traveling with three ladies," Jem teases. "You give us no mind for this entire journey, and here you are asking some random girl on a date."

He shakes his head in amusement. "No winning this one, eh?"

"I don't get why she's so desperate," Di says.

"That's not abnormal behavior," Fire says as she scopes out the town from afar.

Di looks at her in confusion, and Jem explains, "The war ended seven years ago, right? Haven't you noticed a distinct lack of middle-aged males around the Academy?"

She ponders the idea. "Well, now that you mention it, most of the adult men are older."

"So, I guess the special Academy students aren't immune to drafting," Jem snidely observes. "Think about it. There's an overpopulation of women compared to men these days. Unless we want to risk becoming old maids, we have to take matters into our own hands."

"So why haven't you taken matters into *your* own hands?" Era light-heartedly asks. "I've been right here for two years."

"Do you really want me to answer that?" Jem flatly asks.

Changing the subject, Era looks out at the town from his vantage point. "Okay, so how do we safely evaluate this village? We can't let our guard down, even if this town is in the middle of nowhere."

Jem nods. "Towns like these often hire a soldier or two to patrol. There's zero guarantee this town is free from knowledge of our bounties."

"Plus it's unlikely the town sees many visitors," Fire reasons. "The original description for you three was an Allerian, a blond schoolgirl, and an earth shaper. That's a pretty rare mix, so we'll stick out to anyone aware of the bounty."

"Okay," Jem decides, "I'm interested in the rune guy, and Era's crush said he lives to the east. Di and I will look for his house while you two check out the town. As long as Era doesn't shape any earth, he shouldn't be recognized." Looking at Di, she asks, "You okay with your man being alone with another woman?"

"Fire's not a girl. She's a monster," Di mutters as she walks away.

Fire doesn't seem to mind the description as she heads into town. Era offers Jem a wave before following after the mercenary, and it's quickly evident the few people wandering the streets have their eyes set on them. The road cuts straight through town, and the local businesses are strategically placed along this stretch. The buildings are constructed using lumber taken from the forests surrounding the village.

Coming upon a weathered structure, Fire approaches a gruff local standing outside. "Is this the town pub?"

Suspicious of the daytime travelers, he replies, "Looking for a drink?"

"Food, actually," Era interjects. "We heard this town has quite a restaurant."

"Drink or grub, you found it," he says. "The drinks are on the cheap side, but folks travel from all over the hill country for a taste of our stew."

"*Our* stew?" he notes. "You work here?"

"I own the place. Don't get much midday business, but the pot's simmering if you're buying." To Fire's surprise, Era happily enters, motioning for her to follow.

The cozy space sports five round tables made from local pine, matching the exterior. A bar lines one side of the dining area, and a round, unlit fireplace sits on the opposite wall. Era happily takes a seat at a table.

Fire sits with a huff. Keeping her voice low, she asks, "What's the big idea? We're supposed to get in and back out."

"I said I want to be familiar with the place, plus that stew sounds amazing," he says. "It's not like we're in a rush. Jem and Di could be gone for an hour."

She narrows her eyes, wondering what game he's trying to play. Their host arrives with two mugs of water before looking specifically at Fire. "Anything else to drink?"

Fire waves him off. "On the job. Best to stick with the boring stuff."

"Suit yourself. I happen to be roasting a lamb for tomorrow's batch. Happy to toss some in your stew for a bit extra."

Era's mouth waters at the mention of lamb, especially with its delectable aroma in the air, but Fire asks, "How much?"

"Ten venni."

"We'll take the stew as is." Apathetically, the owner returns to the kitchen. Softly, she says, "What a rip-off." When Fire turns back to Era, she notices him watching her with an intense curiosity. "What do you want?"

Her companion is jolted from his thoughts. "It's just that I don't know anything about you."

"And what is it you want to know?"

"Well, anything," he answers. "How old are you, and what's up with your name? Is it a nickname or something?"

Fire is taken aback at his interest, and she tries to decide whether to answer him.

"Just tell me your age, at least," he insists.

"Why?"

"Because I'm sitting here with a master assass-" Hushing himself, he leans forward and admits, "That is, I just want to know how I stack up."

Fire hesitates before answering, "Nineteen."

"Nineteen!?" Era exclaims. "So that only gives me two years to catch up to your level of infamy?" Glancing back at her, he asks, "So what about your hair? Is it actually dark blue?"

She runs her fingers through the short hair extending from beneath her bandanna. "Ever heard of dye?"

"Ah, hadn't thought of that," he admits. "Seems high-maintenance. How often do you dye it?"

"Not often," she says. "Been a while since I last did it, in fact."

"But why dye it that color?" Era asks. "It's practically black. Only in the right light do you even see the blue."

Fire shrugs. "Always been my style."

"Can't say it looks bad on you," he admits. "And, in case you were wondering about my story, I'm-"

"I'm not interested," Fire coldly interrupts.

He pauses for a few seconds before continuing anyway, "Well, I'm the son of a famous thief." Era leans forward on the table and dramatically whispers, "You've heard of the Dark Cloak, right?"

"No."

Era's forehead hits the table, his enthusiasm killed by the blunt response. "I thought for sure you'd have heard of him. Famous thief, practically invented the profession, stole the Jewel of Nerwal... None of this is familiar?"

"I've never heard of any of that, including the Jewel of... whatever." She raises an eyebrow and asks, "How is thievery a profession, anyway?"

"It can be a profession," he insists. "Well, at least according to my father, who raised me to follow in his footsteps. I plan to be as famous a thief as him some day."

"Well, you're on the right track. I've heard of you, and I've never heard of him," she says sarcastically.

Era nods, taking her comment more seriously than intended. "He gave me a lot of advice in life. Actually, this situation reminds me of one of his gems: 'Nothing impresses a pretty girl more than the art of dining and dashing.' He told me I should keep that in mind when I'm out on a date." Era thinks this over, admitting, "Of course, that might not be a good idea in this case, seeing as I'm coming back here tonight."

Fire stares at him in disbelief. "Your father... he sounds like quite a man."

Era blushes and scratches his shaggy hair. "I know! He really is a genius in many ways."

Opting to not respond, Fire instead takes a sip of water. However, she suddenly realizes what Era just dropped into the conversation and slams her glass on the table. "This is not a date."

"I know, I know," Era laughs. "But I'm at least dining with a pretty girl. So, the advice applies, right?"

Fire shoots him a nasty look, making Era regret his words and avoid eye contact. She reconsiders taking the owner up on his offer for something stronger to drink and waves him over.

CHAPTER 13

Di nearly trips over a branch, and she longs for the flat path visible through the trees. "Jem, the road is right there, could we walk on it instead? I don't see anyone around."

"You claim you want to go home, but all you do is complain when we do things to keep you safe," Jem gripes. "If you're fine with being found, then have it your way, Princess. I'm sick of forcing you to care."

She sighs, tired of never getting any sympathy. Once she returns to Canterin, it'll be too soon if she never walks through another forest.

"At last, there it is," Jem calls back, pointing through the trees. "Stay here while I check it out."

Di obeys while Jem approaches the log cabin, built in a clearing next to the main pathway. A trail extends to the road, which Jem uses to casually approach the front door. She takes a moment to glance into a window, in which she can make out shelves and shelves of runes. Confident she has the right place, she knocks twice on the door, and it swings open to reveal an elderly fellow with thinning gray hair and spectacles. Standing over Jem with a wiry frame and wrinkled clothes, he adjusts his glasses and looks his visitor over carefully. "May I help you?"

Jem nods toward the shelves behind the man. "I'm here for the runes."

The collector scans her over with suspicion. Jem has seen the look before; he's processing whether he wants to entertain an Allerian, but he ultimately steps aside, beckoning her to enter. "Welcome to my shop, then. My name is Tulon. How is it I can help you?"

"I have something to show you, and I'm actually here with someone else." Turning back to the woods, Jem waves her hand, and Di steps out from behind a tree.

"Two pretty young ladies interested in runes?" Tulon asks in surprise. "I don't think I've had such a pleasure before now. I'm rather accustomed to smelly old men, much like myself."

The Allerian enjoys the compliment as she and Di enter the quaint home. A musty odor fills the air, reminding Jem of a pawn shop. Just inside the entrance are shelves lined with runes of all different shapes and sizes. It's all but impossible to guess their functions without knowing the meaning of the symbols etched into their surfaces. Jem glances at Di, whose expression lights up at the sight of so many treasures.

The store owner notices Di's interest. "Now, what gets you so excited about runes, young one? Don't tell me you're a rune scholar?"

Before she can respond, Jem cuts in and answers, "We were visiting a friend in the area and heard about your shop. We found an old rune that I want you to evaluate." She retrieves the rune that spawned the water creature and hands it to him.

"This is remarkable," he mumbles. He hurries to his desk, where he places it under a magnifying glass. In the meantime, Di peruses the shelves of runes that stand on display. She used to have full access to such a collection at the Academy, and she finds her nerves calmed to be surrounded with something familiar. Suddenly, she stumbles backward with a yelp as something jumps at her from the pile of runes.

"Don't mind Windy, she doesn't bite," Tulon calls out as he continues his analysis.

The cat rubs against Di's leg as she eyes it carefully. "Windy means it's an air cat? Not a fire cat, I hope."

"You got it. Hasn't made any wind since it was a kitten, so you're safe." Di can't resist stroking the purring feline, and she giggles as it climbs on her lap.

Jem leans over her host's shoulder, but he doesn't seem to notice her as he studies the tiny symbols etched into the rock. Bouncing on her toes and tapping her hands against her thighs, she finally asks, "So, what do you think?"

Tulon jumps at the interruption. "Oh, it's... Well, frankly, this is unlike anything I've seen. Where did you find this?"

"I would actually say that it found *us*," Jem corrects. "The rune was controlling a giant water creature, we stumbled onto it in a cave near Ugorzi."

The rune expert is perplexed by such a casually-stated revelation. "A water creature, you say? What was it like?"

"It was big and scary and tried to kill us," Di cries out.

"Oh, my," Tulon mumbles, not sure whether to believe them. "Well, this is a special rune, that much is certain. I've never seen most of these symbols, and I can't even read them without my magnifying glass. Frankly, this feels like a prank."

"This is no prank," Jem insists. "That thing was designed to be a killing machine. It only stopped when I hacked at the rune at this spot here."

"That was Era's work!" Di interjects, ruining Jem's bluff. "Don't take credit for that."

Jem shoots Di a dirty look and admits, "Fine, so it was our guardian-for-hire who killed it. Either way, it dispelled the moment he hit the rune, which was floating around inside the thing."

Tulon is caught between wonder and disbelief. "Again, I've never seen anything like this. Could it be a...? Maybe it's a relic from the Third Kingdom?"

Jem frowns. "That old fairy tale? Come on, you can do better than that."

"The Third Kingdom was real, Jem," Di snaps, setting the cat aside, "and their technology was more advanced than ours. There are ruins that prove that."

"A bunch of crumbled ruins just proves it existed," Jem argues. "The legend says it was centuries ahead of the rest of the world, and yet it just collapses at the peak of its power? I don't buy any of that."

"There was a great war that took it out," Di explains, annoyed by Jem's stubborn attitude.

"Despite having weapons like this?" Jem sneers while pointing at her rune. "Come on, Di. You're supposed to be smart."

"It happened," Di insists. "According to lore, Alleria and Valvoren allied against it."

"Ha! Now I know it's a myth."

Tulon continues to look it over. "Regardless of the legend, this is far more advanced than any of our runes, so I suppose it lends credence to the theory."

"So there really isn't anything else like this?" Jem asks with excitement.

"Not that I've ever seen or heard." The collector continues to gaze at the treasure before him. "The Third Kingdom is well studied by the Three Pillars Academy, being part of its namesake and all that. Even if it's not related, you could probably set their rune research forward significantly with this discovery."

Jem impatiently taps her fingers on her arm. "Look, I don't care about research. Any idea what it's worth?"

Tulon swings around, aghast by her comment. "You can't be serious! A treasure like this… All you want to do is sell it?"

"I know, she's awful," Di says, glad to have found a kindred spirit. "I don't understand why she won't donate it to the Academy. I know my professors could all learn so much from it."

Tulon looks to Di in surprise. "You're an Academy student?"

Jem shoots Di yet another dirty look. "Oh, yeah. Forgot to mention that."

"And you haven't seen anything like this?" He looks down at the rune with further confusion. "I'd think the Academy of all places would have one."

Di puffs her cheeks. "Infusing obelite with an element starts a degradation process that eventually leads to the rock crumbling, which makes it difficult to study runes from ages past." Helping herself to Jem's bag, she pulls out the shards she'd taken from the underground caverns. "Take these, for instance."

"Wait, have I been carrying those this whole time?" Jem scolds. "I told you to put those in Era's bag!"

Ignoring her, Di offers one to Tulon. "Here, look it over. Based on what we know about the Third Kingdom, the war happened three hundred years ago. There's nothing left from that time, or at the very least, the runes would look like this."

"So why was that thing still active, then?" Jem challenges. "It must not be all that old."

"Obelite hardens and keeps its form while activated," Tulon half-mindedly replies while fawning over the piece of rock. "We can reason that if one exists, there could be others like it."

Jem shudders at the thought of more killing machines hiding across the land. "Regardless, this thing sounds rare, so stop delaying and tell me what price tag you would place on it."

162

The expert is both saddened and stumped by the request. "I've no precedent for anything like this. If you insist on selling it, you'll need to have someone make you an offer."

"And what would yours be?"

Tulon scratches his head. "I guess I'd give you five hundred for it."

"Five hundred?" Jem whines in disappointment. "That's all?"

"I'm a dealer in working runes, and this can no longer be activated. The type of people wandering into my store would never buy such a thing. Sadly, I'm neither rich nor a collector of ancient artifacts."

"That's why we should donate it to the Academy," Di offers as she becomes once more distracted by Windy the cat.

Jem folds her arms, unsure of what to think about the conversation. Rare though it may be, it's almost *too* rare, since selling it would either require significant research or a high-profile auction. "Well, I can't let it go for that little. Thanks for your time, old man."

The rune dealer reluctantly hands the treasure back, and he gazes longingly after the disc as she closes it up in her bag, lamenting the loss of such potential. "Researchers could learn a lot from studying that rune, you know."

"Whoever buys it from me can learn whatever they want," she joyfully replies as she swings her bag to her back. "And for what it's worth, the Academy might be a good place to sell it. They have piles and piles of money, right?"

Di looks despairingly at Tulon. "See? This is what I've had to deal with. All she cares about is money."

Tulon pats Di's head. "Well, next time you're visiting the area, let me know where it ended up. I'd love to see it on display and find out what they've discovered." He holds the shard out for Di to take back.

"No, you keep it," Di says with a smile, pushing his hand back. "I've got more, and I can tell you would appreciate it."

Tulon smiles excitedly. "Do you mean that? Thanks ever so much... erm, what was your name?"

"Her name is mud," Jem says as she drags Di by the arm. "I'm about to make you carry my bag for pulling that little stunt. No wonder it's been so heavy!"

"Era is the one who snuck them in there!" Di insists as they hurry away from the house, offering a quick wave farewell to her feline friend.

Tulon waves after his enigmatic guests before hurrying inside to inspect his new treasure.

* * *

Era stretches and rubs his full stomach as they meander down the town's main road. "That was delicious, and I get to eat here tonight as well! This day is going to be the best one I've had in a while."

Fire ignores her companion, enjoying the light buzz from her drink. It's been a while since she last took pleasure in the sensation. "It wasn't a bad stew," she admits.

"Hey," Era says as he walks alongside her, "I feel like that's the first positive thing I've heard you say."

"I'm not a positive person," she says, apparently not bothered by the comment.

"Still, a smile now and again wouldn't hurt, would it?" he asks.

Fire gives him a warning look. "You'd better stop that."

"Stop what?"

"Stop whatever it is you're doing. We're business partners, nothing more. Quit making idle conversation."

Era gives her a sideways glance. "Okay, so one last question for you." Pausing to consider his words, he asks, "Why are you an... That is, why are you in this profession?"

Fire averts her eyes. "Don't ask about things you don't want to know."

Era swallows hard, but he can't squelch his curiosity. "I want to know. You're really young to be a master assassin."

"I'm not a master assassin. Besides, you're not much younger than me, and you want to be a master thief," she comments, annoyed by the conversation.

"I'm not a master thief, though," Era points out. "And besides that, I want to follow my lineage. You can't possibly come from a long line of assassins. What made you want to be one?"

Fire's eyes glaze over as Era's words cause unpleasant memories to resurface. "Sometimes circumstances force your hand." Suddenly upset she let those words slip, she turns away from him and increases her speed.

164

Era yearns to know more, but he can tell that now isn't the time. He follows her in silence to the edge of town, where they hear a whisper call out to them from the trees. Heading back into the foliage, they find Jem impatiently sitting against a tree.

"Uh oh," Era says. "Been waiting a while?"

"We've been waiting a half-hour!" Jem barks, crossing her arms.

Di scoffs at Jem's exaggeration. "Try five minutes."

"You shut up! I've had enough of you ruining my fun."

"You two not getting along?" Era needlessly asks as a staring contest ensues. "What did you find out about the rune?"

"Nothing," Jem groans. "It's definitely rare, but I don't know who would buy it. It should fetch a good price from the right person, at least."

"Well, that's a start," Era offers enthusiastically. "I'm sure we'll find someone to buy it. But for now, we should head back or I'll be late."

"We're not going back yet," Jem announces while pointing at Era. "What have you been doing this whole time? I can smell you from here! Go back into town and take a bath."

Era's jaw drops. "Wait, you were serious about that? But where am I going to find a place to do that?"

"Pay someone to use their house for all I care," Jem says, shooing him away with her hand. "Go figure something out, Master Thief."

He relents and slinks back toward the village. Jem takes great pleasure in his obedience, but she finds Di giving her a death stare. "What, you're still upset?"

"Not about the rune. You're too mean to Era."

"He's my apprentice, so he has to do what I say. Get over it already."

"He deserves better than you! He's a nice, sweet guy, and he-"

"He's a thief, Di!" Jem heckles. "Your crush is a petty thief!"

Angry, Di turns away with a huff. Satisfied, Jem glances over to find Fire still watching after Era. "You're being awfully quiet over there. Something wrong?"

Fire jumps, snapping back to reality. "Oh, I... No."

"You alright?"

"I'm fine," she snaps. "I'll scout the path back." Without waiting for a response, she runs into the woods, disappearing from view.

Taken aback by the exchange, Jem wonders what has Fire so worked up. Shrugging it off, she leans against a tree, content to enjoy the peace of the moment as Di continues to give her the silent treatment.

*   *   *

Six o'clock comes and goes, but with his date nowhere to be seen, Era sits on a tree stump and hopes he's waiting in the right place. After traveling so much, all the trees blend together, so he can't be certain he's in the correct spot. He sniffs his armpits one more time, content with the results of washing in the bathhouse of a tiny inn. It wasn't a cheap rental, and he calculates how much this date is going to cost him. Jem certainly isn't going to help pay for any of this.

He scans the woods, looking for where his companions are positioned. The plan is for Jem and Di to follow and watch from a reasonable distance. Meanwhile, Fire will continuously scout around the area for trouble, since no one is particularly comfortable waiting so long in one place.

"6:15," he reads to himself, glancing again at his pocket watch. Eventually, the sound of crunching leaves approaches, and he spots Pearl coming to meet him. Now wearing a brown dress, her hair is tied with a red ribbon, holding it up at neck level. She grows excited when she finds Era, and he hurries to meet her.

"Wow, you sure do look nice," Era says, impressed with the appearance of his date. He now feels self-conscious about his own garb, sporting the outfit he wears when performing heists. His black, cotton shirt fits tightly against his skin, and his dark leather pants are intended to help him blend into the night. *'At least I smell nice.'*

"Thanks, Era," Pearl replies, pleased by the compliment. "I'm sorry I'm late. I was waiting back over there, I guess I got mixed up."

As she points back, Era does his best to keep from slapping his forehead as he realizes he's indeed been waiting in the wrong spot, instead opting to let her take the blame. "No worries, I'm just glad we were able to find one another." Offering his elbow, he asks, "Shall we?"

Pearl places her hand tenderly onto his arm, and, after lending a helpful pointer, Era leads the way, aiding his date over the rough terrain. They hike in silence for the better part of the trip, but when Era glances to Pearl, she seems happy. He hopes the whole date goes this smoothly.

166

"So Era," Pearl starts, breaking the silence, "I know nothing about you. Tell me about yourself."

Era eagerly gives her his prepared answer. "I'm a traveling guard-for-hire. I've been contracted by Jem and her sister to-"

"You don't have to lie," Pearl interrupts. "You can tell me if you and your friends all, how do I say this... make a dishonest living?"

Era beams with a grin that stretches from ear to ear. "You're right, I'm a thief! You could tell?"

His enthusiasm surprises her. "Well, it's as much about the makeup of your companions as anything. That and your desire for fast transport. We just don't get many requests for travel, so I always assume such clients are hiding something." Hesitating for a moment, she adds, "We're not exactly operating cleanly ourselves, you know."

"You're smugglers, right?"

"Is it that obvious?" Pearl asks in alarm.

Era shrugs. "Well, your operation is in the middle of nowhere. Even if sky boats are banned from most towns, it seems like you could be located closer to one if you wanted." With pleasure, he adds, "It's good to be in the company of a fellow crook."

Pearl laughs. "Indeed, it is."

Eagerly, he asks, "So tell me, since I assume you're involved with the Merc Market and such, have you ever heard of the Dark Cloak?"

Pearl shakes her head. "No, what is that? Some kind of new fashion accessory?"

The excitement disappears from Era's face. "It's not a... well, never mind. I was just curious."

Pearl shrugs and keeps walking, holding onto Era's arm for balance. She's glad she decided to wear her traveling boots despite the dress. Though thrilled to be on such a rendezvous, she silently wishes it didn't require hiking through a forest. *'Then I could have worn my cute shoes.'*

*   *   *

Jem watches from a distance as Era and Pearl take their stroll through the woods. "He's enjoying himself far too much," she gripes, annoyed he gets to have a fun evening while she's stuck babysitting.

Di follows from a designated distance, having been banned from getting close enough to watch Era on his date. After what seems like an eternity of hiking, Jem beckons for Di to come forward. Excitedly, she rushes up, only to find the edge of town. "Where are they?"

Jem points with her thumb toward the city entrance. "Already in the restaurant."

Di scowls at Jem. "I wanted to see them!"

"All they've been doing is talking to each other about nothing. You didn't miss a thing."

"Okay, but what was Pearl wearing? How was her hair?"

Jem stares at her blanky. "Can't say I noticed. Maybe a dress, and her hair was... well, I'm not sure. Why do you want to know?"

Di slaps her forehead in dismay. "Are you even a girl?"

"I just don't get wrapped up in trivial stuff like that." Sternly, she adds, "And you shouldn't, either! You're only thirteen."

"I'm almost *fourteen*."

Jem smirks, getting the exact reaction she wanted. Di plants herself on a log, wondering how long until this evening is over.

*   *   *

"Thank you," says the host, giving a curious glance to Era before retreating to the kitchen with their orders.

Pearl notices and leans forward, keeping her voice low. "I think that barkeep was eyeing you."

Era says, "Well, I should probably confess to you that I was here earlier. One of my companions and I checked the restaurant out for lunch."

"Ah," Pearl says with a frown. "One of your companions? Aren't you traveling with three girls?"

"Oh yeah," Era awkwardly confesses. "Well, it wasn't a date, if that's what you're implying."

"But it was just the two of you?" she asks, her face showing a tinge of jealousy.

168

Era pauses, unsure of how to properly answer the question. "I think this is a dangerous conversation."

Pearl gasps. "Wait, are you courting one of your companions?"

"N-No!" Era shakes his head vehemently. "Absolutely not! I'm just a guardian-for-hire, like I said before. I'm escorting them back home."

"You just told me you were a thief."

Era's eyes widen as he glances at the nearby patrons. "Hey, keep it down about that."

"Tell me the truth, Era! I don't want to be on a date with you if you already belong to someone else."

He looks Pearl in the eye and assures her, "I'm not courting any of my companions, Pearl. We have a business relationship, that's it."

Pearl studies him at length before crossing her arms and blushing, embarrassed by her overreaction. "Very well. We can continue the date."

Relieved, Era relaxes as the tension eases. Even as they sit in awkward silence, Era feels like he's living a normal life. He's on a date, he's eating food that hasn't been plucked off a bush or picked off the ground, and just sitting under a roof is never a guarantee. He looks at his companion, suddenly appreciating her strange request but still curious as to the nature of it. "So why the date? You don't know me, I could have been a jerk."

"It was risky. I just..." Her voice fades, and she admits, "I have a lot of downtime, and my father procures books for me to fill that time. I've enjoyed many stories involving a fanciful rendezvous between a boy and girl. I've long wanted to experience it for myself, and, when I saw you, I seized the chance."

"You seemed to have it already planned out where we'd go. Are you from this town, then?" he asks.

"Lentien? No, I enjoy the stew here, but I'm from Yugar, originally."

"So how did you end up out here?"

"Well, my father was in the war, and afterward he didn't feel any great love for the military, so he didn't want to move back to his home in Satari. He actually lived in Canterin for a while, working on a merchant ship."

"Oh, so you lived in Satari during the war?"

Pearl grimaces. "Sorry, I should have clarified that my father, the one you met back at the operation... he isn't my real dad. He adopted me just about a year and a half ago."

Era raises an eyebrow. "Wait. How old are you?"

"I'm sixteen. It's abnormal, I know," she agrees. "I've been an orphan all my life, and I had found a home in a traveling act at a young age. I bounced among a few groups over the years, and when my father saw my act, he asked if I wanted to work for him in a more lucrative position."

"Ah, so it's more of a business arrangement?"

"I suppose it is," Pearl admits. "Performance was all I had ever known, but the allure of flying through the sky..." Her gaze wanders as she breathes deeply. "It's like nothing else, Era."

"The romance of the open skies, huh?" he comments, having never before considered such a notion. "So if you lived your whole life as an orphan, why the late adoption?"

"That was more for my protection, considering the type of clientele he supports."

Era leans forward with great interest. "What act did you do?"

Pearl blushes. "It wasn't anything great. I was somewhat of a trapeze artist."

"Whoa!" Era exclaims. "That sounds cool!"

Pearl's face continues to redden. "I wasn't that good at the trapeze, though. I mostly cheated."

"...cheated?" Era asks, confused. "How can you cheat the trapeze?"

"I have a talent," she sheepishly acknowledges. "I'm a pretty decent air maker."

Era tries to figure out what she means. "So, what, you'd blow the trapezes around?"

Pearl laughs at the suggestion. "No, I mean that I could perform all kinds of tricks just by blowing myself around the arena. The audience loved it."

Era's eyes widen. "You can fly?"

"Of course not! I just used my talents to create strong breezes. I'd do flips, loops, and all that. Fake falls but suddenly swoop up and land on my feet..."

"Amazing," Era says in awe. "I've never heard of people flying."

"I wasn't flying!" she insists with a laugh. "It was more like propelling myself around, I suppose."

"Well, I guess that makes you an ideal candidate for flying a sky boat," Era notes.

Pearl nods. "Sky boats aren't exactly reliable. Runes are fragile, and there's no real way to gauge how much power they have left. Given the cost of the runes, it's a balance between replacing them only as often as needed, but without pushing them too far."

"So what happens if you lose a rune?"

Pearl's eyes drop. "The talented pilots might be able to land, depending on which rune was lost and what functionality it had. Most pilots just go down with the ship. All in all, saying it's a dangerous job is a serious understatement." Era now understands why Di dreads riding in a sky boat, and Pearl perks up and explains, "But that's why I'm a good candidate! I can survive a fall by mimicking my midair acrobatics. I can float like a feather from nearly any height."

Era's eyes sparkle. "Incredible. Have you ever fallen before?"

"Once, about six months after I started flying. A key rune just ran out of power midflight. I was probably about a thousand feet up, and I had to abandon the sky boat. I unharnessed myself and floated to the ground." Somberly, she adds, "Father wasn't happy we lost the craft and the load, of course, but he was glad I survived. If it was anyone else, they'd have been dead, and he'd need to hire a new pilot, train him from scratch... the whole bit."

Era grasps the shrewd nature of Pearl's adoptive father. The tavern owner chooses this moment to emerge with their food, the aroma of the roasted lamb prompting Era to nearly drool as Pearl gets her plate first. *Take that, Fire!* he thinks as the two hungrily dive into their meals.

*   *   *

"No way!" Pearl brings a hand up over her mouth, surprised by the volume of her own exclamation amidst the darkening woods. This time keeping her voice down, she whispers, "Is that true?"

"I'm not lying. It was huge, I swear," Era boasts, assisting Pearl over a fallen log as they head back to the operation. "It could control the water around it. Like a water shaper."

"So how did you escape it?"

"Escape it?" he repeats, offended. "I slew the beast, naturally. I had to protect my weak and fragile companions."

171

Pearl grips his arm tighter. "Yes, of course you did. So how did you do it?"

Era pauses, unsure of how many details he should be giving out. "Well, as it turns out, one strike to its center was enough to kill it. If it hadn't, I'm not sure what we'd have done."

"What a brave feat," she says as she rubs Era's forearm. She wonders what kind of person he is, realizing everything he's said about himself could well be a lie. Crafting this story about the water beast is proof he's prone to exaggerations, she tells herself.

As they approach the operation's clearing, Pearl slows her walk. "I'm so sad the date is already over." She leans against her date while looking into his eyes. Her gaze is tender and vulnerable, and Era's heart pounds as he wonders what exactly Pearl has planned. His date stands on her tiptoes and leans in, giving him plenty of time to let his imagination run. Placing her mouth near his ear, she whispers, "Want to go up in the sky boat?"

"W-W-What?" Era stammers.

Excitedly, she steps away from Era and says, "Just a quick trip! I can tell my father I noticed something wrong with one of the ballast runes."

"Didn't you say it's dangerous to go up after dark?" he asks.

"We'll just go up and down. There's no harm in doing that." With a mischievous grin, she asks, "Think you can sneak onto the roof of the sky boat while I go talk to my father, Master Thief?"

Era can't reject the opportunity to show off his skills, plus he admits to himself that he'd like the date to continue a little while longer. He puffs his chest and brags, "Sure thing, it'll be easy for me."

Pearl eagerly heads into the clearing, and Era thinks she must have planned this from the beginning.

*   *   *

Fire emerges from the brush next to Jem and Di, who are crouched over a log while watching from a distance. "Date's over?"

Jem furrows her brow. "I think so, but Era is just staring after her." Turning around, she slumps against the log next to Di and lets out a groan. "Ugh, what a long day. I hope the jerk enjoyed his meal."

Fire sits on the other side of Di. "I haven't seen any movement, but the military isn't known for its expediency."

Jem frowns. "Or maybe those two hunters are still chasing after us?"

"There's no way those oafs could avoid my detection," Fire insists. "If they're giving chase, they're miserably lost."

Di finally takes her eyes off Era. "I'm just glad it's over."

"Oh, let it rest, Di," Jem scoffs. "Era isn't even a great catch."

"How is he not great?"

Jem starts counting fingers. "He's bumbling, slow…"

"…stubborn, idiotic," Fire chimes in.

"…he sleeps in, he's lethargic,"

"…naïve, presumptuous,"

"…and he's totally useless!" Jem finishes.

Di glances at each one, a smile curling at her lips. Turning back toward Era, she gasps as loudly as she can. "Whoa, they're kissing!"

"What!?" they cry out in unison, stumbling to get to their knees so they can peek over the log. However, all they see is Era standing alone at the edge of the clearing, and they look to Di in annoyance.

She giggles at her own mischief as her eye catches motion. "Hey, that's weird. Era just ran into the clearing."

"What's that moron doing?" Fire grumbles as she hurries off.

Di watches as Fire leaves. "I expected to get a reaction from you, but not from her."

Jem hadn't even noticed Fire's response to Di's ruse, but the notion seems ludicrous. She sternly scolds, "Di, you acted like a child. Grow up."

"Think what you want," Di says, waving Jem off. Staring after Era, she wonders aloud, "Just where did he go, anyway?"

*   *   *

Era darts from tent to tent as dusk settles, taking care to avoid any chance of being seen as he approaches the sky boat. The craft hardly looks sturdy; if not for the network of tubing, it would just be a giant box sitting there in the grass. It has no wheels, no windows, and it lacks any sense of style or design. He resists backing out of the extended date, getting more nervous about Jem's reaction with each passing moment.

Sensing an opportunity, he dashes to the converted carriage. He pulls himself onto the roof and lays prone next to the pilot's seat. The workers' voices fade as they enter their tents and turn in for the night. Era sees a tent flap open as Pearl emerges and heads his way. She uses the built-in steps to hoist herself to the top, and she's pleased to find Era waiting for her.

She straps herself in and whispers, "Good job. Just hang tight for a few minutes." She loops the straps around Era's legs, securing him to her seat. After tightening the ribbon in her hair and strapping on her goggles, she asks, "Ready?"

He offers a nervous thumbs-up, and Pearl engages the affixed runes on the console, prompting them to expel wind at incredible velocities and even more incredible noise. Some of the workers withdraw from their tents in alarm, but, when they find Pearl at the helm, they disappear once more.

Her pre-flight checks complete, she crouches low and whispers, "Hold on tight!"

An even louder blast erupts from the console, and Era resists the urge to release his hold and cover his ears. His shaggy brown hair whips around his eyes from the wind, and he grips the straps tightly as he feels upward acceleration. He watches Pearl masterfully tap the console, her fingers moving as if it were a musical instrument.

Slowly and steadily, the speed of the ascension increases. He looks out over the roof just as the tops of the trees disappear behind the edge of the craft. Era starts to feel queasy, but Pearl shows no sign of slowing down.

After what feels like an eternity, Pearl shouts, "High enough?" Clinging tightly to the harness, Era fervently nods as Pearl reduces the output of the wind. The craft loses its upward momentum and comes to a standing hover. In its current state, the sound of the jets isn't so overwhelming. The boat rocks back and forth, and Era stares at the roof in an effort to keep his dinner inside.

Pearl removes her goggles and motions around. "Well, come on! Take a look around."

He reluctantly obeys, peering into the darkness of the night, and his eyes widen at the vast expanse before him. The stars are crystal clear in the cloudless night, and the nearly-full moon looks all the larger as it dominates one side of the sky. Era's jaw drops as he can no longer tell

174

where the ground meets the sky, and small lights from the many tiny villages in the region dot the expanse. He had no idea there were so many towns in this part of the country.

"Over there is the Lidoran Sea," Pearl shouts as she points out in a particular direction, though it's impossible to make anything out. "Sorry, it's pretty dark, but we could probably see the shoreline if it was light out." She then points in the opposite direction and says, "And over there is the Impal mountain range! Or... well, it's too dark to see." She shrugs sheepishly, realizing there's a lot less to take in after dusk.

Even without the sights of a daytime excursion, the stars are simply brilliant, and Era can get a sense from the village lights just how high up they are. "This is amazing."

Pearl nods. "I never get tired of this view. It makes me want to break my own limitations. I want to fly faster, I want to fly higher!" She stretches her hand skyward and says, "Maybe one day I'll have the power to touch the stars."

While he's able to understand Pearl's sentiment, Era experiences a different emotion. Since first meeting Di, it has felt like the world is shrinking on them as they've been pursued. Seeing the countryside like this allows him to breathe, and an anxiety he hadn't noticed begins to fade.

Pearl leans back and admires the view for herself. "When flying a load, I only go about half this altitude because the winds up here can be rocky. But it isn't hard to fly this high if I'm not going anywhere."

Era crawls to the edge and glances briefly down before retreating inward. "Can we see Canterin from here?"

Pearl looks north. "Not at this height. The country is far bigger than you'd expect."

As Era finds the courage to sit upright, Pearl's face swings into his field of view, making him jump in surprise.

"Hey," she says as softly as she can while still being heard. Her tied hair whips around her neck as she sits beside him, apparently trusting the controls to keep the craft steady. She slides close and says, "I'm glad you came up here with me." Her silver hair sparkles in the moonlight, and she meets him with large, vulnerable eyes. "Maybe you can hold me? So I feel safe?"

Is that a joke? Era wonders, watching as Pearl sits fearlessly near the edge of the sky boat while he clutches the harness. Still, he does his best to play the role, and he reluctantly releases the strap from one hand and swings his arm around her slender shoulders. He watches out over the dark horizon, and his mind begins to wander.

Pearl leans into him. "What are you thinking about?"

Era shrugs. "Life isn't turning out quite how I expected."

"Oh? You didn't expect to sit hundreds of feet above the ground with such a fair maiden?"

He can't help but chuckle. "Well, that's certainly true."

"What else, then?"

It's difficult for him to sort through his thoughts, but he finally says, "Since I was young, I had always committed myself to a particular path in life, and I've never once doubted it. My time with my partner has been fun, but we have different goals, so I know I'll need to part ways with her. For some reason, that makes me sad."

"Why wouldn't it?" Pearl asks. "We grow fond of those around us."

He shrugs. "A thief's life requires isolation from others, right? My dad left his family to pursue his dream. I've always known this, and yet... it's hard."

"What if the life you want could be had without isolation?" she asks. "Do you think that's a scenario worth exploring?"

He reflects on his time with Jem, and then his travels with Di and Fire. The journey has been eventful, and these friendships have changed the way he envisions his future. "It isn't so simple," he finally answers. "Jem and I want very different things. Eventually, we'll split ways. We have to, right?"

"Then let it happen," she says. "Nothing lasts forever. Maybe it's time for your next phase of life."

"My next phase, huh?" he wonders. "Yeah, maybe it really is time for me to embrace that solitary life."

"Sure, or..." She leans against him and says, "Maybe you were never meant to be alone, or to follow your father's path. Maybe you were meant to be with others. With someone."

His brow furrows. "What are you saying?"

"I'm saying that, after you take Di home and you part with those other companions of yours, you could come back here, and you could work for the operation. Smuggling is close enough to thievery, right?"

"Be a smuggler? With you?" The notion is a strange one. "I figured I would leave Jem one day to be on my own. But should I really leave her for something like that?"

"Jem can take care of herself," she insists. "What she wants doesn't matter."

"Well, I'm not sure I should just-"

"What do you want for yourself, Era?" she asks, cutting him off.

"What do I want?" he wonders aloud, and their eyes meet in the moonlight. Her soft expression invites him in, and Era again feels his heart race as he gazes upon his date. Her bangs whip playfully around an expression that reflects a bold sense of adventure. His breath trembles as she leans in, and their lips connect. For a perfect moment, all is quiet in the sky as the inexperienced youths maintain their tight-lipped kiss.

However, craft makes a sudden jolt, and Pearl dashes to the console to balance the craft. "We should head back down," she shouts, disappointed. Era gives an appreciative nod as the craft begins descending. He clings to the harnesses, his heart still racing as a curl forms on his lips.

*　　　*　　　*

The boat comes to a rest on the ground, bouncing Era as the landing is anything but soft. Pearl crouches and presses her hand against Era's back as she waves to someone nearby. She then unstraps her harness and lowers her voice. "There's always one night watchman, but these guys must be pretty poor at it since I can sneak past them. Just do what you're good at and you'll be fine getting away." As she continues to act like she's straightening the harnesses, she continues, "I'll unlock the hold below. The four of you need to be inside by daybreak. I'll fly you to the outskirts of Kemplen at first light." Era nods his understanding.

Pearl pauses, somberly accepting the night is at its end. "Thanks for the date, Era. I had a great time." With one last touch on his shoulder, she climbs over the edge and dismounts the sky boat. After quietly unlatching the door below, she retreats to her tent.

Era watches her from his vantage point, waiting until she's safely in her tent to begin planning his escape. The designated guard is sitting on a set of crates, a lantern at his side as his head bobs with drowsiness. Era sighs, his excitement for a challenge diminished. Rolling quietly to the back of the craft, he slips down and stealthily retreats into the woods, ensuring the sleepy watchman never has a chance of noticing him.

As he enters the tree line, he looks back to where he last saw Pearl. Her suggestion of working for the operation echoes in his mind, and he wonders if this really should be his last adventure with his thieving partner. Though he feels he could be happy here with Pearl, his heart sinks at the notion of adopting a lifestyle he's never wanted.

As he retreats further into the darkness of the woods, his heart finally slows from the exhilaration of the flight when Fire abruptly emerges from a nearby bush, and Era nearly jumps out of his skin. "You sure took your time with that," Fire says with arms folded.

"Y-Yeah, I… We were-"

"Save it. I don't care." She looks past Era and says, "Here come the ice queen and princess."

Era turns to his other two companions emerging from the brush. "What's the big idea, Era?" Jem barks. "You could have gotten caught!"

"It was Pearl's idea," he calmly explains. "She insisted we do it or the deal was off."

For once, Jem fails to pick up on his exaggeration. "Okay, fine. It went well, then?"

He nods. "The plan is on. We need to be in the hold by sunrise. We could probably sneak in now if we wanted."

"No, we wait until as close to daybreak as we can," Fire asserts. "If we go too early, we'll be sitting ducks if the military decides to show up. A bootleg sky boat operation is going to catch their eye pretty quickly."

Era is surprised by her comment. "Bootleg? Wait, you heard what Pearl said about smuggling?"

"I heard the entire date," Fire says with a piercing glare. "I saw everything." Era's heart races as she withdraws a timepiece from her pocket and checks it. "I'll scout the surrounding area and come back if there's danger. Otherwise we'll load up a half-hour before sunrise. You three should sleep while you can."

"We'll sleep in shifts," Jem snidely remarks, eyeing the crafty mercenary.

After giving Era one last glance, Fire disappears into the woods. He recounts her words as he tries to convince himself she couldn't possibly have seen what transpired in the sky. Unless she has a spyglass? But no, it's too dark, right? And even then, he had stripped her of everything when they first met. Or did he miss it somehow!?

"Everything okay?" Jem asks, oblivious to the nature of his panic.

Era swallows hard and opts to change the subject. "So, things went well on your end? No sign of trouble?"

Jem waves her hand in the air. "Everything went fine, though Di's constant whining was draining. I'm ready for sleep. You want first or second shift?"

His adrenaline still surging, Era says, "I'll take the first shift. Go sleep." Appreciative of the offer, Jem heads off to set up camp, but Di hangs back. Era asks, "Nervous about flying tomorrow, or are you still upset about the date?"

"Maybe both," she answers before quietly adding, "Didn't realize I had so much competition."

"Pearl?" he asks. "The date was fun, but there probably won't be a second one."

She eyes him for a moment before giving him a hug. Surprised, Era awkwardly returns the gesture, but she releases her hold and hurries after Jem. He gives a wave as she takes off, then turns and sets out to do a round of scouting.

*   *   *

Fire pulls herself onto a branch in the darkness of night. She keeps replaying the moment in the woods when Di had tricked her into an overreaction. It's not just the momentary lapse in control of her emotions, but also that she can't figure out why she even reacted. She shakes off the thought, attributing it to a severe lack of sleep.

She further scales the tree, pulling herself up branch by branch until she approaches the peak. Inching her way as high as she can, the skillful tree climber looks out over the treetops. As she scans the moonlit horizon, she notices a plume of smoke rising a short distance away.

Fire grimaces, wondering if trouble has found them as she descends from her perch and begins seeking it out. When she comes upon the source, she can hardly believe her eyes. Jaras is sitting on a log, stoking the fire. Her blood boils at the sight of the bounty hunter. Gripping her dagger, she boldly leaps into the open from behind the hunter. As he spins around, he deflects her strike with his sword, but the impact causes him to stumble backward. It's all he can do to avoid falling into the flames.

Fire points her dagger at her victim as he slides away from the heat, her muscles twitching at the thought of slicing him to pieces. "You've got a lot of guts to follow me around, Jaras."

The hunter's usual demeanor is strangely absent as he stands and confidently brushes himself off, and it just now dawns on Fire that Jaras already had his sword drawn. Just as she wonders if she just fell into a trap, a figure emerges from the forest behind Jaras, and Fire staggers backward in alarm.

Commander Galen marches in, his hands in the air. "I'm not here to fight, Fire. I just want to talk."

CHAPTER 14

Fire lowers her blade, aware a retreat will make her appear all the more guilty. "Well? Out with it, already. I'm in the middle of a hunt, as you know."

Galen relaxes, but Jaras points at Fire in accusation. "You're working with the targets, and now everyone knows it. You're finished, Fire! You might as well-"

"Lieutenant Commander Bowen, please remove this brigand," Galen calls out to his subordinate behind him.

"Wait just a minute!" the bounty hunter protests as Bowen moves closer. "I thought-"

"You arranged the meeting, and you will be paid for your efforts as agreed upon," Galen interrupts. "Your presence is no longer required." Jaras huffs his annoyance as Bowen prods him away, leaving the two in private next to the small flame.

Galen turns back to his desired audience. "His report is disturbing, so I asked him to set up this meeting for us. He strongly believed you would come out if he made himself visible."

Fire curses her inability to silence Jaras earlier. "How much did he charge you for being my secretary?"

Galen pauses before answering. "Twelve hundred."

She smirks. "You wasted your money. That slob is a pathetic excuse for a bounty hunter. He can't even make a fire, let alone hunt such highly valued targets. When he failed to capture them himself, he made up a little story and sold it to you gullible idiots."

The commander doesn't seem fazed by her words. "Then you deny his claims?"

"There is nothing to deny. His words aren't worth a venni, let alone twelve hundred of them."

Galen picks up a stick to stoke the flames. "So how is your own hunt coming? Have you found the targets yet?"

"Once. I lost them, but I'm already back on their trail."

"Please fill me in on the details. Where did you last see them?"

Pausing, Fire realizes she may well have backed herself into a corner. "Outside Ugorzi. Jaras and Shem interfered with my attempt to capture them, and they got away."

"So, they *are* in the region," he says, deep in thought. "Look, Fire, I'd be a fool to think you allied with the targets, because you know as well as I do that they have no future. Working with them would be suicide."

Fire doesn't have to feign her agreement. With the military on the hunt, Di will be recaptured eventually, and the two thieves will thereafter find themselves in a jail cell. Or worse.

"Money isn't everything we have to offer, you know. If the bounty isn't enough, we can negotiate."

"The money is enough," Fire grunts in frustration. "And none of this means anything since I'm not in league with the felons. Now, unless you're going to stand by while I cut down Jaras, I'm returning to the hunt."

As she turns to leave, Galen informs her, "We have a camp established outside Canterin. You can bring them there once you've rounded them up." Choosing to seize the opportunity to escape, she offers a brief acknowledgement and dashes into the darkness.

Galen watches after her as Bowen appears and signals a flurry of scouts to chase after the mercenary. "At least we know their destination. If they're in this region, they're likely headed to Alleria. That clears the path to the border."

"But why would she protect them?" Galen asks aloud, searching for an answer.

"You think she is?" he asks. "You offered her the world, yet she insisted-"

"It's not what she said, but what she didn't say," he declares with certainty. "Her goal was to prove herself innocent from the beginning, even before the accusation had been made. The fact that she didn't accept a better offer is proof of that."

"Well then, all the better," Bowen says. "Our scouts will track her right back to the asset."

"I'm not optimistic about their chances," he admits. "The mercenary's file labeled her as an expert in tracking, which means she's also an expert at evading trackers. Still, the targets are in this region, so it is reasonable to think they're headed to Canterin by foot."

"Unless they're planning to take a ship," Bowen suggests. "They're only two days out from the nearest port town."

"Agreed. We can have extra platoons at the ports by tomorrow night, but our best hope may be to wait for Fire to bring them to us."

"You think she will, then?"

Galen doesn't give an answer. The shaper pulls back his sleeve and sticks his bare hand into the fire, bending the flames to his will and pulling them entirely onto his arm, leaving the cold, charred logs behind. He extends his engulfed arm, using it as a torch as he and Bowen retreat into the darkness of the woods.

*   *   *

"Get up already!"

Jem's hushed shout stirs Era from his deep sleep. Realizing the sky is still pitch black, he rolls over and plants his face into his arm.

She looks at the half-awake Di in disgust. "You get him up. I'm going to freshen up before stuffing myself into that cramped box." With that, Jem grabs her bag and hikes into the trees for privacy.

"Ugh, this has been one giant experiment in sleep deprivation," Di laments to herself, realizing her late nights studying at the Academy were tame in comparison. She taps her cheeks to wake up, yet she finds the forest floor has never looked so inviting. Crawling to her guardian, she shakes him and urges, "Era, get up already! Jem will be mad."

Era snaps awake and looks around frantically. "Jem's mad!? Where is she?"

Di is taken aback by the reaction. "No, I said… well, never mind. She's freshening up."

"Freshening up?" Era's groggy brain struggles to process her words. After a lengthy silence, the dazed thief pointedly asks, "So why are you worth sixty thousand venni?"

"What? I'm only worth twenty thousand, aren't I?"

"The entire bounty is directed at you. You know that."

"I've already told you that I don't know! I'm good at air shaping, but…"

"There's nothing else?" he asks suspiciously before relenting. "I'm sorry, it's just… There has to be a reason for the bounty. It's huge!" Thinking for a moment, he wonders aloud, "Maybe it's because you're a super Academy student? You're young to be a student there, right?"

"I'm not that great a student." Though her comment is meant mostly for herself, she realizes Era is looking at her intently, expecting an explanation. "It's just that… well, I don't get the best grades."

"You don't?" Era is surprised to hear it. "Well, you've had us fooled. But you're still something special just to be there, right?"

"I'm nothing special, intellectually," she laments. "The other students don't need to…"

"…need to what?"

Di balks. "Nothing! They just don't need to study as hard."

"Come out with it, already."

She sighs. "They don't need to cheat. Like I do."

Era's eyes bulge. "You cheat? At the Three Pillars Academy?"

She frantically shushes him. "Please, Era! Don't tell Jem. She'll make fun of me!"

Era laughs out loud, which seems to further embarrass her. Reining in his reaction, he says, "I'm sorry, Di. It's just that you've painted yourself as quite the student. Not that you're a bad one," he quickly adds. "I mean, I'm sure you're still talented and all."

"I'm not, okay? I'm just lucky they don't realize I'm…" Tears welling up in her eyes, she looks to her guardian. "I just get so scared I'll disappoint Daddy, so I just… I can't stop myself…"

Era pats her shoulder. "Look, Di, this is good news! Maybe they're just after you because they think you're a model student. When we get you home, they'll realize the entire thing was a mistake."

Di scrunches her knees up and buries her face in her arms. "I just… I really don't know why they're after me. I'm not smart, and my air shaping talents aren't useful or anything. I'm not special at all."

"Your eyes are golden," Era offers. "That's not exactly normal. Erm, I mean…" he mumbles awkwardly, realizing he should choose his wording more carefully.

"It's actually an indicator of elemental skill," she explains. "The masters' eyes change with developed skill, though generally it manifests as mere flakes of color. Mine are certainly unique."

"Well, that would match the skill we've seen in you," he says. "I don't know, Di. You seem like you could be special to someone."

The familiar rustle of leaves indicates Fire's arrival. "Everyone ready?" she asks.

"Ready!" Jem calls as she reappears, her bag slung over her shoulder. "Good work, Di, I didn't actually expect you'd be able to get him up." She turns to Fire in anticipation. "Any trouble last night?"

"There was nothing," Fire answers. "The military must be incompetent."

"Or maybe those hunters didn't report us like you thought they would," Era suggests.

Jem shrugs it off. "What matters is that we're in the clear for now. Let's get into that sky boat."

Jem and Fire turn to head out, and, as Era stands, Di grabs his pants and gives them a tug. "Please don't tell," she whispers. He nods and offers to help her stand, deciding it isn't exactly a secret worth telling, anyway. Unfortunately, he still has no idea why they might be after the so-called princess. As always, if Di knows, she isn't letting on.

Leading the way, Jem heads back toward the operation's clearing. The sky had grown overcast as they slept, its darkness making it difficult to traverse the terrain even as it aids their stealth. Coming to the clearing's edge, the group finds the crew members are still in their tents. The guard-on-duty is also sound asleep, making it all the easier for them to sneak in.

Jem signals for the others to wait while she approaches the sky boat and searches for the door. Finding a latch, she quietly pops it open and checks inside with her light rune. Content with the state of the interior, she signals for the rest of the group to approach. Era leads Di to the boat, and Fire brings up the rear. They crawl into the small craft, and Jem quietly closes the hatch behind them.

Jem grins in the darkness as she keeps her voice low. "Cozy, isn't it?"

"Shh!" Fire isn't amused, worried about being cooped up in such a confined space. She knows if things don't go according to plan that they aren't in a position to defend themselves.

The companions sit in silence as the cabin warms from their body heat. Light starts to shine through the cracks in the doorway, indicating that their ride should begin shortly. However, as it continues to get brighter, the only thing that changes is the continuous rise in temperature. Jem and Di fan themselves in vain, and Era leans his head against the door in hopes of catching any fresh air that might sneak in.

Voices can eventually be heard outside, and Fire curses to herself. Pearl was supposed to sneak them off before anyone else awoke. They could be in for a fight if they're discovered.

Finally, Pearl's voice can be heard calling out to someone as she approaches. She hurries to the hold and knocks softly. Everyone looks at Era in anticipation, but he shrugs in confusion. He softly knocks back once, which is apparently what Pearl was expecting. She latches the door and scales the outside of the craft. Era turns to Di with enthusiasm and mouths the words, "Here we go." She grips his arm tightly and prepares for the worst.

A loud blast of wind erupts from the top of the sky boat, rushing through the network of tubes encircling the cabin. A welcome breeze rushes in as the door rattles, and the boat begins to lift off. Losing the security of the ground isn't a welcome sensation for any of the travelers. The craft shakes and rocks as it continues to accelerate upward for quite some time before beginning to move forward.

The noise forces the schoolgirl to release Era and grab her ears. "How long will this flight be?"

Era lets go of one of his ears. "What was that?"

Straining herself, she screams, "How long with this take?"

"Oh!" Era looks at Jem and Fire and shrugs. "I figured an hour or two."

"Huh?"

Era leans closer and projects his voice. "An hour or two!"

"Two hours?" Di flops against her guardian and fights against hyperventilation. Era sympathetically pats her head with his free hand, hoping she doesn't lose her last meal all over him.

After a painfully long trip, the craft begins its descent. The inevitable landing feels more like a crash to the group as they bounce violently before coming to rest. However, no one complains about being on the ground once more.

Pearl's footsteps can be heard coming down the side of the sky boat, and Fire grips her dagger as the door is unlatched, still preparing for an ambush. However, when the door swings open, their pilot's beaming face is the only sight to see. With goggles over her eyes and her silvery hair shining brightly in the morning sun, she steps aside and beckons for everyone to exit. "Good morning, everyone. Welcome to Kemplen!"

Di dives over Era and out of the craft, plopping on the ground and sucking deep breaths as she enjoys the cool grass against her skin. Era waits for Jem and Fire before stepping outside himself, discovering that Pearl found a clearing to land in.

The operator removes her goggles and straightens her messy hair. "I obviously can't land in Kemplen without drawing attention, so I landed outside of town. It's just a short walk north of here."

Fire aggressively gets in Pearl's face and shouts, "And what's the big idea with making us wait this morning? You said we'd leave at first light."

"Hey, now, Fire," Era says as he steps in to defend his date. "I'm sure she has a good reason."

Pearl sheepishly averts her eyes. "I'm sorry, I kind of overslept."

Jem laughs aloud. "You and Era should date for real. You'd get along fine." Pearl blushes at the comment.

Fire suppresses the urge to continue arguing. "I'll confirm Kemplen's location," she says as she turns to Pearl. "Don't leave until I get back." With that, she disappears into the trees.

Di jumps up and makes a mad dash into the woods, her hand over her mouth. Jem shares a glance with her partner and remarks, "That poor child has had quite a journey."

Taking the opportunity, Pearl leans into Era. "Thanks again for last night. Don't forget about my offer."

Era awkwardly hugs Pearl, and she presses into his shoulder and closes her eyes, enjoying the embrace even as Era's mind races at the thought of leaving Jem in favor of the sky boat operation.

Hearing the stomp of a boot, Era finds Fire is standing right behind him. "Kemplen is a short walk. She can go."

Knowing their time for leisure is over, he says, "Take care, Pearl. Hopefully you won't get into trouble with your dad."

Pearl laughs. "Oh, I'll be in a heap of trouble for this. But it was worth it." Bouncing up the steps, she straps herself into her seat, adjusts her goggles, and offers a final wave. Era returns the gesture, as does Di, who is just reentering the clearing. Pearl activates the rune console, and a gush of wind floods the area. The craft lifts into the sky, propelling itself upward until well above the trees.

Fire claps her hands loudly as the sky boat disappears from view. "Come on, let's move. We missed our opportunity to sneak into the city early. Now we have to take extra caution."

"Shouldn't be hard," Jem says as the group follows Fire into the woods. "We've done this before."

Fire glares back at Jem. "You're the one who stands out in a crowd. If anyone is looking for us, you'll be the giveaway."

"You picked this town because it's large and it would be easy to hide in the crowds," Jem contests. "This was your plan, so what do you suggest we do?"

"Wouldn't hurt my feelings if you stayed behind."

The Allerian's eyes narrow. "Care to say that again?"

"Hey, if you can get in, it's no problem. Meanwhile, the three of us can walk through the main gate. As long as we're not together, we won't draw attention. I saw a large tower near the coast that we'll use as our rendezvous point." Motioning back to Jem, she says, "As for you, Ice Queen, you'll just need to get in on your own."

Jem beams confidently. "Is that supposed to make me mad? I'll take it as a challenge to get into the city before any of you do." As she finishes her assertion, the group comes to the edge of the forest, high up on the hillside. The hill country runs right up to the Lidoran Sea, with a steep drop-off leading down to the beach. Kemplen lies at the bottom of the slope, spreading up and down the coast. The tower Fire described is plainly visible and apparently serves as a lighthouse. It will work well as a meeting place.

"Fire," Jem grumbles, "that city has a wall."

"Ah, so it does," she says, her voice lacking surprise. "I guess that'll help with the whole challenge thing." With that, she heads back into the woods.

Di looks to Era, but he just shrugs and follows Fire. Jem stares down at the city as her companions tread off without her, cursing the day she let Fire join their team.

*　　*　　*

As a major sea port on the Lidoran Sea, Kemplen draws early morning crowds through its wide town gates. The wall itself is built up against the sloping hills to the east that descend toward the sea, creating an ideal opportunity for growth along the western coastline. The southern boundary reveals a noticeable decrease in quality as it cuts toward the water's edge, indicating this portion of the wall is regularly demolished and rebuilt as the city expands.

Before venturing onto the main path, Fire motions for Di to come close, keeping her voice low as she offers some last-minute advice. "You'll stick out worse than the ice queen if you travel alone. But if they think you're with a group, especially one without an Allerian, they'll likely pass you right by. They can't stop and check every child entering the city."

"I'm not a child," she grumbles.

Looking out over Kemplen, Fire observes the current foot traffic. "It's early, so there are more people entering the town than leaving. Find a group to shadow and stick with them well past the city gate."

Di nods her understanding, growing anxious. This is the first time she's been asked to perform a solo task.

"We'll take turns going in. The brat will go first, followed by the idiot."

"We're standing right here," Era says in annoyance.

"I'll take the rear," she finishes, ignoring him. "Remember, the tower by the sea is the rendezvous point. We'll meet there in two hours."

Era checks his pocket watch as Di asks, "Two hours? Will I really be fine on my own until then?"

"Group up any sooner and there's no point in walking in separately," Fire explains. "Besides, I need time to find us a ride."

"Hold up, Fire," Era says. "Jem and I were going to find transport. What makes you-"

"Because, besides being amateurs, you two are the unluckiest people I have ever met," Fire states, her dark blue eyes glaring at him. "There is no way I'm letting you select which ship to board."

Di emphatically nods her agreement, and Era finds himself unable to argue. "Fine."

Fire looks out over the sea and says, "I'll need to find a smuggling craft harboring after dark. Inspectors won't allow a transport to unload its goods after sundown, but they aren't typically looking for *people*. We should be able to sneak off the ship under cover of darkness, one way or another."

Era scratches his head. "Why do we need to smuggle ourselves in? Couldn't we just take a normal transport vessel? We could hide below deck until dark."

"Three reasons," she says. "First, you can bet smugglers will know whether the military has recently increased inspections to find Di. Second, are you willing to leave your Allerian friend behind? Because she tends to draw attention in close quarters. Third, it's not uncommon for military officers to use civilian transport, so they would be our traveling companions for the voyage."

Era raises his eyebrows. "Those are good reasons."

"We've gotten this far, but Canterin will be a different story," she states. "They know she's headed there. It was in the initial information." She studies Di and notes, "Come to think of it, do you always wear your hair like that?"

Di runs her hand through her long, blond hair. "Yes, it's been a while since I've gotten it cut. Why?"

"The town guards might have descriptions of what you look like. Let me cut it off."

"No way!" Di grabs her hair and runs behind Era. "Can't I just tie it up?"

Fire sighs. "Fine, whatever. But if the guards spot you in the crowd because of it, I'm running up to claim your bounty."

Era pats Di's head, reassuring her. "Don't worry. If that happens, I'll come to your rescue."

Di appreciates the reassurance. She finds some long grass, ties her hair into a ponytail, and triumphantly shows it to Fire. "Look better?"

She shrugs her indifference. "You ready to go?"

The inexperienced traveler looks down over the city, nervous to be separated from her guardians for so long. "Tonight. Tonight," she whispers, encouraging herself with the hope of returning home.

Fire and Era creep closer to the road, remaining hidden while muttering to each other as various passers-by come and go. They scrutinize every group that happens past them, taking their time in selecting a candidate to serve as an adoptive family. Di's anxiety nearly turns to boredom by the time Era beckons for her to join them.

"See that group headed this way?" Era asks as he points up the path for Di to see.

"The one with all the kids?"

"That's them," Fire confirms. "Just run out of the woods and act like you're trying to catch up to them. People will assume you were relieving yourself."

Di nods, but her feet refuse to move. Fire unsympathetically gives her a hard shove, sending her careening out onto the road. Di shoots Fire a dirty look before jogging to catch up to her cover family.

Era is impressed at Di's ability to get close. "She did a good job."

Fire nods. "Now we wait and see if she gets in."

They watch the gate closely for activity as Di and her family group approach the town. Her blond ponytail is easy to pick out, and they each feel relief when she makes it well into the city and out of sight.

Era sits back and rests against the ground, his arms propping him up. "Guess I'm next, huh?"

Fire sits cross-legged next to Era. "We wait another few minutes, naturally. But if she can get in, we should all be able to get in. The brat and Allerian were the only ones who had any real description when they explained the job. All they knew of you was your earth shaping."

Era glances at Fire, who has taken to drawing patterns in the sand to pass the time, and he smirks at the sight of a reputed assassin doing something so juvenile. "Do you think it will be difficult getting into Canterin?"

"You tell me. Surely you and the ice queen had a plan for this part."

Era sheepishly scratches his head. "We've been taking it one step at a time. Can't say we've ever had a plan for that part of it. Or any of it, for that matter."

"I'd be upset if that was the least bit surprising." Continuing with her sketching, she says, "Canterin won't be easy, especially since we don't know why they're after her. If it's a family affair, they may already have her rich daddy locked up, so even if we get in there's no guarantee we'll be able to claim any reward money."

Era hadn't considered that possibility. "We'll figure something out. Reward money aside, we-"

"There is no 'reward money aside'," Fire loudly interrupts. "You may be attached to the runt and want to see her get home safely, but all I care about is my cut. The ice queen feels the same way."

"Look, I know that we're not doing this out of the goodness of our hearts," he sternly says, "but we owe it to her to-"

"We owe her nothing."

"Would you let me finish a thought?" Era snaps as his body tenses. "You may have mastered a complete emotional detachment, but that's not who I am, okay? All you care about is self-preservation."

"Self-preservation is what keeps you alive," Fire argues as she stretches to get in Era's face. "You're too naïve and it's going to get you killed."

"How exactly am I naïve?"

"Would you stop and think about things for once?" she harshly replies. "The Valvoran military wants your whiny princess, and they want you too. You think that will change once you drop her off? They'll go to Canterin and capture her again, and they'll leave the twenty thousand venni bounties on you and the ice queen for the rest of your miserably short lives." She sits back down with a fuming huff. "And none of that is my concern. Once she's in Canterin, I'm out."

Era slowly sits, reeling from the reality Fire so brutally unloaded. He really had been naïve to think that Canterin was the end goal. Somehow, he figured Di would be safe at home, and laying low for a while would allow them to return to their normal lives. He wonders if such a thing is even possible at this point.

Fire notices the silence. "Did you not consider any of that? What amateurs."

Clenching his fist, Era forces himself to move past his doubt. "All we can do is keep moving forward, one step at a time. It's gotten us this far." He heads toward the road and mutters, "See you inside."

Fire watches Era as he ducks into the moving crowds. "Complete emotional detachment, huh?" She wipes away her doodles and lies on her back, staring through the tree branches at the sky above as the commander's words from last night echo in her mind.

*   *   *

Di wanders aimlessly through the bustling streets of Kemplen, and the port town atmosphere floods her with nostalgia for her hometown. She pauses to take in the smells of the seaside city, allowing memories of her childhood to come flowing into her mind. Her time at the Academy has been one of such devotion to her studies and refinement of her abilities that she had barely given any thought to her home, and now she's returning under such circumstances. Despite what she knows will be a difficult finale to her journey, she wells up with tears at the hope of seeing her father once again.

Though it has certainly not been two hours, Di decides to head toward the designated rendezvous point. The lighthouse is easily visible, towering in the distance. Glancing skyward, she marvels at how high they must have flown on their way here. She's surprisingly envious Era got a private ride with a view last night, though she would never consider setting foot in one again.

Before she knows it, she finds herself at the lighthouse. Situated against the beach, it sports a busy courtyard with wooden tables available for patrons of a nearby refreshment stand. To her surprise, Era is already reclining at a table, quietly sipping a drink. As she approaches, he finishes his water and sets the empty glass on the table. "You're early."

"You too. Fire's going to be mad, huh?"

Era shrugs and leans back in his chair. "She'll be fine. By now she's used to us not listening."

A breeze comes across the water, bringing the smell of the sea along with it. Era closes his eyes to take it in with delight. "Have I told you I'm from a port city as well?"

Her eyes light up. "Which one?"

"Demantura," he proudly replies.

"On the other side of the sea?" she recalls. "What was your childhood like?"

"As normal as possible when your dad is so infamous. I was ten or so when we had to leave town to protect ourselves. Mom was never happy about that." His eyes soften as his mind wanders to the past. "We moved from Demantura to the outskirts of Maaman, where my father garnered an even greater reputation, and he provided for us while I grew up. I set out on my own a couple years ago, wanting to follow in his footsteps." He looks to Di with interest. "What about you? What was your childhood like? I assume it was more normal than mine."

Di leans on the table and looks over the sea. "I'm the daughter of a mayor of a wealthy town, so I probably haven't had a normal life either. But it was good. Daddy always took care of me, even after my mother passed away." She glances to their meeting landmark. "There's a tower like this in Canterin called the Lidoran Lighthouse. Since I was seven years old, whenever I was upset, I would run into it and hide. There were stairs leading all the way up with windows that overlooked the sea. I would relish a moment of self-pity before going back home." Saddened, she adds, "I did that when my father told me I was going to the Academy. I didn't want to go."

"Why did he send you? Was it because of your air shaping?"

Di's eyes sparkle as she speaks. "Part of it was to develop my natural talent, but there's also a large market in port towns for runes, since ships benefit so much from them. Daddy knew he would get old and step down from being mayor one day, and he wanted to set me up so I could provide for myself." She folds her arms with a huff. "But I was twelve! Do you think a twelve-year-old would understand that? I barely understand it now, and I'm almost fourteen."

Era places his hands behind his head. "Maybe you'll understand when you're *actually* fourteen. I think your dad did a good thing for you. One day you'll realize that."

The student nods, but she remains sad. "You would think he'd at least visit me now and again. I haven't seen him in almost two years, but I guess it's hard for a mayor to leave a big town like that."

"Well, you'll get to berate him for that soon enough. Maybe even tonight!" Era happily exclaims. Di takes a deep breath, trying not to get too excited by the thought.

Covered in mud from head to toe, Jem stomps up to Era like she's ready to smack him. He eyes her and asks, "What happened to you?"

"Don't ask," Jem barks as she drops her bag and grabs a seat. Withdrawing a brush, she pulls at her matted hair, trying in vain to detangle it.

Di snidely remarks, "But Jem, didn't you want a challenge?"

"Not in the mood, Di," Jem grunts as she continues her work. Era leans forward and touches the larger dirt smudges, shaping the mud and sucking the earth to his hand, leaving only the water behind. Jem gives him an appreciative nod as he continues his work.

"What in the name of...?" Fire storms furiously up to the group, slamming her hands on the table while trying unsuccessfully to keep her voice low. "Of all the idiotic, amateurish things to do! What did we just discuss about being seen together?"

Era glances around sheepishly. "But, this was the rendezvous-"

"And you're shaping in public, you moron!" She swings her arms and points all around the deck. "Could you not sit at different tables?"

"They're all full," Era continues to argue, against his better judgment.

Fire clenches her fists. "You are the most incompetent bunch I have ever met. Why can't I be tracking you instead of trying in vain to protect you?"

Jem smugly enjoys Fire's exasperation, but Era decides to change the subject so as not to extend the scene. "So? Did you find us a boat?"

"No, I didn't." Resigning herself to the group's clustering, she sits with annoyance. "Almost everyone was willing to talk price, but the cheapest came in at two thousand a head. Two thousand!"

Era sighs. "We definitely don't have that much."

"And even if we did, there's no telling whether our reward money would be worth that kind of expense," Fire points out. "We'll have to wait for another group of ships to dock. Hopefully one of them is willing to negotiate."

"If we wait too long, we'll lose whatever advantage we just gained by flying here," Era points out. "The military will eventually catch up."

"What choice do we have?" Fire grunts. "We've already established that traveling by ship is our best chance of getting there."

"Why not just stow away?" Jem asks.

"Sneaking on is easy enough, but what if we're caught? They'll turn us in the moment we harbor," Fire challenges. "Do you ever think ahead, or do you just do whatever creeps into that tiny brain of yours?"

"You arrogant, low-life scum," Jem snarls. "You think you're so smart, yet look how many times we've had to bail you out of trouble."

"You haven't bailed me out of anything," Fire argues, meeting Jem's gaze.

"Era and I did fine on our own before you joined up, so our ideas must not be all that bad."

"How would you even know which ship is going to Canterin?"

"Well, that ship is probably going to Canterin," Di interjects, pointing toward the harbor.

Everyone's eyes fall on the largest ship in the dock, which boasts three sails and a quarterdeck. The crew is loading crates marked "obelite" in bold, painted letters that can be clearly read even from their vantage point. The lower hold must be full, because several boxes are being tied to the central mast.

"Runes are one of Canterin's biggest exports," Di explains. "No other town on the Lidoran Sea would need that much obelite."

Jem frowns. "Why would they mark the crates so clearly and store them on the deck? Do they want to get boarded by pirates?"

"Okay, Allerian," Fire concedes, "we'll try it your way. Let's stowaway on that ship."

"Well, that was a quick turnaround," Era notes in amusement. "Why the change in heart?"

She explains, "That ship is large enough that we should be able to remain undetected for the duration of the trip. On top of that, they likely won't be finished unloading by nightfall. Inspections will keep them overnight, and we'll sneak off once the crew is asleep."

"So, I guess it comes down to stowing away or waiting till tomorrow for a better option," Era says. "What's it going to be?"

"Like we said earlier, we can't wait around," Jem replies. "The military is closing in, right?"

Era glances around. "Yeah, about that. There aren't many soldiers here. I'm not even sure it was necessary for Di to tie her hair up like that."

Jem glares at Fire. "Are you saying I snuck in for nothing?"

"It was precautionary. We had no idea what we were going to find," she says in defense. "It takes active effort to keep the military off the scent."

"The military doesn't have a clue where we are," Jem insists. "We lost them, if they were ever even on our trail."

Fire sneers but holds her tongue. Last night's encounter with Galen would indicate otherwise.

"Okay, I'm in," Era says. "The worst thing that can happen is we end up at another city. Then we just board another ship. That would throw the military for an even bigger loop."

"I know I'm the one who suggested this," Jem says, "but how are we going to sneak onto a ship, anyway?"

Fire nods her head toward to the harbor. "Just a few crewmen are loading the last of the crates. Seems like the rest of the crew members are going off to eat one last meal before departing."

Jem looks at Era with uncertainty. "It won't be easy."

"What part of this journey has been easy?" he pointedly asks. Still, he looks to the ship in excitement, ready for the next part of their adventure.

CHAPTER 15

Jem quietly hurries down the stairs of the ship to where her three companions are waiting, and she preemptively clamps her hand over Era's mouth to prevent him from loudly proclaiming success. The lower deck is vast and dark, lit only by the few lanterns scattered about. The ship gently rocks in the mild harbor waves, and the hull's creaking effectively masks the group's noises as they move.

Fire leads the group further down the companionway, and they descend into the cargo hold. The space spans the full length of the ship, poorly lit by a single lantern hung on the near wall. The crates that were loaded are roped together and fill half the room.

Jem doesn't like what she sees. "They're loading cargo up top when the hold is this empty? That's a strange thing to do, isn't it?"

Era scratches his head. "I don't know how ships work. Maybe they didn't want to lower them all down?"

Fire glances up to the closed hatch above, but she ultimately shrugs it off. "I think we're safe down here," she says, moving toward the back. "I'm sleeping."

"Are you serious?" Era asks. "Now doesn't seem like the right time."

"Do you have any idea how many hours of sleep I've had these past days?" she challenges. "Don't you dare get yourselves caught. Stay hidden until nightfall, then we'll sneak off the vessel. With any luck, we'll be safely in Canterin." With that, she heads off in search of a place to lie down in private.

Di sits down, and Jem notices her queasy expression. "You grew up in a port town. Don't you have sea legs?"

"I'll be fine. I'm still unsettled from the sky boat ride, is all."

"Hopefully so, because it's going to be a lot worse than this out on the sea," Era warns. "Don't go losing your lunch down here."

"I haven't even had lunch. Or breakfast for that matter."

Jem slings her bag to the ground. "It's been a busy day, I guess. I'm hungry, too." She hands out pieces of stale bread, and her companions gratefully partake.

Voices soon sound out from the main deck above, and the stowaways hide among then crates in case anyone decides to come down to the hold. After a short time, the ship begins its movement out to sea. The rocking of the boat in concert with the flickering lanterns creates an ideal situation for slumber to overtake each sleep-deprived stowaway. Lying silently in the dark hold, each finds it impossible to resist drifting off to sleep.

After a time, a flurry of footsteps from the deck above startles Era from his rest. As he groggily rubs his eyes, Jem and Di also stir.

"Are we here?" Di quietly asks with a yawn.

"It's only been two hours," Era says with a glance to his pocket watch. "That's far too early, right?"

Jem stretches and asks, "It feels like we're still out in open water to me. Maybe there's a storm rolling in?"

The comment doesn't sit well with Era. "I'll go check."

"Hey, I'm coming too," Jem says, "but just for a quick peek. Fire's right that we need to lay low."

Era nods his understanding and creeps to the stairs. Though he can only see up to the next deck, it sounds like the entire crew might be on the top level. He crawls up with Jem in tow, and he's grateful for the ship's natural groaning. It disguises their movements well.

When they arrive at the second level, Era signals to Jem and makes his move, swiftly escaping the hatchway and moving into one nearby room while Jem darts into another across the hall. He moves to the porthole and peers outside, finding nothing but the open sea. There's no storm coming from this side of the ship.

As he turns to leave, the sound of footsteps running down the stairs echoes out. He presses himself against the wall near the doorway, and Jem does the same from her entryway across the hall. He watches the stairs in hopes of timing an escape, but dashing to safety would be risky with sailors nearby. Jem catches his eye and signals him to wait, and he acknowledges. They remain quietly hidden while the crew seems to frantically move about between the decks. Era can tell they're anxious about something, and he continues to wonder what it could be.

A sailor suddenly calls out to one of his buddies, and Di's shriek cries out amidst the sound of a scuffle. Era glances out the doorway in alarm as sailors stream down the stairs in response.

"Stowaway, eh?" one calls out as the sailors drag her up the stairs to the upper deck. "Search for others!"

Era scrambles for a hiding spot, but it's too late. "Found another one!" the sailor calls as he jumps at Era, tackling him as his crewmates rush in.

"Here too! An Allerian!" The cry causes an uproar among the men as they drag Jem and Era up the stairs. The sailors form a path to the quarterdeck, and the two are thrown down next to Di.

Jem wastes no time in grabbing the collar of Di's blouse. "Di! Why in the world were you on the stairs?"

"I'm sorry! I was worried about you and came looking."

Now appearing before them is a woman wearing a deep blue overcoat, and she sports a matching hat covering her long, dark hair. Towering over the trio, she glares at them with penetrating eyes. "What is the meaning of this?"

"Stowaways, ma'am."

"I can see that," she says through gritted teeth. "I mean how the blazes did you allow stowaways on my ship?" she shouts, her face turning crimson as she glares at Jem in disgust. "And an Allerian? There's an *Allerian* on my ship?" She turns to her second-in-command and screams, "Giarva, why is there an Allerian on my ship?"

Jem smirks, but the gesture is short-lived as a sailor grabs her neck from behind and shoves her face into the deck. Era lashes out to aid her, but two sailors jump on him. They hold his arms and force him to his knees.

The captain grabs Era by the chin. "Is this it, or are there more of you?"

Era meets her gaze defiantly, but Jem laughs from her position next to him. "There are twenty more of us down there! Your crew must be incompetent to let so many aboard."

The captain presses her foot down on the back of Jem's head. Era struggles against his captives, but he can't escape their grasp.

"So are the three of you spies?"

200

"Spies?" Era asks in disbelief. "Why would we be spying on a cargo ship?"

"Then what's an Allerian doing here?"

"What's that got to do with anything? We were just trying to get to Canterin," Era pleads, not knowing what else to say. "We stowed away because we couldn't afford transport. That's the truth!"

"Canterin?" the captain repeats in confusion. "What made you think we were going to Canterin?"

Era looks around, locating the crates tied down against the main mast. "Well, the cargo. We thought that since you were carrying obelite…"

The captain crouches to get in his face. "You three have no idea what you've gotten yourselves into."

"Captain," the scout in the crow's nest calls down, "there's a ship off starboard!"

The captain rushes to the rail. "It's early! Could it already be him?"

"Hard to say, Captain," she replies, "but it matches the description."

"Stay on course!" she orders as the crew starts murmuring. "And stay focused, all. Prepare yourselves!"

A crewman arrives with the handcuffs. "Could only find two, ma'am."

"Well then?" she huffs in annoyance. "Put them on and get them to the brig. We'll deal with them later."

"Yes ma'am." He turns and clamps one set on Era's wrists, and he turns to the other two with the remaining set. Placing one shackle on Jem's right wrist, he stretches it out and clamps the other end onto Di's left.

"Now get them out of here," the captain barks as she watches the incoming ship. The crewmen force Era, Jem, and Di to their feet and begin carting them toward the stairs.

"Captain, they've raised the black flag!" The entire crew rushes to the starboard side to get a glance, dragging the three captives along with them.

"Make it look good," the captain calls to her helmsman. "Pull hard away!" Turning back to the rest of the crew, she shouts, "Hoist the mainsail! They'll outrun us, so we don't need to hold anything back. Secondary crew to the below!"

Cast aside amidst the distraction, the stowaways watch as the abnormally large crew goes to work, and half the sailors retreat down the stairs. Given a window of opportunity, they slide toward the crates tied to the mast, ducking in among them and hoping to stay hidden.

As the pirate ship continues to gain ground, the crew becomes visibly anxious. Jem watches them carefully from her vantage point, trying to gauge what might be transpiring. Whatever the case, it seems they want to get caught by this particular pirate vessel.

"Okay, enough," the captain calls out, trembling with anticipation. "Lower the mainsail and hoist the surrender flag. Everyone, be ready!"

The approaching craft soon closes the gap, its pirate crew jeering menacingly with swords raised. The crew appears to consist entirely of Allerians.

A pair of smaller boats are lowered from the vessel, each with a dozen pirates aboard. "Step away from the port side!" bellows one of the raiders. The cargo crew obediently backs away as the pirates use the riggings to hoist themselves to the deck. The surrendering crewmen place their hands in the air to satisfy the invading pirates.

A burly specimen steps to the forefront of the crowd. His head is wrapped in a bandanna, and he wears a dark vest over his white shirt. He grips the sword sheathed at his side while raising a hand in the air. "Stay calm and you won't be injured," he announces in a husky voice, the guttural Allerian accent thick on his tongue. "Now, where is your captain?"

"I'm right here, Captain Turk." Now standing tall at the edge of the quarterdeck, she crows, "It's so good to finally meet you and lay eyes on the *Freedom's Cry*, that notorious vessel of yours. I am Captain Marin."

Perplexed yet entertained, Turk raises his hand in respect. "Well met, Captain. I see my reputation has preceded me in these waters." He motions to the crates of obelite as he struts around them. "I'm afraid we'll be taking your cargo, good Captain, but fear not! Your precious lives are spared." Suddenly, he spots Jem, Di, and Era crouching among the crates. "Is that a fellow Allerian I see? And here I was beginning to think the obelite was the only treasure."

Marin pounds her fist into the railing. "You know our captives? I should have suspected as such."

A pirate forces them from their hiding place as Turk turns back to his rival captain. "Suspected as such?" he mumbles to himself. "Just what is going on, here?"

Marin points aggressively at the invader. "You're a scourge on this sea, you wretched vermin, raiding countless vessels while evading the

Valvoran navy for over a year like the coward you are. You have earned yourself a slow and painful death." Marin draws her sword aggressively and screams, "Captain Turk, your time has come! I hereby order your execution at the hands of the Valvoran Navy. Naval forces, attack!"

Raising a loud cheer, the cargo crewmen draw their weapons and engage the bewildered pirates in battle. Blindsided by the assault, Turk finds a group of assailants headed straight for him. "Bring it on!" he cries as he extends his palms, producing a billowing rush of water from his hands. The torrent rages forth, smashing into the mass of soldiers with an intent to sweep them over the railing. However, the naval sailors boldly meet the water with open palms and shape the element into a barrier. Turk halts his attack, realizing he's simply providing ammunition to these shapers.

"These are the best water shapers in the navy! Your power is useless against this crew," Marin devilishly boasts. Cupping her hands to her mouth, she barks, "All forces, engage!" At her order, the rest of her forces emerge from below deck, raising a cheer as they meet the overwhelmed pirates in combat.

Her trap sprung, Marin leaps from the quarterdeck and lands in a pool of water. Reaching her hand into it, she shapes the liquid into a whip and cracks it at Turk, who barely sees it in time to deflect the attack. Marin whips again, this time enwrapping Turk's sword and tugging as the two face off.

Once more hidden among the crates, Jem shakes her head in disbelief as the sound of dueling swords rings out all around them. "How do we keep finding ourselves in these absurd situations?"

"Fire was right about our luck," Di laments.

Era tugs at his handcuffs, but they hold tight despite their rust. "Freeze these chains, Jem! Then I should be able to snap them."

"You're crazy! Those are made of tempered steel. Ice won't do anything but frostbite you."

"Then let's find Fire and get off this ship."

"And then what? We're in the middle of the Lidoran Sea!"

Di looks back and forth between her two guardians. "Can I just say-"

"No!" they cry in unison, venting their anger over Di getting them into such a predicament.

Era looks back at Jem. "Look, we at least need to find Fire."

"What good will that do?" she asks.

"Would you rather stay here and get skewered?"

"Of course not! But I-"

"Then come on!" Era urges, and he makes a dash for the stairs amidst the chaos. Just when he gets close, he gets inadvertently tackled by a staggering combatant.

As Jem hurries to aid her partner, someone backs into her, and he spins and shoves his sword to her neck. She finds the Allerian captain, still engaged with his naval nemesis, looking on her in surprise. Without warning, he grabs her arm and pulls her along as he dashes back toward his ship. Handcuffed to Jem, Di shrieks and stumbles along, barely managing to stay on her feet.

"Get back here!" Marin cries out as her path is cut off by a skirmish.

"Hey, let me go!" Jem screams while struggling in vain against the burly pirate.

As if conceding to her wishes, he shoves her over the rail, and she shrieks as she and Di fall into one of the small boats waiting below. Turning back to survey the scene, Turk recognizes the hopelessness of the situation and bellows, "Retreat! All men pull back!"

"Jem!" Era cries as he shoves the downed sailor off him and gets up, only to be tossed aside by two combatants engaged in a furious spar. He hits the deck and covers his head, hoping he doesn't find himself on the wrong end of a misaimed swipe.

The surviving pirates leap from the deck, landing in the waters below and scrambling to get into one of the two boats. The naval forces look for orders from their captain, who bears a sinister grin. "Helmsman," she forcefully says, "hard to starboard." He calls out orders to the crewmen, who pull the sails to catch the wind while he spins the wheel to match.

As the pirates row furiously to their ship, they cry out in terror as they find the naval vessel swinging toward them. Turk bites his tongue, realizing he and his men are about to be crushed between the hulls of the two ships. They bump against the pirate vessel, and Turk braces himself against it while pointing both palms outward. With a roar, he unleashes a mighty blast of water into the approaching ship.

Jem watches in bewilderment as the water maker pours every drop of energy into creating a force that redirects the approach of the menacing craft. He screams from the effort as his muscles tremble, desperately clinging to consciousness. Miraculously, the waters are enough to push the stern back such that it passes in front of them, narrowly avoiding a collision with the smaller vessels.

Turk ceases his effort and collapses to his knees in exhaustion as his men scramble to pull themselves to their deck. They grab Jem and Di before hoisting their captain up, all while barking at their helmsman to abandon the empty boats and retreat.

Aggravated by the turn of events, Marin screams at her crew, "Hoist the mainsail! We're not letting them get away!"

The pirate ship catches the wind and begins cruising, but the naval craft is in hot pursuit. Turk wipes his sweat-drenched brow and looks back at his former target, grimacing at how many of his men were lost in the skirmish. His fists clenched, he utters, "Lower the mainsail. Engage the propulsion rune."

As the pirates lower their sails, the helmsman pulls a lever, which is tied to a rope that leads down to the aft of the ship. The rope pulls taut, and a clapper at the end connects with a thick rune embedded into the hull below the water's edge. The moment the clapper connects, the rune unleashes a powerful volley of water, propelling the ship forward at high velocity. Everyone clings to the rails to avoid flying off the ship.

Marin watches the pirate vessel accelerate, a smile curling at her lips. "He thinks he's getting away. Activate the rune!"

The helmsman pulls a lever, but nothing happens. He repeatedly pulls the lever to no avail, and Marin yanks him aside and tugs at the lever herself. She slams the rail and screams, "Who installed the rune?"

The crew stands silent until, reluctantly, a crewman raises his hand. Marin's water whip snatches his wrist in an instant, and she flings him over the edge of the ship with a yelp. As the crew members scramble to toss him a rope, she asks her second-in-command, "We can fix it, right?"

"Y-Yes ma'am!" Giarva yelps with a salute. "Problem's likely with the mechanism, but fixing it while at sea is dangerous and will take time."

"Get it done," she growls. The lieutenant scurries away, shouting orders as he gathers sailors to perform the task. Pointing out over the deck, she barks, "Clean up the deck. Throw all dead pirates overboard and throw the rest in the brig!"

Marin turns and glares after the pirate ship, keeping her voice low as she mutters to herself, "Run while you can, Turk. I'm coming for you."

*   *   *

The *Freedom's Edge* slows to a stop as the helmsman disengages the rune. The atmosphere is somber as the injured pirates nurse their wounds and mourn the loss of their comrades. Turk walks halfway up the quarterdeck's stairs and turns to face his diminished crew, silently noting which members are missing. "We lost good men today, but the rest of us were able to escape with our lives. And for that, we owe those we lost a moment of silence."

The pirate captain removes his bandanna, revealing a shaved scalp as he bows his head and closes his eyes. After a time, he refastens the bandanna and says to the helmsman, "They may try to follow, and we know nothing of their ship's capabilities. Hoist the mainsail and make haste for Allerian waters."

"Allerian?" Di's young voice cries out, the only Valvoran amidst the band of foreigners.

Turk notes the handcuffs and asks Jem, "She's with you?" Jem cautiously nods an affirmation, and Turk pats Di's head. "Don't worry, little one. You're among friends here. We don't turn our backs on fellow Allerians in these waters, nor their comrades." Turning to the crew, he announces, "Men, we have ladies on this ship! I expect you to be on your best behavior."

Not one of the brigands seems particularly trustworthy with such a request. With their glares impossible to ignore, Di nervously steps behind Jem.

The crew's reaction isn't missed by the captain. Leaning to Jem, he says, "On second thought, I'll keep you two in my cabin." He finds his second-in-command and orders, "Jenkit, I want you to take a count of the missing. It looks like we may have lost a quarter of our crew to that psychotic demon."

"Pardon, Captain Turk," replies the grizzled seaman, "but methinks it might be a tad more."

"Never one for optimism, eh Jenkit? Just take the count."

"Aye, Cap'n."

Turning to his new companions, he motions toward his cabin. "Shall we?" He guides them forward amidst the jealous gazes of his crewmates, and he closes the door behind them. The room is lightly decorated, with maps and clothes strewn about the floor. A mat serves in place of a bed, and two large windows in the back allow sunlight to stream directly in.

"Sorry for the mess," the captain says sheepishly. "I don't have many guests in here, as you might imagine. Please have a seat anywhere." With

206

a polite bow, he says, "As you may have caught wind, my name is Captain Turk. Welcome aboard my humble vessel, the *Freedom's Cry*. What we lack in manners and cleanliness, we make up for in hubris," he awkwardly jokes. "What are your names?"

Safe from the mob, Jem's anger boils to the surface. "Why did you drag us over here? What do you want with us?"

"Well, you're a fellow Allerian, and you were a captive on a Valvoran vessel. I thought it only right to save you."

"Save me? You kidnapped me! Our friends are back there!"

The captain is alarmed. "There were more Allerians with you?"

"Get over the Allerian thing!" Jem yells while throwing her arms in the air, forcing Di to do the same with one hand. "Why are you so obsessed with that?"

Still tired from his earlier exertion, Turk flops onto his mat, propping himself up with one elbow. "I consider it a matter of pride to aid any Allerians I find in distress. After all, many Valvoran vessels use Allerians as slaves."

"What? Really?" Jem asks in surprise.

"About three years ago, the Valvoran military sold off their Allerian prisoners-of-war to the sea trade. Didn't want to keep them in their jails any longer, I guess. During our raids, we make it a point to save any Allerians we find. Nearly half my crewmen are former slaves."

Jem slinks against the opposite wall, and Di does the same, thanks again to the handcuffs. "I didn't know Valvoren did that."

"The reason we sail so deep into the Lidoran is to liberate our comrades, but apparently word of our operation has spread. We pushed our luck too far."

"Do Allerians do the same thing?" Jem abruptly asks. "Do they enslave Valvorans?"

"Sure, but that's different," Turk says indignantly. "I've seen what Valvoran pigs can do. They deserve everything they get."

"And so the hatred never ends," Jem whispers.

Eyeing his guest suspiciously, he asks, "So what's your story, then? Why were you prisoners on that naval vessel?"

"We have a knack for landing in trouble," Di answers.

"Can't disagree with that," Jem says. "We're merely stowaways who got caught. We thought we were hiding on a cargo ship, and I'm still not sure what we found. Two members of our group are…" Whispering to herself, she says, "They're still back there."

Turk ponders the situation. "Why are you so deep into Valvoren? And traveling with Valvorans, no less? Even your accent is Valvoran."

"It's a long story," Jem says, doing her best to look vulnerable, "but we need to get to Canterin if at all possible. That's our best chance of meeting up with our friends. Can you… Can you help us?"

"Canterin? That big Valvoran city on the coast?" Turk starts searching one of his maps lying on the ground. He locates the city and taps it. "No can do, missy. Not with a naval vessel hot on our heels. We gotta break for open waters and get back to friendlier seas. You'll come with us to Glouak, and we can figure something out from there."

"Glouak?" Jem asks. "I haven't heard of it."

"Not surprising. It's a tiny town over on the Truitt peninsula. We set up port there."

"You mean in Alleria?" Di realizes, aghast at the thought of traveling to the foreign nation. "I can't go there. I need to go home!"

Turk grimaces. "Sorry, little lady, but I just lost nearly half my crew, and I'm not about to risk the rest of them in a gesture of goodwill."

Jem bites her lip, knowing there's little point in arguing with the pirate captain. They're at his mercy. "Can you drop us off at Canterin after harboring at Glouak?"

Turk frowns. "We'll be steering clear of Valvoran waters for a time, if indeed that crazy captain is out there hunting us. You'd probably be best to find another option."

Di slumps backward, banging her head into the wall. Jem also finds herself distressed as her thoughts turn to Era. He may well be facing the wrath of the captain who thought them to be spies.

Turk notices their sinking emotional state. "Hey now! I'll give you two full run of the ship, and I'll see if I can find you faster transport once we're home." As Di starts to sniffle uncontrollably, Turk rises and slips toward the door. "I uhh… I gotta go do something," he says, making his exit with great haste.

Curling her knees to her chest, Di chokes back the tears as she buries her face into her arms. "I thought I was finally going home, but now I'm…"

Jem is surprised it's taken this long for the journey to emotionally break the young child. As the sniffling turns to sobbing, Jem places her arm around Di's shoulders, taking care to maneuver the cuff chains in front of her face.

"And Era! He's gone, Jem." Di looks at her with red, teary eyes. "He's gone for good, isn't he?"

Despite her deep desire to do so, Jem is unable to argue the point. As the ship carries them further from Valvoran shores, it strikes her that she could possibly never see her partner again, and the thought brings tears to her eyes.

*   *   *

The crew works frantically to replace the rune under Marin's watching eye. "How much longer?" she barks at Giarva as he oversees the implementation.

"We should be ready in about twenty more minutes, ma'am."

Marin looks up at the mainsail, her eyes narrowed. "They're undoubtedly headed for Allerian waters, but they're deep in our territory. We'll catch up to them before they make it past the boundary." Turning to survey the deck, she asks, "How many did we get?"

Giarva pulls a crumpled paper from his pocket. "Eight dead, three in the brig," he reads. "Probably about a third of their crew."

"And our losses?"

He hesitates before reporting, "They killed seven of ours, ma'am. Another five have serious injuries."

Marin's clenches her fists and glares at her second-in-command. "We outnumbered them, ambushed them, and they came out ahead?" Slamming her fist into the rail, she turns and marches briskly away. "Lieutenant, I'm headed to the hold, and I'm not to be disturbed. I want the rune ready by the time I return."

"Yes, ma'am," Giarva replies with a salute, knowing full well what it means when his captain is not to be disturbed.

CHAPTER 16

Era collapses against one of the many crates in the hold, exhausted from his fruitless search. Scared to raise his voice, he had hoped to quickly find Fire, but the poor lighting has made it impossible to find his ally. He wonders in disbelief if she really slept through the commotion as voices continue to loudly echo from above.

Though guilt consumes him over abandoning Jem, he reaffirms to himself that he could have done nothing to help once they were on the pirates' ship. Finding the lower deck void of soldiers, he had raced to a porthole just in time to watch the pirate vessel accelerate away. Though desperate to find Fire, he recognizes she won't have an answer for how to get them back.

Era clumsily stands, his hands still shackled, this time deciding to call out for his companion. "Fire," he calls, keeping his voice just above a whisper. "Fire, where are you?"

The loud stomping of boots on the stairs interrupts his search. Era's heart races as he dives behind a crate, and he gawks at the sight of Marin storming into the hold. Rattled, he presses his back against the crate and holds still to prevent his shackles from clinking. He carefully pulls his pouch of sand open and dips his fingers into it.

Marin approaches the crates with a canteen withdrawn. As she pours it out over her hand, she molds the water into a long whip. Her breath trembling, she flings the canteen aside, takes aim at a crate, and looses the whip with a scream of frustration. Unleashing her pent-up rage, she cracks the crates over and over again, reducing them to splintered rubble. Marin's rage takes her around the room, and she inevitably comes to Era's hiding place. Oblivious to his presence, she strikes it with the same explosive force, and Era finds himself with little choice but to dive to a new hiding place.

The movement doesn't escape the captain's notice. "Who's there?" she calls out, cracking her whip for effect, yet she's faced with only silence in response. "Come out!"

Era grips his weapon with shackles hands, his palms growing sweaty as he holds his breath.

With a growl, Marin unleashes a barrage of strikes against the crates until she creates enough havoc that Era is forced to dash from his hiding spot to avoid taking a blow. He makes a desperate charge, but Marin snaps her whip around his blade and flings him to the ground.

"The spy?" Marin exclaims in surprise. "Ah, so you were left behind by your friends." She yanks back with her water whip, ripping the sword from his hands. Sand scatters around the hold as the blade loses its form, leaving Era defenseless. "An earth shaper," Marin realizes. She snaps her whip at Era, who brings his arms up to shield himself, and the weapon wraps itself tightly around one of his wrists.

Marin grins with delight as she pulls her whip taut. "This is going to feel better than tearing up a bunch of crates!" Yanking back, she forces Era to stumble toward her and slams him in the gut. He staggers backward before she uses her whip to twist and fling him into a crate.

"This is what justice feels like!" she taunts as she slams him into one crate after another. Though Era does his best to brace himself before each collision, he's powerless to do anything to reduce the impact, and he cries out in agony with each collision.

Marin brings him to a rest, and her watery whip snakes up his body and around his neck until it pulls him to his knees. He tugs on the line, gasping for air as the amusement disappears from Marin's face. "I've had my fun. Now you're going to tell me who you are and how you're related to Turk."

"I'm... telling you, we're... not..."

"Lies! You were with an Allerian. That makes you-"

Marin's rant is cut off as a figure appears next to Era and promptly chops her hand through the whip. Her weapon snapped in two, the naval captain falls backward from momentum, and Era hits the floor as the water loses form and splashes around him.

Era chokes and coughs as he sets eyes on his savior. "About time."

Despite the rescue, Fire appears completely dazed. The handkerchief she normally wears over her head is around her neck, and her short hair is plastered to one side of her face. She slaps her cheeks to wake up and looks down at Era with a slur in her voice. "You idiot. I told you to stay out of trouble, and this is what I find when I wake up?"

"Wait, you've been sleeping?"

"Yes! And that's what you should be doing as well." Groggily, she points at Era's opponent and asks, "Who is this person? Why are you in a fight with her?"

"Fire?" Marin repeats as she stands, her whip now half as long as it was before. "You're Fire the assassin."

Fire studies her in alarm. "You've heard of me?"

"You're a menace to the crown. You assassinated the mayor of Trebulin. He was a strong ally of the Valvoran navy."

Her eyes narrow to slits. "How do you know about that?"

"The military knows everything about villains like you," Marin utters with disgust. "I've read your profile. I am Captain Marin of the Valvoran Naval Forces."

Fire glares back at Era. "You picked a fight with a naval captain? Are you insane?"

Before Era can defend himself, Marin interrupts the conversation with a crack of her whip. "I despise scum like you. I'm going to break you like I broke your idiot friend."

"He may be an idiot, but he's not my friend," Fire retorts.

"I don't think that was her point," Era comments.

Marin snags the canteen from the floor and pours the rest of its contents over her shortened weapon, allowing it to absorb the extra water before cracking it against the floor. "I don't know how you snapped my whip, but it won't happen again."

Fire's lips curl smugly at the taunt. She withdraws her dagger and crouches low as Marin spins her whip in a circle. In the dim light of the hold, Fire notices the end of the whip thicken, taking the form of a flail. She backs off as Marin makes her approach, moving the spinning weapon from side to side as she pushes Fire toward a row of crates. Era tries desperately to will himself to his feet so he can help his ally, but his body rejects his efforts.

Her back against the wall, Fire runs out of space to retreat, and Marin pushes her advantage. She flings the flail at Fire, who deflects the strike with impeccable reaction. Bewildered, Marin tries to slam it down on her opponent's head, but Fire spins to the side and chops through the whip once more with her bare hand. Water sprays everywhere, and Marin scrambles to form what little element she has left into a dagger. She makes a wide cut, but Fire's weapon intercepts and shatters Marin's with ease.

Turning to offense, Fire slashes at Marin's side, but the desperate captain catches it with a water rope, gripped tightly by both hands. This time her shaping holds true, and she twists the blade from Fire's hand, only to receive a forceful jab to her abdomen. As she bends over in reflex, Fire's knee meets her forehead, knocking her out.

Era can hardly believe his eyes. "Fire, that was amazing! I can't believe I've beaten you twice."

"You haven't beaten me," Fire barks. She gets in his face and quietly informs him, "But if you want to back that up, I'm game for a duel right now." Era frantically shakes his head. "Thought so."

Era says, "Either way, there's a lot that makes sense all of a sudden." She looks to him quizzically, and he points out over the floor. Alarmed, Fire finds tiny ice crystals littering the battlefield, each fragment shimmering in the light of the flickering lanterns. "You're an ice elementalist," Era realizes. "No wonder you can snap water weapons like twigs! Between the whip and how you shattered that monster's arms in the caverns at Ugorzi, you're freezing them through?" She spins back to Era with wide eyes, who playfully asks, "What, did I figure out your secret? Jem's going to go nuts when she finds out you two have something in common. And to think you've been calling her 'Ice Queen'."

Fire grabs the collar of his shirt. "You will tell no one about this. Do you understand?"

Era is delighted. "Sure, sure."

"I'm serious, Idiot!" Giving him a shove, Fire points sharply at Marin. "That woman had a file on me. If she had known what I can do, she would never have engaged me like that. Secrets like this can mean life or death in my line of work."

Era is taken aback by the gravity of Fire's demand. "Erm… yeah, I guess you're right about that."

She looks back at Era with cold eyes. "So are you going to keep my secret, or do I need to silence you?"

Era finds himself alarmed at the sincerity in Fire's gaze. He swallows hard, realizing he's in no position to negotiate. "Fine, I won't tell anyone. But wow, Di would love to see you in action knowing you're an elementalist. Chopping water ropes with your bare hands? She'd flip out."

Fire nods. "It's not that I'm strong enough to snap an elemental weapon. Water shapers can't shape ice, so I just froze through the whip at the moment of contact. That's the whole trick, but I can't freeze the waters close to their hands. The more control they have over the element, the more it wants to maintain its state."

"Guess that's why she was able to deflect your attack at the end," he notes as she walks over to Marin, unsheathing her dagger. "Wait, Fire," Era calls out, "what are you doing?"

"Just look away, Era. This will only take a moment." She kneels behind Marin and pulls her head back, positioning her dagger across the front of the captain's neck.

"I will not!" Era screams as he runs straight for Fire. However, his injured legs give out halfway there, and Fire releases Marin just before Era crashes into her.

Fire glares at him in annoyance. "Now isn't the time for this."

"You're not killing her, Fire."

"You're so against killing, but just what did you expect by hiring an assassin?"

"Yeah, I hired you. And since I'm paying you, I expect you'll follow my rules."

She scowls and points at her fallen opponent. "That woman is a naval captain! She's going to report us! Leaving her alive will cause us problems."

Era doesn't back down. "That's not a reason to kill her."

"It's not a-? What is with you?" Fire shouts as she stamps her foot. "Do you have any idea what kind of trouble you're in? Do you think you and the ice queen are going to drop the princess off and just go back to your happy old lives? You're in so far over your head, and you don't even realize it!"

"That doesn't mean I have the right to take her life, even if it ends up saving my own." Before Fire can object, Era adds, "My father taught me a lot in my life-"

"Great. More brilliant advice from the loser dad."

The comment strikes a nerve. "Hey, I know he taught me a lot of unconventional things, but he also instilled in me that, no matter what I

214

take from others, I never have the right to take a life. No one does." Softly, he admits, "I don't know why, but that one stuck with me."

Fire doesn't back down. "You think anyone else you fight feels the same way? If you respect the lives of your enemies, it's going to get you killed."

Firmly, he says, "That doesn't make it right, and you never know... maybe killing them will come back to haunt you some day."

"Not killing your enemies will come back to haunt you *immediately*," Fire insists. "You're naïve if you think that anything good can come from showing your enemies mercy."

"Well," Era suggests, "if I thought like you do, you'd be dead right now. So that logic saved your life, right?"

The simple revelation takes Fire aback, and she aggressively points her dagger at him with a wild look in her eye. "Era, you let me kill her, or I'm going to-"

"How many enemies have you killed, Fire? And has it made your life easy?" her companion pointedly asks. "If I'd done that... If I'd let you die in the woods that night..." Contentedly, he tells her, "Then I wouldn't have you as my companion, as someone I can trust."

Fire's heart sinks deep into her gut, and she averts her eyes as Era's gaze fills her with shame. Her inner voice screams at her to finish the job. Allowing the captain to report back to the military will make it impossible to deny their suspicions about her. And yet, glancing back at Era, she finds her heart pounding.

Marin groans and stirs, but Era stomps on her head, slamming it back into the floor and ensuring she stays out. "Fortunately, my father never outright condemned violence," he admits.

Fire turns away in resignation. "Fine, do what you want," she says. "Where are the ice queen and the whiny princess, anyway?"

Era's smile fades. "So, yeah... they were taken by pirates."

She watches him, at first taking it as a bad joke. Realizing he's serious, she growls, "I seriously, *seriously* hate you guys."

*　　*　　*

A lurch by the ship stirs Marin from her slumber. In alarm, she jumps up and looks for her adversaries, but she finds herself alone in the low-lit chamber. From the rhythmic bumping of the ship, it appears the propulsion rune has been affixed and activated.

Marin darts up the stairs, carefully watching for signs of the intruders. Confused and frustrated, she arrives on deck to find the crew watching out over the sea as they speed along. She finds Giarva and demands, "Just what is going on?"

Her subordinate salutes. "We're chasing the pirate Turk, ma'am. The rune was installed successfully, just as you requested."

"And why did you not come find me?" Marin barks.

"You were not to be disturbed, Captain. Surely you felt the ship accelerate? We started mere moments before you arrived."

Marin looks out at the waves speeding by their vessel. "How long was I down there?"

"Half an hour or so, ma'am."

She slams the rail. "We have a problem. One of the spies from earlier is still on this ship." Marin lowers her voice to finish. "And he has a friend. Fire, the assassin."

Her lieutenant is taken aback, but he doesn't act terribly impressed. "Should I know who this assassin is?"

"Do you not read over the warrants? She is dangerous, and she is on this ship." Turning to address the crew, she shouts, "Everyone, back to your stations! We've a pair of stowaways on board, and you are to bring them to me before we catch up with the pirate vessel. Do you understand?"

A chorus of "Yes ma'ams!" rings out, and everyone scrambles. Marin ascends the stairs to the quarterdeck and watches out over the bow as the wind whips through her hair, cursing the luck she's had in her mission to find and execute the pirate captain. She swears to herself that she'll have Turk's head within the hour.

*   *   *

A slow creak catches Turk's attention. Standing on the quarterdeck above his cabin, he steps to the rail and glances down to find Jem quietly closing the door behind herself. "She done crying?"

Jem looks up, startled by his voice. "Yeah, she fell asleep." Closing the door almost all the way, she sits with her back to the cabin.

"Why not come up here and see the view?"

Jem wiggles her hand, which is still chained to the wrist on the other side of the door. "Took me a long time to move her next to the door. I imagine she might wake up if I move her up the stairs."

The pirate offers a hearty laugh. Leaping over the rail, he lands softly and sits cross-legged in front of Jem. "Don't worry, we'll get those chains off when we harbor. Our two lock pickers were… Erm, well, they were lost in the battle." Jem offers a sympathetic nod as she watches over the sea from her vantage point. He studies her and asks, "Why are you so hesitant to return to Alleria? How long has it been since you left?"

"I crossed over when I was young," she explains. "I haven't been back."

Turk scratches his cheek. "Was that during the war?" Jem nods a confirmation. Not wanting to push the subject, he says, "You know, you never told me your names."

"Oh, sorry about that. My name is Jem, and the short one is Di."

"Jem?" Turk repeats in confusion. "Doesn't sound like an Allerian name."

"It's not," she affirms. "Jem is kind of a nickname."

"What's your real name?"

"Lost to time, I guess," she says with a shrug.

"Sounds like you're more Valvoran than Allerian, but I guess that's to be expected if you've been living there most your life." Curious, he asks, "What do you have in Valvoren, anyway? What keeps you there?"

Era immediately comes to her mind, but beyond that is very little. "I have nothing," Jem answers, her eyes glazed over. "Alleria, Valvoren… they mean nothing to me. I have no family, no home, and no allegiance."

Turk is taken aback. "But Valvorans are brutal, disgusting creatures. Look at that captain we just encountered, and look at what they did to Alleria during the war! They burned dozens of cities to the ground."

"Do you think Allerians are innocent?" she challenges. "They're not, you know. Don't assume I want to go to Alleria just because I'm Allerian."

The captain leans back. "Well, like it or not, we'll be in Alleria by tomorrow."

Jem bites her lip as a sailor in the crow's nest cries out, "It's them! The naval ship!"

The crew starts murmuring fearfully, and Turk calls out, "You're sure?"

"They're gaining on us fast, whoever they are."

Someone hands Turk an extendable telescope, and he sprints up the stairs to look out over the stern. Jem jumps to her feet as well, momentarily forgetting about the chains and pulling her attached companion through the cabin door with a shriek. Jem offers the dazed girl a sheepish apology.

"What's going on?" Di asks, trying to get her bearings.

"Not sure yet, but I think that naval captain might be catching up."

Di's eyes light up. "With Era?"

Jem grimaces. "Assuming he's alive."

"It's her, alright." Turk lowers his telescope and orders, "Engage the propulsion rune!"

The helmsman is already prepared for the order. He pulls the lever to activate it, and the ship starts bouncing violently over the waves as it speeds away from the approaching craft.

Turk continues to watch through his looking glass before folding it in resignation. "They're still gaining on us," he calls out over the noise of the rune's spraying. "They must have a better rune than we have."

His second-in-command gives him a glance. "I told you we shoulda' got the bigger one."

"Shut up, Jenkit." The captain draws his sword and raises it in the air. "Men, it's been an honor. Today, we fight for our right to live!" The men applaud. "We fight to avenge our fallen comrades!" The men cheer. "Are you with me?" A deafening roar erupts as the remaining pirates enthusiastically raise their blades in the air, ready to follow their captain to their deaths.

Jem places a hand on her terrified companion's head. "Don't worry, Di," she says reassuringly. "You're the only Valvoran on this ship. Tell them you're Canterin's princess and you'll be safe."

Trembling, Di looks up at her protector. "B-But, even if that's true, you'll be killed along with the pirates!"

Jem offers a sad smile. "No one lives forever. I've had a fun journey, and if it ends today, I think that wouldn't be so bad."

Di's eyes fill with tears as she hugs Jem. Subtly wiping her own eyes, Jem calls out, "Hey, captain! Got a sword for me to use?"

"Not on your life! You two lasses are staying below deck."

"Hey, I can fight!"

"Not with that anchor around your wrist you can't."

"I'll cut my hand off if I have to! There's no way I'm sitting back and-"

"Jenkit! Take the girls to the hold," Turk calls out to his second-in-command. "Tie them up if you have to! Don't let them get back up here."

Jenkit moves to contain the girls. Jem meets his eye, daring him on, but the burly pirate just hoists the girls over his shoulders in one swift movement. Jem kicks and screams, giving Jenkit a fair amount of trouble as he hauls the two down the stairs.

"I'd say we have fifteen minutes at the most," Turk calls to his men before forming a mischievous grin. "But we'll be ready with some tricks up our sleeves."

*   *   *

Marin watches triumphantly from the bow as they gain on the pirate ship. "There will be no failure this time," she calls to her ready crewmen. "No one will escape, no one will survive!" The naval soldiers raise their swords in the air, letting loose a rallying cheer in response.

Ascending the stairs to the quarterdeck, Marin takes her place next to her lieutenant. "How have we not found those spies yet, Giarva?"

"I... I'm not sure, ma'am. We've scoured the ship for them, and all the landing craft are accounted for. Is it... I mean, is it at all possible they were never-"

"They're on my ship, lieutenant. I'm not wrong."

"Aye, Captain. But with the pirate vessel nearing range, I think it would be wise to direct our focus to that."

Marin watches Turk's ship as they rapidly close the distance. "Fine, we'll find them after we execute the pirates. Tell the men to abandon their search for now and prepare for battle." As Giarva scampers off, Marin stomps the deck in frustration, questioning how the two stowaways found a hiding place on her vessel.

*　　*　　*

The stomp of the captain's foot echoes loudly into her personal cabin below the quarterdeck, making Fire and Era glance upward in curiosity. Shrugging it off, Fire returns to her work.

"Ow!" Era yelps as he pulls his hands away from Fire and shakes them in pain.

"Shut up," she whispers, yanking his hands back to continue picking the locks on the handcuffs. "Would you man up, already?"

"You pinched me," Era whispers back. "Are you sure you can pick these? You're good, but maybe you're not-"

Before he finishes his sentence, Fire successfully pops the latch and opens one side of the handcuffs. She eyes him and mutters, "You're lucky you didn't discard my pick along with the rest of my gear."

Era sheepishly laughs, but he says nothing as she continues to work. It doesn't take her long to pop the other latch, freeing Era from his bonds. He grips each wrist in sequence, twisting and stretching them out.

Fire squats by the open window in the back, ready to escape in case someone tries to enter the locked cabin. "We're lucky the captain likes her privacy," she comments. "No windows facing the deck makes hiding in here a lot easier. Seems the crew won't set foot in here either, considering they must be looking for us by now."

"That's good," Era says in relief. "So, what now? We just stay in here until…?"

"They'll search in here eventually. We'll stay here a bit longer, then we'll sneak back into the cargo hold. The ship will harbor, and we'll get off. Somehow."

Era shakes his head. "No, not about that. Jem and Di are-"

"They're gone," she says coldly. "Mourn your loss later. Much as I don't like it, I'll need you in a fight if it comes to that. So stay focused."

The notion of losing Jem shakes Era to his core. He feels the guilt rushing back at his decision to dash below deck, even as he watched them get dragged to the other ship. He knows in his heart that there was nothing he could have done in that moment, but the logic does nothing to deter his emotions.

Trying to distract himself, he offers, "That was pretty impressive though, scaling the outer hull by freezing grips into the side. Your arm must be feeling a lot better."

Fire twists her wrist around. "Yeah, it's mostly healed."

"And to think we thought it was broken at first," Era recalls.

"You thought it was broken. I just let you think it was."

"Still," he says, looking at his hands, "I wish I had gloves. Those grips were cold."

Fire grunts in annoyance that Era knows her most closely-guarded secret, even if that meant she was able to use her ability in front of him. "You're dead if you tell anyone."

Era sighs. "With all we've been through, I expect you to stop constantly threatening my life at some point. It's clear you're not used to working with others."

Fire hesitates at the comment. "You're certainly in limited company," she admits.

Before Era can reply, the ship bounces violently as yet another cheer is raised by the crew. Fire glances out the window, able to make out the propulsion rune below as it sprays water out the back. "They've been accelerated for quite some time now. Could they still be pursuing the pirates?"

Era's eyes widen at the possibility. "If so, we can meet up with-"

"This isn't good news," Fire says, cutting him off. "Even if we meet up with them, there's no way for us to escape. We might be in Allerian waters by now, if not the middle of the Narubi Ocean."

"Ugh, that isn't a pleasant situation," Era realizes while looking down at the rune. "Say, I've never seen a rune like that before. Do you suppose that's how the pirates got away earlier?"

The comment sparks an idea in the mercenary. "What if we-" Fire starts being getting interrupted by a sharp turn of the vessel, forcing her to tumble into Era. She shoves him away just in time for another jolt to knock her to the floor.

Era offers his hand in amusement. "You were saying?"

Fire begrudgingly accepts his help, wincing as she massages her sore backside. "It's time to take control of the situation."

*   *   *

The disguised naval vessel glances off the pirate ship, crashing bulkheads as the crews of both ships tumble to their respective decks. Marin's helmsman disengages the rune, as the pirate ship has already abandoned use of its own.

"Shape the boarding planks and advance!" Marin shouts.

Watery tendrils lash out at the rival vessel, manipulated by the water shapers on Marin's craft. The fluid enwraps the rails and riggings on both sides, locking the ships together. Once secured, the skilled shaper mold the thick waters into boarding planks. With a loud rallying cry, the naval sailors use the planks to launch their assault.

As the front lines clash blades, Turk desperately beckons for a special squad to move forward. Each member wields a shield-like rune, and they activate the runes to unleash vicious flames upon the advancing naval soldiers, catching many on fire and forcing them to leap into the water for salvation. The pirates start to celebrate until a line of sailors on the naval quarterdeck start firing flare runes at the pirates that forces them to scatter and allow more soldiers onto their ship.

Turk jumps into the mix and unleashes a torrent of water. "Bolster the boarding defense!" he cries as two of his flame-throwers fall. He takes aim at the nearby boarding plank and blasts a group of opponents into the ocean, but more adversaries just take their place. Turk angrily glances to Marin, who stands smugly at her helm. "Won't get your hands dirty, eh?" he mutters with disdain.

Turk dodges a sword strike and shoves his open palm into the soldier's gut, unleashing a blast of water that vaults his opponent high into the air before dropping into the ocean. Taking a moment to survey the scene, the pirate captain can tell it's a hopeless scenario for his crew. They were already severely outnumbered, and the odds aren't moving in their favor quickly enough. Drawing his sword, he charges a group of soldiers, spraying their faces with water as he unleashes a flurry of sword strikes, determined to take as many of them down as possible.

Motion suddenly catches his eye, and Turk watches in surprise as two newcomers appear from over the outer railing of the quarterdeck. They catch one of the naval soldiers off guard and kick him over the rail.

Fire shoves another soldier off the ship while Era hurries to the rail and spots Turk. He cups his hands and shouts over the clamor of the battle, "We're here to help! How do we activate the rune?"

Bewildered, Turk reasons these must be the allies Jem had mentioned. "Won't work," he grunts as he blasts another sailor with a jet of water, "their rune is better!"

With Era having drawn attention to himself, a group of soldiers charges the set of stairs to get to him. Fire aggressively kicks the first one in the face, who stumbles back into the rest, knocking them all back down to the deck.

"Just tell me!" Era insists.

"It's the lever behind you. Pull it!"

Era finds the lever and gives it a tug, and the mechanisms below deck take care of the rest. The rune blasts its stream of water out, but the two ships remain conjoined by the elemental bindings. They start rotating around one another as if caught in a whirlpool.

Recognizing the problem, Era leaps down to the main deck. He draws an earth dagger formed from what he was able to retrieve following his fight with Marin, and he races toward the nearest mass of water and hacks away at it. The shapers on the other side maintain their focus on the element, ensuring their bindings hold firm.

A group of naval sailors charge across the elemental plank to attack Era, but Turk steps in and washes them away before further clearing the area around his new ally. Era turns to thank him, but his eye catches Marin swinging their way, her water whip wrapped around the pirates' mainsail and a metal sword drawn. He tackles Turk just in time to save the pirate's head as she slices at them in passing. Undeterred, Marin lands and snaps her whip around Turk's wrist. "You're not escaping," she vows as she flings him into the mast. Era makes an attempt to tackle the naval captain, but she flips him over her head and slams him into the deck.

A loud commotion breaks out as something like a massive plow emerges from the companionway, shoving soldiers and pirates alike out of the way. Holding Di perpendicularly as she extends a shield of air, Jem charges forward while letting loose a battle cry.

"What the blazes?" Marin cries as they crash into her and push her over the nearby railing. As she falls, she snaps her whip to the rails on her own ship, saving herself from plunging into the ocean.

"Jem? Di!" Era exclaims in disbelief.

"Era!" they shriek in unison as they run toward him, but a soldier cuts them off. Di lifts a shield in defense, and Era slams the sailor's head into the hard wall of air from behind. Their opponent deposed, the three hug one another awkwardly amidst the clashing swords.

"Not the time, people!" Turk cries as he duels with a soldier.

Era sheepishly releases his hold. "Right! We need to cut the pirate ship loose from those water bindings."

Jem pumps her fist excitedly. "Time to use the hammer again, Di."

Di resolutely nods, trying to reconcile her immense joy at their reunion with the terror of finding herself on such a battlefield. She holds both hands outward and solidifies the air into the form of a hammer-like club, which shimmers in the sunlight as if made from glass.

"Clear the boarding ramps!" Turk bellows. "Protect our new friends!"

Screaming as they run, Era, Jem, and Di charge forward while reeling the giant hammer back. They swing it forward and smash the railing to pieces, which causes the water to dissipate and fall into the ocean below. The ships instantly begin to separate, placing additional strain on the remaining binding as the shapers struggle to hold on.

As they move to smash the remaining plank, Marin leaps onto the shaped surface and whips the handle of the elemental hammer, pulling it tight and preventing the three from reeling it back.

"Di, just make a new one," Jem grunts as she and Era desperately pull back against Marin's hold.

"Oh, right," Di realizes as she drops the tool, causing everyone to stagger backward from the release of momentum. The three allies tumble to the deck, and the off-balance Marin dives back to her own side in an effort to keep from falling into the ocean.

Jem yanks Di to her feet and forces her hands together. "Again, quickly!" When she does so, the quick-witted Allerian first swings the weapon back around the opposite direction to slam an approaching soldier in the stomach, after which Era hurries to also grab hold of the weapon.

"Protect them!" Turk cries as he shoves a naval sailor out of the way.

"Stop them!" Marin shouts as she scrambles to react.

A pair of soldiers moves to intercept, but Fire leaps down on them from the quarterdeck and yells, "Go!"

Screaming as they run, they together guide the bulky weapon to its remaining target, smashing the spot where the watery mass is attached. The wooden rail explodes into a mess of splintered fragments, and the pirate vessel lurches away from the military ship, blasting a powerful spray of water in its wake.

224

Marin reaches out in desperation as the spray rains down on them. "Match their speed!" she orders. The helmsman frantically works at the console, but the rune fails to activate. The crew can do nothing but watch as their coveted prize escapes, and Marin's fists tremble with rage as she pieces together what must have transpired.

Back on the pirate ship, two of the remaining naval soldiers charge the helm in order to disable the rune, but Fire greets them and skillfully knocks each of them to the ground with a single strike. She admires her handiwork while rubbing her knuckles, clearly enjoying herself while members of the pirate crew arrive to take them captive.

"Fight on, men!" Turk cries as he unleashes a jet of water on his nearby opponents, sweeping their feet out from under them. The pirates let out a cheer, and it doesn't take long for Marin's men to surrender. The pirates herd them to the bow of the ship, where they strip them of their swords and force them to their knees. Their victory achieved, the crew lets loose a thunderous shout of triumph.

Turk climbs to the quarterdeck and watches back after the cargo ship in confusion. "Why are they not giving chase?"

Fire smirks, twirling her dagger for Turk to see. "Someone may have cut the propulsion mechanism to shreds." Sheathing the weapon, she adds, "And that same person may have scratched the symbols off the rune. Just in case."

Turk abruptly embraces her in a joyous hug that lifts her into the air. She lets out a yelp as he swings her around and drops her back to the deck. Her arms freed, she slams the pirate captain in the abdomen, making him double over in pain. "Never touch me," she mutters as she turns to look over the main deck.

While half the pirates are busy tying up their prisoners, the other crewmen have surrounded Era, Jem, and Di, cheering and hugging their saviors. Fire watches Era as he sheepishly scratches his head at the attention, a recurring habit of his that she's noticed during their travels together. "The idiot was right. It all worked out in the end," she whispers to herself. She finds her mind wandering back to their conversation in the cargo hold, and the conviction once more stabs at her like a knife through her heart. The more she watches him and his new friends celebrate their victory, the more shameful she feels.

Turk stumbles next to her while rubbing his stomach. Weakly, he groans, "Quite a crew you have there, Captain."

"Captain?" Fire scoffs. "What makes you think I'm in charge?"

"You're cut from a different cloth than the others, that's an easy tell. The way you took control of that fight was nothing short of impressive."

"Controlling a fight is easy. Controlling those three is like herding wild frost boars. It can't be done."

"Welcome to being a captain." Reluctantly, he relents, "Look, I owe you all for what you did."

"I was hoping you'd say that," Fire says.

"You saved my life, not to mention the lives of my crew. You're going to Canterin, right? Giving you a ride is about the easiest I should come out." Looking to the late-day sun, he adds, "I can drop you off a few miles outside the city. The darkness should aid your cover as you sneak in. Unless you have something else in mind?"

A chill runs down Fire's spine as she recalls the commander's words regarding troop deployment surrounding the city. Going straight to the shores of Canterin will almost assuredly result in a military encounter, so the better option would be to head to a different port town and follow the original plan to smuggle in via cargo ship. Her breath trembles as she considers her options.

"Just tell me what you want," Turk offers, interrupting her thoughts.

"What I want?" Fire looks down once more to her companions as the celebration dies down. Oblivious to her inner turmoil, Era enthusiastically points her out to the pirates standing nearby, and they raise a cheer in her honor. In that moment, she knows exactly what she wants. "Take us to Canterin."

Turk raises a fist in the air. "To Canterin, then!"

Era celebrates the announcement with Jem and the pirates, and Fire turns away from him while Turk barks orders to his crew, steering them toward their final destination.

CHAPTER 17

Jem stretches and massages her wrist, ecstatic to be freed of the bindings that long held her to Di. "It feels so good! Thanks Fire."

Fire moves to Di's wrist. "Now, hold still. The lighting is getting worse."

Di glances at the reddening sky as the mercenary works to unlatch her cuff. It feels like time is crawling as they cruise along under normal sail power. "I can't believe I'm finally going home. Is this really happening?"

"Geez Di, have a little faith. Didn't we tell you we'd get you there?" Jem asks.

"Let her be excited, Jem," Era says, placing a hand on his partner's shoulder. "She's finally going to see her father again!"

"Ow!" Di exclaims with a wince as Fire's hands jerk.

"This side is rusted," Fire mumbles to herself.

Jem shoots Era a nasty look. "Hey, why did it take you an hour to mention that Fire could pick our locks?"

He shrugs. "Didn't think about it, I guess."

"And my necklace! My rune! Those were going to make me a fortune," she groans. "How could you leave my bag behind?"

Era frowns as he realizes his belongings were also left in Marin's hold. "Well, it would have been hard to manage those hefty bags while swimming between ships and all that. But look!" He reaches into his wet boot and retrieves the emerald necklace.

Jem gasps and snatches it. "When did you-?"

"Ah-ah! A thief never reveals his secrets," he says with a wink. "I swiped it some time ago and, well, kinda forgot about it."

"You swiped it?" she grunts in annoyance, though she hardly sounds upset as she caresses her recovered treasure. "Well, at least I still have my necklace."

"That's Andrea's necklace," Di insists. "You stole it."

"And that's what makes it mine," she smugly responds.

Era furrows his brow. "Doesn't that make it mine, then?"

Jem ignores his comment as she wraps the jewelry around her forearm. "So, what happened after we got taken? You two met up, and then what?"

"We hid in the captain's cabin," Era explains. "No one ever thought to look there."

"But how did you get in there without being spotted?"

"Well, we were able to scale the hull," Era starts to explain, but Fire shoots him a look, reminding him of the penalty for revealing her secret.

"Scale the hull?" Jem asks, already interested. "How do you scale the outside of a ship?"

"That's what I want to know," Turk chimes in as he approaches. "You did that on my ship as well, showing up on the quarterdeck behind those naval sailors."

Era glances around as everyone watches him expectantly. "W-Well, if you just... I mean, if you grip it really tightly..."

"We found climbing hooks in the hold," Fire interjects nonchalantly while picking Di's lock. "They slipped into the sea after we climbed aboard this ship."

Everyone seems to take her at her word, and Era marvels at how her fabrications go unchallenged, though it certainly helps to maintain such an intimidating aura.

Turk claps his hands, drawing attention back to himself. "Well, we should be gettin' to Canterin within the hour. Sit tight!" he shouts as he heads back to the quarterdeck.

"Ow!" Di again yelps as she yanks her hand away from Fire. "Stop pinching me, will you?"

Fire stands in frustration. "Come talk to me when you're ready to have that thing off." She walks to the far rail to watch out over the sea.

Di pouts as she massages her wrist, and Era places a hand on her arm. "Better go apologize, Di. Unless you want that thing still dangling there when you greet your father." With a groan, the weary traveler saunters over to Fire.

Jem takes a moment to study Era, alone with him for the first time since they started this journey. She's relieved they managed to find their way back together. Just two years back, she couldn't imagine worrying about someone in this way.

"I'm so glad I found you, Jem," Era says, as if reading her thoughts. "The way things have been going... I thought that was it for us."

Jem nods, reserving her enthusiasm. "I'm ready for this adventure to be over."

Concern washes over Era as he remembers Fire's words from earlier that day. "Jem, this won't end after we return Di."

"It better end!" Jem exclaims. "I want nothing to do with that girl anymore. She's nothing but trouble."

"But won't the military keep pursuing us?" he asks. "Returning her won't wipe out our bounties."

Surprised, Jem glances over to where Di is begging for Fire's help. "Are you saying you want to sell out to the military?"

"No, not anymore," Era says. "I mean, it keeps crossing my mind, but... Jem, I just can't do it. Even if it costs me my life."

"It might cost me my life too, you know. Think about me for once!" With a huff, she says, "Those are our only choices, Era. Turn her in or be on the run. Indefinitely."

He sighs. "I doubt we'd last long on the run. We don't exactly plan well."

"Hey, I know you don't plan well, but I can keep us alive just fine." Reflectively, Jem says, "You don't need to worry, Era. Once we have that reward money, we can survive just fine running from the military. After all we've been through, I think we can handle anything together."

Era is taken aback by Jem's demeanor. "So, turning in Di is off the table?"

"It's never been on the table, Era," she says. "I know you don't think much of my compassion, but I don't want to turn her in, either. That child may be a handful, but no one so young deserves that kind of fate."

Era feels a burden lift that he's been carrying since he first considered the option. With relief, he playfully says, "Looks like I'm starting to rub off on you."

"And why do you think kindness is something you need to teach me?"

"Well, I also taught you sympathy, a sense of humor…"

Shaking her finger at him, she argues, "You haven't taught me a thing in nearly two years! I've still got a lot to teach you, so…" Quietly, she adds, "So stick with me, Era. We'll get through all this together, somehow."

Warmly, he says, "I like being with you, too. Thanks, Jem."

She glances back to Fire and Di. "Don't thank me yet. We'll have our hands full, for sure. That nasty assassin might pursue us for our bounties once Di is home."

"Fire's good, but we can beat her together."

"Yes, *together*," Jem stresses. "No more solo stuff." After a moment, she adds, "I'm glad I met you, Era. You're pretty special… in your own way."

"In my own way?" he asks, raising an eyebrow. "That's a poor attempt at hitting on me."

The Allerian bursts into laughter. "Hitting on you," she says in glee as she walks away, leaving Era to wonder what's so funny about the idea.

As Jem wanders past the quarterdeck, she hears the captain call out from above, "Hey lass, come up here."

Curious, Jem climbs the stairs. "What is it, Captain?"

"Call me Turk," he responds. "I wanted to… errmmm, you know, see how you like the ship?"

Jem smirks at the pathetic attempt at conversation. "Just how long has it been since you've seen an Allerian woman?"

Turk wants to take offense at the question, but he kicks at the deck and admits, "Aye, it's been a while."

"Well, I'll still take the attention as a compliment," she offers. "And look, I want to say thanks. I know this is risky for your crew, and I'm sure they'd rather go home right now than sail deeper into Valvoran waters."

Turk grunts his disagreement. "You think my men just want to go home? We live a dangerous life, Jem. A day like today is what makes us feel alive."

"All the same, thank you. This means a lot to us."

230

As she turns away, he blurts out, "You could always come with us!" Jem stops in her tracks, and he continues, "You know, come back to Alleria, live among friends? You don't belong in Valvoren."

Softly, she says, "I don't belong in Alleria, either." She glances back to Era and says, "I belong with them, for now at least."

Turk reluctantly nods. "I belong with my crew, and you with yours. I can respect that."

"For what it's worth," Jem adds with appreciation, "it was nicer than I thought, being with other Allerians. It's tiring to always be singled out in a crowd."

The captain extends a hand. "Well, if you ever end up on my side of the border, look me up. You know we harbor in Glouak."

Jem clasps hands with the pirate. "I will, Turk. Thanks for everything."

He watches her return to her companions as his second-in-command joins his side. "Too bad the pretty girl won't come with you, eh Captain?"

"Shut up, Jenkit."

*   *   *

Barefooted, Era hops out of the landing boat into the dark, shallow waters, only to find a painfully rocky beach floor. Dancing as he seeks softer sands, he pulls the boat onto the beach and extends a hand to help his partners get out. "Careful here."

"We're lucky we found a beachfront in the darkness," Turk says as he and Jenkit join the group out of the boat. "The trip to town should be short, too. Canterin can't be more than a few miles to the east."

After strapping his boots back on, Era extends a hand to Turk. "Thanks, Captain. We owe you for this."

"You owe me?" Turk scoffs as he refuses Era's hand. "I still owe you ten times over. You're as gutsy as anyone on my crew, doing what you did."

Era scratches his head, embarrassed by the compliment. "Actually, this might be the least crazy thing that has happened to us recently."

Turk raises an eyebrow. "If that's true, I'd love to know what else you've been up to." To Jem he says, "Last chance, lass. No second thoughts?"

With a glance to Era, she answers, "None."

"Then my business is done here," he says regretfully. "Stay safe, my friends."

The group heads up the beach, but Jem lingers. "Say, Turk, what are you going to do with your Valvoran prisoners?"

"Why do you care?" he asks in surprise. "I figured I'd take them back to Alleria with us, maybe sell them to a shipping operation. See how they enjoy being treated like animals."

Jem grimaces. "You would do the same thing to them? You can't vilify the Valvorans and then commit the same atrocities. You're adding to a cycle of hatred that will never end."

"That cycle will exist whether I release those men or take them back to Alleria," Turk contends. "It's just a handful of captives. We can't end all the hatred with something so insignificant."

"Maybe not, but you could end it for those soldiers by setting them free."

"They killed my men!" he continues to argue. "Besides that, they're soldiers who will go back to the military and kill more Allerians one day. I can't just let them go."

"And that's why the cycle will never end." Dejected, she turns and follows after her companions.

The pirate grits his teeth and stomps the ground, failing to suppress the urge welling within. "I mean, I said I still owed you," he grunts. Jem turns back in surprise, and Turk adds, "If I let those prisoners go, we're even. You got that?"

Jem beams brilliantly. "You've got a deal, Captain!" With that, she offers an enthusiastic wave as she disappears into the woods.

"Pardon, Captain," Jenkit says as he steps next to Turk, "but you don't actually intend on following through with that, do you?"

"I've no choice," Turk states. "I'm a man of my word, and I honor a debt. The men will have to understand."

"The only thing they'll understand is that you was entranced with a young dame," he replies.

"Th-That had nothing to do with it!"

"Aye, Captain. Aye."

*　　*　　*

"Come on, Jem!" Di calls out as her guardian catches up. "Let's hurry, I'm almost home!"

Era laughs at the display of enthusiasm. "What's it been? Two years? This should be a heartwarming reunion to witness."

"We have to be careful," Jem sternly warns. "Sneaking into Canterin is going to be our hardest challenge yet." She turns to Fire and says, "Okay, I hate to admit this, but you're a big part of why we've gotten this far. What's the plan for tonight?"

Curtly, she answers, "I'll scout ahead. You three follow."

"That's it? I thought you'd-" Fire dashes into the darkness before Jem can finish her thought, much to her confusion. "Okay, what's with her?"

"Must be focused on the task at hand," Era reasons. "Let's advance carefully."

Jem looks to Di. "You know where we are?"

Di boasts a huge grin. "I used to play on this beach growing up! Canterin is under an hour's hike from here."

Era politely bows and motions ahead. "Lead the way, Princess."

Di gladly marches into the dark woods, and Era follows. Jem turns back and watches Turk as he and Jenkit row back to their ship. The moonlight shimmers off the water, illuminating both their small craft and the pirate ship in the distance. She waves one more time, just in case he's watching.

As Jem turns back, Di slyly says, "You're taken by him, aren't you?"

"Lay off, now," Jem scolds. "Let a girl enjoy her childish crush."

"Hey, what's he got that I don't?" Era asks.

"Muscles, for one. Manners, for two."

"A rugged, unshaven jaw," Di adds.

"Regardless," he interjects, wishing he had held his tongue, "there's no point in falling for someone you'll never see again."

"I'm not falling for him, Era," Jem says. "He was a nice guy and the first Allerian I've truly met in a long time. That's all there is to it, and you're right to say I'm never going to see him again."

233

Era shrugs. "Maybe the winds of fate will-"

Jem gives him a shove. "Just drop it already."

He grabs Di's shoulders to catch himself, nearly tripping her in the process. She glances up at him, her heart throbbing at her guardian's touch. However, in that moment, she saddens at the thought of parting ways with him. "Era, we're going to see each other again, right?"

"Hey, I told you that I'd visit. I even said we'd have a date."

"You promise?"

"Absolutely. Jem rarely lets me sleep in an inn, so keep an empty bed and I'll come often."

Di finds herself comforted by those words. The journey home has felt like it was never going to end. However, now that she's mere miles from her destination, she's confronted by the reality that she will miss her protectors. *'Though at least I won't be around Fire anymore,'* she thinks with relief.

"Okay, okay, that's enough chatter," Jem says. "Let's keep our wits about us."

They walk in silence, each traveler's thoughts consumed with nervous anticipation of what it might take to get into the city. If the military is expecting Di to return, getting in will be a challenge. And besides that, Canterin has a wall, which will complicate their infiltration.

After some time, Jem finds her mind wandering back to Turk's return to his ship. Though they came in under cover of night, she could clearly make him out from her position, even seeing the silhouette of the ship far offshore. If the military was scouting the shoreline, it's entirely possible that they were spotted.

Jem snaps her fingers to catch the attention of Era and Di. She leans in close and keeps her voice just above a whisper. "I don't like this. Something doesn't feel right."

Era furrows his brow. "Fire is scouting ahead. If she finds anyone, she'll let us know."

Jem's heart sinks as Era's words spark a realization within her. "We have to get out of here."

"Leave?" he asks in confusion. "But we're so close to-"

"Era! We've been trusting Fire because she was injured, but it would take nothing for her to lead the military to us. We need to leave!"

"What? No, she wouldn't do that."

234

"She would, and she is!" Jem looks to Di and asks, "Where could we go to hide ourselves-"

The distant rustling of leaves cuts her off. They wait in silence as a distant glow of torchlight indicates a group is approaching from the east.

Jem grabs Di's hand and whispers, "Come on, we can outrun them!" However, more groups are swarming from all directions.

Di stumbles backward, trembling. "We're surrounded?"

"We can still hide," Era says as he pulls a new sword from the ground. "And if we have to, we can fight."

Jem swallows hard, wondering how many soldiers there are. "Fire really sold us out," she says, her voice quavering.

"You don't know that," Era contests. "Just wait, she'll come back and-"

"You're an idiot, Era! You trusted her, and you got us to trust her as well! But this was her plan all along. It was the only reason she was helping us."

Clouded with doubt, he says, "Look, either way, we have to hide. Now!"

They search furiously for a good hiding place, but the best they can do is dive into a thick bush. Era's mind races to think of a plan, and as he glances at Jem, he can tell she's doing the same thing. Yet, in that moment, he realizes there is truly no plan that can get them out of this situation. He takes Jem's hand, catching her by surprise. He offers a warm smile, and the same conclusion dawns on her. They have probably come to the end of their time together.

A military private comes into view, confirming their fears. The soldier holds a torch at his side, scanning the darkness as he moves through the area. More soldiers appear as well, and another line is behind them.

Era holds Di closely as their adversaries come within arm's reach of their hiding spot. Despite one passing them by, another soldier approaches and peers into the brush. He stares for several seconds before calling out, "Captain! I think I-"

Era doesn't wait. He leaps at the soldier and smashes him in the side of the head with a blunt club. He turns to another, who starts to draw his sword, but Era knocks the wind out of him before he can use it.

"Over there!"

"Hurry!"

"I see him!"

Hoping to use himself as bait, Era dashes straight for the line of soldiers, engaging one in combat as he quickly finds himself surrounded.

"Is this the one?" a soldier calls, pulling the shrieking Di out by the arm. As soon as he gets her in the open, Jem leaps out and punches him square in the face. She follows it up with an elbow to the gut, dropping him.

"Run!" Era shouts as the soldiers overwhelm and tackle him, shaking his club loose. They shove his face into the dirt and force his arms behind his back.

"Era!" Jem cries out. She turns to Di and yells, "Run away! Go!" The frightened teen obediently takes off into the darkness.

Jem turns back and charges the soldiers around Era. She throws herself into two of them in an attack that leaves Era with only one soldier pinning him down.

"Jem, just run!" her partner screams as he desperately struggles to escape the soldier's grip.

However, his partner is quickly overcome by reinforcements. The bulk of the group has now surrounded the area, giving the wanted criminals no chance for escape. They're yanked to their feet, but Jem kicks furiously at her captors until a soldier jams the hilt of his sword into her gut. Her body goes limp, held between a pair of soldiers as she struggles to catch her breath.

"Infernal Allerian," the soldier mutters as he smacks her across the face.

"Leave her alone!" Era screams. Enraged, he kicks and struggles against his captors, but the same officer gets in his face.

"You insolent scum! Where is the girl?"

"She's over here, sir," a soldier calls out, showing the captain their prize. The girl hangs limply between two men.

The captain looks her over in shock. "She's young! Did she give you trouble?"

"Err... no sir. But she struggled enough that we were forced to knock the wind out of her."

"Where is she?" someone cries out while marching furiously through the masses.

The captain steps next to Di as he salutes his superior. "Commander Galen! Over here, sir."

Di summons the strength to lift her head, and she quakes in fear of the villain who took her from the Academy. "This is her," Galen confirms. "Take her away." Squad leaders shout their orders, and most of the troops leave to provide Di with a heavy escort.

"Bring her back!" Era screams as he fights against the soldiers holding him.

The clamor draws Galen's attention. Furious, he storms over to the thief and flings him to the ground.

"No!" Jem groans, tears welling in her eyes.

Galen glares down at the source of his woes. All the frustration, stress, and exertion of the last week boils to the surface as he pulls back his sleeves. "Bowen!"

The lieutenant commander steps forward from the crowd and ignites a flame that lashes out at Galen, who catches it in his hands. The crackling fire dances up and down his arm as he moves it at will, and the flames illuminate the commander's demeanor, reflecting the resolve of an experienced warrior hungry for battle. "Stand up," he demands. "You're going to pay for your crimes against the Valvoran military."

Era knows just how different the situation is compared to the last time they battled, as the flickering fire reveals the sheer number of reinforcements present to join in if needed. He claws at the ground, scraping up fistfuls of earth. "Why did you take her? What do you want with her!?"

"That's none of your concern." Galen unleashes a fireball at Era, who forms an earth shield from the forest floor and deflects the shot. Without hesitation, the commander charges and leaps over the barrier, and he slams his flame-covered fist into his opponent's chest that sends him staggering backward.

"Stop it!" Jem shrieks, tears streaming down her cheeks.

As Era tries to stand, Galen mercilessly flings a fireball into his arm, which sends him spiraling back to the ground. Desperately, Era screams and grabs at the earth, forming a sword as he stands. He points the blade at his opponent, a feral gleam in his eye.

Galen is undeterred by the challenge. With both arms engulfed in fire, he sends the flames out like a projectile. Era jukes wide to dodge the attack and dashes at the unarmed Galen.

However, the experienced fire shaper reels the flames back in like a spring, and he unleashes them once again into the thief. Era has no choice but to shield his face from the surprise attack, and Galen takes advantage by delivering a sharp kick to Era's side. He lands hard and screams in pain as Galen shoves his flame-covered fist into his face, forcing him to feel every bit of the searing heat.

"Please," Jem begs of her captors. "Please, let me go to him. Please!" Yet her words fall on deaf ears.

Galen's eyes reveal a determination to finish the job. He dispels the flames and grips his hilt, unsheathing his sword for the first time in the fight. The glint of the torchlight flickers off the cold steel as he extends the blade, ready to declare judgment on the criminal.

Clinging to consciousness, Era digs his trembling fingers into the soft earth below him, but, in that moment, he finds himself using his remaining strength to lift his eyes to Jem. Though she's shouting, he can't make out her words. He's grateful to her for all she did for him. In the end, he wasn't strong enough to protect her, and he feels the sting of that regret.

Galen raises his sword. Jem screams out as Era squeezes his eyes and braces for the strike.

Leaves rustle, and the sound of metal against metal rings out. Era looks up, stunned to find Fire standing over him. Her dagger in hand, she holds Galen's blade back, preventing him from dealing his finishing blow. The pummeled combatant is overcome with relief at the sight of his ally. "Fire, you came," he mutters weakly.

Fire glares at Galen, but she doesn't fight him. "We had a deal, Commander."

He scowls. "These two committed a grievous crime. This is justice."

"No, killing petty thieves to satisfy your vengeance is murder," she challenges. "Stand by your word."

Glancing back at his battered victim, Fire's words appear to strike a chord with him. Calming himself, he motions to the soldiers holding Jem, and they drop her to the ground. "We're done here," he calls. "Report back to camp." The soldiers are perplexed by the order, but they begin their retreat.

Jem scurries over to Era. He's burned and bruised all over, and he cringes with every movement. It's all he can do to keep himself from screaming in pain.

238

The commander makes eye contact with his victim one last time. "If I ever see you two again, I will cut you down. There will be no mercy."

Alarmed, Bowen asks, "Commander Galen, sir, you can't seriously be letting them go?"

Galen ignores his lieutenant commander and glances instead at Fire. "That you would choose this as your reward..." He sheathes his sword and moves briskly to rendezvous with his men. Bowen reluctantly follows, and they disappear into the darkness, taking the last of the torchlight with them.

Fire spits in Galen's direction and extends a hand to Era. "Are you able to stand?"

Era weakly slaps Fire's hand away. "You... You really sold us out?"

"I didn't sell you out, I saved your life," she says.

"They took Di!" Era cries, his voice trembling as he summons what strength he has left. "You betrayed her. You betrayed me! How could you do something so...?"

"Look, I did what I had to do. What you could never have done for yourself."

He glares at her in disgust. "You're the most cold-blooded person I've ever met. Are you even human?"

He tries to stand, but the pain is too much to bear. Jem forces him back and says, "Hey, Era, I think Fire just saved us. Let's all calm down and-"

"She didn't save us, she led them right to us! She sold out a child!"

Fire clenches her fists, her anger rising. "The princess was fated to end up in their hands. Sacrificing her was necessary for you to survive."

"Di's life isn't something you can-"

"This is the military, fool!" Fire screams. "Were you going to protect her forever? They would have gotten her eventually, and you two as well. This was the only way! You know this!"

Through sheer will, Era stands upright enough to gaze into Fire's eyes. "Get out of my sight."

"You stubborn, arrogant...!" Fire turns and storms off with a huff. "We're even now! I owe you nothing."

As Era watches her disappear into the surrounding darkness, the dizziness becomes too great to bear, and he collapses into Jem. She eases him to the ground, and she's comforted to find him merely passed out.

The silence of the forest brings a peace to the long day, and she wipes the tears as a strange relief settles in. "It's over," she whispers. "It's finally over."

*   *   *

Galen marches briskly into the encampment that had been established to recover the missing asset. Now that she's back in custody, it will be torn down and its soldiers relocated to their original deployments.

"Commander Galen," a soft voice calls from the shadows. "It seems your mission is a success."

"Yes, thanks in no small part to your efforts here, Commander Talkem," Galen says, not particularly pleased to be interacting with his peer.

Talkem approaches Galen, his expression difficult to make out due to a scarf pulled tightly over his mouth and nose. The middle-aged commander has his graying hair cut short, and his bright blue eyes sparkle with golden flakes. "I'm pleased to see the Raging Flame making full use of Merc Market resources."

"Please do not call me that," Galen utters with disdain. "Yes, I used your resources. They didn't come cheap."

"But they worked," Talkem says as he leans close and lowers his voice. "There is no shame in what you did, young Commander. They are resources to be used. That is all." With that, he turns and says, "I will return to Yugar, then. Do your best not to lose her again."

Galen watches Talkem leave the camp. Originally a renowned mercenary, the Merc Market leader was drafted as the war dragged on, and he benefited from the leadership vacuum existing after the treaty was signed. Galen has often wondered just how deep his underworld connections run.

Shaking that off, he flings the tent flap aside and finds his asset on the ground, bound by ropes and surrounded by soldiers. She trembles at the bright orange flecks that highlight his green eyes, yet she summons the courage to speak. "What did you do to my friends?"

"You need not worry about them anymore," he coldly replies. "You won't see them again."

Di's heart sinks at the answer, and her head hangs low as all the hope she had mustered comes crashing down on her. She squeezes her eyes shut, refusing to mourn before her captor.

"Needless to say, I will not be letting you out of my sight," Galen says. "Now, if you please, we must complete our original journey."

The soldiers force Di to her feet and lead her from the tent as Galen follows. He barks an order, and two platoons of soldiers accompany the entourage out of camp.

CHAPTER 18

Era opens his eyes to find himself lying on the hard forest floor, staring up at a cloudy noonday sky. He cringes as his severe burns provide a painful reminder of the previous evening's events. "Jem," he calls out, frantic to find his partner. "Jem, where are you?"

"Right behind you," the Allerian answers with a yawn. Era twists his head to find Jem reclined against a tree, wiping the sleep from her eyes.

"Where's Fire?"

Jem scoots next to her partner. "Gone. You made it pretty clear that's what you wanted."

Era recalls the end of their exchange. "And then?"

"Then you collapsed from your injuries, and I set myself up as a sentry." Rubbing her swollen cheek, she admits, "Guess I dozed off, myself. We were both in pretty bad shape last night, though I can't hold a candle to what you experienced."

He squeezes his eyes shut as those horrible images flood his mind. Dozens of soldiers. Jem captured and beaten. Di dragged away. The commander's flames, and the intensity of his assault. "I never stood a chance against that guy," Era realizes.

"No, you didn't," Jem bluntly states. "Frankly, I don't think we could have won if we had double-teamed him. He fought like one of the four commanders, all right. In the end, he got what he set out to get."

"Only because of Fire," Era laments. "You were right about her, Jem. I can't believe I trusted her."

Jem leans back on her hands. "Era, I spent a lot of time thinking about things last night. I don't think Fire cashed in on the reward money. It's pretty clear she asked for her payment to be... well, that our crimes against the military would be absolved."

Era pauses at the thought. "Even if that's true, she sacrificed Di to do it. How cold-hearted do you have to be to sell out a teenaged schoolgirl?"

"She decided Di would never be able to escape the military," Jem surmises. "Even if her calculations were cold-hearted, that doesn't mean she was wrong." Reluctantly, she adds, "I think maybe... she made the right decision."

Era's jaw drops. "Jem, you can't be serious! She sacrificed a person... she sacrificed *Di* to-"

"What is Di to us, Era?" his partner demands. "We just met her a week ago. She was a client who hired our services, and without a down payment! Protecting her was never worth throwing away our lives."

"But on the ship you said-"

"I was wrong, okay?" Jem bursts out. "I mean, I'm not saying we should have turned her in, but the military would have captured her eventually, right? And we'd be dead for our troubles." Softly, she adds, "I almost watched you die last night, Era. She wasn't worth that cost. Not to me."

Era squeezes his eyes shut. "Even if they would have captured her eventually... Even if there was a chance I'd be killed for it, I can't accept the decision to abandon her just so I can live." He grimaces and says, "You were right about me, Jem. I was never able to separate myself emotionally from her. I'll never be like Fire. She doesn't have an emotional bone in her body."

"You think Fire wasn't emotional?" Jem asks. "Era, the only reason she saved us was because she wanted you to live. She started caring about you."

Era blinks in surprise. "I think that's impossible."

"Got a better theory?" Jem asks. "You changed her somehow. I know she didn't give up thousands of venni for *me*."

"She cared about me?" he squeaks. The notion is a sharp contrast to the narrative he had constructed.

"She's human, Era. She was probably planning a betrayal all along, but somewhere along the way she decided that she didn't want to see you dead. She traded the money for our lives." She leans back and looks at the sky. "She gave us a second chance. We should be grateful."

"Grateful!?" Era forces himself up to his knees, powering through the pain. "Jem, she sacrificed Di. Like her life had no value!" Sternly, he adds, "I know what Fire did made sense. I know it kept us alive. But my father once gave me some good advice-"

"Era, look," she says impatiently, "your father was a great man and all, but his advice was-"

"He said to value all life, Jem," he continues. "He said that I... that *nobody* has the right to take a life, to decide who lives and who dies. Fire chose our lives over Di, and I can't accept that."

Jem is stunned that such words could come from such a bastion of misguidance. "Even then, what's done is done. We have to move on."

"No, I can't move on, Jem. I can't just abandon Di," he grunts as he manages to stand. "I need to report this to her father, or the Canterin police, or *somebody*."

"That entire platoon of soldiers from last night could still be in town," she argues. "Remember what the commander said to us last night? We need them to forget about us, Era. We had a plan, so let's stick to it."

"That would be smart," he agrees, "but I'm going to Canterin. And from there I'll go to Satari if I must. I have to get her back."

He starts walking, but Jem stays behind, watching her partner painstakingly force his legs to move. "Era," she says, her voice trembling, "Era, I can't do it. I can't..."

Era offers an empathetic nod. "This is my choice, Jem. I'm not going to ask you to risk your life for me."

Now angry, Jem shouts, "You might die, Era! Last night, you really almost died! If you go to Satari, you won't come back in one piece. I just know it."

He pauses to reflect on her words. "That could happen, I know."

Jem plants her hands on her hips. "So that's it? After two years of my superior tutelage, you're just going to leave me for that girl? After Fire gave up all that money to let you keep your life, you're going to throw it away? For crying out loud, Era! What about your dream to become a world-renowned thief? Are you going to throw that away, too?"

Somberly, he replies, "What kind of thief would I be if I can't steal Di back?"

The simple response shatters Jem's resolve, and she turns away to hide her crimson face. "Fine, go then. Go steal her back."

"Jem, I-"

"Just go!" she yells.

Era nods his understanding. "Thanks Jem. For everything. You're the best teacher I've ever had." With that, he limps gingerly toward Canterin, and, as his footsteps fade into the quiet of the forest, Jem finds herself truly alone for the first time since meeting Era.

*   *   *

As the train rattles beneath her, Di thinks back to the previous night, when they escorted her into Canterin. To think she had finally returned home after such an ordeal, only to be back in the custody of her kidnappers. She desperately wanted to scream out for help, but the commander had wisely gagged her before entering the city. She searched desperately for anyone who might recognize her, but the hour was so late that few people were in the streets. The train departed before sunrise, allowing them to leave under cover of darkness.

Their ride grinds to a halt at its destination, and Galen prompts Di to stand and exit. She reluctantly complies, terrified about what's in store for her. After descending to the dusty ground, she's surprised to find their destination is such a remote town, if one can even call it that. The houses are made of caked mud, and there's little foliage as far as she can see. A weathered sign next to the stop says, "Welcome to Grasis".

Di is led into town, where she's guided toward a run-down building with "PUB" painted in thick, black letters above the door. She steps into the poorly lit tavern, which sports only a single patron.

Commander Galen gently prods Di toward the individual enjoying his drink in the back of the bar. Resting his glass on the table, he studies her with a dubious glare.

Galen salutes. "General Graff, sir! I've retrieved the asset per your request."

The general stands and plants his hand on Galen's shoulder. "Excellent work, Commander." Towering over his coveted target, he offers his hand and says, "My name is Worren Graff, and I serve as general over the entire Valvoran military. Pleased to meet you, Miss...?"

Di looks back at Galen, who nudges her to prompt a response. Reluctantly, she takes the general's hand, finding skin that has been roughed by decades of callouses from handling a sword. "My name is Di. Di Venelli."

"Di? There's a name I've not heard." He indicates for her hands to be untied, and a soldier obliges. "And just who are you, Di?"

Confused, Di wonders if he really doesn't know. "I'm a student of the Three Pillars Academy, and I'm from Canterin. My father is the mayor."

Graff beckons for her to take a seat, and she dares not disobey. The general's heavy presence is instilled with an authority felt even by a civilian such as Di, and she finds an intense purpose in his gaze. He watches her, studies her, and waits for her to understand that he is someone to fear. It is not a long wait.

The general ultimately folds his hands on the table and says, "Di, I apologize tremendously for the way you have been treated. Please know that we would not be so desperate to bring you here, except that there are reports of Allerian mobilization." Taking another drink from his mug, he slams it down loudly. "War is coming, Di. And you're purportedly the means to our victory."

Di's confusion doesn't escape his notice. "You don't know what I'm talking about." It isn't a question, yet she musters the strength to shake her head, and he says, "Frankly, I haven't placed stock in the reports being true. But if our informant is to be believed," he says, disdainfully, "you are the key to powerful technology located deep in this desert country of the Berev. A Third Kingdom weapon, if you can believe it."

In shock, she glances at Galen, but he remains stoically focused.

"So here we are, in this remote blemish on the map of our great nation, with a youth who grasps nothing." Finishing his drink, he stands and starts toward the exit. "Rest assured, little lady, you will be returned home when all this is done. Weapon or not, I can only assume you'll be of little use to us once we're through."

Di follows after him in disbelief. "I'll go home?" she whispers to herself.

The general adjusts his cap and shields his eyes as they step into the sun. "Accursed cloudless sky." Turning back to Di, he says, "I'm afraid the location is a two-hour hike from here."

As they begin their march into the desert, the general's words haunt Di. Tears stream down her cheeks as she thinks back to her guardians. Any comfort at the thought of returning home is negated by the haunting realization that Era and Jem risked and lost everything to protect her, yet perhaps, in the end, she never needed to be protected.

"What do you mean I can't see him?" Era challenges, his voice raised in anger. "He's a public official, which means that-"

"You can't see him because he isn't here," the receptionist interrupts, annoyed by the commotion. "He's at the beachside festival today. You can find him over there."

"Oh," Era says sheepishly. "Thanks then." He retreats from City Hall, still limping as he maps out his new destination. Planted on a hill sloping to the shore, Canterin is more populous than he'd imagined, and the oceanfront stretches as far as the eye can see. Impressive stone buildings line the streets, and the size of the crowds milling about in the midday atmosphere is enough to overwhelm a visitor like himself.

As he walks briskly down the street, watching all the passers-by and merchants selling their wares, he sees countless rune shops open for business. Just as Di described, runecrafting is clearly a major part of the local economy. One shop in particular is displaying a pyramidal figurine that could be made of glass, but the base is a water rune programmed to shape the element. His mind wanders back to the catacombs under Ugorzi, and the frightening water creature that was programmed to be a killing machine. Such a rune must be thousands of times more advanced than the pyramid rune.

The beachside festival is easy to spot. Kids dart around with runes that spray water at each other while dozens of young adults are engaged in a runecrafting competition, frantically etching symbols into their otherwise dormant rocks. Nearby, Era finds a judges table with a placard that reads "Mayor Venelli", where a crowd surrounds an elderly official bearing a red judge's ribbon. He is much older than expected, and Era wonders at what age he must have fathered Di. Still, Era marches forward, fighting back the dread of telling the father about his kidnapped child. Squeezing himself to the front of the crowd, he cries, "Mister Mayor, I have urgent business to discuss!"

The city's leader is surprised by the declaration. "Young man, I appreciate your desire to speak, but if you could just wait your turn-"

"It's regarding your daughter, sir. Err... Mister Mayor." Era realizes he has no idea how to properly address a mayor.

"My daughter?" he asks, perplexed. "Young man, I have no daughter."

Era is startled. "You have no...? I'm talking about Di! Short girl, long blond hair. Excellent air shaper? You sent her to the Three Pillars Academy."

He eyes Era's torn and burned clothes, clearly wondering about this disrupter's mental health. "I've never had a daughter, lad. You must have me confused with someone else."

"A-Aren't you the mayor?" he stammers.

"Well, yes, I am Canterin's mayor."

Era's mind spins as he searches desperately for an explanation. "How long have you been mayor?"

"I have been the mayor for thirty-seven years. I have three sons and no daughter," he says with concern. "I'm not sure what else to tell you."

Era is at a loss. "Di is... she's the mayor's daughter! She's spoiled, hates the outdoors, and is almost fourteen!" As he looks around in frustration, his eyes land on a lighthouse tower, almost identical to the tower they used as a rendezvous point in Kemplen. "There, that tower there! She used to hide in that tower growing up."

By now, the crowd around the mayor is growing restless over Era's insistence on continuing the conversation. "While growing up?" the mayor asks. "That tower was just finished three years ago."

Era's heart sinks straight into his gut. "I was told that... I mean, she's from Canterin, and she's-"

"Our City Hall has a department of records. If your friend grew up here, she should have a record there," he says. "Maybe you can learn more if you take a look."

Era silently nods, still in shock as he leaves the crowd, questioning whether Di really was lying to them the entire time. He glances back at the tower, which is exactly as described by Di. Convinced she at least has ties here, he heads back toward the city's center in hopes of finding the truth behind his companion's identity.

CHAPTER 19

The sun is at mid-afternoon when Era drags himself out the city gate. Frustrated and defeated, he finds the first tree on the path and slumps down against it. He stares back into the city he had been so desperate to reach, amazed by how things turned out.

The humming of a familiar tune catches his ear, and he's bewildered to find Jem wandering from the woods. She gives him a wink and does a spin. "Hey, Era! How are my new clothes?" She showcases a leather vest tied over a black tunic, and leather shorts sit over black cotton leggings extending to her knees. Her emerald necklace drapes loosely over her vest.

"N-Nice," the confused Era stammers.

"It's the latest in fashion, and my necklace looks amazing with it. This will be great for when I-"

"Jem, why are you here?" he asks, cutting to the chase.

The Allerian tries to act surprised. "Why am I here? I went shopping in Canterin, and you just happened to be here when I got done, so..."

"You came from the woods," Era points out. "Were you waiting for me?"

"Of course not! I was trying out my new clothes."

"In the woods?"

"That's where I spend all my time, isn't it?" Jem asks, getting testy.

"It's just that I thought you were-"

"We're partners, Era," she says. "We don't go abandoning each other. I... I want to help you."

"Thank goodness," he sighs in relief. "Because I don't think I can save her on my own."

"Don't get me wrong," Jem says with a huff. "I'm not in this to save Di. I'm in this to keep you alive. That's my only goal here."

Her partner grimaces. "Sorry, but I have to get her back, Jem. I'm not going to abandon-"

"I know, I know. You're as stubborn as ever, I get it," she says. "I'll help you get her back because I want you to stay alive, and you'd get killed doing it on your own." She flashes her confident grin and says, "Don't worry, I'm in."

He musters an appreciative smile. "Thanks, Jem. I wouldn't know what to do without you."

She rubs her nose awkwardly. "So anyway, you look depressed. I take it you didn't get far in there?"

"Is it that obvious?" he asks as he sits back against the tree. "Di doesn't exist."

"She doesn't exist?" Jem repeats. "Well, we know that isn't true. We traveled with her for a week, and it was annoying."

"I'm serious, Jem!" Era shouts, showing his frustration. "The mayor has no daughter. The hall of records verified it, plus I looked at every single birth record from thirteen years ago." He hangs his head and says, "I even checked the twelves and fourteens. If she was born in Canterin, it was with a different name, which I guess could be expected considering she lied about everything else."

Jem takes a seat next to Era. "So, the princess was never a princess." A sour look on her face, she gripes, "Girl sure played us."

Era slaps his forehead. "I'm such an idiot. First Fire, and now Di! They both had me completely duped."

His partner frowns. "And you still want to save her after all that?"

He reflects on this. "I guess I do." Relaxing, he rests his head back on the tree while chuckling. "Honestly, what was her plan, anyway? What did she think Fire was going to do when there was no reward? Maybe getting recaptured saved her life."

A devilish grin creeps across Jem's face. "I'd have loved to watch Fire find out there was no reward."

Era mulls the situation over in his head. "We're facing a steep task," he thinks aloud. "We need to go to Satari. To the barracks."

Jem balks. "You can't possibly be serious."

He shrugs. "Di said the military was taking her to their headquarters. We know where she is, now we just need to break her out."

"And what exactly is your plan for that?"

"I'm going to sneak in, of course," he replies, insulted. "I'll find Di, and we'll make our escape. It'll be like any other thieving operation."

"But with your poor stealth, you won't even make it past the-" Cutting herself off, she snaps her fingers and says, "Wait, I've got it! But we're going to need help." She drops a new set of clothes onto her partner's lap and gets to her feet. "You might need to get dressed up for this, depending on her mood."

Era looks to her in confusion. "Wait, all our money was left on the ship. How'd you buy these?"

"Since when do we shop with money? Now get dressed and meet me at the train station." With that, she starts her hike back into Canterin.

"Wait, Jem! What do you mean, 'depending on her mood'?" Getting no response, he looks back to the clothes in his lap and feels an incredible relief wash over him. He's sure glad she came back.

*   *   *

The southern region is far less generous than the hill countries Di and her guardians traveled. There are few trees to offer shade, and the ground is hard as rock. They long passed the last of the quarry fields, which are the only reason the tracks extend so far south.

As they come to the crest of a hill, Di takes in the view of the surrounding area. The arid land sports patches of green here and there. Rock formations begin to dot the landscape, but to the south is a flat horizon, where the hills end and an endless expanse of sand stretches as far as she can see. She reasons that those must be the wastelands, recalling that legends of the Third Kingdom are based primarily on ruins found deep within that region.

They come to two towering boulders leaning into each other. The shade is welcome as the group heads between the rocks, where another troop of soldiers is waiting. They salute the general and move aside, revealing a passage cut into the side of the craggy surface.

The general is handed a light rune, and he leads the way, motioning for Di and Galen to follow. They step into the entryway, and Di marvels at how precisely the rock has been cut. While she's gawking, she nearly falls as the ground sharply lowers. Galen steadies her shoulders, allowing their captive to regain her footing as the steep decline takes them underground.

After descending the ramp, Graff holds the rune out to illuminate a dead end. Di observes the wall, and she instantly notices a copy of the elemental dodecagram etched into the rock. Or at least she assumes as such, as the symbols are different from what she learned at the Academy, and her academic mind searches for answers. Each manipulation is marked by a unique symbol, with a thirteenth in the center where there is usually none.

"We've had no success displacing this wall," the general explains. "You're supposedly the only one who can open it."

Di is startled. "Me? How am I supposed to do something like that?"

"That's what we're here to find out." Graff motions for Di to step forward. "Please, see what you can do."

"I have no idea how to do this, even if you ask me to-"

"I'm not asking you," the general corrects, his voice turning aggressive. "I'm ordering you to open this door."

"But that doesn't change anything!" she argues. "I can't just-"

"Our source was accurate about everything, even down to your description. A young, blond-haired Academy student who pretends to be the daughter of the mayor of Canterin."

Her brow furrows. "What did you just say?"

"I'm afraid your story doesn't check out, my dear," Graff explains. "The mayor of Canterin has no daughter."

Galen is taken aback. "Then why did she head back to Canterin?"

"Because he's wrong. My father is the mayor," Di insists, not backing down.

"Look," the general sighs, rubbing the bridge of his nose, "I don't care who you are. Perhaps you're an illegitimate child he kept secret, or otherwise some kind of adopted heir. All I'm saying is that we have compelling evidence that you're the key to whatever lies beyond this door. As such, I expect you to open it."

Di swallows hard, shaken by the accusation. Faced with little other choice, she extends an open palm to the general. "Light, please?" He hands it to her, and she studies the inscribed etchings. The new symbols are unlike any she has studied. If there's a puzzle to be solved, she's stumped, and she rests her hand against the carvings to apply force to it.

The moment her fingers touch the cold, stone surface, the back of her hand begins to glow. Startled by the bizarre phenomenon, Di jumps back, her heart pounding as the glow fades. "What was that?"

"Again!" Graff shouts, stepping forward and grabbing the rune from her. "Do that again."

Di obeys, and the back of her hand once more shines. Staring at it in wonder, she realizes one of the wall's foreign symbols is now emblazoned on her skin: an outer circle with a diagonal chord and two inner circles tangent to it, one larger than the other. As it glows, the matching symbol on the wall illuminates in tandem.

The wall abruptly crumbles into a pile of rock and sand. As the dust clears, the bewildered academic finds the glowing symbol has vanished. The sound of clapping breaks into her thoughts, and she turns to find Graff displaying his approval. "Looks like you were special after all, Di."

"Sir, that was…" Galen starts, but he cannot find the words to describe what he just witnessed. "Did you know?"

"I'm learning right alongside you," Graff admits. He turns back and whistles loudly, signaling for troops to descend the ramp and proceed into the corridor with light runes. Stepping through the pile of sand left behind by the door, the group plunges into the catacombs. Di glances at the general as they walk, but he shows no sign of awe or reverence. He marches with a purpose, his intention set on finding his prize.

Di follows the soldiers until she finds herself on a platform overlooking a large room, filled with an eerie glow produced by four distinct barriers of light against the far wall. The soldiers mutter amongst themselves at the strange sight.

"What kind of place is this?" the general mumbles, running his hand along the smooth walls as he descends the stairs to the floor below.

Metallic furniture is strewn about the room, intact and ready for use despite one corner of the facility having collapsed. Glass panels line the walls, and a multitude of consoles rise from the ground before the four barriers. Each pulsating wall is translucent, revealing a small chamber on the other side. Above each barrier is one of the four new symbols from earlier, as if providing a unique label to each of the protected alcoves.

"This must be it," the general declares.

Puzzled, Galen wonders about the meaning of the symbols and their respective barriers. "Are there four weapons, then?"

"Regardless, it appears the girl matches with only one of these symbols." He motions for Di to move up. "If you would."

Di is far more intimidated by the wall of light than the wall of stone. Cringing, she reaches her hand out to the barrier, and a powerful electric bolt zaps her the moment she touches it. She shrieks and jams her finger into her mouth with a whimper.

"It didn't work?" the general asks, not showing any concern for her injury. "Then how are we supposed to get in there?"

Galen's eyes fall to a dark panel on the wall separating two of the light barriers. "Maybe this?"

The general studies it before glancing to Di. "Come take a look."

Still teary-eyed from the jolt, Di approaches the panel, wary of the barriers of light to either side as she carefully reaches for the glass pane. She touches it with a single finger before resting her entire palm on it, and the cool surface begins to glow.

The light barrier corresponding to Di's symbol disappears with a loud pop, revealing what lies within. A wide, cylindrical pillar is at the center of the inner chamber. It stands about as tall as Di, and a section is carved out of the back wall, where metallic instruments and restraints are left hanging open, as if a prisoner was once held here against his or her will.

The general studies the pillar and the space around it with disapproval. "Nothing in here looks like a weapon. Perhaps the key needs to work more magic."

Di grows frustrated by the constant demands. "I already opened the doors. What else can I do? Maybe it's gone."

"With this security, it's impossible anyone managed to get in before us. Not without you, at least." He studies her suspiciously and asks, "Have you been here before?"

"No!"

"Then find my weapon," he impatiently demands.

Di hurries into the cramped chamber and begins searching for anything interesting. "Is this obelite?" she wonders aloud, resting her hand atop the centerpiece. She comes back to the front and finds a pair of gaping holes in the stone pillar, as if inviting her to insert her hands. An unnerving glance from the general tells her that she has better give it a try, and she pushes her clenched fists inside.

The contact triggers a mechanism within to clench down over her wrists. She yelps in response as a loud buzzing begins vibrating the room, and the pillar illuminates brilliantly. Di shrieks loudly as the bystanders can do nothing but shield their eyes.

Just when it all becomes too great to bear, the buzzing stops and the light fades. As their eyes readjust, Graff finds Di leaning against the pillar, still standing under her own power as she withdraws her arms. More noticeable than Di, however, is a brilliant ball of light sitting atop the pillar. It glows a beautiful shade of yellow, and everyone beholds the sight in awe.

Graff storms in and flings Di behind him. Galen catches her, though his focus remains on the mysterious object.

Puzzled, Di finds that her forearms now bear bronze bands, intricately engraved with the same symbol emblazoned on her hands. A radiant gemstone is embedded near each of her wrists, and she marvels at how these accessories abruptly appeared. She yanks at the armlets, but she's unable to remove them.

"This is the weapon?" the general exclaims. The perfectly-formed orb appears sized to fit in the palm of one's hand. It gives off no heat, no sound, and it doesn't seem to affect the pillar as it rests atop it.

His curiosity piqued, the general reaches out and touches it with his right hand. The instant he makes contact, the orb cracks loudly and disappears with a blinding flash of light. The general snaps his hand back as a sharp pain penetrates into his flesh. It's all he can do to prevent himself from screaming in front of his subordinates, and he furiously massages his hand to dull the pain. The symbol they've all grown accustomed to seeing is now emblazoned where the pain entered his hand, printed in the two o'clock position on his palm.

"General, are you okay?" Galen calls out.

"I'm fine," Graff answers, staring at the place where the glowing orb once sat, "but where did the weapon go?"

"The weapon is right in front of you."

The soldiers draw their swords and point them at the newcomer, who seems unfazed by the display of aggression. Bearing a smile, he places his hands in the air as he walks into the room. "Good to see you again, General Graff. And good to see you too… Di, was it? Is your guardian not with you?" A chill runs down Di's spine as she comes face-to-face with the traveler she met in the woods outside Ugorzi.

"Ares," Graff mutters with disdain. "How did you get past my men outside?"

"I have my ways," he explains as he casually strolls into their midst. "More importantly, I see you've found the weapon. Excellent work."

"What do you mean, we've found it? The weapon just disappeared before our eyes!"

Ares looks at him with exaggerated confusion. "Disappeared? But General, the weapon stands right before you." He looks at the pillar again, and Ares sighs. "The weapon is short, blond, wears a tattered outfit... Need I go on?"

All eyes shift to Di, and the bewildered youth's heart races at the attention. "What?"

Frustrated, Graff grabs Ares by his collar. "What do you mean by calling this runt a weapon? What's she good for besides opening doors?"

"General, the proof is right there," Ares says playfully, pointing at the general's hand. "The object absorbed into your hand was the key that makes you her wielder. You own her now."

"Own her?"

"Your will is her will. Diamond is a weapon, and you, my good general, are the conductor of this weapon."

"Diamond!?"

"Right. The weapon's name is Diamond."

"You're making no sense!" Graff shouts as he shoves Ares back. "You had better start explaining yourself or-"

"Look, let me start over," Ares calmly interrupts. "Diamond is the weapon you sought. As her conductor, you now wield this powerful weapon, and you can use her in any way you desire. Go ahead and give a command!" When Graff's confusion persists, he adds, "Order her to do something out of the ordinary, a physical feat you wouldn't expect her to be able to do. Trust me."

The general's nostrils flare. "It will cost you dearly if you're trying to make a fool of me." He turns to Di, tying to make sense of Ares' claims. He clears his throat and states, "Diamond, go... do a backflip."

Di just stares back, at a loss. "I can't do a backflip," she squeaks.

Graff turns and glares at Ares, who already has his hands in the air waving. "Hey, hey, you can't just tell her to do something. You need to will it. Use her like you would a weapon."

Furious, the general moves at Ares aggressively. "I've had enough nonsense out of you-"

"Your sword is an extension of your body, right?" Ares asks. "You don't ask it to do something. You take it in your hand, and you *make* it do what you want. The sword is an extension of your will." Motioning to Di he says, "Do the same thing with this weapon."

Graff looks at his hand, again eyeing the symbol engraved into his palm. Somehow, what Ares says feels right. He extends his arm toward Di's forehead and meets her eyes.

Di feels a heavy sense of dread as she finds herself unable to look away from the intimidating war veteran. His presence exudes a dominating authority. She wants desperately to run away, yet she finds herself frozen where she stands.

The general opens his palm, and the symbol on his hand begins glowing. The symbols on the back of Di's hands reappear and glow in response as he forcefully speaks. "Do... a... backflip."

The order barely escapes his lips before Di leaps vertically into the air, performing a perfect backflip. She lands gracefully with her arms poised out to her sides, her demeanor one of great satisfaction, as if the act was nothing abnormal to perform. However, the moment passes, and a bewildered expression returns to her. "What? How did I just...?"

"Diamond is a weapon like no other," Ares chimes in. "If you want her to sing, she'll sing. If you want her to dance, she'll dance." Pausing for effect, he adds, "If you want her to kill, she'll kill."

Di is horrified by his words as she tries to figure out how and why she just performed the backflip at Graff's command. It wasn't that she was forced to do it. She wanted to do it, and she took great pleasure in doing so.

Graff isn't impressed with Ares' suggestion. "What's she going to do, scratch someone to death?"

"Did you not notice the backflip, general?" Ares asks while extending a finger and spinning it around in the air. "Flawless. Perfectly timed and executed. Complete control of momentum and balance. This isn't the weak little schoolgirl who's been slipping through your fingers. This is a weapon, designed to kill."

"I'm a person!" Di cries out, tears welling in her eyes. "Stop calling me a 'weapon' and talking about me like I'm not here!"

Ares frowns. "I expected you to remember everything the moment you received your bonds, but I guess there was no such revelation. Needless to say, you're not the person you think you are. You're Diamond."

"And stop calling me Diamond! My name is Di! I'm just… I'm just a normal girl from Canterin."

"You're not the daughter of a mayor, Diamond," he says.

"Then who is she?" the general barks.

"Isn't it obvious?" Ares asks. "She's from the Third Kingdom. A weapon used in the war three hundred years ago. She's been asleep in this very chamber ever since, having only resurfaced two years ago."

"You're speaking nonsense," Graff insists. "How is it possible for someone to sleep for three hundred years without aging?"

"The answer is simpler than you'd think," Ares answers, his smile twisting into something more sinister. "Diamond isn't human. She's a rune."

CHAPTER 20

The declaration prompts everyone to turn to Di. Tears now stream down her cheeks as she fails to understand the bizarre claim.

"Technically, she's a very special kind of rune," Ares explains. "She's a runic, created and programmed by the Third Kingdom."

Di can only manage to stammer weakly in defense. "That... That makes no sense! I'm not three hundred years old. I was born in Canterin! Fourteen years ago."

"Your memories are nothing more than a construct meant to strengthen your alibi," Ares explains. "They are not real."

Her gaze turns wild. "I'm from Canterin! Daddy... Daddy is the mayor! I grew up in Canterin!" She collapses to her knees, overwhelmed and dizzy.

"Stand up," the general barks, and her hands glow in response as she instantly jumps to her feet. Her eyes are filled with a lonely sadness as she chokes back tears.

"Remember, General, she's a weapon," Ares points out. "Her air shaping capability is elite. Use that to your advantage!"

Graff grows annoyed by the informant. "We're done here. Ares, you will be escorted back to the capital. You have held back critical knowledge until now, and you will tell us everything you know." The soldiers surround Ares with weapons drawn.

Ares drops his smile. "I'll play along for now, but don't leave me bored for too long." Graff waves them away, opting not to give him the satisfaction of a retort.

Galen studies Di, fuming at the turn of events. Never would he have imagined that this was the reason he was pursuing this child. He looks to his superior and says, "Surely you don't take him at his word, General."

"I would be crazy to do that," he replies. "However, we've seen for ourselves that something strange is going on here. I want another test without that aggravating fool present." He pats the commander's shoulder and says, "You're going to duel her."

Galen is aghast. "Sir! You can't possibly expect me to spar with a child."

"Whether she's a child or not is what I want to verify," Graff explains. "We must validate his claims."

"General, I cannot-"

"You will do this, Commander," Graff demands. "Now give us some space as I prepare the weapon." Frustrated, Galen storms to the other side of the room.

The general looks at Di in the pulsating light from the three remaining barriers illuminating the chamber. "What do you know of all this? Surely you must know something."

Di lowers her eyes. "I know nothing."

Not satisfied, Graff extends a hand toward her, the symbol on his hand aglow. "Tell me what you know about yourself."

Her hands shine in response, and Di looks up with sadness. "I know absolutely nothing."

Graff sighs, annoyed that Ares remains his only source of information. He had hoped to make the arrogant youth irrelevant. "Well, regardless, I want to see what you can do. Your opponent is one of my most elite soldiers, so you'd best not hold back, Diamond."

She shivers at the name that seems so cold and foreign, and she glances to the diamonds embedded into her new armlets. Her mind wanders to her father, growing up by the sea, hiding away in the lighthouse, the beachside festivals every year… She yearns to break away and run home. She can't begin to imagine a scenario where her father isn't waiting for her with open arms.

"General," Galen calls out, "with all due respect, I wish to decline this order. Please have respect for my dignity."

Di finds a devilish grin spread across the general's face. "Perhaps your appearance is one of your greatest assets as a weapon, Diamond," he suggests. "Go knock him unconscious."

Graff's words penetrate her mentality as her hand symbols glow in response to the command. Suddenly, nothing else matters to her. Not her father, not her humanity, but only the mission to take the commander

260

out. Inwardly scoffing at how weak Galen now appears, she wonders why she was ever afraid of him.

Di's shift in demeanor doesn't go unnoticed by the general. He raises his eyebrows as his purported weapon sprints at her opponent with a burst of speed.

"You've got to be kidding me," Galen mutters to himself as he shifts to a defensive stance.

Di lunges at him, her fist extended. He sidesteps the attack and reaches to restrain her, but she reacts quickly and slaps his hand away. She unleashes two sharp jabs, which he blocks, though he's taken aback by the force she delivers with each blow.

As she continues her one-sided assault, Galen calls out, "General, please stop this! I'm not interested in-oomph!" Di lands a successful punch to Galen's gut, prompting him to take a defensive swipe at her. She dodges and slams her target forcefully in the chest, then kicks his knees out from behind, grabs his uniform, and yanks him backward. He hits the floor with a slam that echoes throughout the chamber.

The commander groans, revealing to Di that her mission is not yet complete. She raises her foot above her downed opponent's forehead, but Graff calls out, "Diamond, stop!"

As her mentality returns, Di stares down at the villain who had pursued her relentlessly, bewildered by how harmless he now seems. She feels proud of the victory and her newfound capabilities until the general exclaims, "Well done, Diamond! I think things are starting to become clearer."

The excitement fades as she is reminded of the greater reality of her situation. She looks at her hands, noticing again the armlets around her wrists, and her mind spins as she tries to reconcile what just happened. She never lost awareness as she executed the general's order, yet everything within her gave way to a desire to accomplish the mission, as if the general's will had become her own until she accomplished her directive.

With Galen on the ground, it occurs to her that only one of her captors remains. Seizing the opportunity, she charges at her newfound master, catching him by surprise as she throws a punch straight toward his gut.

The general glares at his assailant. "What was that supposed to be, Diamond?"

Di is panting heavily, her fist mere inches from the general's stomach, but she can't force herself to make contact. Blinking back tears of frustration, she tries to uppercut his chin, but her fist swings wide and misses, as if a mental barrier is preventing her from landing a hit.

The general backhands Di across the cheek, sending her to the floor. "Fortunately, it seems you cannot attack your master, though apparently the inverse isn't true." He places a foot on Di's hand, making her squirm as he presses down on it. "Insolent girl, I will not let such an act go unpunished."

As Di cries out in pain, Galen calls, "Sir, she's just a child!"

Graff pauses in contemplation. Ultimately, he steps over his new weapon and motions for her to follow. "We're headed back to Satari. Come along, Diamond."

The order isn't a forced one, but Di knows there is little point in disobeying. "Satari," she whispers to herself, sobbing as she comes to grasp the hopelessness of her situation.

As they disappear into the tunnels, Galen slams the ground in frustration. He looks to the pulsating barriers, trying to process Ares' claims, Graff's actions, and what he should believe about it all.

*   *   *

Era sips his water, once again enjoying the small amount of luxury. He happily watches as the tavern owner returns to the kitchen to retrieve his stew.

"And just how are you planning on paying for that?" Jem asks in annoyance.

He leans forward, keeping his voice low. "I already ate here twice, and I paid for it both times. The way I see it, they owe me a free meal."

"But we're not here to eat, you dummy."

"Then we should have eaten earlier. I'm hungry."

Jem sits back with in annoyance. "We need to get some cash. We barely had enough to pay for the train ride to Duroshe."

"And that was only after spending an hour shoplifting," Era admits. "Good thing the pawn shop didn't ask too many questions."

The door opens, and Jem and Era find their guest has arrived. The silver-haired Pearl sees Era and excitedly waves to him, though she scrunches her nose at the sight of Jem.

Era hopes his face isn't crimson as he fights off the memory of that special moment on the sky boat. He stands and pulls a chair out for his guest.

"Ugh, Era, you're not on a date tonight," Jem bemoans, resting her chin on one hand. "Get over yourself."

"You're just mad I didn't help you to your seat," Era snidely responds as he sits.

"Darn right, I am. What's the matter, am I not feminine enough for you?"

"You? Ha! You act like you were raised by a pack of fire wolves."

Pearl sits back as the partners bicker, and their host comes to deliver a water. She politely turns down anything more and waits for the pair to finish their argument.

"Fine, whatever," Jem finishes with a huff. "Pearl's here, so let's talk business."

"Yes, please," Pearl jumps in. "The note you left in my pilot seat said nothing other than where to meet you." Quietly, she adds, "You didn't mention you had company with you."

Era sheepishly shrugs. "Sorry for being so secretive. We didn't want to approach in plain sight and get you into more trouble. I assume your father was angry about taking us to Kemplen?"

"Oh, he was furious!" Pearl exclaims with her gray eyes open wide. "But that's my fault. If I'd not overslept, I would have been back in time to conduct business." Pausing, she realizes, "You haven't been gone long at all. Why are you back?"

Era looks to Jem to get the go-ahead to fill Pearl in. "Well, when we were here last, we were kind of on the run."

"Yes, that was obvious," Pearl says.

"From one of the four commanders."

She crosses her arms and smirks. "Was he in league with the water monsters you dispatched so bravely?"

His brow furrows. "No, and it was just one water monster," he corrects matter-of-factly. "Galen was after Di for some reason. They ambushed us in the forest outside Canterin and took her to Satari."

"Fortunately, they started the trains back up once they recaptured her," Jem says.

"That was because of you?" she asks in disbelief.

"It was no coincidence," Era insists with an edge in his tone. "They sent an entire platoon of soldiers to surround and capture us. They were desperate to get her back."

"So, wait, all this is the truth?" Pearl realizes. "How did you escape?"

Era's head droops, and Jem jumps in. "Fire saved us, but she wasn't able to save Di."

"Oh yes, the mean one," Pearl recalls. "She was mean."

Keeping his voice low, Era leans close to Pearl and says, "We're going to get Di back. We want to raid the military barracks." Pointing skyward, he adds, "From above."

Pearl laughs aloud. "You want me to land on top of the military headquarters?"

"Don't be ridiculous," Jem scoffs. "Your death trap makes far too much noise to land on it. All you need to do is fly us over it."

Excitement creeps across her face. "You're going to jump?"

Era nods his acknowledgment. "We know this is risky. We're storming the military headquarters of all places. There's no easy way to do it, but this is the best way."

Pearl studies him closely. "You two are taking an awful risk for this girl. Just what is she to you, anyway?"

Era frowns as he searches for the answer. "It's complicated, I guess. She's a friend. One worth fighting for."

"But Satari is a trip," Jem says. "Can you sneak off for that long?"

"It's a sixteen hour flight," Pearl agrees. "Still, the timing isn't bad. I'm taking a haul to Pigo in two days. From there it's just a three hour flight to Satari, so it's doable." She contemplates the idea before shaking it off. "No... No, this isn't a good idea. I mean no offense, Era, but this just seems too dangerous."

Era leans forward, placing his hand on her arm. "Pearl, I know this is a lot to ask. We're asking a huge favor we could never repay. But if you don't help us, we'll sneak into that barracks the hard way. Dropping us in might actually help us to live."

Pearl looks at his hand. "You want to save her that badly, huh?" Summoning her determination, she says, "Then I want something in return for my help."

"Fine, you can have another date," Jem says.

"I'm not interested in buying another date." She eyes Era and says, "I want you to take a job with the operation."

"Huh?" Jem asks. "What job? What are you talking about?"

Era furrows his brow. "Pearl, you're serious about that?"

Jem pounds the table. "What job?" she demands.

"We need someone like Era at the operation," Pearl explains. "We're short-handed, and he would be a great fit."

"Absolutely not," Jem tells her. "A great fit? Have you met Era?"

"You may think him incapable, but I know he'll do great."

"I'm not talking about that," Jem argues. "Era wants to be a master thief. He'll never accomplish that while working for you."

"Smuggling is like thievery," she says, not backing down. "He'll adapt, I'm sure he will."

"Adapt?" she shouts, standing in anger. "I'll have you know that Era comes from a long line of-"

Era places his hand on his partner's arm. "Jem, please." When she sits with a huff, he asks Pearl, "How long would you want me to work there?"

She contemplates this and answers, "One year. But I know you'll love it, Era. I know you'll want to stay longer if you give it a chance."

Jem opens her mouth to speak, but Era cuts her off and says, "I'll do it." He looks to Jem and says, "This isn't about me, Jem. I might not even survive all this. If I come out alive and Di is safe, I'll gladly trade a year of my life."

"Era, she's a manipulative con artist!" Jem shouts. "She won't let you go after a year, and you're far too loyal to leave without her permission."

"Even so, we need Pearl's help," he says, turning back to the pilot. "You'll do this for us if I agree?"

She extends her hand. "I will."

"And Jem and Di, I want them to have jobs too."

Pearl hesitates but says, "They're welcome as well."

Without hesitation, Era shakes her hand. "Deal."

Jem sits in disbelief at the exchange. The owner chooses that moment to deliver Era's bowl of soup, and he happily partakes. Pearl sits back in her seat with great satisfaction, leaving Jem to stew over the exchange as the group now sits in heated silence.

*　　*　　*

Though the majority of the military's prisoners are held outside the city, a small holding room in the barracks is used for military prisoners of special interest. A guard stands and salutes Graff on his arrival, and the general marches to the only populated cell, finding his prisoner lying on the floor, his arm draped over his eyes. "Okay, Ares. It's time to talk."

He energetically sits and meets his interrogator expectantly. "Talking is what I want to do, General. What do you want to talk about?"

Graff crosses his arms in disgust. "The most obvious questions are 'how' and 'why'. How do you know so much, and why have you given the information away? If you're planning to collect on this debt in the future-"

Ares cuts him off with an upheld hand. "General, we've already discussed this. I'm simply concerned about the growing Allerian threat."

"I'm not buying that," Graff snaps. "Why not claim the weapon for yourself? Don't tell me you were above such a temptation."

"To answer your question directly, I'm simply not capable of being a conductor. Only those with special stature can lay claim to a runic. You know: kings, princes, dukes." His expression turns sly as he adds, "Generals."

The claim is surprising, but Graff is certain there must be a good reason for Ares not taking Di for himself. "Then explain how you know all this. You knew everything about the weapon: where to find it, what it looks like, how to use it…"

"Ah, already calling the weapon an 'it', are you, General?" Ares stretches out and reclines against the back wall. "I mean, you're technically right. Diamond is no more a girl than a rune that produces a statue of a girl."

"Quit dawdling and answer the question."

"You're so impatient, General," he chides. "If you must know, I merely inherited this knowledge. My master before me devoted his life to it, only to make his most significant discoveries at the end of his days. He left everything to me in hopes I would make good use of the information."

"Who was this master of yours?" the general demands to know.

"He was a nobody," Ares responds. "A dropout of the Three Pillars Academy nearly sixty years ago. While he was there, he stumbled onto crucial information deep within the school's vast archives. He became so obsessed with his research that he couldn't bear to spend any time on his studies, and he was expelled. Fortunately, he was able to smuggle his notes and resources out so he could continue his research."

"And you? What's your story?"

"You want to know about me? I'm honored, General," he says. "I'm also a nobody, someone who wouldn't have known an air rune from a water one. I was desperate to learn a trade in the wake of the war's end, and we happened upon one another. I was his apprentice until the day he died."

The general grows frustrated with Ares' surprisingly reasonable answers, none of which explains his near-supernatural ability to sneak around so effectively.

"What's your impression so far, General?" Ares asks, turning the conversation around. "Do you like your new weapon?"

The general rubs the bridge of his nose. "The weapon has strength, but its personality is a great weakness. I intend to see how effectively I can erase its memories and persona, then maybe it will be-"

"Ah-ah, I wouldn't do that, General."

Graff raises an eyebrow. "Oh? And why should I leave the whiny brat as it is?"

Ares eagerly replies, "Free will is essential to a runic's development. You must give it the ability to make its own decisions."

"Yes, I know that in the heat of battle, it can't be relying on my commands to-"

"It goes far deeper than that, I'm afraid," Ares interrupts, prompting an icy stare from the frustrated general. "A runic is capable of tremendous growth, but that growth is directly tied to its personality and free will. You have the power to squelch the personality if desired, but that will have a negative effect on its potential."

"You're saying I need to leave the personality alone?" Graff asks, greatly aggravated by the prospect.

"Not at all. You can do whatever you want with the personality," Ares counters. "Just don't do it using commands."

"So, I need to harden it," Graff mutters, turning toward the exit.

"Wait, General, you're going to leave me here?"

Graff glares at his prisoner. "You'll be freed later today, with high expectations that you'll deliver the other weapons. *High* expectations."

"So why not let me out now?"

"Because I hate you," he says, slamming the door as he exits.

*   *   *

"Well, if it isn't General Graff," the captain of the guard says with a salute as the officer enters the royal receiving room. "What has you visiting His Majesty today?"

"The successful conclusion to a long and arduous mission," he triumphantly declares. "All things considered, I'm feeling quite young for the first time since the war."

"Good. It'd be a shame if you keeled over from old age before I did," says Larimar as a small troop streams into the chamber. Behind them walks Di, now boasting a military uniform, alongside a military tailor. The guard captain catches sight of the youth and shakes his head, mumbling something about recruits getting younger and younger.

The general applauds at the sight of his weapon. "That uniform suits you, Diamond."

Di looks herself over with contempt. The dark garb has been perfectly sized for her frame, making her look and feel like a toy soldier. Her hair is tied back in a ponytail, and she was even given a pair of leather boots to wear. The only missing element is the armored breastplate the soldiers wear, likely because it would weigh as much as her.

"The uniform is perfect," Graff observes, "but I thought you would cut the hair short, Lairdly."

The lanky tailor salutes the general. "Sorry, sir. She refused to let me cut it off."

The general raises an eyebrow. "She refused? I instructed you to make a soldier out of her, not ask her opinion."

He rubs his stomach tenderly. "Girl has a mean punch."

Graff waves him off. "You're dismissed, Lairdly. Go back to whatever it is you do here." The unranked member of the military salutes and slinks back, grateful for the chance to make an exit. The general looks down at Di condescendingly. "You punched Lairdly? That flunky isn't worth the effort."

Di puffs her cheeks. "Nobody touches my hair."

"Excellent, Diamond, you've finally started to embrace your role as a weapon," he declares.

Agitated, she asks, "What is this all about, anyway? No one will take me seriously like this."

"You will start looking and behaving like a soldier," Graff calmly responds. "That is the purpose of today's exercise, after all."

"Exercise?" she repeats with concern.

"Nothing to fret." He nods toward the throne room doors and asks, "Are you ready for your audience with His Majesty?"

Di stands at the entrance to the king's audience chamber, studying the five seals inscribed into the towering doors. She takes a deep breath, trembling with anticipation. Never in her life did she think she would have an audience with the king of Valvoren, and she finds herself eager despite her circumstances. "Y-Yes," she stutters as her knees continue to shake.

Graff impatiently stamps his foot. "Diamond, you're not a little girl from Canterin. Ludicrous as it sounds, you're now an elite soldier in this fine military machine. You must act the part."

Di nods, but her demeanor remains anxious. Graff is annoyed by the display of weakness, and he's reminded of Ares' words about personality reconstruction. Still, he wonders if a compromise would work for this situation. He extends his palm and says, "Diamond, you will not be nervous in front of the king."

His weapon's hands glow, and the order takes effect immediately. Di is stunned at how quickly the anxiety leaves her, to the extent that she can't even remember what she was nervous about. Glancing at the back of her hands, she finds the glowing symbols fade without dropping the effect.

Graff motions to the guards, and they push the heavy doors open for the two to enter, leaving Larimar's contingent to decipher what they just witnessed.

Di is in awe of the grandeur of the throne room. Everything feels gigantic, from the ceiling height to the pillars extending along either side of the path leading to the two thrones. Light runes shine brilliantly from the ceiling above, illuminating the expansive space. There are no windows, and, as best Di can tell, there is no way in or out other than the entrance. The hall was likely built to safeguard the king should the city come under assault.

King Haran and his queen sit on their respective thrones, each planted on the raised platform at the end of the hall and anxiously awaiting the arrival of their guests. Two guards stand on either side of the throne, each bearing a long spear poised vertically. Though Di's audience is with the king, she finds herself unable to take her eyes off his radiant wife. The queen has brilliantly blond hair tied up and back, and she wears a flowing white dress that only accentuates her pale skin. A miniature version of her husband's crown rests on her head, fashioned from gold and silver, and she exudes a quiet elegance most fitting for a queen. She smiles warmly at Di, though she's clearly confused by the young soldier's presence.

Next to the thrones are four ceremonial chairs, three of which are populated by the king's advisors: Meskel Reece, the foreign minister. Crin Laffel, the science minister. Fenger Nagel, the finance minister. The fourth chair sits empty, belonging to the general when not presenting.

Di gasps at the sight of a familiar face from her days at the Academy. "Headmaster Laffel?"

The elderly advisor adjusts his spectacles. "You do look familiar. How is it I know you, young lady?"

Knowing she has only met him a handful of times, Di says, "From the Academy! I was-"

Graff clears his throat to silence Di, and he kneels before the throne. "Your Majesty, it is an honor as always." Glancing up, he adds, "And I'm glad to see Her Majesty is also feeling well enough to join us."

The king motions for him to stand. "General Graff, congratulations on your mission's success. Your report was perhaps the most optimistic I've ever received from you. I'm looking forward to your demonstration."

"As am I, my liege. But first, an introduction." Graff motions to his companion and announces, "This is Diamond." Di takes a bow, still fascinated by the magnificence of the royal pair. Graff boasts, "She is the weapon we have been hunting."

The king and queen glance at each other, and the ministers begin mumbling at the strange declaration. "Explain yourself, General," the king commands.

"This is no ordinary youngster," he says. "Diamond is far more capable in combat than perhaps even my best commanders. We have a top-notch warrior at our beck and call."

With his audience baffled, Graff extends his arm. "If you would have it, please allow me to give you a demonstration."

"I think that would be wise," the king says.

Di has started to become accustomed to receiving his orders, but she still cringes as Graff extends his palm, angling it so the king and queen can see the symbol glow in response. "Diamond, I command you to perform a series of backflips to the entrance." The symbols on her hands illuminate as she executes the feat, keeping in perfect form all the way to the doors and finishing with grace.

"Come!" the general barks, again causing their hands to glow in tandem. She runs back to him and stands at attention.

The audience is more perplexed than impressed. "Perhaps the mission wasn't a success after all," Reece scornfully suggests.

Even Haran loses patience. "I don't get it, General. Is she part of a circus act?"

"I don't understand it fully, myself," Graff admits. "However, it seems that any order I give to Diamond is executed without pause. Mysteriously, the object we found deep underground bound her to my will." He extends his open palm to the king and queen, showing them the emblazoned symbol. "This is the point of control by which she can be given any order. She must obey my commands, regardless of her own desires."

"What good is it to give orders to a child?" Laffel scoffs. "I'm disappointed, General. You claimed to discover a Third Kingdom treasure!"

"Allow me to give you the most effective demonstration I could devise," Graff calmly says. He claps his hands together three times, and the throne room doors creak open, where six prisoners are led into the throne room. Graff motions toward the new arrivals and says, "These men are captured convicts. Each one is a murderer."

The queen's eyes bulge, and even Haran looks uneasy at the declaration. The guards by the king tense at the arrival. However, the convicts themselves appear bewildered as to why they've been summoned. Several even look afraid. Di watches as the felons come closer, worried about the nature of this exercise.

The general turns and addresses the men before him. "Each of you has been convicted of murder. Your death sentences will be executed tomorrow at sunrise," he announces, which is apparently news to the group. "However, I've decided to lend you a chance to keep your life." Pausing for effect, he explains, "You will do battle with an opponent of my choice. If you win, you are free to go. Does anyone object?"

Di gulps, now seeing exactly what the general has planned. The convicts are confused, but no one is willing to turn down such an offer.

Graff looks to a guard. "Give them your sword."

The soldier is bewildered by the order, but, when it becomes apparent his superior isn't joking, he unsheathes his weapon and tosses it in front of the group. It clangs loudly in the chamber, shimmering in the glow of the hall's light runes.

The gruffest specimen doesn't hesitate to take it, tightly gripping the handle. His muscles bulge while he skillfully twirls the blade in his hand. He points the sword at Graff and growls, "Come, let me kill you."

"Me?" the general asks with contempt. "Oh no, I have no intention of fighting you." He prods Di forward. "You'll be fighting this one."

The queen gasps, and the king shifts uncomfortably in his seat. The convict looks in confusion at the petite soldier in front of him. "Her? No, I said I will kill *you!*" He flings Di aside and dashes toward Graff, who curses at the demonstration gone wrong as he unsheathes his sword in defense.

In the blink of an eye, Di appears between the general and his aggressor. The symbols on her hands aglow, she raises a palm and intercepts the strike with a thick shield of air. The assailant's blade deflects, allowing Di to drop the wall and elbow him in the stomach. She unleashes three quick strikes to the chin in succession before swiping the convict's feet out from under him. He hits the ground, and Di stomps on his head to knock him out.

The audience chamber fills with murmurs from the ministers and prisoners alike. Graff sheaths his sword, stunned by the sudden aid he received from the weapon who had just been flung to the ground. He never gave her an order, and he refuses to believe her actions stemmed from goodwill. "Take that man back to his cell," he orders, delighted to be back in control of the situation.

As the soldiers drag the unconscious prisoner out of the hall, the other convicts stand in bewilderment. Determining this time to play by the general's rules, one grabs the sword from the ground and charges Di.

Pleased, the general orders, "Diamond, knock him out."

This convict strikes boldly at Di, intending to cut through whatever barrier she had constructed before. However, instead of performing that particular defensive maneuver, she merely sidesteps the aggressive strike and elbows him in the side of the head, finishing the fight with a single blow.

"This is going too fast," Graff mutters to himself. He calls out to the guards, "More swords! One for each of them!"

The soldiers eagerly volunteer their weapons. The convicts hesitate, so Graff declares, "If any one of you kills her, you'll all be set free! So come at her, all four at once!" Desperation kicking in, they each scramble for a sword, and Graff says, "Have at it, Diamond. Take them all out."

The diminutive combatant eagerly calculates how best to take out each of her opponents. She deflects each strike with miniature shields of air while perfectly counterattacking each one.

Graff looks expectantly to the king, whose expression says it all. He's awestruck at the sight of this youth taking out convicted felons three times her age. Still, Graff feels like the demonstration is lacking something, and he looks back at Di with a frown. Having already dispatched half her opponents, she's facing off with the last two.

"Diamond, I wish to give you a new order," Graff calls out. "I want you to kill those men."

The order startles the convicts. Desperate to survive, one barrages his opponent with heavy attacks. However, she perfectly blocks each hit while fully maintaining her balance.

Eventually, Di deflects one of his attacks with a single hand, a shield of air protecting her from the blade. She steps into the convict and punches him square in the stomach, and her assault ends there. The convict drops his sword and groans as he leans into his opponent. Graff strains his eyes, trying to figure out why the fight ended so abruptly, and it becomes apparent that Di didn't simply land a punch. A blade of solidified air is penetrating her victim's back, visible only because of the blood streaming down its sides. Mercilessly, Di dissipates the weapon and lets the murderer fall.

Her remaining opponent tries to blindside her with a heaving strike across her side. Di flips into the air just in time to avoid the attack, leaping over the blade and landing cleanly on her feet. The convict recovers and prepares to strike again, but Di meets his blade with her own. There is no deflection; her sword cuts cleanly through the steel blade of her opponent. Apparently expecting this, she uses her momentum to swing around and cut her adversary across his chest. Her second victim collapses, and Di extends the air blade to her side. She dispels the weapon, freeing the blood on it to fall to the ground. Each drip echoes out in the dead silence of the chamber.

Soldiers rush to each of the felled opponents, checking for life signs. One calls out to the general, "He's dead, sir." The other one confirms this as well.

As Di regains her senses, she stares in horror at those she just killed. Tears well in her eyes as her knees grow weak.

Seeing her state, Graff hurriedly orders, "Diamond, wait outside." She immediately obeys, running to the end of the hall and flinging the thick doors aside with ease as she escapes the throne room.

The general turns to his awestruck audience as the soldiers begin dragging the convicts away. "Your Majesties," he boasts, "that is the power of this weapon."

Haran stands and applauds, prompting his officials to do the same. "General, that was the most amazing feat my eyes have ever seen!"

Graff hides his approval at the praise. "I suspect she is capable of far more than what we've witnessed. As you've now seen, she is an air shaper on top of everything else. We must push her harder and see what she can do."

"I concur," says the finance minister.

"Such finesse," Reece adds. "We must test her."

"Indeed, General," the king agrees. "Give her more of these tests-"

"You're horrible, all of you," the queen interrupts, forgoing protocol as she wipes away tears. "She's a child!"

"Saleen, remember your place," Haran urges, perturbed by the outburst.

The general's brow furrows. "Actually, Your Majesties, that leads me to my final piece of information I have to share. The source who led us to Diamond claims that she is not a human child. Of all things, she may be a rune from the Third Kingdom. A special rune called a runic."

"That girl, a rune?" Haran asks, eyeing his science advisor.

Laffel adjusts his thick spectacles. "That isn't possible. It's more likely the Third Kingdom weapon somehow infused this ability within her."

"Unfortunately, we have no way to know for sure," the general somberly admits. "What we know is what I have demonstrated."

Queen Saleen abruptly stands and bows to her husband. "I'll take my leave, Your Majesty." She descends the stairs, giving Graff a cold stare as she rounds the platform and heads for a private chamber in the back of the hall.

Haran sighs. "Her compassion is both her greatest strength and her greatest weakness. I can understand her concerns, but if that girl can prevent another war, we must use her. Alleria will have nothing like this on their side."

"Agreed, we must find a way to make its power known to the Allerians," Graff says, "but based on my observations in the Berev, I believe there are at least three other weapons like Diamond. We must secure them for ourselves before the Allerians are made aware of this power."

"The Academy should have first access to this purported Third Kingdom chamber," Laffel interjects. "We will decipher this puzzle with expediency, Your Highness."

Haran nods. "You have my permission to devote any resources necessary to this task. Excellent demonstration today, General. Have you anything else for us?"

"No, Sire. In fact, if you would allow it, I should tend to the weapon."

"Then you're dismissed."

He bows and turns to leave, but Reece calls out, "General, one more question. Your command over the weapon is absolute, as we've seen. What happens if you were to sustain injuries in battle? Can the power be transferred?"

Graff knows the intent behind the question, and he shrewdly answers, "Ares has claimed that the power can be transferred."

"Can you offer a demonstration?"

He grimaces. "I cannot. Our esteemed informant failed to give me the details before disappearing. I will interrogate him when next he shows himself."

"And what of the remaining weapons?" Reece further asks, eyeing him suspiciously. "Do you intend to bind them yourself?"

"As we collect the remaining weapons, I plan to divide them among my four commanders," he replies before turning his eyes to Haran. "Does that suit Your Majesty?"

The king nods. "Thank you, General."

With that, Graff continues his retreat from the hall. As the guard closes the throne room doors behind him, he wonders whether the power truly can be transferred. He expects Reece will one day demand proof of this.

His thoughts are interrupted by the sound of sobbing. The soldiers guarding the throne room doors are all staring at the dreaded warrior now curled up against the stone wall, her face buried into her arms. Bemoaning that his great weapon has the appearance and fortitude of a teenager, he stands over Di and barks, "How long will this take, Diamond?" Di looks up, startled. "Those were cold-blooded killers you slew. One murdered his wife and two others before he was apprehended. You delivered justice."

Di chokes back tears. "Doesn't matter. You're going to make me kill more people."

"My will is now yours, Diamond," the general coldly states. "You will do what I have spent my entire life doing. You will serve this great nation and keep it safe."

"Safe from what?" Di demands. "From the Allerians? You want to go to war as much as they do. You're no different than they are!"

Graff backhands Di across the face, sending her to the floor. "Do not compare me to those filthy animals. I've seen firsthand what Allerians are capable of doing. They aren't in the same echelon as you and me." Graff glances back to the throne room doors and says, "We left four convicts alive in there. You will carry out their sentences in the morning, this time without a command."

Di rubs her cheek as a shiver runs down her spine. "No, I couldn't... I'll never kill unless you make me."

"You must learn how to kill if you are to survive on the battlefield. I won't always be there to issue commands to you," Graff lectures. "Now stand up." She reluctantly complies, not wanting to endure another forced command. Graff folds his arms expectantly and says, "Show me the blade you used back there."

The air shaper swings her arm to the side and forms a shimmering blade of air that extends another arm's length beyond her fingers. It takes the form of a thin triangle, and the air forms a seal around her wrists and hand, giving her control over the blade without needing to grip it.

"From the wrists?" Graff observes. Impressed with the flawless blade, he's again tantalized by the prospect of using Di in combat. "Can you do it on both arms?" Di looks defeated as she extends her other arm to the side and forms an identical blade.

"Now you're becoming a real weapon, Diamond." He turns to leave the receiving room, motioning for her to follow. "Come along, then."

Di dispels the blades and wipes the remainder of her tears from her eyes. Her fears of being made to kill now realized, she finds herself resigning to the notion that there is no escaping this new reality.

CHAPTER 21

Era steps away from the busy market district, clutching his purchase as he heads back to the busy city entrance. He can hardly believe the atmosphere of Satari, even Canterin pales in comparison to the cultural ambience the capital exudes. The streets are packed with travelers and locals alike, and the peaks of the palace can be seen towering above the sizeable structures.

Leaving the town gate, he watches the guards from the corner of his eye, but they continue to pay him no mind. It's true he's no longer wanted, but he tenses up just the same. Prior to meeting Di, he would always playfully sneak around the town guards as if they would instantly recognize him for the infamous thief he aimed to be. However, now that he's had a high-profile conflict with the military, he can't help but be legitimately cautious. As soon as he's out of sight of the soldiers, he ducks off the path and into the woods.

Clear of danger, he asks himself for the hundredth time whether this is something he should be doing, especially with Jem and Pearl now involved. Yet, hiking through the brush, the silence is terrible compared to the round of complaining he's grown to expect. He's amazed at how much he misses Di, and he can't shake the feeling that he would forever regret abandoning her.

"About time," Jem calls out from behind a tree. "I was actually starting to worry."

"I wasn't gone that long," he argues as he hands the goods to Jem.

"The guards didn't give you any trouble?"

"Nothing. Didn't even bat an eye at me. You probably could have come with me."

His partner points to herself. "Allerian, remember?"

Era shrugs. "There were plenty of Allerians in there. It's really multicultural."

Jem is upset as she looks the packages over. "Can't believe I'm buying more pressure packs. It's your fault we lost both of them, you know? You should pay for these yourself."

"I *did* pay for them both," Era contests. "Three days' worth of stealing and pawning along the way, and I still barely had enough to buy them. Why couldn't I have just stolen these?"

"Because if you failed, you'd have drawn attention to yourself in the capital," Jem explains. "Didn't we already go over this?"

"I wouldn't have gotten caught," he pouts. He glances skyward and says, "Pearl is coming tonight."

The mention of the sky boat pilot irks Jem. "Era, you can't go through with that selfish girl's proposal. She doesn't-"

"Like I keep saying, it's not worth discussing," he interrupts. "I had no choice."

Her emotions well within her as she blurts, "Forget that! Era, you're blind to what's happening here. That sneaky smuggler is trying to-"

"-manipulate me into staying for longer than I year? Yeah, I know."

She blinks in surprise. "Okay, so maybe you're not as naïve as I thought. But then how could you go through with that agreement if you know what's she's up to?"

"How could I not?" he asks. "If we pull this off, we're going to be more wanted than ever. What better place to hide than a smuggling operation in the middle of nowhere?"

The notion is unexpectedly astute. "You thought that far ahead?"

"From the moment we decided to approach Pearl, I had a feeling she was going to want something like that in return," he explains, "so I had plenty of time to think about what I'd do in response. But in the end, we'll never get to Di without Pearl's help. On top of that, Di might not have a place to go after we rescue her, seeing as her hometown was a lie. Securing a future for all of us was the best move."

"But your dream of becoming an infamous thief will be on hold, maybe permanently if Pearls gets her way," Jem says. "You're really willing to give all that up for Di?"

"Not just Di," he warmly tells her. "You're worth it too, Jem. I'd give it all up if we can be together after this. I'd do it in a heartbeat."

She leans forward and says, "You're something else, Era."

"Right back at you. I know you don't need to be here," he says. After a moment's consideration, he asks, "Jem, if I can ask, why *are* you coming along with me? This mission isn't likely to, you know…"

"Succeed?" she asks with a straight face.

"I was going to say, 'be easy', but that's probably closer to the truth," he admits.

"You wouldn't stand a chance without me," she replies. "You should be thankful I'm coming along."

"I am," Era says, "but I don't understand why you are."

She hesitates, as if seeking an answer, herself. "I don't know for sure. You and I have been traveling together for so long that I… well, I didn't want to go back to a life of solitude."

"But you were alone for years before we met," he says in surprise. "I always figured you were anxious to ditch me and return to that lifestyle."

"Turns out it's more fun to have someone to yell at along the way," she teases. "Besides, you were doing it with or without me, and you're far too dense to pull off something like this yourself, Master Thief."

"That's because I still have lots to learn from you," Era offers.

"Don't you forget it! And don't think I have any intention of dying for you or Di. We're getting in and getting out. Alive."

Era nods in agreement. "I just hope we can find her after all this. She might not even be in there."

"We'll get information at least," Jem says, "but if things get rough then we're retreating. No unnecessary fighting! This is a stealth mission, so act like a thief for once."

"Don't worry," he says. "This one isn't for fun. Di is relying on us."

"Okay," Jem declares while patting Era's leg, "you'd better get going. You need to spend the entire rest of the day exploring Satari."

"Eh?" he asks, confused. "Why do I need to do that?"

"We're going to be jumping from a sky boat at night, and we need to be able to find the barracks to land on it," she explains. "In other words, you need to know this city inside and out. Find landmarks, measure distances. Be able to find our target in the dark of night, from above."

"I guess that makes sense," he agrees while getting to his feet and stretching. "Okay, I'll be back at dusk so we can head to the rendezvous point."

Jem watches as Era walks back toward the city. Anxiety begins to overtake her, and she takes a deep breath to calm herself. All she can do now is wait.

*   *   *

Graff chomps on an apple as a knock sounds at his door. He swallows his bite without chewing and barks, "Come!"

The door swings open to reveal Galen standing in the doorway with a salute. "You wanted to see me, sir?"

"Commander, come in." Galen enters and closes the door to Graff's quaint office. He shifts uncomfortably, unsure as to why he's been summoned. Graff takes another bite of his fruit as he continues to review a document in his hand, apparently in no rush to address the commander. Accustomed to this, Galen waits patiently for his superior.

The general places the paper on his desk and glares at Galen. "Commander, as you know, I've placed an order for you and the other commanders to gather tonight. They need to see a demonstration of the new weapon."

Galen affirms his understanding, perplexed as to why he's been singled out. "I saw the notice. I'll be there."

Graff looses a sigh. "Galen, the one thing I cannot do with the weapon is fight it. It cannot attack me, and I've now validated it has a preprogrammed mechanism to protect its master."

"So, she will automatically defend you? Even without a command?"

"Exactly. If it perceives a threat to me, it will zero in and neutralize it." Leaning forward, he admits, "But Galen, I wish I could fight it. I want a true test of its skill, but I have no way to do that myself. As such, you're going to fight it in front of the other three commanders."

The prospect isn't a welcome one. "That didn't go in my favor last time."

Graff waves his hand in the air. "No, that doesn't count. You weren't trying, and you had no idea what to expect. I want to see a real duel between the two of you."

"But sir, I don't want to fight a-"

"It's not a child, Galen," the general growls. "Diamond is a weapon. A thing. It is a rune made for a purpose."

With disdain, he asks, "Then you've accepted that miscreant's claims as truth?"

Graff shrugs. "It's a convenient explanation, so I've chosen it to be the truth. It helps to keep the respect of the soldiers who see it in action. And besides that, I need the weapon itself to believe it."

"But what if the transformation itself was the weapon?" he challenges. "For all we know, it could have transformed me into an elite warrior had I placed my hands in that stone."

"An unlikely hypothesis. The girl has no identity, and her shaping skills exceed even those of Lieutenant Commander Rex," he argues. "It is a rune, Nayl."

Try as he might, Galen is unable to picture Di as anything but a scared and frail child. "General, with all due respect, I'd prefer if you asked-"

"Who?" Graff asks, clearly not interested in the answer. "Another of the commanders? You're young, Galen, but they're all a step behind you, a fact of which you've been particularly proud in the past." He points at his subordinate and says, "No, you are going to fight it. It will be an excellent demonstration of its power. Naturally, I don't expect you to win, but I do expect you to put up a good fight." When Galen shows frustration, Graff suggests, "It would benefit you to accept this truth, Commander. War will come again, and Diamond will be an integral part of our forces."

The commander knows he can do little to contest that truth. "I'll do my best, sir. And how is… *it* doing with its training?"

Graff rubs the bridge of his nose. "It's a flawless soldier when under direct commands, but it's taking too long to break its weak side. In the last three days, it has executed ten convicts sentenced to death. Three were Allerians," he adds with satisfaction. "However, despite my efforts, it hasn't killed or even harmed a thing when not being commanded to do so." Pausing, he notes, "Well, except for poor Lairdly."

"Can't you just keep it under your command?"

"Ares has claimed the runic's power is tied to its free will. If it becomes too reliant on my commands, it's possible it will lose its power." With a suspicious tone, he admits, "I don't want to trust anything that snake says, but this is a difficult claim to disprove. For now, the weapon is strong even while under my command, and it has thoroughly defeated any opponent I've presented. Which is again why I want it to fight with you."

Galen salutes. "As you wish, sir."

"Dismissed," Graff says with a wave of his hand.

The commander steps into the hallway and closes the door behind him. He walks around the corner before punching the stone wall in frustration. For the first time since joining the military, he finds himself in direct moral opposition to his commanding officer. He rubs his knuckles as he continues on his way, cursing his involvement in all this.

*   *   *

Night comes, and darkness overtakes the woods. The moon and stars are hidden from view in the cloudy sky, much to the delight of the thieves. The darker it is for them when they make their drop, the better.

A screeching whine fills the sky. Jem clutches her flare rune, waiting until the sound intensifies before firing it. The brilliant ball of red light shoots high into the atmosphere, guiding the pilot to their location.

Pearl sets the craft down and disengages the runes. She removes her flight goggles and asks, "Any change in plans?"

"Nope, everything is still in place," Era answers.

"Skies are calm, so it's a good evening for this," she says. "Just promise me you'll be careful in there."

"We'll be fine," Jem interjects.

"I didn't ask you," she snidely states. "Era, promise me you'll come out okay. Even if you don't find Di, I just... I need you to be safe."

"I'll be fine," he insists. "I have Jem with me, after all! She'll keep me out of trouble, as always."

With an annoyed glance to his companion, she leaps off the sky boat and into Era's arms. She leans close and grips his back tightly, and Era reciprocates the hug as the emotion of their evening together floods back to him.

"H-Hey!" Jem shouts, annoyed by the display of affection. "He said he'll be back, so no need for that mush."

Pearl releases her friend and gazes into his eyes. "I know he will." With that, she leans in and gives him a kiss on the cheek. "For luck," she whispers, her eyes drifting to Jem, who fails to hide her disgust.

His face red, Era uncomfortably scratches his head. "Th-Thanks," he stutters. "Are you set for this?"

"Yep," Pearl says, her excitement building. "I'll circle the city slowly so you can best time your jump. I take it this is also the rendezvous point for afterward?"

"It is," Jem affirms, "but keep in mind that Satari is an hour's walk from here. Give us enough time to make it back."

"Got it," Pearl says with a nod. The pilot straps her goggles back over her eyes and climbs to her perch on the craft. "Hop inside! I'll stomp the roof three times when we're over the capital."

As she fires up the runes, Jem jabs Era with his elbow and shoots him a look, as if to demand an explanation for the kiss. He offers an awkward shrug and hurriedly opens the hatch for them to enter, grateful for once that the sky boat noise is so overbearing.

*   *   *

A loud knocking prompts Era to shove the door open, filling the cabin with wind. Fighting his fear, he carefully leans outside and observes the moonlit city below. He locates a particular pair of spiral towers, and he follows those north to locate the palace and adjoined military barracks.

He turns to Jem, shouting over the wind. "Ready?" Jem nods, and Era slams the roof, indicating to Pearl they're jumping. Taking a deep breath, he squeezes his eyes shut and dives from the sky boat. He activates his pressure pack, and the high volume of wind works to slow his descent. He aims the jets to take him toward his desired destination.

As he gets closer to the roof, he can start to make out the details. Watching carefully for patrols as he lands, his feet touch ground with a surprising amount of momentum, and he frantically works to cut the rune off before being yanked off the opposite edge of the building. The rune deactivates, and he comes to a stop just in time to avoid a fall. Jem lands behind him, and they stash the packs next to the edge of the roof, having planned to use them to escape if necessary.

Crouching low in the darkness, they take a planned break to evaluate the situation before proceeding, but there are no indications they were noticed. They bump fists and move quietly along the rooftop until they find a hatch. Jem rests her ear to it before signaling her partner to move it. Era pops a latch and removes the wooden covering. After confirming the room below is empty, she slides her legs off and lowers herself into the opening.

Era waits up top while dangling his arms down, ready to instantly pull Jem out if needed. When she signals for him to descend, he does so with uncharacteristic grace. Jem points to a small table in the corner, which Era retrieves. He places it below the opened hatch and climbs on top to test it, ensuring they can use it to escape.

The intruders pause to take in their surroundings. Large crates line one wall of the room, and military uniforms hang over the edges. A lantern is lit next to a sewing machine that has fabric positioned below the needle. It becomes apparent this is the studio of a tailor.

Footsteps approach from the hallway outside. Era and Jem each dive behind a box on opposite sides of the room. The door creaks open, and a tall, lanky fellow walks in. He gets about halfway into the room when he notices the moved table. As he walks up to it, he barely notices the opened hatch above before Jem grabs him and shoves him against a wall, covering his mouth while Era hurries to close the door.

Jem draws her shattered dagger and brings it to the tailor's neck. "Tell me where you keep your prisoners," she mutters in a low voice. She uncovers his mouth slowly while adding pressure with her knife.

His eyes widen in shock at the sight of an Allerian. "I-I-I'm just a tailor! I'm not armed-"

Jem covers his mouth and twirls her blade in intimidating fashion. "You only get one more chance. Tell me where you keep your prisoners!"

He nods his head, and Jem removes her hand once more. "Th-The jail is outside town."

"Outside?" Jem repeats. "There are no prison cells here?"

"There are s-some in the basement, but those are only used for high-profile prisoners."

"We're looking for a short, blond girl named Di," Era says with hushed urgency, cutting to the chase. "Do you know of her?"

"Y-Yes, she's in the basement as well."

A wave of excitement sweeps through Era's body. "Where are the stairs?" he demands.

"Outside. To your left."

285

Era glances to Jem. "Anything else?" When she shakes her head, he grabs some cloth and gags their new informant. Jem ties his hands behind his back, and they lift and dump him into one of the crates full of uniforms.

They move to the door, again confirming no one is in sight before making a dash for the stairwell. They descend quickly but quietly down the stone stairs, masking their sound as best they can. The barracks is built four stories high, creating a long trek to the basement.

Upon reaching the bottom, Era finds a narrow hallway illuminated by light runes embedded in the ceiling. There's no choice but to run all the way down without any cover. He signals the information to Jem, and she nods in confirmation. They dash into the open, with Era taking the lead and Jem watching their backs.

It feels like it takes an eternity to reach the end of the hall, but they manage to do it without anyone happening upon them. Surveying his options, Era targets a heavy, metal door. He pushes it open and hurries inside, and Jem files in behind her partner.

"Hey!" a guard calls out from the back corner, and it quickly becomes obvious that they cells are empty. "Who are you?"

Era wastes no time tackling the private while Jem closes the door. "Help! Help!" the guard cries as he kicks Era into a nearby cage wall, causing further racket. Era manages to trip him, and Jem swiftly brings her dagger's handle down on his head to end the fight. They freeze, desperately hoping no one heard the ruckus, but they soon hear a set of footsteps approaching. Jem dives behind the desk, and Era hurries to hide behind the door.

The metal door swings open, hiding Era from view as the new arrival steps into the entryway and notices the unconscious warden. Rather than rushing inside, he carefully searches the room from his vantage point before pulling the door back and slamming it into the hidden intruder.

As Era staggers out from his position, his opponent grabs him and flings him to the ground before drawing a sword. Jem leaps over the desk to engage, but she halts herself when she realizes who their opponent is. "Oh, no," she utters.

Blade in hand, Commander Galen appears just as taken aback by their presence. "You two?"

Era scrambles to his feet, cursing their luck at stumbling onto such an opponent. The commander's last words to him echo in his head, promising he would kill them if he ever saw them again.

And yet their adversary just watches them, making no aggressive movements as he especially seems to study Jem. In the end, he sheathes his sword, his expression a cross of amusement and disdain. "You two are here for the girl? I'm impressed you've made it this far."

Surprised by the attempt at conversation, Era forms his earth sword and directs it at the skilled warrior. "Surrender! We have you outnumbered."

Amazingly, Galen raises his hands in the air. "If I may ask, what exactly is your plan here?"

"We're asking the questions here," Era insists as he awkwardly acts intimidating. "Tell me where-"

"What is your relationship with that girl?" he asks. "How is it you know her?"

"Di is just a child who wants to go home to her father, and we're trying to get her there," Era spouts. "Why do you even want her? You're inhuman for putting her through all this."

"So, you truly have no idea," Galen mumbles, confirming his suspicions. "You're involving yourselves in something you'd do well to forget. If you want to survive, forget about her and leave now, before you're found out."

Jem is confused by the casual nature of the conversation, but Era isn't so taken in. "You'd sure like that, wouldn't you?"

"That girl isn't who you think she is. She's no daughter of a mayor, and that's the least of her surprises." Solemnly, he adds, "She will not leave with you."

The partners meet eyes. Their knowledge of what they found in Canterin gives weight to Galen's words. However, Era's determination outweighs his uncertainty. "She's our friend. We won't abandon her."

Galen remains unmoved by the display. "Then your lives are forfeit."

Era aggressively pushes his earth blade forward. "Where can we find Di?"

"Head into the hall and turn left. Take that until you find the large sparring room. You'll find her there, but you should hurry, because she's due for an audience shortly." Galen surveys his surroundings and asks, "So will you lock me up in one of these cells?"

Era grows frustrated by Galen's mild response to his predicament. "Yeah, we're locking you up. Shut up, already." Galen meanders into a cell, allowing Era to close it behind him. He turns to Jem and whispers, "That won't hold him for long. It's likely he has a way to create fire."

Jem shakes the cell door. "But these bars won't just melt, either. We should have time." She looks at Galen, annoyed to find him gazing at her. Ignoring him, she makes her way to the door and verifies the hallway is again clear. "Come on, let's go."

Galen sits on the stone floor as he watches the two intruders exit the prison room. He crosses his arms and thinks about the Allerian, realizing it's the first time he's seen her in good lighting. "There's no mistaking it," he mutters to himself. "That's definitely her."

CHAPTER 22

Era and Jem creep down the hallway, moving swiftly while looking for the room Galen described. Though Era is intent on finding their friend, Jem's thoughts are stuck on the way the commander had acted. Dread starts to creep in as she wonders if this is their last chance to make a clean escape. "Era, do you think we should-"

Era signals for Jem to stop and wait as they approach an entryway. He peeks around the corner, observing the room inside. "She's in there!" he eagerly whispers.

Jem peeks around Era, finding Di amidst a group of soldiers. "What is she doing?"

"Who cares? Are you ready?" His partner swallows hard, and Era's enthusiasm drops as he watches her hesitate. "What is it?"

"It's just what the commander said." Shaking it off, she looks back at Era resolutely. "No, never mind that. We've come this far, so let's go get her."

Without hesitating, he dashes boldly into the room, an earth club drawn and ready. He runs behind a soldier, who turns just in time to get smashed in the face by Era's blunt weapon. He turns to another and slams him in the gut as Jem sweeps her opponent's legs out from under him.

The rest of the soldiers clumsily draw their blades and rush toward the two aggressors, leaving Di to watch in disbelief as her guardians pick a fight. "Era? Jem? You're alive!" she squeals with excitement. However, realizing her friends are still outnumbered, Di clenches her fists and hurries to join in. She assaults a soldier from behind by kicking out his knees and yanking him forcefully into the wall. She moves to Jem's opponent and slugs him in the back of the head with solidified air around her fists.

Jem's jaw drops. "Di, what in the world?"

Di beams proudly as Era smashes the remaining soldier in the side with his club and kicks him to the floor. Not wasting any time, he runs to Di and embraces her. She hugs him back, clinging tightly to him as she holds back tears. "Era, I thought you were dead!"

"Not yet, at least." He places his hands on her shoulders and looks into her eyes. "We've come to save you. Let's get you home."

Di's heart sinks as she grasps the reality of the situation. "No, Era, I can't leave!"

"It's okay. We've got a safe way out, but we have to move!"

Era tries to tug at Di's arm, but she pulls back, refusing to go. "Era, I can't explain it right now, but you have to leave me here. I'm not... I'm not who you think I am. I can't go with you."

A wave of terror crashes over Jem. "That's what the commander said," she realizes. "What's going on here? Why are you wearing a military uniform?"

"I have to listen to him! He's making me fight... and kill. And he'll make me fight you, I know it!"

Era furrows his brow. "You're not making any sense, Di. Just explain it later, but come with us now!"

"She isn't capable of leaving," someone calls out from the entrance of the room. "That's what she's trying to say."

Di's eyes widen in terror at the sound of Graff's voice. Desperately, she urges her friends, "Hurry! Leave now!"

Era refuses to heed Di's pleas, instead stepping between her and the general, holding his sword ready. "Who are you?"

Graff ignores Era, instead setting his sights on the one behind him. "See, Diamond, this is what I'm talking about. Here's an Allerian criminal, standing right before you, and you haven't dispatched her yet? Shameful."

Di throws herself on the ground. "Please, I'm begging you! Let them go, they don't understand!"

The general raises his head back and strokes his chin. "Ah, now I get it. So, these two were the ones who caused poor Commander Galen all that stress." Addressing the intruders, he says, "How brave of you to infiltrate this place. You were her abductors?"

Era points his sword at the general. "*You* were the abductors!"

"You grasp nothing," Graff says as soldiers enter from behind him. Era and Jem watch helplessly as the privates swarm in, prompting flashbacks to the forest outside Canterin. However, when the soldiers see Graff and Di, they merely step back to the wall and observe.

"Don't worry about them. They were coming for a demonstration," Graff says as he motions around. "It seems we'll be starting early, but this should be even more effective than what I had in mind."

Di turns and hugs Era, gripping him tightly. "I'm so sorry, Era," she squeaks out, her voice trembling. "I never meant for you or Jem to be hurt."

"Jem?" Graff asks, interested. "Is your name truly Jem?"

"None of your business," she sneers.

"I once knew a man by the name of Colonel Jemson. Perhaps you've heard of him?" Jem's eyes widen, prompting a scoff from the general. "Your reaction is enough. So, you're Colonel Jemson's daughter, all grown up? I wonder if Galen ever realized it was you he was pursuing."

Focused on the threat around them, Era whispers, "Di, you can fight. You two need to break through the line and make a run for it. I'll keep this guy back."

Di once again pleads, "Era! You have to listen, I can't-"

"To everyone who has now gathered," the general announces, "these brigands are personal friends of the weapon. It wants desperately for them to be safe. Keep that in mind as we move forward." He looks to Di with cold eyes. "Diamond, I think it's time to begin our demonstration."

Tears streaming down her face, Di falls to her knees. "Please! I'll do anything!" she shrieks.

"You already do that," he says with a devilish grin. Graff extends his hand outward, his hand symbol glowing as he orders, "Let's start out slowly. Diamond, disarm that man."

Confused, Era glances at Di just in time to notice her make a diving lunge at him. He stumbles backward as she assaults him, kicking him in the gut before punching hard at his left shoulder. Jem watches in shock as Di shows no sign of letting up.

"Di! What are you doing?" he calls, but his friend continues her attack, and it's all he can do to defend the strikes without dropping his sword. He desperately tries to grapple Di, but the runic twirls around him and knees him in the side.

Stumbling aside, he tries to put space between them. "What did you do to her?" he shouts at the general.

"I did nothing," he coldly states. "This is what Diamond is."

Di solidifies the air around her hands into blades, and Jem watches in horror as she charges Era, swiping at him with her deadly weapons as he skillfully deflects each attack with his own elemental sword. As the sounds from the skirmish echo out, even more soldiers pour into the room. Cut off from any chance of escape, all Jem can do is watch her two friends duel.

"Di!" Era cries as he gasps for breath, growing exhausted from the struggle. "Di, snap out of it! It's me!"

The air shaper swings at him harder and harder, clearly taking great pleasure in each blow. Era finds himself barely keeping up with his diminutive opponent, and he becomes desperate to take the offensive. He defends an attack and swings a club at Di's side, but she deflects the strike with both blades and knees him in the stomach. She slams her a weapon into his earth blade, which sends his left arm out, leaving him entirely defenseless.

Mercilessly, Di steps forward and swings her blade up alongside Era's body, cutting into the underside of his left shoulder. Her weapon passes through the tissue as if it isn't there, and, for a moment, Era doesn't even realize he's been cut.

Jem shrieks as Era's arm lands beside him. The combatant grabs his shoulder with his remaining hand and screams in pain. Not letting up, Di follows through with her momentum and kicks him so hard that he rolls along the ground before coming to a stop. Jem rushes to him and slides to her knees. She rips her vest off and forces it against his shoulder as she pulls him up into her lap. Tears stream down her cheeks as Era's face twists in agony. "No, Era…" she squeaks out.

Di dispels her blades, and Era's blood splatters to the ground next to her. However, her mission complete, the warmth returns to her expression, and tears flow instantly as she realizes what she just did to her friend.

"Ha!" Graff bellows. "That was a literal interpretation of 'disarm'! Well done, Diamond."

Di grabs the sides of her head and falls to her knees. "No! I… I…"

Jem caresses Era's head as her vest soaks with blood, and he bites his tongue as he continues to grip his wound. His blood covers her, but she holds him tightly as her own tears drip onto his cheek. "It's really over…"

"Diamond," the general calls out. She squeezes her eyes shut and covers her ears, horrified of what she knows is coming next. "He's suffered enough. Kill him."

The entire room watches in silence as the weapon stands. She forms her blades and readies herself to strike.

Jem lays Era's head gently back against the stone floor. "Jem, don't…" he groans as she gets to her feet.

She wipes her eyes and whispers, "It's okay". Despite the situation, she feels no regret as she draws her broken dagger and steps between Era and his aggressor. With determination, she screams at Di, "You think you can treat him like this? After all he did for you!? I won't let you touch him. I won't!"

Di races at Jem, her blades pulled back as she closes in on her target. The Allerian brings her weapon up in defense, but Di stops short and spins, bringing her blades jointly from the side. Jem has no time to react. She squeezes her eyes and braces herself for the fatal strike.

"Stop!" Graff bellows, and Di freezes in place, her blade mere inches from Jem's neck. All the soldiers in the room are murmuring as they point at something off to the side. Even Jem and Di, despite their situation, realize something is amiss and turn to find Era's dismembered arm engulfed in flames.

When Graff approaches, it abruptly extinguishes as a gust of wind breaks forth from the limb, and the entire arm crumbles. "What the blazes?" he mumbles as he kneels beside it. He touches the pile of wet dirt that used to be an arm, confirming it is as it appears. "Mud?"

"Congratulations, General," a voice calls out from the back. The soldiers step aside, and Ares strolls into the room.

The general glares at his informant, who appears to bolster as much confidence as ever. "What do you want, Ares? I thought you were searching for the other weapons."

Ares grins. "I was indeed, and I found one. Then I followed him here." He points at the arm on the ground and says, "I guess I was too late. I see you already broke it."

"What?" Graff asks, glaring at Era. "This kid is another weapon?"

Recovered from her commands, Di's eyes widen in shock at the revelation. "He's the same as me?" she whispers.

"What do you think will happen if a rune loses a limb?" Ares asks, playfully teasing his audience. "Earth, water, air, and fire comprise these weapons, and to these elements they return, as you just bore witness."

Though perplexed by what's transpiring, Jem notices most of Era's blood on her clothes has turned to earth. She glances back to Era and finds her once bloodied vest is now a muddy mess. Even Era's hand is covered with a mix of dirt and blood.

"I don't…" Era starts, fighting through the pain. "What's going on?"

Graff eagerly turns to Era. "It seems you're a rune, just like your friend here. What luck that you should bring yourself to us."

"Too bad you had to cut off his arm to find out," Ares chides, "but that won't slow him down. He'll be as effective as Diamond, even with a single arm. Runics are extraordinary."

"Yes, I would believe that," Graff says as he moves toward Era.

Alarmed, Jem shifts to place herself in his path, brandishing her shattered dagger with trembling hands. Unamused, the general raises his hand toward Di, intent on making the Allerian move aside. However, before he can issue an order, a loud clamor emanates from the hallway outside. "What's going on out there?" he demands to know.

Soldiers start streaming into the hallway, but a small figure bursts into view. Fire shoves her way past the soldiers and races for the group in the middle. She leans close and orders them, "Close your eyes."

"Contain her!" Graff shouts.

As the mass of soldiers moves in at her, Fire reaches into her pocket and withdraws three small, white orbs. Squeezing her eyes shut and turning her head away, she throws them into the floor.

A blinding flash floods the room. The soldiers start running into each other as they grab at their eyes in agony. Even Graff falls prey to the attack.

"Move!" Fire screams as she grabs Di's arm and stumbles through the masses. Jem gets Era to his feet and helps him escape, stepping over the victims as they writhe in pain. The group races down the long hallway and up the stairs, with Fire dragging Di as Jem helps Era with each step. The mercenary turns and beckons with her arm, not happy with how slowly the other two are moving. "Come on, come on!"

Di snaps her hand away from Fire, glaring at her betrayer with no small amount of hatred. She wipes her tears and tells Jem and Era, "I can't go with you. Now you understand why."

Fire realizes for the first time that Di is dressed the part of a soldier. "Wait, just what's going on here?"

"I have to do whatever he says! And I..." Sniffling, she tells Fire, "Just get them out of here. Don't stop, because I'm sure I'll be coming for you right away. You can't let him get Era."

Jem wants desperately to say something, but no words come. She hurries her wounded partner past the runic, and as they move, Era meets Di's eyes. With just a look, the two exchange an entire conversation: Di's regret, Era's pain, and their mutual confusion over all this. Di shifts her gaze to his wound, and then to the floor.

"Di," Era groans. "I'm going to... come back... for you..." The words are like arrows in her heart, and she takes one last look at him as Jem hurries him further up the stairs. Fire is unable to grasp the situation, but, with Era and Jem willing to leave her behind, she also abandons their former companion.

Di listens to their echoing footsteps as her tears drip to the stone floor below. It doesn't take long for Graff to barge into the stairwell, still furiously rubbing his eyes. "What are you doing, Diamond? Go bring him back!"

Her hands glow, and she wipes away the tears. "Yes sir," she shouts as she runs after them, her sorrow replaced by an intense focus on retrieving the newfound runic for her conductor.

*   *   *

The three companions race for the tailoring office, stepping over several downed soldiers on the way. Jem realizes Fire had quite a time getting down to the basement, which is odd since this floor had been abandoned not long ago. It doesn't seem characteristic of Fire that they would hear her break in.

Fire leaps onto the table and hoists herself with ease to the rooftop above. She lies on the roof and reaches down with both hands. "This is going to hurt, so be a man about it."

Era forces himself to bear the pain as he steps onto the table and stretches his arm up. Fire grips his hand while Jem lifts him from below. He grits his teeth as they haul him up, but he manages to keep most of his screams from escaping his lips. Safely on the roof, he rolls to the side as Fire helps Jem up.

"The pressure packs are over here," Jem calls out as she starts to make a run for them.

"Whoa, whoa. That was your plan?" Fire calls out. She smugly points behind her and says, "I like mine better."

Jem peers into the darkness, spotting the sky boat parked at the building's far edge. Her mouth drops as she realizes just how Fire got inside, not to mention why she had attracted so many soldiers when she did it.

"Hurry!" Fire calls out, prodding them along.

"Era?" Pearl screams out at her injured friend, and she starts to dismount her craft.

"Shut up and start your boat!" Fire bellows. Pearl reverses course and scrambles to her chair while Jem helps Era climb inside.

Fire starts to close the door from the outside, and Jem reaches a hand out. "Wait, aren't you coming?"

"No way am I getting in that thing again. I'm riding up top," Fire shouts over the noise of the runes, slamming the door and latching it from the outside. She scales the footholds and grabs onto Pearl's harness. "Go! Go!"

"I'm going, already!" Pearl shouts back as she starts the liftoff. The boat ascends, and Fire intently watches the hatch in the roof. Though she expected soldiers, it's Di who appears, leaping skillfully to the rooftop, and she races after them without hesitation. The runic gets within jumping distance mere moments too late to reach the craft. They take to the dark sky, leaving Di and the barracks behind.

Graff catches up to his weapon as they escape. "They got away?" he shouts, panting from exertion.

"No," the runic answers. She casually kicks off her boots and places her bare feet on the cold roof. "I'll retrieve him." Without further explanation, she races along the rooftop and leaps off the edge, making Graff's heart skip a beat as he expects her to fall. However, she runs straight past the roof's edge, ascending as she moves, shaping the air beneath her feet. Graff has no choice but to stand and watch as both sky boat and weapon disappear into the cloudy night.

*   *   *

296

Fire grabs a lengthy harness strap and ties it around her waist. She leans close to Pearl and yells over the wind, "Take us as far as you can go. All the way to your operation if you can."

"That's a sixteen-hour flight!" Pearl shouts back. "Doesn't Era need to see a doctor?"

"You're right. Take us Nadar, then."

As she glances behind her, she spots a light dot chasing after them. She strains her eyes, and she's shocked to find Di running to catch up to them. She leans back to Pearl and shouts, "We have incoming! Can you go any faster?"

"Incoming?" Pearl screams back. "What's coming at us?"

"Just answer the question!"

"This is as fast as I can go!"

Fire grimaces as she turns back to Di, wondering what the military did to her. Realizing she's in for a fight, she draws her dagger from her waist, grateful to be restocked on weapons.

Di catches up as the sky boat reaches the city limits. Her two blades shimmer in the faint moonlight, giving Fire a warning of what's to come. She covers her blade in a thick layer of ice, and she maintains her hold on it as she prepares to receive Di's attack.

However, their pursuer merely runs alongside the sky boat, apparently more interested in getting inside than fighting with the combatant on top. As she takes a swipe at the door latch, Fire reaches down and intercepts the strike with her enhanced weapon. Di's blade deflects off it, and she loses some momentum. Fire finds the single strike nearly penetrated the layer of ice on her blade despite her attempt to maintain its form. Thankful she'd taken the precaution, she repairs the protective shielding and turns her attention back to her opponent.

Now with a new target, Di makes a dash for the rooftop, her sights locked onto Fire. The markswoman flings darts at her target, but Di molds a blade into a shield and deflects each one without losing any speed. She gets close enough to swing at Fire, who guards the strike and tries to kick Di back, but the nimble warrior dodges. The runic gets a foot on the roof and swings her other blade around, which Fire again defends. However, this time the force is enough to send her staggering to the side, and Pearl watches in horror as Fire tumbles over the edge of the craft.

"No!" she shrieks as she gives a nervous glance back to Di. The short soldier looks at Pearl with cold eyes, holding her blades at her side. Pearl knows she has no way to defend herself, and her heart races.

However, Di ignores the pilot, instead jamming one of her blades into the roof and carving a wide circle. She kicks it in and peers inside, finding Jem again standing in the way of Era. Di smirks at the pitiful attempt to protect her target.

Her eye catches motion; she narrowly intercepts an ice-enhanced blade, but the follow-up kick sends her flying off the side of the sky boat. Fire watches as the air shaper tumbles and falls behind the craft. To her dismay, Di eventually catches her footing and starts making her way back.

"Thank goodness," Pearl exclaims. "How did you get back?"

The veteran fighter gives a grateful tug on her harness. However, as she watches Di coming after them, she knows her luck is going to run out eventually. She runs several scenarios through her mind, but none end in her favor. Reluctantly, she unties her harness and leans close to Pearl. "Change of plans. The military knows I work out of Nadar, so take Era to Duroshe." After pausing, Fire adds, "Do not turn this craft around, or I will kill you. You got that?" Pearl fervently nods, wondering why Fire thinks she would consider such a thing.

Jem's head appears through the hole in the roof. "How did Di get on the craft?" Fire nods toward the runic running through the sky, and Jem can hardly believe her eyes. "How can she do that?"

"That's what I want to know." She crouches next to Jem and says, "Get Era to a doctor. Pearl is taking you to Duroshe."

"What?" Jem shouts, confused. "What do you mean?"

"Tell him I'm sorry, both for earlier... and for now." With that, she steps past the confused Jem and stands at the edge, clutching her dagger and encasing it in ice once more.

Di comes full-on, aiming for a quick kill. She strikes at her opponent twice, but Fire skillfully deflects each attack and dives into her assailant, taking both of them off the roof. Jem watches them plummet, this time with no harness attached. "Fire!" she shrieks. She scrambles to the edge of the sky boat, watching helplessly as the combatants plunge into the darkness.

"Pearl, bring us back around! Fire took Di off the edge!" Jem screams.

Pearl's eyes widen, now understanding Fire's orders. "She said not to! And besides, what can we do?"

Jem slams the roof in frustration, staring after the last place she had seen the two before they were swallowed by the night. Reluctantly, she returns to Era, leaving Pearl to guide them to their destination.

CHAPTER 23

The embattled fighters tussle as they plummet, each struggling to gain the upper-hand. Fire grips Di tightly, pinning her arms as she tries desperately to take the runic all the way down. The winds whip them in all directions as they spiral towards the earth below.

Unable to break free from Fire, Di kicks furiously to get air-shaped holds beneath her feet. She bounces off solidified platforms, slowing their descent significantly by the time they reach the treetops. They crash through the branches and slam into the ground below.

The impact knocks the wind out of Fire, who gasps desperately for air while Di slowly stands, gripping her side with a groan. Her ponytail is undone, and her long hair hangs loosely. She glances upward and listens for the sky boat, but she hears nothing, which tells her the mission is over. Her mentality restored, she forms a blade and extends it at Fire, stopping just short of her forehead. "Not so tough now, are you?" The injured mercenary meets her glare with silence, and Di continues, "You sold us out... You sold me out! And now I'm-" She cuts herself off and looks herself over. "Now I'm this."

She dispels her blade and wipes her eyes. "And yet, if you hadn't sold me out, Era would probably have been captured or killed when we got to Canterin. I hate you for it, but I also have to thank you, Fire."

Fire stares at Di in awe. "What are you?"

"What am I?" She runs her hand through her hair as the answer echoes in her mind, and Fire is startled as the air shaper reforms one of her blades. Without hesitation, Di pulls her long hair tight and slices cleanly through her thick locks. The golden strands float to the ground, each one shimmering in the faint moonlight, and Fire watches with disbelief as they turn to wisps of air and disappear into the atmosphere.

Her hair now at shoulder length, Di faces Fire in resignation. "I'm a weapon. A rune, and I've been programmed to obey whatever General

Graff says. If Era is really the same as me, you can't let him get caught or they'll do the same thing to him." Feeling her hair with one hand, she says, "Don't let him come after me again. Protect Era from them, and from me."

Bewildered, Fire watches as Di marches into the woods. Finding herself alone on the forest floor, she tries to get up, but she's in far too much pain to be able to do so. She feels her consciousness slipping, and she doesn't find the strength to fight it. *'Just a quick rest,'* she tells herself as her vision fades to darkness.

*   *   *

Graff paces the entry hall in the barracks, tapping his foot and watching the clock as he waits impatiently for his weapon to return.

Galen hurries into the chamber and approaches his superior. "General Graff, I-"

"Where the devil have you been, Commander?" Graff barks.

"Sir, I-"

"Save it," he snaps. "Diamond's traveling companions broke into the barracks before escaping again. Of all things, the boy turned out to be another runic."

Galen's brow furrows. "That guy?"

"That accursed Ares also made an appearance, though it appears he slipped out amidst the chaos." Confidently, he says, "They may have escaped, but Diamond is retrieving them as we-" He cuts himself off as Di marches into the hall, and a scowl forms when he finds her alone.

The short-haired soldier marches to the general. "I failed," she reports, her expression cold and unyielding. Smugly, she adds, "He got away."

Graff backhands her, though she maintains her footing. "You dare to take pleasure in defeat? And how could you fail? You are the military's greatest weapon!"

Di indignantly rubs her cheek and says, "Fire defeated me in combat."

"No," the general scowls, "you are not defeated until you are dead. Assuming a rune can even die."

"You ordered me to retrieve him, but I could not. Once that order was nullified, your command to remain in the barracks brought me back."

Graff's nostrils flare. "You knew what I desired of you. You will start obeying me even without a command, Diamond."

"My name is Di," she defiantly growls. "I may be a rune, but I will never, *never* obey you unless you force me. There's nothing you can do about that."

"Nothing I can do?" He extends his open palm, revealing his emblem of power over her. "Go into the city and slaughter a dozen civilians in their sleep. We'll blame the Allerians, so be sure to carve each one up mercilessly."

Di panics when she hears the command, and Galen is equally alarmed. However, both realize that, despite Graff's words, the seal doesn't light, nor does Di make any movements toward the door.

"Do you think I wouldn't do that?" he bellows. "Do you think I can't force you to commit atrocities that will be forever burned into that tiny brain of yours? You will obey me or I will break you, Diamond."

Her breath trembles with anger, yet she says nothing. She knows what he says is true.

The general notices her hair but chooses not to acknowledge it. "You'll make it up to me, Diamond. You will find the other weapons as we receive information on them. And you will retrieve your friend for me eventually."

She nods her understanding, not out of forced obedience, but because she knows he's right. No matter where Era runs, Graff and his military will follow, and she'll be leading the charge.

"Turn in for the night. Tomorrow you'll begin hunting the new weapon." With that, Graff briskly retreats, his powerful footsteps echoing as he leaves.

Di gives one last glance to Galen, who averts his eyes in response to her gaze. She then turns and marches toward her private quarters.

*   *   *

The sky boat shakes violently as it lands in the tiny clearing. Pearl disengages the runes and rips off her harness. Pulling her goggles up, she jumps over the edge and swings the door open, then helps Jem ease Era from the craft.

Though Era is still gripping his shoulder, the bleeding has stopped, and the pain has largely subsided. He says nothing as his friends help him to a tree and then collapse next to him, succumbing to their mutual exhaustion.

"They're both dead, aren't they?" Era asks, breaking the silence.

Jem swallows hard. She wants to say something to the contrary, to encourage her friend to maintain his hope, but her mind is blank.

"I killed them," Era realizes aloud. "My foolishness killed them, and it almost got you two killed as well." He squeezes his eyes shut and says, "How stupid was I to think I could keep everyone safe?"

Jem places her hand on his knee. "Era, something big is going on here. There's no way we could have predicted any of that would happen. That Di would..." She cuts herself off, glancing at Era's left shoulder.

Pearl can't fight back her curiosity. "What happened in there, anyway?"

Era looks to the sky, watching as the clouds give way to the stars. "Di wasn't Di, anymore. They did something to make her into a soldier, and it seems she couldn't disobey that guy's commands." Pausing, he asks, "Who was he, anyway?"

"That Ares guy called him the general. If that's true, he's the leader of the entire military," Jem informs him. Looking to Pearl, she says, "He somehow made Di fight Era, and she did this to him with those elemental blades."

Pearl studies his covered wound. "Di did this?"

"It's more than that," Era says, holding his muddy hand up for Pearl to see. "This used to be my blood. Now it's just dried dirt."

"Is that some kind of joke?" she asks, glancing to Jem, whose expression tells her otherwise.

"Blood aside, my arm turned to mud as well," Era says. "My body doesn't seem to be fully real. The general called us runes."

"Runes?" Pearl repeats. "What does that even mean?"

"I have no idea," Era says in dismay. He wants to discredit the suggestion, yet he finds the evidence impossible to deny.

Wanting to change the subject, Jem asks Pearl, "How did you and Fire meet up?"

Pearl grows visibly agitated at the mention of it. "She was so mean! The moment I returned to that clearing, she jumped me and forced me at knifepoint to go back and land on the barracks. Land on it! Soldiers started pouring onto the rooftop thanks to the noise, just like I said they would." With a frown, she admits, "But she took them all out. She's scary good."

Era can't help but be amused. "That sounds like her, all right. Did she... Did she say why?" Pearl shakes her head.

Finding the group in silence once more, Pearl asks the question on everyone's mind. "So, what now?"

"At the very least, we've put you through enough," Jem says. "You should get yourself home."

"Hey!" Pearl protests, taking offense. "I'm involved in this as much as any of you. You can't just get rid of me." Pondering the situation, she asks, "Why not come back with me to the operation? It might be the safest place for you at the moment."

"And what if Di survived that fall?" Jem asks. "I mean, that's great news if she did," she says, eyeing Era, "but she's working for the military now and knows you saved us."

Pearl's eyes widen in alarm. "We'll need to move the operation immediately," she realizes. "Ugh, Father's going to kill me!"

Era returns to his depression. "Pearl, you and Fire both suffered so much because of my foolishness." He buries his face in his knees, wishing he could disappear.

She places a hand on him. "Era, I don't know about all this rune stuff, but I do know you're special. I'd do it again for you, if you asked." Era looks at her in wonderment, and her silver hair reflects the moonlight as she looks back to her sky boat. "Moving the operation is something we've done before, we'll survive. But the offer stands if you still want to come back with me."

Era thinks about this and says, "I think it's best if we kept a low profile, for now. Besides, Fire knew we were coming here. If there's any chance she survived..."

Disheartened, Pearl says, "Given everything that's happened, I guess I have no choice but to cancel our deal." Holding a finger up, she says, "But you'd better make it up to me, one day."

"I'll try," he says with sincerity. "Still, maybe this is all for the best. The military knows what I am, so it'll be dangerous to be associated with me."

"Era, for being so selfless, you're just so selfish!" she abruptly declares. "Do you think that Jem or I or even Fire care about that? Quit assuming that all we want is to be safe. We also want you to be safe, and to be our friend." Glancing at Jem, she asks, "Right?"

Jem is taken aback by the admonishment, but she grins in agreement. "Sorry, Era, but I agree."

Era finds solace in their words. "You two are weird." He stands and wraps his arm around the pilot. "Thanks, Pearl. I hope to see you again."

"Me too, Era," she responds, hugging him back. When he releases her, she hugs Jem as well, much to her surprise. "Best of luck, you two."

"We'll be fine," Jem assures her, pushing her off. "Now get going."

Pearl climbs onto her sky boat, straps her goggles on, and activates the runes. With a wave, she lifts off and ascends to the skies. Era and Jem watch as the craft accelerates and disappears from view.

Jem turns back to her partner. "She'll be okay."

Era sits back down, returning to his prior gloom. "She's being brave, but her life is in danger now. I just hope they don't find her and-"

"Hey, your rune body has already healed that wound, so you don't seem to need a doctor, now," Jem abruptly notes. "Let's just spend the night out here, and tomorrow I'll check out the town. Fire is the one who told Pearl to bring us Duroshe. Like you said, if she survived, she should meet us here, right?"

A glimmer of hope finds its way into his eyes. "Yeah, let's wait for her here." He reclines and tries to clear his mind. "Thanks, Jem. You're an amazing friend."

"You're worth it, Era," she says, lying down next to him. "So quit beating yourself up and get some sleep. We'll figure things out, just like we always do."

He smiles, grateful for the strength of his partner as he watches the stars twinkle in the sky. "I'll do my best."

*   *   *

Though the tall buildings of Duroshe boast prominence, the city feels smaller to Jem than Canterin or even Kemplen. Still, the noonday crowds pack the market, which Jem uses to blend in. The occasional Allerian gives her confidence she won't be identified by military personnel, plus the town seems to lack a significant number of soldiers. She laments that her three days of *not* being a wanted criminal are over. It seems she'll forever be hunted by the military now.

Despite the situation, Jem finds herself in good spirits. She glances to her bag, tallying up the goods she procured while 'shopping'. Fruit, bread, and a fresh garment for Era are all within. '*Not to mention the bag itself,*' she smugly thinks. However, with no sign of their mercenary friend, she doesn't expect to see a shift in Era's mood.

Exiting the town gate, she walks off the path into the woods, humming the tune that always brings her comfort. Her thoughts travel in endless circles during her solitary walk, and she soon finds her partner at the base of a decline, still leaning against the same tree in depression.

A rustle from behind prompts her to eagerly turn around, hoping to find a certain someone emerging from the brush. However, she's met only with a dead branch that must have fallen from the trees. With a sigh, she turns back to her original course, this time coming face to face with an exasperated Fire.

"Have you learned nothing from me?" the mercenary barks. "You go into a major city, you walk the main paths, and you-"

"Hey! I'm…" Jem starts, but she can't hide her sense of relief.

Fire raises an eyebrow. "Say, Allerian, are you happy to see me?"

"Of course not," she responds with a sniffle. "I just-"

"I take it the idiot is with you?" she interrupts, to which Jem nods. "He's okay?"

"Physically, yes, but he's in a bad place otherwise." Excitedly, she exclaims, "This is just what he needs! To see you and-"

"Pass," Fire replies, holding up her hand. "I just came to confirm you two survived. I'm not talking to that bull-headed, moronic-gyah!" she screams as Jem grabs her collar and drags her down the hill. "Hey, don't-Stop! What are you doing?"

"I'm not in the mood for drama. You're going to see him," Jem growls back.

"I don't want to-agh!" she yelps as Jem flings her in front of Era, who came to investigate the commotion.

She shoots Jem a death stare as Era shouts, "Fire, you're really okay!"

"Fine, yes! I'm alive, you're alive, we're all alive," she huffs. "Let's all hug and- Are you crying?"

Era wipes the tears from his eyes. "Fire, you're alive, thank goodness."

Fire appears genuinely stunned by the response. "What is it with you two, anyway?" She slumps against a tree, giving up on a quick getaway. "Yes, I survived the fall."

"And Di?" Era eagerly asks.

"Alive, naturally," she answers, waving her hand in the air. "I don't know where she got that kind of power, but, well, by saving herself she saved me as well. She left me in the woods and returned to the capital."

Era collapses to his knees. "Everyone is alive," he says as he chokes back more tears.

"That's great and all, but you two owe me a serious explanation," Fire says. "The brat is now siding with the military, her air shaping ability is beyond belief, and she's calling herself a rune. What gives?"

Era's head drops, and Jem admits, "We're still trying to figure it out, ourselves."

"A person can't be a rune, can they?" she wonders out loud as she folds her arms. "Then again, that water monster was a rune, and it had a consciousness. Is it possible a rune could produce something as complex as a human?"

"Oh, it's possible," Era says. "When that water creature lost its limbs, the water would spread along the ground, lifeless. After all, whether it's a shaper or a rune, there needs to be contact in order for there to be control, right?"

"So?"

He plucks a strand of hair and hands it to Fire, who watches in fascination as it turns to sand and crumbles. "This is what Di meant?" she cries in alarm, jumping to her feet. "She said Era was the same as her!"

"Relax," Jem says. "He's not an enemy. He isn't like Di."

"Di wasn't like Di either," Fire reminds her.

"Something changed when they captured her," Era says. "I'm still the same guy. So far, at least. But I'm a rune."

"I still don't get it," Jem huffs in frustration. "What about your history? You even have a famous father! You can't have a father and be a rune."

"You mean the famous father no one seems to know," Fire realizes aloud.

Somberly, Era says, "Di had a history, too, but when we went to Canterin, she didn't exist. Like her, I don't exist. My dad doesn't exist. None of our memories are real."

Jem argues, "No, you exist, Era. We've traveled together for a year-and-a-half. You're stubborn, ignorant, and overconfident." Warmly, she adds, "But you're loyal, caring, and, frankly, you're amazing. You exist."

"But what am I?" he asks.

"You're Era. You are what you are, and that's all that matters to me." She glances at Fire, who averts her eyes. "Okay, I'm going for a walk. You two work out this thing you've got going on."

As she leaves, Era and Fire sit in stubborn silence. Eventually, Era gives in and asks the question that has been burning in his mind since last night. "Fire, why? Why save us again?"

With a shrug, she says, "I figured I still owed you one."

"Why?" Era asks again, but Fire ignores the question. "Look, I'm sorry for, you know, those things I said. You really did save us back at Canterin. There was no other way, and I see that now."

Fire slams the ground and glares at Era. "Would you grow a spine already? Of course there was no other way, but you wanted to save the princess so badly that you were willing to throw your life away for her." Hesitating, she adds, "And I had no right to take that decision away from you. So I still owed you one."

Era shakes his head, amused that he finds satisfaction with that answer. "Fire, I wish I could figure you out."

"Right back at you."

He thinks back to the previous evening. "But, wait, have you been following us since we parted at Canterin?"

"You surprised? It was pretty obvious what you were going to do."

"So you followed us to Satari and got the jump on poor Pearl after she landed at the rendezvous point? You're persistent."

"I see a job through to the end."

Era nods gratefully. "How'd you get here, anyway?"

She leans forward, crossing her legs as she sketches absent-mindedly in the sand. "Took a quick nap, then walked through the night and caught a train to Duroshe. How else would I get here?"

308

"Well, I'm glad you found us," he says quietly. As a cool breeze sweeps through the trees, Era closes his eyes and deeply breathes in the fresh air. "Fire, thanks." The sound of uncomfortable shifting is her only response.

"Well, one thing's for sure," Era says, changing the subject. "I'll need to learn how to use a sword right-handed. You might actually stand a chance in a fight against me as I am."

"Don't tempt me to beat a cripple," she retorts as Jem approaches. "That was a short walk, Allerian."

"That's because it came to me!" Jem proclaims. "We want to know what's going on, right? So we'll go to the one place that might have answers for any of this."

Era looks at her expectantly. "And that's...?"

"Come on, Era! Use that rune-brain of yours. What's the one place full of super-smart people who study nothing but elements and runes?" With a wink, she adds, "As a bonus, they already spent two years studying Di."

"You want to go to the Academy?" Era realizes. "What do you expect to find there?"

Jem acts offended by the question. "Don't be so negative! We'll figure out what you are. You don't think they'll have a lead?"

"I guess they should," he reasons. "If nothing else, didn't Di say they had ties to the Academy in Alleria? Surely they've compared research notes, being allowed to travel back and forth like that."

Fire's eyes bulge, and she gives a subconscious glance to the west, realizing she'd heard those rumors once before.

"Exactly," Jem states. "Between the two Academies, someone should know something about you."

"Say," Fire says, choosing her words carefully, "I'm going to come with you." When they look at her in surprise, she explains, "The brat knows I survived, so there's certain to be a bounty on my head. I need to find something I can use as leverage." Era and Jem both eye her suspiciously, and she quickly adds, "Not you! Sheesh, you think I'm going to turn you in after all that? I dove off a sky boat for you."

"Well, I guess we can let you come along," Jem says, but if Era turns into an obelite disc, I call dibs. Think of how much that would be worth!"

"Fine, you can have your Idiot rune," Fire replies with a smirk.

Era stands and brushes himself off. "Jem, Fire, by some miracle, we all managed to survive last night's adventure. It's just too dangerous to keep you involved. I should do this on my own from here on out."

Jem glances at Fire, and they simultaneously burst out laughing. "You? On your own?" Jem scoffs.

"Seriously, you'd get lost trying to figure out which way is north," Fire adds.

"Hey, joking aside, I'm the one they're after. I can't just let you two continue to put yourselves in-"

"Save it, Era," Jem says. "I'm coming along, whether you like it or not. We're partners, after all."

"And at this point, you owe *me*," Fire claims, "so I'm coming, too."

Era gratefully relents. He stretches his lone arm and looks skyward, cupping his hand to shield his eyes from the sun. "The Academy, huh?"

Jem reaches into her bag and withdraws an article of clothing. "Here," she offers. "Can't let your opponents know you're gimped."

Era takes the black material and lets it unfold, revealing a cloak that extends to his knees. The neck is already fastened by a familiar emerald necklace. "Jem, isn't this your-"

"It was getting in the way," she says, waving it off. "It'll look good on you."

He slips the cloak on and rotates it, allowing the garment to cover his left side and conceal his handicap. "What do you think? Should I call myself the Dark Cloak, now?"

"I guess someone might as well use the nickname," Jem replies. "Just don't start spouting terrible advice."

Era looks himself over. The emerald necklace, though a subtle addition, sparkles as the sunlight catches it. "Thanks, Jem. This is great."

"Now stop getting your clothes all torn up. I can't keep stealing you new ones," she scolds.

Era's mind wanders again to his young friend and their fateful meeting that started it all. "Once we've found our answers, there's still Di. We need to save her."

"We will," Jem promises.

Fire raises an eyebrow. "You realize she cut off your arm, right? You still want to rescue her?"

Era sheepishly asks, "Is that weird?"

"Not for you."

"We'd better get moving," Jem says as she motions along. "We've got to stay a step ahead of the military. Again. At least this time they won't know where we're going."

"Doesn't mean it will be easy," Era reasons as he marches alongside his partner. "But, like my made-up father used to say, 'An easy steal is a steal not worth stealing.'"

"What does that even mean?" Jem asks.

"It means that maybe this whole thing will be worth it. I think."

"Worth it in what way? Financially?"

"Ugh, can you two not shut up for two minutes?" Fire gripes.

"And there it is," Era says. "Fire already regrets coming."

"That's fine. Gotta keep her on her toes, or it won't even be a challenge," Jem says. "Hmmm… maybe that's what your fake father meant?"

"I don't know what he ever meant," Era admits. "With him gone, I guess I'm left to figure things out on my own."

"Not on your own, Era," Jem says, patting his shoulder. "You're never on your own."

"Yeah," he says, a smile forming. "I'm glad for that."

EPILOGUE

The dark hallway is covered with ancient symbols, each one's representation lost to time. Ares marches down the tunnel, undaunted, accustomed to the dank atmosphere of the cavern. He rounds the corner and enters the foyer of the underground facility.

"Guess I'm late," he says to the Allerian woman impatiently waiting for him. "Sorry, sis!"

"You're always late, Ares," his black-haired cohort bemoans, glaring at him with deep, dark eyes. She stands as tall as Ares, and her hair is tied into two ponytails that each extend to her lower back.

"Don't be such a nag, Athena," he says. "Besides, I have a good excuse. Just wait until I make my report."

"Whatever you say, dear," she says snidely as she knocks on the steel double-doors before them. The two travelers each step back in anticipation.

The doors open, revealing an elderly fellow wearing a leather coat that buttons down the front. His gray hair is unkempt, and he isn't pleased. They kneel as he gruffly states, "You're late. Report."

Athena starts. "I just delivered a second runic to the Allerians. She'll soon be bound, same as the first."

Ares' mouth drops at the report, and he scrambles to present himself positively. "I've had contact with three. One is bound, and, if you can believe it, the other two are traveling together! I naturally have leads on the others as well."

The old man grunts his disapproval. "How long have we awaited their awakening, and I'm to find satisfaction with three bound runics? Leads are nothing. Bind the rest."

"Yes, sir," they affirm. Without another word, he slams the doors shut.

The siblings turn to march out through the tunnel, and Athena smirks at Ares' report. "Only one? That was your big announcement?"

"Shut up, Athena," Ares snaps. "I'll have mine all bound before you." His usual smile returning, he adds, "And that's when the real fun begins."

APPENDIX 1:
MAP OF VALVOREN

APPENDIX 2:
MAP OF THE HILL COUNTRY

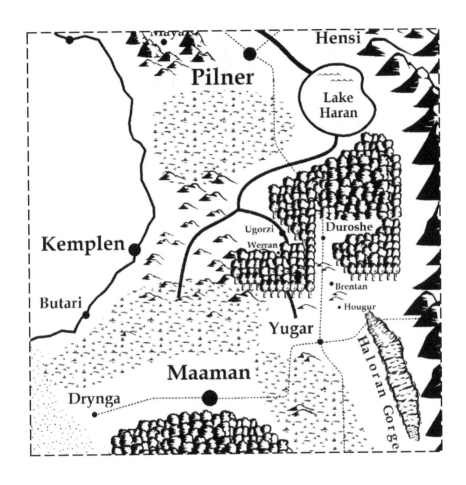

APPENDIX 3:
ELEMENTAL DODECAGRAM

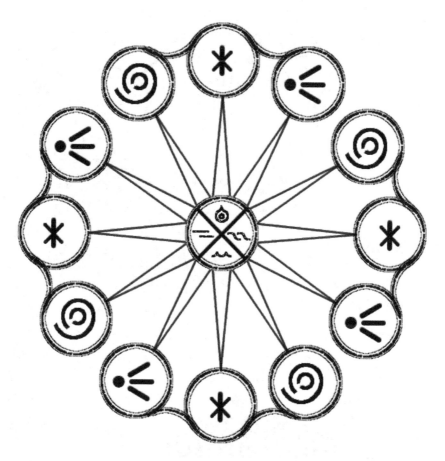

CORE ELEMENTS

 FIRE

 AIR

 WATER

EARTH

MANIPULATIONS

 CONTORTION

 INSTANTIATION

 DERIVATIVE

About the author

Jeff has been a storyteller all his life, dating back to the fourth grade when he wrote two choose-your-own adventure books. He regularly consumes fantasy stories in their many forms, with a particular love for anime and video games.

Outside of writing, Jeff tries his best as a Christ-follower, husband, and father. When not crafting a new chapter, Jeff is usually studying for a Cisco exam, enjoying Notre Dame Football, or competing in Super Smash Bros. tournaments.

Acknowledgements

I owe many thanks to the creation of my first book. As it turns out, writing a novel is much harder than throwing out nearly 200,000 words and expecting it to be a masterpiece. Who knew?

First and foremost, thanks to Emily for fostering my desire to give this a shot. You were my encouragement as I delivered a few chapters at a time for review. A single unfavorable word would have ended all this before it started, yet I heard nothing but the love and respect you always show me.

Second, my thanks and appreciation go out to Tim. You were my first true reader and most enthusiastic believer that my early blathering could be refined into such a story. You worked tirelessly with me on character consistency and trimming the fat, and in doing so you saved me thousands in editing fees! You did not spare the rod in your efforts to beat my writing into tolerable shape. This book would have been insufferable if not for you.

Special thanks to Madelyn for your enthusiasm in getting this book into the hands of others, and to Jeff for being an early guidance on proper grammar and writing. Thanks to Trevor and Jess for the detailed feedback, and to all my beta readers – the list of which is particularly long and even includes Grace, my 93-year-old grandmother. I believe in this story and these characters because of all of you and your enthusiasm.

A letter to you

Dear Reader,

Thank you for reading the first entry in the Runics Series. The next book, Sapphire Ambition, is already available! An excerpt has been included below. Get it today!

Please stay connected! You can do so by:

- Joining the mailing list via mailer.runicsbook.com to receive updates on new releases and events.

- Following me on Twitter: @KishSquared

- Emailing me directly at runicsbook@gmail.com. I love hearing from readers and will always do my best to reply.

All the best,

Jeff

An excerpt from Book 2: Sapphire Ambition

The escaping fugitives charge through the brush, seeking the safety of the woods, but Era eventually succumbs to the throbbing in his legs and stoops to catch his breath. "Fire, I don't think they're following us. I need a break."

Her hostage still in tow, Fire turns back to her ally in exasperation. "Really, Era? Aren't you literally built better than that? Even this Academy buffoon is in better shape than you are."

"The knife in my back was proper motivation," Ospif retorts, quite winded. He barely drops his heavy package before Fire shoves him aside and kneels beside it. "Hey!" he cries. "How rude."

"Shut up," she growls as she counts her treasure.

"I've never seen a creven before, and now we have five hundred of them," Era gloats. "Are they made from silver?"

"Partially," Fire replies as she closes the bag and studies the surrounding forest. "Where is the ice queen? We need to keep moving."

Ospif brushes himself off and announces, "If you villains have had your fill, I'll be returning to the Academy now. And I'd request you deliver that rune back to me."

Era fumbles in his pocket for the rune blade. "You want it back? I'm not sure. It's a pretty great find on my part."

"A find? That rune is the product of years of research and dedication! You'll give it back or... or..."

"...or what?" Era asks, genuinely curious.

"It's irrelevant," Fire states, "because his journey with us is far from over. He's still our hostage moving forward."

"B-Beg your pardon?" Ospif stutters. "I have served my purpose in assisting your escape. What else do you have in mind for me?"

"First, you're going to show me your seal," Fire states. "Prove you're royalty like that fat oaf claimed."

"How insolent! The seal is a sacred image of-"

Fire cuts him off by grabbing his collar. "Show it to me or I'll find it myself."

Ospif grunts his disapproval as he lifts his pant leg. On his calf is a faded, stretched tattoo of the royal family's crest.

"I assume that makes him a Haran?" Era asks.

"That or a counterfeiter," Fire replies. "Either way, he should be worth good coin."

"Good coin?" he exclaims. "You have good coin in that very satchel. Why do you need me in addition?"

"You're our insurance policy," she answers. "In case this isn't enough."

"Enough for what, pray tell?" he demands. "You have fifty thousand venni in your possession!"

"We have how much?" Jem calls out as she emerges from the brush.

"An Allerian!" Ospif shrieks, stumbling backward and tripping over a log. He points at Fire with a shaking finger and exclaims, "You're conspiring with the Allerians? I should have known."

Era snickers and turns to his friend. "Hey, Jem. That went well-ish."

"I witnessed your grand escape from afar," she scolds. "I take it the billowing smoke pouring from the Academy was your doing?"

The adventure continues –

check it out today!

Made in the USA
Middletown, DE
12 June 2023

32498497R00179